OWNING JETT

LUCY LENNOX

ISBN: 978-1-954857-79-7

Cover Art: Najla Qamber | Qamber Designs
Cover Image: Wander Aguiar
Editing: One Love Editing
Proofreading: Jodi Duggan

OWNING JETT

Two weeks. One villa. A dangerous game of seduction and lies.

My job is simple: get close, get the intel, get out.

Then Locke Maris walks into my op.

He's cold. Controlled. Heir to a billion-dollar shipping fortune.
And so aggressively straight he doesn't even look at me twice...

Until he does.

Locke makes me an offer: play his assistant by day, be his secret
lover by night, at a house party where the world's elite will gather
to sip champagne, enjoy the Italian sun... and play a dangerous
game called Paxis.

In this ancient variation of chess, humans are pawns and each coded move could start or stop wars. I should report this to my agency immediately. Walk away clean.

But I can't walk away.

Because in the privacy of his suite, the moves Locke makes are just as dangerous, the words he murmurs in my ear as devastating, and the growing devotion I feel as destructive as any global war.

At the end of this, I'll have to disappear like I always do.
I don't get to want things that could ruin my cover—or my career.

But Locke Maris is ruthless about protecting what's his, and as far as he's concerned he owns me.

When everything falls apart, I'll find out exactly how far he'll go to keep me.

AUTHOR'S NOTE

Special Thanks to Rachel W. for suggesting the name Rocky, and
to Kelsey M. for suggesting the names Kida and Makani for use on
characters in this story.

1

JETT - FOUR YEARS AGO

IT WASN'T a stretch to play a go-go boy. I loved sex, and I was proud of my body. Win-win. Not that my bosses at ESP knew either of those things.

Fortunately for them, I was also only twenty-three, so I could pass easily as a dancer in a gentleman's club.

Unfortunately for me, I was new enough at the agency to not have a choice in my assignments. Might as well enjoy it as much as I could.

I rolled my hips at my mark—Ronald Gillen, cargo-smuggling union boss and all-around shitheel—and felt his eyes follow the curve of my ass and thighs in my booty shorts. Loud club music flooded my system and loosened my already warm muscles.

I bit back a laugh at the thought of telling a younger Jett Marian that one day he'd be paid good money to shake his assets for men in a gentleman's club. Talk about a dream job. After two particularly shit breakups in college, I'd determined that playing the field was a thousand times better than being in a relationship. And the past several years had only proven me right.

Some old guy reached over and pinched my ass before shoving a twenty in the waistband of my jock and making a lewd comment about how I'd look even better on my knees for him.

Okay, so maybe not all of it was dreamlike. In fact, after spending the past four nights dancing in expectation of Ronald appearing in this club, I was ready to get the information I needed from him so my professional dancing days could be over.

I made a big production of licking a finger and trailing it down my bare chest, regretting it a moment later when I realized my fingertip still had leftover glitter eye shadow on it. *Blech.*

"Such a pretty boy," Ronald murmured, eying me over his fat cigar. "Are you new here, sweetheart?"

"I came especially for you, Daddy," I teased with a flirty grin before turning and leaning over, moving my hips from side to side so he could get a peek of bare cheek at the edge of my shorts. I reached back with one hand and ran my fingers along my skin just under the edge of the fabric while holding on to the pole with the other hand. "You like what you see?"

My goal was to get him into a private room for a lap dance where I could distract him while getting close enough to scan his phone with the device embedded in my leather bracelet.

He was with several other men, half of whom were obviously more interested in the women dancing around the room, while the other half either lasered their attention on me or were too busy courting Ronald's favor to pay attention to the dancers at all.

I turned around to face him and leaned the top of my back against the pole, moving my hands down my front and into the top of my shorts. I closed my eyes and tilted my head back, pushing the shorts down enough to show the jock underneath them and a hint of pubic hair.

When the Ecumene Stability Project had recruited me out of college a little over a year ago, I'd gone through the kind of intense training program used by the CIA, MI6, and Mossad—which made sense, since the massive global intelligence agency had a budget larger than all of them put together. Among other things, that training had honed my body into a tool—efficient, strong, ready for anything.

Including luring alcoholic old men into private rooms.

I just needed to seal the deal.

I bit my lower lip and slowly dragged my gaze up from Ronald's black leather wing tips to his crotch and lifted my eyebrows in pleasant surprise as if I saw something impressive there.

I did not.

My tongue came out to wet my lips, and I exhaled, keeping my eyes on his crotch for another moment before sighing and whimpering a little. Then I continued my perusal up over his beer belly to his chest and thick neck. I forced myself to imagine letting this man do dirty things to me, and the image was horrifying enough to heat my cheeks.

Which was exactly what I was going for.

I blinked at him innocently and turned away in faux-embarrassment for having been caught looking. More ass-shaking and pole-humping, then I'd face him again and play with my nipples. It was important to have a plan.

"He's a pretty one, isn't he?" I heard Ronald say to someone in his smoke-roughened voice. I wasn't sure why I was surprised he sounded like a New Jersey dockworker when that was literally what he was. Or had been before moving up to union steward.

He was the guy who managed the list and the line, knew every ghost container on every ship, and accepted envelopes of cash to get favorable movement for all three.

Ronald Gillen was a small fish. A known quantity. Which meant ESP allowed him to keep doing what he was doing.

The man was also an easy mark.

He kept two phones, and neither used biometric security measures—no FaceID or fingerprints for old Ronnie. In fact, he'd once been overheard saying, "They ain't chopping my finger off to get in the damned phone just to see Sheila's nagging texts about being late for dinner."

I'd learned his passcode by simply standing behind him in line at Olivo's Deli two weeks ago, and it happened to be his daughter's birthdate. *Dumbass.*

I finished my spin and lowered into an open-kneed squat in front of Ronald when I saw a new man in his group. He was tall and fit, dark-haired and sexy as fuck. Even though he looked like he was only about thirty, the man oozed money.

Not just money, old money.

Power.

His presence seemed to suck all of the air out of the room and set everything to vibrating.

What the fuck was *Locke Maris*, the heir to the Maris shipping fortune, doing in a place like this, meeting with a corrupt union boss?

His eyes flicked over me with zero interest, which was no surprise. He probably had a pretty wife or girlfriend at home. I was a little impressed he didn't seem interested in the dancing women nearby either, though. Maybe he was loyal. Or maybe he was simply focused on something else at the moment.

Like whatever he was here to talk to Ronald about.

Was he aware of Ronald's petty grifting? Was he involved in it? In charge of it?

Maris was a much larger fish than Ronald or any of his known associates. And now he was in the middle of my op at the fucking Candy Bar.

I needed to get into Ronald's phone to figure out why.

As I sank further into the squat, opening my knees and rolling my hips, I met Ronald's eyes and winked. "Please," I mouthed in a flirty way, tilting my head subtly toward the private rooms.

He tilted his chin up in agreement, then said something to Maris, who quickly shook his head and spoke again. Ronald lifted his eyebrows and made a joke I couldn't hear over the music. They exchanged a back-and-forth before Ronald finally arranged for a private dance with me. I hopped down from the platform and made my way to the private room, not realizing until it was too late that the man following me wasn't my fucking mark... but Locke Maris himself.

"Oh, uh..." I glanced behind him, trying to stay in character as a flirty dancer looking for a heavy tipper. "Just one person per VIP dance, baby."

He narrowed his eyes. "Do you see anyone else?"

"I thought your friend wanted the dance," I tried.

"Apparently not. And neither do I. If we could get this over with quickly, there's a hundred bucks in it for you."

I blinked at him, trying to look stupid and confused instead of annoyed and frustrated. "Why hire a private dance if you don't want one?"

Maris smiled coldly. "Because my *friend*, as you called him, thinks forcing me into a lap dance with a male stripper will give him the upper hand in the conversation we're about to have."

It was clear from his tone that Ronald had miscalculated. Badly.

I crossed my arms in front of my chest, suddenly less capable of hiding my annoyance. "I'm not a stripper, asshole. I'm a..." I gritted my teeth, wanting so badly to say *highly trained intelligence operative*. "Dancer."

Maris sighed and pinched the bridge of his nose. "Can you just get on with the dancing, then? Better yet, don't. We can sit in here for the duration of a song and call it good."

Well, *that* wasn't happening. If this asshole was going to spend time in a private room with me, I was going to do my best to hack *his* damned phone instead. Which required getting close to him.

"No can do, baby," I purred, stepping closer and fingertip-walking my way up his chest to the cleft in his chin, which I tapped lightly. "I'm required to give you a dance. So, sit your sexy fucking ass down."

He did not look amused, but he sat anyway. I moved over to the music system keypad and selected two songs without asking his preference or how long he wanted the dance for. Let him cut it off early if he noticed the song change. Two songs would give me more time.

If the man wasn't attracted to me, though, this was going to be next to impossible. No horny haze of distraction to take advantage of. And he'd most likely balk at my touching him.

"You want to pretend I'm someone else, baby?" I asked with a grin, moving my hips and shoulders as the opening notes of Ginuwine's "Pony" came over the sound system. "Go right ahead."

He sat back and studied me, large hands open and easy on his long thighs. "You're not going to give me the little talk about not touching?"

My heart rate picked up, but I forced myself to shrug easily. "Maybe I want you to touch me."

This was unfortunately true.

As I moved closer, I caught the expensive scent of him. I saw a few little imperfections like a spot he missed shaving and a scar in his eyebrow that made him even hotter somehow.

There was no doubt, Locke Maris was a tasty treat. And if he ever wanted to touch me... well, I was no saint. I'd let him touch the fuck out of me.

For free. Repeatedly.

"That's not going to happen," he said. The words came out easy. Informative. Not snappy or emotional.

"Suit yourself," I said, raising my arms above my head and shimmying my hips. "But I'm planning on touching *you* unless you tell me not to."

He tilted his head at me before nodding toward the door. "Are you his type?"

"Whose type? Your friend?" I moved between his open knees. Of course I knew he'd met Ronald, but my goal was to act stupid enough to not be suspected of hacking the man's phone if he caught me attempting it.

"My associate. The man with the cigar." Was there a hint of calculation or amusement in his eyes? It was hard to tell.

"I don't know, but I thought he was into me. Would have liked to dance for him privately," I said with a wink.

I danced closer, placing my hands against the wall on either side of his face before leaning in to whisper in his ear. "But I'm happy to be dancing privately for you, even if you haven't had your sexual awakening yet, sweetheart."

The low rumble of his laugh made my dick suddenly feel strangled in the jock I wore under these shorts. As far as I could tell, the man's phone was in his inside jacket pocket.

"Let's get this jacket off," I urged, smoothing my palms over his chest and pushing the jacket open. The firm muscles of his chest were impressive. "In case you get... hot."

Thankfully, it really was warm in here. He allowed me to pull the jacket off and set it on the sofa next to his hip, where I'd be able to reach it when I got onto his lap. The music's bass pounded through the room and our bodies as I locked eyes with him and moved to the beat.

I ran my fingertips down his chest again and across his broad shoulders before moving his knees together and kneeling up on the sofa on either side of his thighs.

He relaxed back into the velvet cushions and lifted an eyebrow. "You're determined to dance for me despite my lack of interest," he said.

I pursed my lips and then tapped them with a finger as I leaned back and ran my other hand down my chest to my abs to draw attention to them. I had fucking V-cuts for god's sake. He could at least *envy* them, even if he didn't want to touch them.

"How much will you give me if I can make your dick hard?" I teased, gyrating over his lap without sitting on it, then moving off him again to slowly unbutton my shorts.

He huffed out a laugh. "You? Make me hard?" He pretended to think on it before rolling his eyes. "A thousand dollars. In cash."

My own eyebrows shot up. "A cool grand just for making you hard? Deal."

His dark eyes met mine. "You're awfully sure of yourself. I bet high because it's not happening. Unless you bring one of your lady friends in here."

Well, now he'd triggered my obstinate stubborn streak.

I grinned and began a sultry striptease, pulling my shorts down enough to reveal my white cotton jock. After four nights of dancing here, I'd learned that many men had a secret locker room fantasy. And so far, this athletic jock had a 100 percent success rate on making men lose their fucking minds.

"Challenge accepted."

2

LOCKE

THIS KID WAS A DISTRACTION. Something about him got on my nerves. Maybe it was his cocky assumption that he could "turn" me, as if that was something a person could do.

He couldn't. I loved women. Had been enjoying sex with women since I was fifteen and one of the assistants at my grandfather's office had offered to blow me in a back room at the company Christmas party.

I considered myself to have a higher-than-normal sex drive but was only ever driven toward women. Period.

The dancer was attractive, I'd give him that. Muscular and fit. Eyes such an impossible blue I wondered if they were colored contacts. His lips reminded me of a phrase my sister had tortured me with one long-ago summer on Martha's Vineyard, when she'd first discovered romance novels and wouldn't stop talking about the hero's "bow-shaped lips."

I'd confidently told her that no one in real life used that phrase. But this man's lips were decidedly bow-shaped.

I almost wanted to take a picture and send it to Celeste.

It was no secret that Ronald Gillen was into men, even though he was supposedly closeted. At this point, I was pretty sure even his wife knew he fucked men on the side. That was none of my business. My only reason for being here was to get him to stop harassing one of the women in my office.

Because Ronald was also into women. And Shayla had been the target of his sexual pursuits for a few months now, since she'd been hired to work in the Maris office he had the most dealings with as a longshoreman boss.

Nobody working for me should have to deal with nasty, unprofessional innuendos and pressure to accept a date. My father might not have cared enough to protect our employees back when he was in my position, but I sure as fuck did.

I was here to give Gillen a friendly reminder to treat my people with respect. But this was a one-shot deal. If he wasn't smart enough to take the hint, I'd ruin his fucking life.

His insistence on giving me this lap dance—a thinly veiled attempt to distract and gain some sort of leverage over me—wasn't helping his case. If anything, it was only making me more annoyed.

I ran my eyes over the dancer's fit physique. Cut abs and Adonis belt. Slightly rounded pecs and shoulders. Tanned skin and...

My eyes caught on his brown nipples as he teased them with his fingertips. They crinkled and tightened at his touch. For some reason, that got my attention. Did they remind me of a woman I'd been with? Possibly. Not that I could think of which woman that might be.

I imagined what they would feel like against my tongue. Whether I could make them tighter and harder by sucking on them.

My dick began to stir, and I quickly shifted in my seat. *What the fuck?* Allowing myself to compare him to sexy women I'd been with was a surefire way to lose this damned bet. And that wasn't happening.

"What made you want to become a dancer?" I asked as disinterestedly as I could. Conversation about work was a guaranteed boner killer for everyone.

He peeled his shorts open further, exposing a surprisingly dull cotton jock. That certainly wasn't going to turn me on. I'd seen a million of them over the years in various locker rooms and had never gotten hard for one. They reminded me of the grassy, sweaty smell of soccer practice from years ago.

He pushed the shorts down and shimmied out of them, turning to show me his bare ass, which I had to admit was impressive. Squats on the pole clearly worked for him.

"I like to move my body," he said, backing up until his ass was swaying over my lap. "I like to touch myself." He turned back to face me and climbed over me again, his knees on either side of my thighs.

Then he lowered his voice to a sultry whisper and leaned in to brush his lips against my ear. "I like to fuck."

My eyes drifted closed. There was something about that word spoken in his voice that made my skin prickle. Maybe it was the music or the room. Maybe it was simply the idea of sex and all the skin on display.

"Fuck or be fucked?" I challenged. But it came out sounding rougher than usual.

He leaned further into me until his hands were down by his knees and his nose was brushing the skin of my neck. "Depends which one you're into, baby. Do you want to hold me down and fuck my tight hole? Is that what you're thinking about right now? How you'd force me to take it? Put me on my hands and knees for you? Maybe wrap one of your big hands around the back of my neck and teach me a little lesson?"

His voice was breathy, which made my heart pound harder and my own breaths more shallow.

"You seem to be begging for a lesson of some kind," I said coolly.

The fact that he seemed to be getting under my skin annoyed me. But I couldn't deny he was alluring in a certain kind of way. I could see why someone like Ronald would be into him. Into this.

The image of Ronald touching this beautiful man with his perpetually sweaty hands annoyed the fuck out of me.

The dancer continued, moving his body in a way that was hard to ignore. Sultry and languid as the music shifted to something slower. He straightened up so I was staring at those nipples again. They were close enough to lean over and taste, which of course I would never do.

I caught a whiff of his deodorant as he lifted his arms above my head on the wall and looked down at me. My eyes strayed to his armpit and the brown hair there.

He smelled good. I was half-inclined to ask him what products he used.

A tiny dark mole peeked out from the edge of the armpit hair, matching a somewhat lighter one above his lip. My stomach clenched.

No wonder he'd been hired here. He was undeniably, objectively sexy. Hiring him was a solid business decision for this place. How much did dancers get paid, anyway? Was profit sharing involved? There really should be, because the ROI of—

I felt another tightening in my gut as the dancer's eyelids fluttered closed and he mouthed a snippet of the lyrics.

"I'm so used to being used..."

Did those lyrics mean something to him, personally? Was he in a bad situation? Of course, I'd heard horror stories of people being taken advantage of in jobs like this. Usually those were women, but maybe the same held true for men in powerless situations.

Not that it mattered to me, obviously. None of us got to choose the situations we were born into, and we all had to make the best of the hands we were dealt. Besides, the man had admitted to enjoying being watched. Enjoying fucking, even.

I glanced down his body to the cotton jock, imagining what it would look like if the sex act he was miming right now was actually happening.

Just as a point of intellectual curiosity.

Simply because the biology of gay sex was something I'd never had reason to consider before.

And because thinking about it passed the time—*god, how could the music still be going?*

Not for any other reason.

Something about that cotton jock kept drawing my attention, though. The bulge in the front was impressive. Surprisingly so. But then again, the man had been hired to show it off.

"You like what you see, baby?" he teased, a hint of laughter in his voice.

Every time he called me baby, it set my teeth on edge.

"Not much to see at all," I said, trying to sound bored.

In reality, I wasn't bored. I was entertained against my will.

There was no denying the man had rhythm. He moved his body like liquid lava, thick and warm, curving over every surface it crawled across and leaving bright, charred destruction in its path.

His fingers moved across my neck until I realized he was gently clasping the front of my throat. I met his eyes with a glare.

"Inferiority complexes are so unattractive," he purred with a knowing grin.

I huffed out a laugh, which made his fingers press harder against my throat for the barest moment. "I do okay."

"I'm sure you do." He ground down on my lap, pressing his ass into my groin before rolling his hips forward. His cock pressed into my lower stomach, surprising me with its firmness.

"You getting hard for *me... baby*?" I teased back. "Now who owes who a grand?"

I realized my hands were squeezing my own thighs tightly enough to wrinkle my suit pants. I smoothed out the fabric and moved my hands to the back of my head to keep from touching him by accident.

Heat from his body swirled around us, scented with a hint of masculine sweat that didn't turn me off the way it should. My eyes returned to the jock, curious to see whether I was actually making him hard or if he was just naturally... gifted.

The top edge of the jock's elastic strap had moved low enough for me to see a line of soft brown pubic hair above it. A thin trail of it roamed up to his belly button. I realized he wasn't waxed or shaved like a woman would be at a club like this.

Why not? Did gay men prefer their dancers to have body hair?

I trailed my eyes up to his chest, trying to consider whether I would prefer hair on a man if I were gay.

He moved the hand from my throat down my chest and to his jock, where he squeezed himself and let out a little moan. My heart rate shot up as I stared at what he was doing.

"Yes," he said in a breathy voice.

I glanced up at his eyes, only to find them closed and his head tilted back. His cheeks were flushed pink, and his lips were moist like he'd just licked them. His chest heaved with rapid, shallow breaths. The music poured around us with its low beat and dirty lyrics.

"Yes, what?" I asked before reminding myself I didn't care. My voice sounded like broken glass scattered across gravel.

"Yes, you make me hard. Yes, you make me want to touch myself. Get off to the image of your fat cock shoved deep in my hole. Of you holding me down and fucking me. Of you telling me to *shut up and come* before someone finds us together. Of you clapping a hand over my mouth and whispering filthy words in my ear as you take me from behind."

My chest heaved as the oxygen in the room thinned. He moved his hand again, and I realized he'd snuck his fingers inside his jock to touch himself. He was still perched in my lap, his ass brushing against my cock with every move he made to the sultry music.

"Keep going," I said gruffly.

Clearly, he was enjoying himself, right? So why not let him fantasize since we were stuck in here together anyway.

He leaned forward and rested his forehead on one of my shoulders, bracing a hand on the sofa by my hip. With his other hand, he continued to tease and stroke himself under the jock. We both stared at what he was doing, and I caught glimpses of his cock where the jock was pulled away from him.

Then he started making... *noises.*

Tiny little breathy whimpers.

A sucked-in breath.

A muffled gasp.

The head of his cock poked out of the top of the jock, and for some reason, he nearly stumbled off my lap. I quickly reached out and grabbed him around the waist to keep him from falling.

"Oh god," he breathed, reaching for his cock again. "Fuck, fuck, fuck."

I couldn't believe this guy was jacking off right here during a VIP dance. On top of me. *In my lap.* It made my stomach flip.

Turn. I meant, it made my stomach *turn.*

"You always perform sex acts when you bring people in here?" I demanded.

He didn't pick his head up from my shoulder and glare at me like I would have expected. Instead, he tilted his head a little and spoke with his soft lips against my neck. The sensation made my skin itch.

"Never. *Fuck.* Get mad at me again." He added the last part with a breathy chuckle. "It's doing it for me."

"You're crossing so many lines right now," I warned.

"Don't you want to make me come, Daddy?"

There was still a hint of amusement in his voice, and it made me want to laugh. "Don't call me that," I said with my sternest voice. "I'm not your fucking daddy."

"Will you be angry if I come? Punish me? Put me over your lap and take it out on my ass?"

My hands tightened, and that's when I realized I was still holding his waist. In fact, one of my hands was somehow fisted in the strap of his jock.

I quickly let go and moved my hands back to my thighs, but they landed on his bare legs instead.

His eyes widened as I looked at him quickly in apology and pulled my hands back like they'd been burned.

The sound of his laughter filled the small room. "The skin cops aren't coming, big guy," he assured me. "I promise."

Then he eyed me carefully. "And you can't catch gay from me either, FYI."

"That's not what... I didn't..." I cleared my throat. "There are rules."

"I liked your hands on me," he confessed. And for some

reason, he sounded more real in that moment than he had this whole time. "Even if *you* didn't."

The seduction scene seemed to be over. I glanced down at the cotton jock and noticed it was no longer as full as before. His cock had deflated, understandably.

When I'd recoiled from him, I'd come off as disgusted by him. In reality, I'd been disgusted by myself. I never wanted to take advantage of anyone, especially someone doing their job.

Hell, that was why I was here in the first place.

"I should probably go," I said, shifting a little to remind him he was still on my lap. "Thank you for the... ah... dance... I'm sorry, I didn't catch your name."

"Jett," he said, before his eyes widened in surprise. "Thro. *Jethro*. My name is Jethro. Jethro Davis."

He moved off me and shimmied his hips a little while adjusting himself. "Fucking blue balls," he muttered before turning to look for his shorts. As he bent over to pick them up, his ass cheeks opened, revealing a clean, pink hole. In that flash of a moment, it squeezed tight, the skin wrinkling and releasing in a way that went straight to my dick.

I stared at it, suddenly imagining myself doing everything he'd described. Grabbing his hips and driving my cock deep inside him. Telling him to be quiet and take it while he let out more of those breathy whimpers and grunts.

Blood rushed south and filled my cock so fast my head wobbled like a helium balloon losing its string.

When Jett—because there was no way his name was actually Jethro—stood back up and turned to face me, my face flooded with heat. Though where that blood came from since it was all in my dick, I had no idea.

I stared at him.

He caught my expression and tilted his head to the side. "You okay?"

I gritted my teeth and shook my head, opened my wallet, took out a thousand dollars, and dropped it on the sofa behind me.

Then I did what I should have done when goddamned Ronald Gillen first suggested this.

I got the hell out of there and took care of business.

3

JETT

"He's clean," Trevi said as I walked into the conference room a few days later.

"Who?" I sipped the coffee I'd picked up on the walk in this morning. It always took forever for it to get cool enough for me, despite this being one of the coldest Octobers on record in Manhattan.

"J. Locke Maris. The guy whose phone you cloned? Big shipping exec? Nothing in it except basic work shit and a few texts with family, friends, and lovers."

My ears perked up. "Lovers?"

Trevi shrugged. "I mean, there are a few texts arranging dates with a few rich ladies, but he's boring as fuck, honestly. Seems like a workaholic. Which makes no sense, considering he's a trust fund baby."

I nodded, unsurprised. That tracked with the man I'd encountered that night at the Candy Bar. The man who'd been determined to stay rigidly in control, even while I was half-naked and gyrating on top of him.

It also tracked with what I'd found online later. While I was… ah, researching someone associated with an op. As a diligent intelligence agent does.

Locke Maris was one of those rich, powerful people who often got written up in gossip blogs. "Famous for being famous," as my uncle Derek would say.

Sure enough, photo after photo showed the sexy Maris heir dressed to the nines with a model-beautiful woman on his arm, shaking hands with other high-powered executives in boardrooms, or playing golf at exclusive resorts. In every single shot, his face was tense and unsmiling, like he couldn't wait to get back to his spreadsheets.

And fair enough, I supposed. Maris Holdings was a massive conglomerate managing shipping lanes, satellite tracking, and data analytics for global trade, and he would run the whole thing someday. Those were probably some pretty important spreadsheets.

None of that explained why he'd come to a gentleman's club for a conversation with Ronald Gillen, though.

The good news was, I'd managed to clone Ronald's phone later that night when he'd gone to the men's room and the damned thing had fallen out of his pocket onto his chair. I'd rolled my eyes hard at how much effort I'd gone to, only to succeed through dumb luck.

"What about Gillen's phone?" I asked Trevi.

He grinned. "Oh, there was all kinds of shit in his. Names, dates, transactions. What a dumbass. None of it connected to Maris, though, that I could find."

Before he could tell me more, our boss and a few other support staff came in.

Rocky's long blonde hair was pulled up in its usual twist, and the high heels paired with today's dark suit were black with red polka dots. Though ESP agents could wear whatever we wanted as long as we were professional from the waist up for Zoom calls with the Feebs and CIA higher-ups, Rocky only ever let loose with her footwear.

"Good work, everyone. Thanks to Agent Marian here, we now have the names of three longshoremen suspected of moving the drugs off the Meridian Bell before customs inspection. The FBI's picking the suspects up for questioning and pulling surveillance for the dates and times of transactions noted in Gillen's phone."

"And Gillen?" Trevi asked.

Rocky shrugged. "It seems Gillen didn't know the precise nature of the contraband shipment, though he accepted money in exchange for looking the other way while the longshoremen had unauthorized access to the container. They've decided to leave him in play, just in case he can prove helpful again."

Even a year and a half into this job, part of me still expected someone to protest. Gillen might not be the biggest fish in the criminal pool, but he was undoubtedly a criminal.

ESP's job was to gather information, though. Deciding what to do with that information was outside our purview.

Rocky finished up a few last points, then thanked everyone again before moving on.

"Alright, next up is something that just came in this morning. We've been tasked with sending an agent to Nome, Alaska, to check out credible evidence of suspicious drone activity at a remote outpost. Last summer, a joint research exercise was aborted when it became clear it was a cover for unauthorized surveillance. We need to determine if this drone activity is related."

Her eyes met mine, and she gave me an apologetic wince.

"Sorry, Jett. I know the last thing any of us wants is to go somewhere colder than here, but a female agent would stand out too much on this one, and you're closest to being able to grow out a scruffy beard." Her eyes flicked to another agent in the room. "No offense, Thompson."

Thompson's baby face turned pink while Trevi elbowed him and snickered. "Don't worry, boo. You're next up on the college ops."

I thought about the trip home I'd been planning to take in a few weeks. While it wasn't exactly hot in South Carolina this time of year, it was definitely warmer than here. And sure as shit warmer than Alaska. "Yeah, no problem. I can handle it."

"'Course you can. And in exchange for this op, you'll get extra time off when you return, so feel free to start researching discount Caribbean cruises now," she added with a wink.

"Yeah," Trevi said with a snicker. "Maybe having those images in your head will help keep you warm."

It did not, in fact, keep me warm in Nome. Nothing did. Not the high-tech clothes I'd brought or the hot baths I'd taken every night in my hotel room, or even the memories of fondling myself while perched on Locke Maris's lap.

I froze my fucking ass off while spending two weeks running down a group of rogue high schoolers who turned out to be playing an obscure internet game that relied on drone footage to score points.

In addition to freezing to death, I also managed to get food poisoning from bad fish and spent four straight days stuck between my bed and the bathroom.

When I finally got back to New York, I was ready to catch the next flight to Charleston so I could visit my family and recuperate in the house on Rabbit Island. But when I video called my parents to tell them I was coming, they said I couldn't.

"There's a late-season hurricane heading our way," Mav said. My poor dad looked as devastated as I felt. "We're heading out to Napa to visit everyone at the vineyard."

Beau popped his head in the frame. "Hey, kiddo. Come join us in California."

The thought of turning right around to the West Coast made my stomach turn. "Can't do the long flight or the social rah-rah. I think I'm going to stay here and let the jet lag overtake me."

Beau's eyebrows dipped. "At least go out with some friends. Seems like you've been doing nothing but work since you started that job. We know you want to impress the consulting firm, but they have to allow you some personal time."

Mav nodded over Beau's shoulder. "Corporate life in a traveling job's hard enough as it is. Be sure you're taking time for yourself so you don't burn out."

I nodded and grinned. Little did they know I did just fine with personal time. Between cases, I usually managed to go out to bars in the city and pick up men to go home with. I danced, drank, and fucked before it was time to dive into another case.

My cousin JJ claimed I was in my *Sex and the City* era. My brother Gabe claimed I was abusing Grindr. They were both right.

I loved the city. Loved the diversity compared to my small South Carolina town. Loved the anonymity. The opportunity. The shopping and eating. I loved everything about New York. And now here I was, able to suck every bit of marrow out of its bones.

After finishing the call with my parents, I went back to my tiny apartment and slid between rumpled sheets, falling asleep for a solid ten hours before waking up crusty-eyed and gross. I showered for a long time, then dressed before heading to get something to eat.

My uncle Jude was a famous musician who'd given each of his nieces and nephews trust funds to help pay for our education and give us financial security. Other than using some of it to pay for my college tuition, I tried never to spend any of it. But tonight, I allowed myself to splurge on a kick-ass steak dinner. I was worn down from the travel and stomach bug, and I never wanted to see another fish as long as I lived.

Thankfully, Rutherford's had a spot in the very back corner next to the kitchen. I caught up on my social media scrolling while eating my buttery filet and garlic mashed potatoes. After the amazing meal and a few drinks, I headed to the men's room.

Instrumental music filled the dimly lit tiled space, glinting off old brass fixtures. As I pulled myself out at the urinal, someone came in and took the spot at the urinal next to mine.

I was planning to mind my business, but something about the way the man smelled was so familiar I couldn't help but turn my head slightly...

Locke Maris was already looking at me, eyes narrowed like he was trying to place me.

Fortunately, my ESP training kicked in, reminding me that to this man, I was Jethro Davis, go-go boy at the Candy Bar.

"Aren't you the... stripper?" he asked, finishing and putting his dick away before I had a chance to sneak a peek at it.

Annoyance flashed through me. "Dancer," I corrected, putting my own dick away as quickly as possible. "Yes."

"What are you doing here?"

The question wasn't rude. More genuinely curious. And I didn't blame him for wondering, since most of the staff at the Candy Bar—hell, most of the staff at ESP—wouldn't be able to afford a glass of water at Rutherford's.

"I had a... a date." I lifted my chin and tried not to notice the way his suit—possibly custom, definitely expensive—lovingly hugged every inch of his broad frame.

His eyes widened. "A... *date*?"

The way I'd said it was normal. A reference to a man taking me out to dinner for the purpose of romance.

The way he'd said it was different. A reference to a man taking his boy toy out to dinner before fucking him. For cash.

Locke's oh-so-serious face wore an oh-so-serious frown like he was concerned... or more likely judging me. I had to wonder if he'd ever had sex for fun in his oh-so-serious life.

Not that it mattered. His assumption suited my purposes since it fit with the cover.

I stood up straight as if trying not to look ashamed. "Yes. As if it's any of your business. Good night."

I stepped toward the door before remembering to wash my hands. I had to do an embarrassing little sidestep slink to the basin.

Locke stepped up behind me, his larger body making me feel hemmed in. I refused to meet his eyes in the mirror.

"Is your date someone I know?"

The warm air from his words hit the back of my ear and made me shiver. It was cold, surrounded by all that marble tile.

"How would I know if you know him?" I tried putting a flirty tone on my words.

I was actually feeling a little cheated that I couldn't flirt with him for real. *Fucking straights, always ruining a good time.*

"Is it the man from the club?" he asked.

I flicked water off my hands and turned to grab a linen towel from the pristine stack on a silver platter. "As if he could afford me."

"How much is your date paying you?"

I tossed the towel in the nearby basket and turned to face him. "The same amount you paid me for our bet, babe. Maybe after a few more dates, I can afford this place on my own. Excuse me."

As I stepped past him, he caught my wrist in his warm, firm grip. "Wait."

My heart skipped in my chest. Locke didn't scare me in the least. But he did surprise me. And that scared me a little. "What?"

"You're going to let some stranger fuck you for a thousand dollars?"

I lifted my chin and met his eyes. They were just as intense and sexy as I remembered. Every cell in my body wanted this man's attention, even if he currently thought I was a whore.

"Baby, I'm going to suck his dick for a grand. If he wants to fuck me, it'll be five. And right now, you're costing me money."

Not gonna lie, it was a little liberating to get my *Pretty Woman* on. All I needed was a tall pair of zip-up boots and a killer wig.

The fact that I'd suck Locke Maris's dick right here and now for free made me want to laugh my ass off. But mostly, I wanted to disgust him enough to get out of there before blowing my cover.

I wasn't exactly the most experienced operative in the world, and one of our first lessons had been not to bite off more than we could chew. The more lies you told, the larger the cover burden became.

Locke's nostrils flared, and his fingers relaxed, letting my hand fall. He nodded once.

I left the men's room, feeling his eyes burn me the whole way out.

Just in case he was behind me, I made a small production out of going to a now-empty table and looking confused and frustrated that my "date" had seemingly abandoned me.

Then I got the hell out of there.

As soon as the frigid night air hit my skin, I shivered for real and pulled my coat tighter. I hung a right and began walking toward the Lower East Side, tucking my chin down inside my scarf and tugging my beanie out of my pocket. Only three blocks later, a sleek, dark SUV pulled over, and the rear window rolled down.

Locke's frown hadn't changed but had somehow managed to get even sexier. "Get in."

"No way. I don't want a ride."

The vehicle kept pace with me despite someone behind honking their horn.

He stayed calm. "Get. In."

This was a very bad idea, but then again, it *was* fucking freezing out here. Whatever digestive benefits I'd get from walking would be negated by my freezing to death before I made it home.

Besides, WWJD? By which I meant *What Would Go-Go-Boy Jethro Do?*

"Fine," I muttered, yanking the door open and climbing in. The air was blessedly warm, and I couldn't help but groan a little in relief as I slid deep into the buttery leather bucket seat. "Forty-seven Market Street, please," I called up to his driver.

I saw the man make eye contact with Locke, who gave a very faint headshake. "I'd like you to come home with me."

I stared at him. "You *would*?"

"Yes."

"*You* would?"

"You sound like an idiot," he muttered.

Not untrue, but I wasn't sure what was happening here... even though my dick seemed to be stupidly, immaturely, *career-killery* on board with whatever the guy wanted.

Then again, Locke had come up clean in our investigation, and I was on personal time right now.

We'd just be two private citizens... doing *private* citizen things.

"Forgive me if you're shocking me a bit, Mister..." I suddenly realized his driver could hear us. "...*Hypocrite*," I finished vaguely.

"Can you just keep your mouth closed until we get there? Is

that too much to ask?" He blew out a breath and pinched the bridge of his nose, and though it seemed impossible, he somehow frowned harder. "I've had a shit day, and my head's killing me."

Keeping my mouth shut wasn't something I excelled at. But on the off chance I could convince him to let me do something else I *did* excel at later, I stopped talking and enjoyed the ride.

4

LOCKE

I DIDN'T KNOW what I was doing, exactly. All I knew was that in the weeks since seeing this kid in the club, I hadn't been able to stop thinking about him.

More accurately, thinking about his effect on my dick. Because in the end, I'd gotten hard for him.

Even more accurately, I'd gotten hard thinking about fucking his ass. I'd gone out and found a woman to have anal sex with—which had been fine. Good, even. But it hadn't put an end to my thoughts of *this* particular ass.

So when I'd run into him at Rutherford's, I hadn't been surprised at my dick's continued interest. He was even more attractive than I remembered. Still moved with liquid heat despite being at an uptight restaurant, dressed in ten times more clothes than before.

But when he'd mentioned being there with some presumably old-ass sugar daddy, I *had* been surprised at my visceral reaction. At how wrong it had felt.

Jett Whatever-his-name-was seemed like the kind of guy who

could get modeling jobs paying way more than whatever he could make as an escort. Or get a corporate job, depending on his education—hell, even without an education. All he'd need to do was drop a few comments about "preferring hard work over useless degrees," and my grandfather would hire him at Maris.

Not that it was worry over the man's financial future that made the *wrongness* of his plans for the evening sit heavy in my gut.

No, it was the sudden, unshakable conviction that Jett should be coming home with *me*.

I wanted him to suck my cock and help me kick this fucking headache. And maybe kick whatever the hell spell he'd put on me at the Candy Bar while he was at it.

When we arrived at my house, I thanked Demarius and let him know my guest would most likely be ready to go home in the next couple of hours.

Demarius nodded, unsurprised. He was used to waiting around to return women home after I fucked them—not that he'd ever assume that was what this was. Everyone, including my driver, knew I wasn't gay.

"I didn't take you for a Greenwich Village guy," Jett said as I let him into the town house.

"What guy did you take me for?" I tossed my keys aside and led the way up the stairs to the kitchen.

"Meh. I've only been in the city a year and a bit, but I'd guess Upper West Side. Isn't that where all the uptight banker types live?"

I snorted. "Do I look like an uptight banker type? You know what, don't answer that. What would you like to drink?"

"I'm guessing you're out of Natty Light and Boone's Farm, so I'll go with whatever you're having."

I was surprised to hear a slight Southern softness to his voice as he said the names of the beer and cheap wine. "Where are you from?"

He hesitated for a beat before giving me a megawatt smile. "Is this the getting-to-know-you portion of our date?"

I pulled out the bottle of Macallan and two lowball glasses. "Definitely not a date."

"So more like a *date*?" Jett batted his lashes coyly while copying the tone I'd used back at the restaurant.

To my shock, I felt myself blushing slightly, though I couldn't say why. I busied myself pouring scotch, glad he couldn't see my cheeks.

"Charleston, South Carolina," he said when I put the scotch down on the counter and handed him one of the glasses.

I couldn't determine whether or not he was telling the truth. Maybe it was close enough. More likely a shitty small town nearby —one he might have had to leave when they discovered he was into men.

"What brought you to the city?" I asked, handing him one of the glasses of scotch.

He shrugged. "Always wanted to come here. Try my hand at having a big life." Then he winked at me. "Maybe fuck all the pretty boys while I'm at it."

I tossed back the scotch in one swallow. "I'll give you a thousand dollars to suck my cock."

Jett's cheeks flushed, and his eyes brightened. Possibly from the drink. More probably from the knowledge he'd still get a payday tonight, even though I'd noticed back at the restaurant his sugar daddy had run off.

"I'd suck your cock for free," he said. "Gladly. But I thought you were straight."

I could tell he was teasing, but I answered anyway. "I am. But I want my dick sucked, I have zero patience for small talk with a woman right now, and you're easy. Yes or no?"

Jett moved in front of me and immediately lowered to the floor on his knees. The quick obedience made me suck in a breath. Jesus, if only it were this easy with a woman.

I hadn't imagined we'd do it here. In my mind, we'd have a drink to help take the edge off and then go up to my bedroom. The more I thought about it, though, the better this was. It would be over quickly, and I could send him on his way.

He placed his hands on my thighs gently, as if being careful not to scare me off. "You gonna tell me your name, big guy?"

It was strange to not be recognized. Rare, but it certainly happened. It felt like I'd been featured in a thousand articles, social media posts, and magazines as one of the world's richest and most eligible bachelors, and was generally recognized on the street from having been photographed for many of them.

"Locke," I said.

"Nice to meet you, Mr. Locke. I'm Jethro, in case you forgot." His grin was so genuine and engaging, it was hard not to smile back.

"Locke's my first name." I watched him as he moved his hands slowly up my thighs toward my belt. "And if your name's Jethro, I'll suck *your* cock."

His easy laughter filled the kitchen. "Fine, Jett, then."

I yanked my belt open, frustrated that this was moving so slowly. "Stop acting like I'm a delicate flower. I assure you, I'm not."

"A mouth's a mouth?" His smirk drew my attention to his lips.

"Some are better than others," I said. "But they probably all feel warm and wet around a cock."

"Oh, honey. Spoken like someone who's never been blown by a

man who loves sucking cock and knows exactly how to do the job."

I didn't want to think of all the other men he'd blown. He was here now, with me, and that was all that mattered.

That, and getting this over with, of course.

"Can we get on with it?" I grumbled. "I have a splitting headache and would really like to have an orgasm and go to bed."

His smile faltered just enough to make me feel like an ass, but then I noticed the fire in his eyes.

He wasn't hurt—he was pissed.

Fine. I didn't care.

"Sure. Hey, you seem like the kind of guy who likes a little teeth in his beej, yes? Great."

His hands took over unbuttoning my pants, which he did with a little too much vigor. As soon as he got them open, he stopped and made a little sound in his throat that went straight to my balls.

"Oh," he breathed. "Now, that's promising."

He leaned in and rubbed his cheek against the front of my boxer briefs, pressing against my cock and humming in pleasure. Then he sucked in a deep breath through his nose as if sniffing me.

"So good," he said under his breath. "So fucking good."

I moved my fingers into his hair, pushing it back so I could see his expression better. His eyes were closed, and his eyelashes fluttered against the tops of his cheeks. He wet his lips with his tongue, leaving them shiny...

As if he couldn't wait to taste me. *Jesus fuck.*

My breath came in shallow pulls as he continued to rub his face over my cock, nosing my balls and the crease between them and my thigh.

What the fuck even was this? Some kind of cock worship through cotton?

Whatever it was, it seemed to be working. My dick began to fill, shifting against the fabric.

He pulled my suit pants down more until they finally gave up and hit the floor. Then he nudged my feet farther apart and moved his hands up to my groin, pulling his face back and meeting my eyes again. "You sure, Locke?"

The question was serious, but hearing my name in his voice made it even more real.

Fuck yes I'm sure. I'm sure I want a mouth on me, regardless of whose it is.

"Suck my cock, Jett," I growled.

He pulled down the front of my underwear to discover I was already half-hard, which was impressive considering the nearly blinding headache I had. But maybe the loss of blood in my head was helping because I already felt a little bit better. Hell, maybe it was simply the distraction.

Because Jett was distraction incarnate.

His fingers wrapped around my cock and tugged gently before he opened his bow-shaped lips and engulfed the head in his mouth. As soon as his hot, wet tongue hit my skin, I grunted in surprise.

Fuck. *Fuckkk.*

The sensation of his tongue moving along my shaft was indescribable. Maybe it truly didn't matter whether it was a man or a woman doing the sucking because this was fucking incredible.

Or maybe you're just desperate.

My cynical brain was hard to hear over the sound of blood thundering in my ears. Jett's hand cupped my balls, his fingers brushing against my taint.

"Fuck!" I grunted again, unable to keep my reaction private.

"You like that?" he hummed. Then he grinned without taking his eyes off my hard, wet cock. "Good boy."

"Shut the fuck up," I said, trying not to laugh. "Less talking, more working."

When a woman was on her knees for me, I was careful not to say or do anything that could be interpreted as degrading. But Jett didn't seem to give a shit. It was a relief not to have to worry about that.

And this was a transaction, pure and simple. Not a date. Not romance. Just one man doing another man a service for cash.

It was freeing in a way.

He sucked along the length of me, making my toes curl in my shoes. I threaded my fingers in his hair and held on. "Just like that. Fuck, that's good."

Jett's talented mouth made me feel things I hadn't felt before. Sensual pleasure, yes, but it was more than that.

Freedom from social norms.

Curiosity.

Was this why so many men hired sex workers? So they could take their pleasure as they wanted it without any concern for reciprocation?

But even as I thought that, I couldn't help but imagine what it would be like to reciprocate with Jett. What would that look like? What made him feel good?

As soon as the tip of his tongue hit just the right spot under the tip of my cock, I stopped thinking about anyone's pleasure but my own. My balls were full and tight, brushing against Jett's pointed chin when he slid the flat of his tongue down my cock at a certain angle before taking it in his mouth again and dropping over it until the tip was in his throat.

The sound of him happily gagging on my cock was what pushed me over the edge, releasing my orgasm like flicking open a pressure switch. I cried out and cursed as the feeling overtook my entire body, my cum spilling into the man's throat.

The man.

The *man*.

In that moment, I didn't give a single shit. Only that I felt incredible, my headache was nearly gone, and I had a warm, wet tongue bathing me gently as I came down from the momentary high.

Impossible blue eyes peered up at me. And that's when I noticed several things at once.

Jett's cheeks were flushed pink, his eyes glassy with need, and his hand was in his open pants, jacking himself rhythmically.

I stared at the opening of his pants, at the faint peek of the tip of his erection as it poked out from his closed fist. His groan filled the kitchen as he sank lower and rested his head against one of my thighs.

His free hand still held on to one side of my ass, something I hadn't noticed earlier. Now I noticed every millimeter of the connection, his strong fingertips dangerously close to the cleft between my cheeks.

The moment became uncomfortable quickly. Reality crashed down as I realized not only did I have a sexual encounter with a man, which wasn't something I was into, but also that I had a sex worker in my house.

What the fuck had gotten into me? If I wanted a blow job, I could have picked up any woman at any bar between Rutherford's and here.

But when the softest whimper escaped Jett and his glassy eyes sought mine, something in my gut anchored me there to watch. To bear witness to his pleasure and take a little bit of pride in the fact his orgasm was *mine*. He was coming because of *me*. Because he'd found satisfaction in pleasing *me*.

When his orgasm hit, he didn't cry out or grunt. His whimper turned to a soft keening noise, as if he was trying to stay quiet and keep his reaction to himself.

"Give it to me," I growled, glaring down at him. "That orgasm's mine. I want it *now*."

The noise turned into a cry as his hand tightened on my ass, and another spurt of cum spilled from his cock onto his fist. His entire body shuddered as he laid his head on my thigh again.

I ran my hand through his hair and murmured. "Now who's the good boy?"

What the fuck am I saying?

Another soft sound escaped him as his breathing slowed. I cleared my throat and leaned over the counter to grab a dish towel, handing it down to him before tucking myself away and yanking up my pants.

"I'll call Demarius to meet you outside. He'll take you home."

He stood and wiped his hands quickly, tossed the used towel in the nearby sink, before straightening his clothes and zipping his pants.

"Appreciate it, man. Take care." He turned toward the stairs, seemingly unbothered by my dismissiveness.

"Wait," I said, reaching for my wallet. I pulled out ten hundred-dollar bills and handed them over. "Thank you."

He stared at the money for a beat before looking up at me. The pink of his cheeks darkened. "Yeah, er... thanks. See ya." He took the money and hurried down the stairs.

After watching him go, I slunk up to my bedroom, feeling a strange sensation in my chest and stomach that didn't have anything to do with the fact that I'd just let a man suck me off... and everything to do with the fact I already wanted him to do it again.

"Too bad," I muttered to myself as I yanked off my clothes and tossed them in the laundry bin. It was a onetime thing, and now it was done. The next time I needed a quick fuck, there were any number of women I could call without losing a thousand dollars in the process.

Just like after the encounter at the Candy Bar, I vowed not to think of Jett again.

And just like after the night at the Candy Bar, I failed. Epically.

I kept reminding myself it was the skill, not the man. Anyone with a mouth that talented would've gotten me off. The stubble scratching my thighs, the masculine strength in the hands gripping my ass—those were just... details. Irrelevant details.

No matter how many times I repeated it to myself, I couldn't get the kid out of my mind.

Three months later, I finally broke down and went to 47 Market Street. But the woman who answered the door said no one matching Jett's description had ever lived there.

He was a ghost.

5

JETT

THE HAMBURG JOB came at the perfect time. I couldn't get Locke Maris off my mind and had been on the verge of doing something very stupid, like knocking on his front door and begging him to fuck me, when Rocky called me in for an emergency meeting that stole all my focus.

Today's shoes were Big Bird–yellow Crocs thrown on over thick, mismatched wool socks and worn with jeans and an MIT hoodie. Her ensemble, more than anything else, indicated how serious this case was.

"I need you to relocate to Germany for six to eight months," she said, clicking her laptop keyboard until a giant case file flashed on the giant wall monitor at the end of the room. "We have a situation developing near Bremen, but we believe it involves water routes near Hamburg."

As she began explaining the developing situation—environmental activists serving as a distraction for a weapons smuggling ring using the Elbe and Weser Rivers—I felt a familiar excitement wash over me.

This. This was why I'd joined ESP.

I wanted adventure and excitement, challenge and intrigue. I also wanted to help. To make a difference. To be one of the global good guys. And an opportunity like this was pretty rare for an agent without years of experience.

"Why me?" I asked, quickly adding, "I mean, I'm thrilled and totally here for it, but I'm curious why you picked me."

"We think the best position for gathering intel is through an organization called Climate Direct-Action Network, which is primarily comprised of college and grad students. Your cover is Jonas Vogel, a disenchanted marine-biology student taking a gap year between undergrad and grad school to travel around Europe." She slid a tablet over to me. "Here's the bio, but we're sending it to your portal as well. You have three days of travel to study it and become this guy. Your job is to get to know the other members through seemingly random meetings, like striking up conversations at pubs and stuff. Express your discontent with your country's efforts at environmental policy, et cetera."

As she clicked through various images of the leaders of the group and explained the situation, I got a clearer picture. My part in this wasn't a rush. It was a long-game mission to gather intel.

"Why the urgency?" I asked when she took a moment to steal a sip of her coffee. "It seems inconsistent with a six-to-eight-month op."

She blew out a breath and met my eyes. "That's the second part of your mission. We already have an undercover agent in the group, a young woman from the office in Munich. The flow of intel from her has slowly dried up, meaning her reports went from detailed and helpful to vague and useless. We believe she may have been turned."

"Is she okay?" I asked, surprised and concerned.

"Yes. We've seen her and have verified she's healthy and safe.

We've even offered to swap her out in case she needs a break for any reason. She insists she's fine and still working hard in the effort."

Rocky met my eyes. "We need you to figure out what's going on with her. Has the organization truly stopped colluding with the smuggling ring—in which case, why isn't she asking to be reassigned? Is she being kept from the inside information for some reason—in which case, we need to extract her? Or is there something else going on? You know from your training that the most likely scenarios when an agent has been turned are that they disappear completely or they start feeding just enough information to keep the home office from getting suspicious. That's what seems to be happening here. We just can't be sure."

I nodded. "And if you simply pull her off the op, you'll never know."

"Right. We need to know what information she has access to and compare it to what she's passing along to us."

It was exactly the kind of assignment I'd dreamed about. And I was ready.

"Let's get it done," I said, leaning forward to begin studying my cover.

IT TOOK me ten months to finally get proof of Mira Stein's double cross. In that time, I'd had to sink deep into my cover, becoming an angry asshole who spent more money on beer than food, and who got into bar fights at the drop of a hat.

There'd been times I hadn't been able to get in contact with ESP, times I'd had to miss key check-ins, and times I had to spend my cash on bribes instead of food.

By the end of the mission, I was starving for more than just a decent meal. I was starving for sleep in a comfortable bed instead of a blanket-covered pallet in a run-down warehouse, time back home with my family, sex with any man who would have me, and affectionate touch, if I could get it.

My plan was to head to Rabbit Island for a couple of weeks after my debrief in the office. Back home, Mav and Beau would feed me, I'd be able to roast in the white-hot sand of August, and I could get as many hugs as I wanted. My sister, Becca, would probably even agree to give me a shoulder rub as long as I binge-watched whatever show she was into while she did it.

As for the sex, I wasn't willing to wait. As soon as I got to the airport hotel in Amsterdam, I headed to the bar to grab a bite to eat and scroll a hookup app before even checking out my room.

I got lucky as soon as I took a stool at the bar. The man finishing his drink next to me seemed just as eager for attention as I was. As soon as I finished my meal, he invited me up to his room.

Fuck. Yes.

"Let me close out," I said, gesturing to the bartender that I was ready for my check.

The man gave me his room number and excused himself to the restroom. As soon as the card machine spat out a receipt for me to sign, I heard a familiar voice behind me, filled with surprise.

"Jett?"

I turned and nearly fell off my stool. "Locke? What are you doing here?"

His eyes devoured me, roving up and down my body as if taking inventory or making sure everything was where it was supposed to be. When his eyes returned to mine, they were filled with heat.

Locke Maris and his frown were absolute catnip to my touch-starved, normalcy-starved self. I wanted to inhale the fuck out of him and ride the high as long as possible.

I quickly signed the receipt, so distracted I probably signed my real name by mistake, before grabbing my backpack and Locke's hand and pulling him into a nearby alcove half-hidden behind a heavy velvet curtain.

And then I lunged up and kissed him, full on the mouth. My hands clutched at his suit jacket lapels tightly enough to pull him off-balance. He slapped one hand on the wall and reached the other around my back to hold me close.

His mouth stayed on mine, kissing me back with as much pent-up desperation as I had after ten months of celibacy and sacrifice.

"Please take me to your room," I begged. "Please."

I didn't want the handsome stranger from the bar. I wanted familiarity. Someone dominant enough to make all the decisions so I didn't have to think. And someone whose presence overwhelmed me enough not to leave room in my head for anything else.

Locke pulled back and studied me. "Are you in some kind of trouble?"

At that point, I would have said whatever I needed to say to get him to agree. "Yes."

I didn't even feel guilty for the lie because it wasn't one. I'd just spent the better part of a year in life-or-death trouble. I was troubled to the edges of my teeth. And right now, all I wanted was to leave it behind for a night.

"Let's go," he said gruffly, pulling my hands off his lapels and straightening his jacket. He placed a hand on my lower back and steered me toward the elevators, taking my ratty backpack out of my hands and throwing the strap over his shoulder.

Within moments, we were in a large suite with walls of glass probably overlooking something impressive. I didn't care. All I wanted to overlook was Locke Maris, preferably naked.

"Tell me what's wrong," he demanded as soon as we were alone behind a closed door.

"Nothing, I just..." I blew out a breath, feeling more vulnerable than I cared to admit, even to myself. "You're a sight for sore eyes."

He studied me while setting my bag down, pulling off his jacket, and laying it neatly on the back of a chair. "You look awful. Where have you been?"

I let out a weak laugh. "Thanks. Way to romance a guy."

"Is that what I'm trying to do?" He crossed his arms. "Funny. I wasn't aware."

"I want to be fucked," I said, needing to keep this from turning into a conversation about me and what I'd been through the past almost year. I avoided sounding whiny, but only just.

His nostrils flared. "Not happening. Tell me why you're in Amsterdam."

Was I still Jethro Davis, go-go boy from the Candy Bar? Or was I allowed to be Jett?

I knew better than to tell him my last name was Marian. When you meet someone on an op, your connection to them will always be traceable to the op. Which meant I could never be Jett Marian to him, junior consultant for a "global solutions" company.

So I chose to do what my training demanded and stay under the cover he knew.

"You remember the guy I was with at the restaurant in New York?"

His forehead crinkled. "Your date? I never saw him."

"Probably for the best. Anyway, he hired me to go on a business trip with him, only his wife found out about it. He gave me some cash but then took off." I shrugged. "I've been traveling around a little, hoping to see some things, but I found a killer deal on a flight home I can't pass up, so I'm heading back tomorrow."

He uncrossed his arms and stepped toward me, tugging up the hem of the plain black T-shirt I wore.

"You're skin and bones," he said, nostrils flaring. "Haven't you been eating?"

I yanked my shirt back down, suddenly embarrassed. "That's none of your fucking business. And if you don't like what you see, I can take it out of your sight."

As I turned to leave, I tilted my head up to keep the stupid tears in my eyes from spilling out.

I hadn't been eating. Or sleeping. At the end of the op, I'd been alone and scared as fuck, expecting Mira Stein to discover I was with ESP and rat me out to Malte and Timo, who would have beaten me to death and tossed me in the fucking river without giving it a second thought.

"Sit the fuck down," he said, moving to the telephone and picking it up.

I was too tired to argue. I felt like I could sleep standing up. Being in Locke's presence felt like the safest I'd been in ten months.

"Fine," I muttered, dropping onto the sofa, kicking off my shoes, and stretching out. I closed my eyes for a minute, listening to the deep, rhythmic sound of him telling someone to do something. I wasn't quite sure what and honestly didn't care.

Sometime later, I awoke to the light clatter of dishes being set down. I was curled on the sofa with a hotel duvet on top of me, warm and comfortable in the air-conditioned room.

"Come eat," Locke said.

"I already ate," I croaked, voice rough from sleep and exhaustion.

"Don't care. Come eat more."

I sat up and tried to get my bearings.

Amsterdam.

The mission was over, and I was headed home.

"Yeah, okay. Gonna find a bathroom first." I made my way to the first open door I found and moved into the bedroom in search of a toilet. Locke's suitcase was open on a luggage stand, and his Dopp kit was on the bathroom counter.

After emptying my bladder and washing my hands, I snooped through his toiletries, going so far as to take a picture so I could snoop in more detail later.

It wasn't creepy; it was good intelligence work.

When I made my way back to the main room, Locke was sitting at the small dining table, scrolling his phone. "Eat," he said without looking up.

I moved to the table, suddenly interested in whatever smelled so good. It was French onion soup, a fresh Caesar salad, and a basket full of various rolls. Nothing too heavy for this late at night, which I appreciated.

"You're not eating?" I asked as I dipped the spoon under the cheese layer of the soup bowl.

"I'd just come in from a business dinner when I saw you," he said, setting his phone down and reaching for the cocktail in front of him. "Who was the man you were with?"

The soup was incredible. I quickly swallowed another spoonful. "What, at the bar? I didn't catch his name."

His eyes darkened. "The man who left you in Europe. You were with someone at the bar?"

I blinked at him, suddenly realizing my mistake. "Oh. Nobody. Nothing."

He simply stared at me until I confessed. "I picked up a guy at the bar. He was in the men's room when you found me. We were going up to his room."

Locke's eyes flicked to my backpack, which had been part of

my cover. I'd lived out of the one bag the entire time I'd been in Germany. If I never saw the damned thing again, I'd be happy.

I realized he was putting two and two together and getting twelve. He clearly thought I'd come to this hotel bar to pick up a rich guy for a free stay in a nicer place than I'd ever be able to afford. I made a mental note not to let him see the hotel key card in my back pocket.

"Thank you for the food," I said, trying to change the subject.

"You should take better care of yourself." He sounded irked.

"You make it sound so easy," I said, irked, too, for another reason. I'd spent most of this year in degradation and discomfort to keep at least ten large shipments of illegal weapons from reaching mainland Europe and getting into the hands of ultra-right terrorists, which would've destabilized the entire fucking world, including his precious shipping empire.

Locke's jaw flexed, and his frown intensified before he blew out a breath. "I'll take you home."

I stared at him in disbelief. He'd said it like he was doing me some giant favor. What an egotistical ass. "I don't need your fucking charity."

"Don't be ridiculous. I have a plane, and I'm headed to New York in the morning anyway." He lifted an eyebrow. "You really going to waste your money just to save your pride?"

I was so tired, I wanted to cry. If this was how I felt in a temporary moment of weakness, I couldn't imagine how people who really lived in dire straits all the time felt. "I'm going to go."

Locke stood and moved toward me just as I stumbled over the foot of the table.

When he curled his hands into fists instead of reaching to steady me, I couldn't decide if I was relieved or disappointed.

"Stay," he demanded in a tone that probably worked on all his underlings.

I glared at him. "No."

"Please," he ground out. "I already told you we're not having sex. So just fucking... *stay*, okay? Get some decent sleep."

His reminder that he wasn't interested in me sexually should have been a relief. I was too tired, too worn-out, even though I wanted him. Badly.

But it stung nonetheless.

The set of his jaw was counterbalanced by the concern in his eyes and the furrow between his eyebrows.

Always so damn serious.

I wanted to ask him why he cared so much about where I slept. Why he'd somehow made me his responsibility. But I didn't think he'd answer honestly.

Locke Maris was a difficult nut to crack. And he obviously had no interest in me cracking his nut, which was probably for the best. It was too messy, and I cared too much about my career.

For tonight, though, I could at least allow myself to stay with someone I could trust.

"Okay."

6

LOCKE

My thoughts were all over the place. How did this guy manage to get under my skin the way he did?

Maybe he was right. Maybe I saw him as a charity project. But it wasn't pity I felt when I looked at him. It was anger.

I wanted to salt the fucking earth.

He was a completely different Jett than the one I'd known. Skin and bones, weary and exhausted, when he should be smiling and dancing unabashedly. How dare the man he'd been with treat him like shit?

If I had someone under my protection, I'd make sure they had everything they needed. More than that, I'd make them feel special. Precious. Any man who could afford to bring an escort halfway around the world could also afford to treat him right.

Jett would eventually give me the guy's name. And then I'd make sure the asshole rued the day he ever laid eyes on this kid.

"You're welcome to shower," I said, trying hard not to scare Jett off. I could tell he was on the edge of bolting, and the very idea that he'd have to find another man to charm into a free room for the night made me sick to my stomach.

Clearly, he'd needed food and sleep. Not sex.

Not that I didn't want to fuck him. I did. In fact, when I was with Jett, my sexual attraction to women was nonexistent. Like smoke suddenly ripped out of the air by a vacuum—there one minute and gone the next.

I'd thought of sex with Jett Davis many times in the months since I'd seen him last. Getting hard for him twice now had made me question my sexuality, but in almost a year of looking for any sign of any attraction to other men, I hadn't found it. At least not enough to want to act on it.

It was just *him*.

Just this stripper—pardon me, *dancer*—and paid escort.

Which meant it wasn't his maleness that intrigued me. It was something else.

Hell, maybe it was the fact that he challenged me. Most of the women I'd ever been with did whatever they thought I wanted. Jett *should* have done whatever I wanted, but instead gave me attitude —and that teasing, smirky smile—at every turn.

Jett lifted an eyebrow at me. "Are you saying I stink?"

I glanced at the sofa, which was definitely not large or comfortable enough to give him the rest he needed. The man needed to sleep in a bed, and mine was plenty large enough for the two of us.

"I'm saying I don't want to share a bed with someone who could still be covered in another man's jizz," I snapped. "Get in the fucking shower."

He snickered as he headed back to the bedroom. Within moments, the clear sound of the shower spray turning on indicated he hadn't closed the bathroom door.

My curiosity got the best of me, and I wandered into the bedroom to catch a glimpse of him.

He was softly singing the lyrics to what sounded like a German pop song under his breath as steam billowed out of the glass cubicle. His eyes were closed and face tilted to the ceiling as the water cascaded down his hair and onto his back. The rounded shape of his ass drew my attention, but then again, all of him was like a magnet for my eyes, including the cock hanging from a thatch of dark pubic hair, moving a little against his thigh as he swayed to the tune.

As my eyes roamed and he turned to put his face in the spray, I noticed bruises along his sides and back in various shades of yellow, brown, and purple.

What the fuck kind of danger was he putting himself in? Accepting money for sex made people vulnerable to abuse. Had his sugar daddy put hands on him? Or had something happened while he was practically homeless here in Amsterdam?

I knew if I asked him about it, he'd likely leave, so I kept my mouth shut. But the anger in my gut ratcheted up several notches. When I found the asshole responsible for this, I would rip his life into tiny pieces.

I forced myself to move away and stop staring at him like a creep. Jett had been badly used. I refused to be another person who took from him, even if all I was taking was a glimpse of his gorgeous body.

I moved around the room, pulling off my clothes and changing into a pair of sleep shorts. I grabbed two bottles of water from the fridge in the main room of the suite and put one on each nightstand. When Jett was finally out of the shower with a towel wrapped around his waist, I joined him in the bathroom to brush my teeth.

"There's an extra set of everything there if you need it," I said, gesturing to the toiletry kit I'd requested be sent up with the food. There was no telling what was in his ratty backpack.

He thanked me softly and reached for the kit, yanking out the toothbrush and toothpaste before attacking his teeth like he was trying to rid himself of mouth demons.

"Onion soup," he garbled when he caught me staring at him in the mirror. "Thank me later."

I thought back to the kiss he'd planted on me in the bar. Wholly unexpected and raw. Desperate.

All-consuming.

I'd never kissed a man before, so I'd been caught completely off guard. And then I'd been surprised to… not hate it.

Fine, I'd liked it. Very much.

But maybe that was simply the passion he'd put into it. It was hard not to respond to that kind of energy.

It didn't matter, though. I shouldn't have kissed him back. And I definitely shouldn't have been thinking of all the other things I wanted to do to him.

I was dating someone. Two months ago, my grandfather had insisted on setting me up with the very beautiful Kalliope Andros. To my surprise, we'd been compatible—meaning she was as insatiable in bed as I was and remarkably unsentimental, a rare combination.

I hadn't promised Kalliope exclusivity—that wasn't something I did, ever. But I knew after two months of seeing each other fairly regularly, she'd consider it a betrayal if I had sex with someone else. Unlike my wastrel father, I was capable of controlling my urges so I didn't fuck up a good thing…

Even if being here with Jett made it hard to remember why my arrangement with Kalliope *was* a good thing.

Even if Jett was temptation incarnate.

The man was a mystery. After discovering he'd given my driver a false address, I'd tried to track him down. I'd even gone so far as to have my assistant get our security company involved to run a background check on him.

There was no "Jett Davis" to be found. But we'd found plenty on *Jethro* Benjamin Davis. Which meant Jett had been telling the truth when he'd given me that name, even if Jett was the name he chose to go by. He was from Charleston, South Carolina, too, just like he'd said, and the only child of a single mother who worked at a Waffle House.

Since moving to New York almost two and a half years ago, his job history read like holes around a dartboard. He'd been an "entertainer" at the Candy Bar for four months, a DoorDasher for a year before that, a promotional event greeter, a cater-waiter, and various other temporary, low-paying jobs.

But the most interesting piece of information was that he was only twenty-three. This somehow seemed decades younger than my thirty-one. But between the two of us, he seemed to be the one with harsh life experience.

I'd grown up in luxury, with every wish granted and every privilege imagined. My parents hadn't been supportive or caring, even before my father's death, but I'd always had my grandfather, Maris Holdings, and a legacy to uphold.

I stepped slightly behind Jett to floss my teeth after finishing brushing. My eyes caught a drop of water sliding down the back of his shoulder and over the sharp peak of his shoulder blade. It paused for a moment as he leaned over the sink, then continued down his poor, abused spine, before dipping into one of the dimples in his lower back just above the edge of the towel.

I imagined tracing the droplet's path with my tongue. Kissing each bruise, each knob of his vertebrae. Then I imagined my thumbs finding those divots over his ass while I held his hips and drove into him.

My heart rate picked up.

Fuck. What was it about this guy that made me consider fucking another man? Especially when I had a willing woman waiting for me back in the city.

My eyes met his in the mirror. His cheeks and neck were splotchy red.

"You like what you see, Locke?" he asked softly.

I ignored my thickening cock. "Who did this to you? The bruises."

He blinked, the wet, dark lashes tangling before revealing eyes a faded denim blue.

"I need his name, Jett," I said. "I know people who can give him a dose of his own fucking medicine."

He turned to face me and stepped into my personal space, wrapping his arms around my back and hugging me. His nose pressed into the side of my neck.

I froze, my arms down by my side. "What's happening right now?"

"It's a hug," he said with a smile in his voice. "We're hugging."

"I don't hug," I insisted, wrapping my arms around him. If there was something this man seemed like he needed right now, it was a little comfort.

It took me several long moments to realize I'd been had.

I pulled back and put my hand on his chest, holding him away from me. "Tell me who caused these bruises. And no distractions this time."

"That's not going to happen. But I appreciate your concern. I promise I'm fine."

He moved toward the bedroom, pulling his towel off and dropping it on the floor as he went.

I stared at the pale globes of his ass. The dimples above it. The long, slender stretch of his back.

My heart thundered in my ears. My neck. My face.

My cock.

Calm the fuck down, Locke. It isn't any different than seeing Kalliope's naked back and ass.

I sucked in a breath.

Lies.

Jett moved out of the bedroom and past the small dining table, then leaned over to rifle through his backpack, presumably in search of clothes.

As my eyes went straight to the cleft of his ass and the drop of his balls between his legs, I realized I'd been had again.

That rosy-pink hole caught my attention and held it tight. It seemed his mouth wasn't the only thing I was interested in.

My dick hardened painfully at the sight of his body, his vulnerability.

His unexpected need for comfort and protection.

Something about Jett sent rational thought skittering away like a handful of pebbles tossed into gale force winds.

7

JETT

I WAS TOO tired to tease Locke about sex. While I wanted so damn badly to be taken hard and fast from behind and fucked straight to sleep, it was clear Locke didn't want me like that.

Maybe it was the way I looked—vastly different from the man with hot V-cuts and abs back at the Candy Bar. Or maybe Locke's little moment of sexual experimentation had been a bust. One and done, no need for more.

Either way, it was clear that wasn't happening. I pulled on my last clean pair of boxer briefs and slid into the bed.

"I know I should probably offer to sleep on the love seat, but that's not happening," I said without looking at him. I didn't want to risk the look of disappointment or, worse, disgust on his face when he realized I was going to hold him to his earlier offhanded statement about sharing the bed.

"It's fine," he said hoarsely. "Just go to sleep."

I gritted my teeth, turning to face the wall. "Asshole," I muttered under my breath.

The bed behind me dipped, and it took all of my core strength to keep from rolling toward him. Instead, I rode the edge of the bed like my life depended on it.

"You're going to fall off the mattress."

"I'm fine."

Locke sighed like I had worked his very last nerve. "'Course you are."

He turned off the lamp, dousing the room in darkness. Silence slid between us, and for some reason, that made me feel sorry for myself.

Tired, lonely, and rejected. The triple crown of pathetic. I couldn't help the tears that slid down my face or the tiny accompanying hitch in my breathing.

Beside me, Locke froze.

"Are you... crying?" he demanded, horrified.

"No," I sniffled, willing the hot tears back into my eye sockets. *Betraying little fuckers.* "Of course not. Jesus."

After a minute, I couldn't help but sniffle again. It was just exhaustion, that was all.

"Get the fuck over here," he grumbled, reaching a warm hand around my hip and tugging me back until I was engulfed in his arms, little-spoon style. "Go to sleep."

The tears came faster but silently. I thought I'd gotten away with my noiseless pity party until his deep voice murmured, "You're killing me."

I turned in his embrace and buried my face in his neck, reaching my arms around him and hugging him tightly.

"I'm sorry," I half sobbed. "It doesn't mean anything. Ignore me."

His strong hands roamed up and down my back, careful of my bruises. I waited for his gruff demand again to tell him who had hurt me, but it didn't come. Instead, he shushed me gently and murmured reassurances into my ear, his warm, minty breath soothing and welcome on my skin.

And all I could think was... I hadn't known Locke was capable of this. Of simple comfort.

I knew him as a proud, controlled man who sometimes pissed me off with his cool, confident demands. As a man whose perma-frown made it damn near impossible *not* to tease and provoke him. But his deep voice muttering nonsense words—rumbling from his chest directly into mine—was more soothing than anything I could remember.

It reminded me of the way my fathers treated each other, never hesitating to show that the other was beloved and cared for.

I began to calm, wondering if I should pull away again and let him sleep without a clinging spider monkey plastered to his front. Instead, I squeezed my eyes closed and let myself daydream that I was in the arms of someone who loved me. That I was something protected and cherished.

Once upon a time, this was something I'd wanted for myself. Then I'd gotten my heart broken in college—twice—and realized I was happiest when I didn't take things too seriously. Casual sex with no strings was fun and easy. I fucking loved it. Besides, commitment and true love weren't exactly compatible with being an ESP agent.

If I ever *did* want commitment, it wouldn't come from a straight guy like Locke Maris, who lived in a completely different world than I did, or any other straight guy who didn't appreciate how good it was to be with another man.

This was simply a moment of weakness.

"Go the fuck to sleep," he grumbled, tugging my hair a little where his fingers had been running through it.

"Fine, but I'm not moving," I warned him sleepily. "I'm staying right here in your face."

He shifted a little, making his lips accidentally brush my forehead. "I will give you a thousand dollars if you shut up and do as I say."

I snuggled in closer to his warm, reassuring strength. "I will give you a thousand dollars if you suck my cock right now."

He let out a huff of laughter, his breath moving the hair over my forehead. "Baby, if you had a thousand dollars, maybe we could talk."

I fell asleep with a grin on my face and words of my own wealth on the tip of my tongue. I didn't speak them, of course, or believe his offer. But I imagined his hot mouth around my cock anyway. It was enough to set me up for the best dreams possible.

Unfortunately, that wasn't how dreams worked.

The nightmare began as all my nightmares for the past several weeks had. Murky water against the docks in Hamburg. Overcast skies and too-brisk wind off the water. The now-familiar clank of equipment and shout of the hafenarbeiter as they loaded and off-loaded cargo. The forbidding sense of danger and deceit. The knowledge that something wasn't right.

What happened in the dream varied, but the sense of foreboding and danger never did. Sometimes my family would be there. Gabe or Becca or one of my dads. Sometimes it would be my grandmother. My boss. One time, it was the young woman who'd sold me a sandwich a few days earlier.

In the dream, they'd been taken. Or murdered. Or shoved into the impossibly deep port waters, never to be seen again.

I startled awake, as I always did—gasping. An aborted scream of agony on my lips. Sweat covering my body.

But this time when it happened, strong male arms banded around me, exacerbating the terror.

I struggled, sucking in as much air as possible so I could cry for help.

"Jesus fuck. Jett. *Jett*! It's me, Locke. Stop fighting me. For fuck's sake." The sleep-hoarse voice was familiar, and a wave of relief washed over me.

"S-sorry," I said, choking on an inhaled breath while simultaneously trying to huff out a laugh to assure him I was fine. The result was a coughing fit.

Locke loosened his hold, allowing the chill of the room to hit my warm skin where our chests had been pressed together.

I blew out a breath and started to move toward the far side of the bed, but then I realized Locke had only moved away to grab a bottle of water for me. "Drink this."

The water was cool and clean. I gulped down several sips before handing it back to him to put back on the table. "Thanks."

"You want to talk about it?"

"Definitely not."

"Suit yourself. Go back to sleep, then."

I stared at the dark shape of him, only faintly visible in the city lights coming around the edge of one curtain. "You're bossy as fuck. Do you think you run the entire world? Because you sure act like it sometimes."

He rolled flat on the bed beside me and laughed hollowly. "Feel like it sometimes, too."

"Do *you* want to talk about it?" I asked, wondering if I could gather any kind of intel while I was here. Might as well, since the whole sex thing was off the table, and the idea of returning to the murder pier in my dreams was not welcome.

"Nothing to talk about. I manage an arm of my family business. Someday—hopefully no time soon—I'll run the whole thing. And running Maris comes with serious responsibilities."

Calling Maris a "family business" was a massive understatement. Hell, half the ships in the Hamburg port during my mission had been Maris ships, the equipment stamped with Maris logos.

His family was so wealthy, I was surprised he didn't travel with personal security.

"Is that why you were in Amsterdam?" I pressed. "Big ruler-of-the-world meetings?"

"Not exactly." After a brief hesitation, he added, "I was here for a chess tournament."

Unbelievable as this statement seemed, it had the ring of truth. For a moment, I gaped at his shadow in the darkness. Then I scrambled to turn on the bedside lamp.

Locke threw an arm over his eyes with a muffled curse.

"A *chess tournament*? What the fuck?" I demanded with a laugh. "I've been around plenty of chess. No way are you a chess nerd."

Locke pushed himself up to sit against the headboard, rubbing his eyes and glaring at me all the while. His face was adorably sleep-rumpled with a red splotch on his cheek where it must have been pressed against some part of me while we slept.

"It's an old-world variant of chess called Paxis," he explained. "More complicated than regular chess. And I wasn't playing, I was watching. My grandfather's the Paxis player in our family."

My fingers itched to look it up online, but I resisted the urge. "Let me understand. You travel the world to cheer on your grandfather while he plays ultra-nerdy chess?" I teased.

He crossed his arms in front of his chest, and I tried not to appreciate the broad spread of his shoulders and curved muscles of his pecs. Or the masculine hair on his forearms. Or the happy trail I could now see disappearing from his belly button down into the sheets.

"Something like that, yes." He eyed me. "Don't tell me you don't have a nerd hobby because I won't believe you. Everyone has one."

I blinked at him and blurted out the truth. "S-seashells." I cleared my throat. "I'm on the hunt for the tiniest perfect specimen. Specifically, spiral or conch-shaped. So, like, a triton or tulip would work. I like tritons, but they're rare. I've heard they're more common in Hawaii, but I've never been."

"Where have you found them so far?" he asked, looking surprised. "Rockaway Beach in Queens? I've heard of people searching for shells there."

"No, South Carolina. I grew up on the coast there, I think I told you?"

Shit. Had *I told him that?*

After so many months as Jonas Vogel, it was hard to remember Jethro's backstory period, let alone which bits of it Locke and I had discussed.

Fortunately, the stakes were low. I'd wager big money Locke remembered even less about Jethro than I did, and I couldn't imagine a scenario where he'd go looking for info. He'd probably forgotten I existed until we'd run into each other.

Still, it made sense to change the subject.

"Anyway, I haven't been to a shell beach in years," I lied. "Tell me more about Paxis. Is there like an association of players? Is your grandfather ranked? Who puts on the tournaments? Do you play, too? Does your whole family?"

Something shifted in his demeanor. "My grandfather plays with a private group. And yes, I'm... learning. My father had no aptitude for the game while he was alive, and my sister, Celeste, has no interest in it." He shook his head, faintly amused. "Which left me to take it on."

That was an odd way of talking about a hobby. As if playing chess were somehow a heavy responsibility he carried. Maybe the family's reputation in Paxis circles was an important part of his legacy.

But a new, slightly horrifying thought occurred to me. "Is your grandfather here now?" *Is he likely to show up and wonder why I'm in your bed?*

Locke shook his head. "He flew to his house in Italy for a break. I have to return to the city for work. Running the world doesn't just *happen*, you know."

I laughed. Beyond the golden circle of light from the lamp, the room was dark and still, making it feel like the two of us were suspended in a bubble. Maybe that was why Locke was answering my questions honestly. Maybe that was why I wanted to reciprocate.

"My dads are into a cutthroat card game called Egyptian Ratscrew," I blurted. "Have you heard of it?"

Locke's frown intensified like he wasn't sure he'd heard correctly.

"I know, I know, weird name, but you might like it. It's really fun and intense. It involves a lot of slapping and yelling. At least, my family's variation does." I held out my hand and pointed to a needle-thin scar on my pinkie. "This is from my sister's pointy-nail era. Siblings are vicious."

We talked for a little while longer. I explained how the card game worked and regaled him with a few stories of epic games over the years, congratulating myself that I was aware enough not to share any specific identifying details he could use to find my real identity.

Eventually, I turned the light off again, and we continued talking as we sank back down onto the bed, facing each other.

It was... *nice.*

Weirdly domestic, but... good.

As I closed my eyes, I imagined this was how actual couples fell asleep, talking about unimportant things, and I found myself wishing for more of it.

I wondered what it would be like to see Locke again, back in the city.

I even wondered whether there was a chance I could ever tell him who I really was.

As Locke's breathing evened into sleep, my eyes shot open in the dark.

What the fuck was I thinking? Breaking my cover? For... a chance at begging for scraps from a straight man's table?

This op had really fucked me up if this was how low I'd sunk. The fantasies spinning in my head were ridiculous. Not to mention dangerous.

Which was why I waited to be sure Locke was truly asleep and then quietly got the hell out of there to catch my flight home.

And why, two weeks later, I agreed to transfer to the Miami office.

8

LOCKE - PRESENT DAY (THREE YEARS LATER)

I HAD zero patience for pouty women, and the one on my arm was skating close to my limit tonight.

"I told Taylor we'd meet her and Eduardo at the Sky Bar after this. Kizzy Sweet is DJ'ing, and it's gonna be lit! Pretty please, Lockie? It's the least you can do after making me sit through the Marines' dinner party thing."

"Maritime," I corrected for the second time as I guided Willow through the frigid night air toward the entrance to The Glasshouse. "It's the Maritime Foundation benefit."

While she continued to whine and plead, I thumbed the invitation in my coat pocket. It had come by courier just before I'd left the office.

The Paxis Council was calling an unexpected tournament.

After my grandfather's death several months ago, many people had reminisced about him being a formidable chess player. But no one outside the Paxis Council itself had known what was really on the line when he and his powerful friends gathered to play.

The fate of the world. Or at least the stability of it.

It was always unsettling to have the council call for a tournament outside our normal schedule. But this was also the first tournament where I'd be playing the Maris family seat. And on top of that, it was my turn to host the gathering at my grandfather's—now *my*—place in Italy.

The combined pressure had been sitting heavily on my chest for the past hour.

I'd need to go to Italy a few days early to prepare the villa and staff. Then spend at least a week playing in the tournament to hash out the needs of whatever had popped up.

On the one hand, I was looking forward to it. Despite being late spring on the calendar, New York's winter still had a stranglehold on the city, and an almost two-week break in the sun sounded ideal. I also enjoyed the intellectual challenge of the game itself.

On the other hand, I didn't enjoy the immense responsibility that came with what it represented. In this case, trying to foil Russia's latest plot to cause instability in the Baltic region.

And the timing could not have been worse. Just when I was finding my rhythm as the head of Maris Holdings, I had to step away for a couple of weeks.

But the memory of my grandfather's words about the Paxis Council was never far from my mind.

Responsibility chooses the worthy, not the willing.

Russia's provoking activities had been ramping up, and it seemed it was no longer a collection of minor events but something much more serious, which meant it was time for the Paxis Council to do its thing.

Years ago, when my grandfather had finally revealed to me that Paxis was a front for some of the world's wealthiest people to solve critical global challenges, I'd been shocked. I remembered asking him why the council couldn't just solve issues verbally, through discourse and diplomacy the way government leaders did.

Some things are too important to say out loud, Locke. Words are powerful. And they cannot be unspoken.

I hadn't understood at the time, but now I did. Words could be overheard. Translated. Shared. Game moves could be disguised, and the way this particular game was played, with a combination of specially crafted boards and pieces, the moves could only be understood by someone trained for years on the game.

Someone like me.

"I'm not up for a late night," I murmured to the woman beside me as I lifted my chin to an acquaintance at the coat check stand.

After shrugging off her big, feathery coat, Willow looped her arm through mine, pushing her breast against my elbow, and tugged on my necktie. Her breath was hot on my ear. "What if I let you do whatever you want to me back at your place first?" she purred in a voice almost loud enough for people to overhear. "Then can we go back out? You know you'll feel better after a little... exercise."

Her suggestion was laughable since we both knew she'd let me do whatever I wanted to her after this, regardless. But if she wanted to leave after I was done fucking her, that was fine by me. I'd sleep better without her in my bed.

"We'll see."

As soon as we entered the dining room, my distraction changed from the Paxis tournament to the crowd of important benefactors. I greeted people as they approached, introduced them to Willow, and generally made small talk until it was time to sit for the meal.

One of the things I appreciated about the woman on my arm —in addition to her sexy-as-fuck body—was her energy. She chatted with anyone and everyone, gossiping about celebrities just enough to be engaging but not enough to be annoying.

Though I was known as a brilliant business negotiator, smiling and putting people at ease was not a skill I possessed. My sister, Celeste, had inherited all the charm in our generation.

As Willow entertained the people at our table, I ruminated about the Paxis invitation again.

Most people on the council brought a "date" of some kind. Men brought wives or girlfriends, women their husbands or boyfriends. They might also bring practical guests as well: assistants for the work-obsessed, or a chosen successor, as my grandfather had brought me for years.

While the council played in the afternoon and evening hours, those who didn't know the truth of the game kept busy with work or enjoyed their time shopping, skiing, or sunbathing, depending on the tournament location. The game would often pause for an extravagant sit-down dinner at night, where everyone was invited.

In the past, I hadn't brought anyone since I'd been there with my grandfather, but I'd suffered for it. While other men were able to return to their rooms and blow off steam with a willing wife or girlfriend each night, I'd returned to my hand, laptop, and a giant-sized bottle of lube. Like a fucking loser.

After the last tournament—on a remote island in the Caribbean a few weeks before my grandfather's death late last year—I'd sworn to myself I'd bring someone next time to warm my bed.

This time, it would be even more critical for me to have a way of releasing the tension.

Willow was young and beautiful, poised and fashionable. She was currently a successful social media persona, posting stories about celebrity fashion faux pas with humor and an air-headed quality I hadn't yet determined was real or not. She also seemed to be on the hunt for a husband, which was one of the reasons I'd been careful to set expectations with her that I was only interested in casual.

If I invited her to my place in Italy while I hosted some of the world's most powerful people, my warnings to her wouldn't matter. She—and most likely others—would see it as a sign of more serious intentions than I had. Not to mention, the Paxis Council would be nervous about having an influencer there, despite the NDA everyone was required to sign.

But the alternative was a couple of stressful weeks without sex, a situation I was unwilling to consider again.

As they so often did when I thought about sex, my thoughts swung back to the man I'd met several years ago. The one who'd made me question everything about my own sexual identity.

After losing Jett for the second time, I'd returned to the city, eventually finding myself at a gay bar in the Village. *Just research*, I'd told myself. To understand what I'd felt with Jett. Or, hell, maybe in an attempt to find him.

He had an incredible fucking mouth.

I'd nursed one drink and watched. Men kissing, touching, laughing. I'd waited to feel something—attraction, curiosity, disgust, anything.

I'd felt nothing. Yes, the men had been attractive. Objectively so. But I hadn't wanted to take any of them home with me.

It hadn't been any random man I'd wanted. It had been him. *Just him.*

Which was somehow worse, especially considering the man didn't seem to fucking exist, despite my best efforts to locate him.

"Locke said he'd take me, didn't you, babe?" she asked.

My stomach dropped. "Excuse me, I was distracted by something. What are we talking about?"

Her laugh was easy as she leaned a shoulder into my arm.

"The Sky Bar, silly! It's going to be amazing with the city lights and the clear sky tonight." She grinned. "And imagine the content I can get for my accounts. The fashion disasters at an event like that will be epic, am I right?"

The woman next to her shared the laugh, and they returned to celebrity gossip.

No. No fucking way could I take someone like her to Italy.

It was a nonstarter.

I'd have to find someone else.

THREE DAYS LATER, that someone quite literally fell into my lap.

"Oh, shit, sorry," a man said as someone's suitcase tumbled from the overhead bin and knocked him into my personal space.

This is what I get for flying commercial.

I reached out to help him stand back up, muttering, "It's fine," even though it wasn't. The tiny bottle of airline water had splashed onto my shirt and chin as I'd been mid-sip, and my phone had tumbled from my lap to the floor.

When the man got to his feet, he turned to apologize, and the words froze on his lips. "Locke?"

My eyes met familiar denim blue, a bow-shaped mouth I hadn't seen in three years outside of my own memories. "Jett?"

The crowd of passengers surged behind him, mumbling their annoyance that he was holding everyone up. I quickly moved to the empty seat by the window and gestured for him to take my now-empty seat to get out of the aisle.

He reached down to grab my phone before handing it to me and following me into the little row. Then he fell into the seat beside me and blew out a breath. "Hey. Hi. Ah… what… where are you traveling?"

My heart thundered. I took a moment to study him. To drink in the look of him. He was healthy and well, sun-kissed despite the time of year. Filled out and muscular again. Seemingly recovered from Amsterdam.

I cleared my throat. "Home. New York. I was in Atlanta for a meeting. You?"

"Oh, er..." He seemed flustered. "Same. I mean, not home, but flying to the city. New York."

I bit my lip to keep from smiling at the absurdity of the words. "Mm."

He blew out a breath. "I'm staying with a friend. Hoping to find work. You know, same old."

I didn't want to appear overly interested, but I was too curious to stay quiet. "Where've you been living?"

Jett's cheeks flushed as he glanced back at the line of passengers moving slowly past first class. "Oh, you know, just here and there. I stayed near my family for a little while and then came to Atlanta for a job. Was down in Miami a bit." He shrugged. "I go where I find work."

"What kind of work have you found?"

Before he could answer, a woman stopped and eyed me. "I think you're in my seat."

Jett stood and smiled. "He definitely is, and I'm in his. Let me get out of your way."

He turned back to me after I stood to follow him into the aisle so the lady could take her seat.

"It was great seeing you, Locke." He paused before adding with a flirty grin, "You look good. Really good."

Before I could say anything, he was gone, moving off down the aisle toward the back of the plane.

I stared after him until forced to take my seat. Then I spent two hours wondering what strange trick of fate had pushed us together not once, not twice, but three times now.

And how, after the previous two, he'd been impossible to trace.

Against my will, I remembered the feel of his hot mouth on my cock, the way he'd let me fuck into his throat without complaint. How he seemed to have encouraged it, liked it even.

Don't even consider it. That is a very bad idea.

I couldn't help but wonder what it would be like if I could have a willing mouth like that in Italy. Two weeks far away from home with Jett at my beck and call. His mouth on me every night when I came to bed.

It was ridiculous, of course. There was no way I could take a man as my "date" to the Paxis tournament. It was an old-school group, made up of powerful families going back centuries. As far as I knew, there'd never been a gay couple at a tournament. And I knew several current members would probably have a stroke if I showed up with a rent boy on my arm.

And even if it were acceptable to bring a man, I wouldn't. It would give everyone the wrong idea. I wasn't into men. No need to open up a can of worms just because I wanted to fuck the guy again.

I had spent the first two hours of the flight working. My assistant had filled my inbox with questions that needed answers.

But while I worked, I hadn't been able to stop thinking about Jett. About how good he looked but also how uncertain he seemed about his job prospects in the city.

Eventually, I couldn't take it anymore, and I walked to the back of the plane.

Jett was sitting in a window seat next to a heavyset gentleman and a young mom with a sleeping baby strapped to her chest.

"Excuse me," I said softly, nodding toward Jett, whose eyes

were closed and whose ears were covered by large headphones. "I need to ask my friend a question."

The guy elbowed Jett, whose eyes widened in surprise. They widened even more when they landed on me.

"Hi. I wanted to give you this." I handed him a business card I'd written my cell number on the back of. "Text me when you get settled, and I'll help you find work. We always have positions for someone willing to work hard."

He took the card and looked at it. I wondered if he recognized the name and finally realized who I was. Most people had heard of Maris, whether they realized it or not. It was stamped on half the shipping containers in the world and seen on tractor trailers up and down America's highways.

"Er, thanks." He pressed his lips together before meeting my eyes. His sparked with something hot and provoking. "But that's not the kind of work I'm interested in."

Why was he so fucking pretty?

Sex radiated off him like... like some kind of cataclysmic vibration. It reminded me of the time I'd been deep in the bowels of a cargo ship when a container had dropped on the metal deck above. Percussive impact that seemed to rearrange every fucking cell in my brain.

Couldn't everyone around us see it? Feel it?

My chest rose and fell as I battled the graphic images in my head. "Okay," I said. "Well, keep my card in case..." I cleared my throat. "In case you ever need anything."

I nodded like an asshole and moved back up to my seat.

Where I spent the entire rest of the flight fantasizing about giving Jett Davis the kind of work he truly wanted.

9

JETT

Locke Maris was incredibly fun to flirt with. It clearly made him uncomfortable, but just as clearly intrigued him. He was a conundrum. One I knew better than to provoke, but one I couldn't seem to stop provoking anyway.

The woman sitting in my row leaned forward and blinked, absently patting her baby's back to keep them asleep. "That's Locke Maris."

I smiled politely and nodded, distracted by the memory of the way his suit vest had accentuated his wide shoulders and narrow waist or the way his rolled-up sleeves had revealed the ink on his forearm.

Her voice sounded awed. "He was interviewed on WSB yesterday. I saw it on TV when I was waiting for a doctor's appointment. Something about an expansion that creates new jobs in Atlanta and Savannah. Are you friends with him?"

"I've met him a couple of times. I wouldn't say we're friends."

The man between us chimed in. "If I had someone offering me a job at a company like that, I'd take it in a heartbeat. I've heard they pay great. Buddy of mine did an IT consulting gig there and said it was sweet."

"Shipping's not really my thing," I said with a shrug before sliding his business card into my pocket.

But Locke himself? Fucking Christ, was he my thing. My mouth had filled with saliva when I'd realized his was the body I'd fallen onto. Every cell had begged to stay right there in his lap. Thankfully, reality had come screaming in very quickly, and I'd snapped back into my Jethro Davis persona after a few moments of feeling suddenly tongue-tied around him.

Locke Maris had taken on superhuman qualities in my memory. For three years, he'd become my secret crush. My hidden obsession. Yes, *Brenda*, I had seen the interview he'd done on the Atlanta television station yesterday, not because I'd been in Atlanta, but because I had a fucking Google alert set on the man. I'd watched it on my phone this morning while boarding my flight from Biloxi, Mississippi, where I'd finished up my most recent assignment.

I'd also seen the *New York Times* op-ed last month about the "positive global impact" of the "exciting new face of leadership" at Maris Holdings now that Locke's grandfather was gone.

I should have told him I was sorry about his grandfather's death. The news had hit global media outlets when I'd been home last Christmas with my family. We'd come in from spending one of those magically warm winter days out on the beach to discover Reynolds Maris dead of a sudden heart attack.

My heart had gone out to Locke. He'd spoken reverently about his grandfather, and I had to assume the loss would have hit him hard. In addition to losing someone he loved, the death of Reynolds Maris had suddenly thrust Locke into a position of leadership for a global monolith with multiple billions of dollars in revenue and the expectations of high-level financial stakeholders around the world.

Do you think you run the entire world? I'd asked him. *Because you sure act like it sometimes.*

Feel like it sometimes, too, he'd said.

Locke was only thirty-four. But then again, he'd had the bearing of a CEO even at the age of thirty or thirty-one when we'd originally met. Powerful, capable, and driven.

Men like him were catnip. It was one of the reasons I'd requested a transfer back to New York six months ago. The scene in Miami had been too different. Too... easygoing for me. The men there hadn't been as focused or as driven as the men I'd hooked up with in New York. It had been too much like where I'd grown up, with chill vibes that better suited my dads than me.

I shook off thoughts of Locke Maris and focused on the upcoming meetings back at the office. While my reports on the most recent case were completed and had been submitted, I needed to prepare to answer questions during our team debrief, as well as consult with the legal team regarding the arrests made in Mississippi.

As I started my music again and returned to the coded notes I'd been taking in my phone, the casual reference to human trafficking and other horrors in my notes struck me. This kind of shit had become commonplace for me over the past five years. My almost jaded acceptance of it all was one of the reasons Rocky continued to suggest I take some time off.

I'd had ten assignments in two years and had only taken a little time off to visit my family in all that time—a weekend home at Christmas and a week the month before that for my cousin Mattie's wedding in Napa. Working hard suited me just fine, especially when I had cases like a recent one in Spain, where I'd had my evenings and weekends free to find satisfying company.

The sex had been plentiful enough in Spain—and at my cousin's wedding—to make the dry Sahara of Mississippi survivable, but I was definitely looking forward to some time back in New York.

While none of the men waiting for me in the city could hold a candle to Locke Maris, there were plenty of sexy guys to take my mind off him and everything else.

I spent the rest of the flight finishing my notes. By the time I deplaned, he was gone. Locke's business card burned a hole in my pocket, so I pulled it out and studied it while waiting for the train. The cream card stock was velvety thick and engraved with bold, gold foil lettering.

J. LOCKE MARIS
Chief Executive Officer
Maris Holdings International
A Maris Family Enterprise Since 1872
Global Freight | Security Consulting | Port Operations | Arctic &
Pacific Routes
Pier House, Battery Park, NYC
EA: Minerva.Willis@MarisHoldings.com

On the back was a handwritten phone number I would never use.

I ran my finger over the letters, memorizing the information before turning it over and doing the same with his private cell number.

And then I tore the card into tiny pieces and threw bits of them away in various trash cans between LaGuardia and my rental in Chelsea.

As much as I loved fantasizing about Locke Maris, the man was straight. Yes, he'd been willing to experiment with me *once*.

But letting someone suck your dick wasn't quite the same thing as a more involved sexual encounter—the kind I wanted, needed, and deserved.

However, after the following two long days of endless meetings and three nights of absolute shit hookups, I decided I would rather suck Locke's dick in a dank alley than expect a supposedly vers guy from Grindr to top me.

And maybe I'd had three too many heavy-handed cocktails. But while I was drunk enough to text him, I wasn't drunk enough to put his actual name in my contacts.

> This is Jett.

After a few long minutes, a response came in.

CATNIP
> I need to talk to you.

My heart leapt. The look he'd given me on the plane had been heated as fuck. I could tell he wanted me. He'd wanted me in Amsterdam, too. He just hadn't allowed himself to do anything about it.

> About what?

CATNIP
> Tell me where you are and I'll send a car.

> Posh in Hells Kitchen

CATNIP
> Be outside in ten.

When I got to his place, the driver directed me to a wood-paneled study, where Locke was sitting at a large desk, working on a laptop. A fire blazed in a nearby fireplace, surrounded by overstuffed leather seats. The room seemed old and well-worn. It suited him.

He glanced up when I walked in. "Sorry about that," he said, shutting the computer and standing up before indicating the leather chairs. "Have a seat. Are you hungry? Would you like a drink?"

I shook my head. "I'm good."

He looked incredible, as usual, but this time, he was dressed more casually than I'd ever seen him. A faded Columbia University hoodie, dark, late-night stubble on his cheeks and jaw, and his hair messy from running his hands through it.

Catnip. *Jesus fuck.*

I bit my tongue against the urge to lick my lips in anticipation. Last time I'd seen him, he'd rejected any physical encounter between us, but what else would he have called me here for but to suck his cock again?

"I have a business proposition for you," he said as he stood and moved over to the chair opposite mine.

I opened my mouth to remind him I didn't want a job at his company, when I realized maybe he didn't mean business-business. Maybe he meant sex business.

"Okay?"

He leaned forward and clasped his hands together between his knees, resting his elbows on his thighs. He studied the carpet for a beat before glancing back up at me.

"I need you to come with me on a trip."

Before I could ask him what the fuck he was talking about, he continued.

"You'll travel to Italy with me. By day, you'll play my perfect assistant and event coordinator, catering to my guests' needs. But at night..." Locke's voice was hypnotizing, challenging, practically daring me to disagree. "At night, you will cater to *my* needs." His eyes bored into mine. "And I have *very* specific needs."

I stopped breathing.

Locke's jaw tightened. "Complete discretion is required, as well as an NDA. No one will know you're anything more than an employee helping the event run smoothly. In exchange for your service and discretion, I'll pay you one hundred thousand dollars."

My face was on fire, and my fingertips felt strange. "Um. What?" I asked stupidly.

He stood and turned away from me, moving toward a small wet bar in the corner to grab a bottle of water from a hidden mini fridge. When he returned and handed it to me, his face was all business.

"We leave Sunday. If you need a passport, my people can help facilitate an expedited process."

My brain was like a sandwich with no filling. Open and empty. "I, uh… I have a passport. Amsterdam, remember?"

Not that it was relevant. Because you know what else I had? A fucking *job*. As a global intelligence agent. I was not a high-priced —*very, very* high-priced—escort.

"Good. Then you'll simply need to spend the next few days letting my people outfit you with the proper clothing."

He moved back to the bar and poured himself a drink from a heavy glass decanter. "Do you have any questions?"

"No, I…" *Can't do this. Tell him you can't do this.* "I…"

He took a sip of his drink and wandered back toward me before threading his fingers through my hair. "I want to see you on your knees for me again. My cock stretching those pretty lips wide enough to make tears slide down your face."

Oxygen sawed in and out of my lungs as my dick strangled itself in my pants. "*Gurk.*" I choked on my saliva and began to cough.

His lips curved into a lazy grin. "Yes. Exactly like that." Locke's fingers tightened in my hair, tilting my head back, which only made my dick harder. "Say yes, Jett. Let me have you for two weeks. It will solve your money issue and meet my... needs."

He was so fucking cocky. I wanted to knock him down a peg or three.

"I need more information," I said, trying to sound way more nonchalant than I felt.

Locke released my hair and trailed his fingers down the side of my face before turning and retaking the seat across from me. "Like what?"

"Like what the *J* stands for in your name," I said, buying time to seek out my missing brain cells.

"Irrelevant."

I swallowed. "Fine. Then, like where are we going, exactly? What kind of house party is it? Who'll be there?"

I told myself I was only asking these questions out of curiosity. Information gathering was part of my job. Locke Maris was a global power player who had influence on a very high level. The access he could provide my agency was hard to come by.

I was considering this for work reasons only. Work. ESP work.

"Every year, a group of us get together to play Paxis. This year, we've decided to schedule an extra tournament. It's in a secluded villa with views of the Med, an infinity pool and hot tub, gourmet food, and luxury accommodations. There will be a dozen players and their spouses and/or employees. I need someone to be my assistant and help act as a host. I'm not the best at being..."

"Warm?" I teased. "Sociable? *Nice*?"

His eyes narrowed. "I prefer not to use someone from my office to act as my social coordinator in this case. I need someone outside of Maris. Someone outgoing and charming."

"Someone who doesn't mind being your whore," I said, trying to make a joke but falling flat.

"Your word, not mine. I prefer to think of you as a kind of... physical therapist."

I snorted inelegantly, and when I saw his lips curve up and his eyes glint with amusement, I almost agreed right then. But that was impossible. There was no way I could actually say yes.

Rocky has been begging you to take a vacation. The devil on my shoulder wasn't helpful.

Rocky would murder you herself if you took a two-week prostitution break under an old op alias. The angel on my shoulder was a bitch. And most likely a narc as well.

"Explain to me why you need..." I tilted my head at him and tapped my lips with a fingertip. "Therapy."

He steepled his fingers together in front of his chest. "I have a high appetite for... exercise."

So did I. Very high. And even higher when I was around temptation like Locke Maris.

"I'm sure any number of women would be happy to fill that role for you on a fancy-pants trip to Italy with your chess nerd friends."

He pressed his lips together and inhaled through his nose. The flames flickered around the gas logs, and I found myself wishing for the distracting crackle and pop of a real fire like the ones in my family's lodge in Montana.

"I have too much work to do to entertain a woman and give her the attention she would require. Besides, the woman I've been seeing would read too much into it," he finally said. "And she isn't the discreet type."

"Is she the sharing type?" I asked in surprise, suddenly uncomfortable with the knowledge that he was seeing someone.

"We aren't exclusive. She doesn't owe me anything, and that

goes both ways." He eyed me over his lowball glass as he took another sip of the amber liquid. "Does that bother your delicate sensibilities?"

I easily fell into the role he expected of me. "I'm used to being the side piece, Locke. Which is why I know it doesn't usually end well. I prefer not to get my eyes scratched out by someone's expensive manicure."

He set the glass on a low table next to his chair and leaned forward again, just enough to give me the barest whiff of his scent.

As if I needed further temptation.

"You're not attracted to men," I pointed out in a voice a little too breathy.

"No. But I am attracted to your mouth."

I wanted to be offended by that, but it only turned me on more. Maybe I *was* a whore. A happy one if I could have access to this man's willing body for two straight weeks in the Mediterranean in addition to his hundred grand.

Not that I needed the money. But I wouldn't mind reallocating it from the Maris fortune to those less fortunate.

"John," I said, trying again to make a joke. "If you're hiring me for sex, surely the *J* stands for John."

"Are we done here?" He sounded bored.

"What happens when you change your mind a few days in?" I asked.

He lifted an eyebrow. "Do you have so little faith in your ability to satisfy me?"

I met his eyes. "Maybe you should let me blow you right now to see if it's as good as you remember it."

He stood again and moved toward me, standing between my legs. His hand moved through my hair until he cupped the back of my head and brought it toward the front of his pants. Just as I was getting ready to take a deep inhale through my nose, he let out a soft rumble of laughter and leaned down to whisper against my ear.

"Some decisions are best made hungry, Jethro."

The sound of my fake name in his deep voice played me like a fucking fiddle. Why was that?

Locke moved away from me and back over to his desk, where he picked up his phone and tapped something into it. "Demarius will take you home. He'll also be out front of your place Sunday morning at nine to pick you up. In the meantime, text me a list of your measurements so someone on my team can get you decent clothes. Don't bother packing anything. My people will take care of it."

I blinked at him. "I didn't agree."

He opened the laptop and got back to work. "You will," he said without looking up. "Good night, Jett."

10

JETT

I wasn't going to go.

Obviously.

Mostly because I wasn't Julia Roberts, and this wasn't Hollywood. I was a highly respected intelligence officer. My unclaimed accomplishments had been on the front pages of news sites and on the lips of world leaders.

I'd helped dismantle a human-trafficking ring in Venezuela by locating the foothills compound in which they were being held. My work in Germany three years ago had foiled an eco-terrorist attack on the canal locks in Brunsbüttel. I was good at what I did.

And I wasn't about to fuck it up by playing happy hooker to a billionaire.

"Did you have a nice night?" Trevi asked as I hugged my coffee cup at the conference table the next morning.

"Mpfh."

He took the seat next to mine and snickered. "Too many G&Ts?"

Before I could answer, Rocky came striding in. "Where are Rita and CJ? We have a situation brewing in Germany."

The mood in the room immediately shifted. As soon as everyone was present, Rocky began debriefing us about suspicious activity near the Kiel Canal, the vital waterway that allowed an average of ninety vessels a day to take a shortcut from the Baltic to the North Sea.

The canal was critical to the movement of goods in Northern Europe, something I'd seen firsthand three years ago when I'd been on one end of it in Brunsbüttel. It was being used more and more to smuggle goods into and out of Russia, so it was no surprise that it was involved in something.

"We intercepted a shipment of drones, but there's chatter about possible munitions and hazardous chemicals coming on other vessels or by rail. Draković weaponry travels by rail in that region. And so do international aid supplies, all things various groups are eager to get their hands on."

While my gut filled with the usual nervous excitement I experienced at the start of a new mission, it also dropped in extreme disappointment that the decision to go to Italy was now irrevocably made.

Not that I'd been seriously considering going.

The opposite. Obviously.

But if I had, that idea was well and truly nixed now that there was a serious mission in a place I had the most practical knowledge of. I wasn't even sure anyone else on the team was fluent in German.

Rocky turned to CJ, one of the newer recruits. "You're heading out in the morning. You'll be working with one of the inspectors in Brunsbüttel as a gopher of sorts. The inspector is an asset who knows what's going on and will give you access to as many vessels as possible."

I kept my eyes on my boss, waiting for an assignment. She turned to Rita next. "And you'll be in Kiel. The best cover we can get for you is working at a lunch cart on the docks. We need you to make friends with as many dock workers as possible and keep your ears open. At Kiel, we're looking for anyone who is falsifying records, cherry-picking which vessels get inspected, et cetera."

Next, she turned to Trevi. "I need you in constant communication with them. We can't have a repeat of three years ago." Her eyes flicked over to me before landing back on our comms specialist. "Jett should never have been in the dark so long in Hamburg. That's on me. But I don't want a repeat, okay?"

I felt a flush of heat in my face. "I did fine," I clipped, feeling stung, even though I was clear that wasn't her intention.

She glared at me. "Of course you did. You also lost twenty pounds and fucked up your bloodwork because you didn't have adequate nutrition."

"I got the job done."

She took in a slow breath and let it out, clearly trying to keep her cool. "Would you like to revisit the op debrief from three years ago? Because we can do that. But not right now. Right now, we're going to make sure that our agents don't go into the field thinking it's okay to stay dark for that long or starve themselves in the process." She directed her gaze to the others around the table. "Also, I need everyone to be clear that danger to your personal safety on an op doesn't just come from bad guys with guns, okay?"

After the op in Hamburg, she'd ripped me a new one, but Rocky had also taken responsibility for it, claiming she'd sent me out too soon before I'd completed some of the advanced training.

This was somewhat true, but the experience I'd gained on that op had been invaluable. And it had led to my quick ascent in the ranks.

"Where do you need me on this?" I prodded, trying to refocus on the current op.

Rocky pinned me with a look. "On vacation."

I blinked at her. "No, I mean where do you need me in Germany? I'm fluent in German and familiar with Brunsbüttel."

In fact, I was one of the people on the team with the most fluency in European languages. It was part of what had gotten me recruited out of college in the first place.

She tilted her head and looked at me with an expression of disbelief. "I know you are. Which is why you're not on this op."

"That's why I *should* be on this op," I insisted.

"So someone can recognize you as the eco-activist Jonas Vogel, the kid who was literally arrested for loitering on the docks with nefarious intent? Not on your life."

She had a point.

"I can provide support from here, then. I'm an experienced operative. I have information that might help," I said, turning to CJ and Rita. But before I could give them suggestions about being undercover in Germany, Rocky cut me off.

"Except that you're going on mandated leave, and that's final. Listen, Jett. I've tried asking you nicely to take some time off—"

"I just went to my cousin's wedding!"

Trevi snickered, and the edge of Rocky's lip curved up. "Yes, you did. You took an entire week off... *six months ago.*"

"That wasn't six months ago," I insisted, doing the math in my head and realizing I was wrong and she was right. "Shit."

"Yeah, *shit.* So you're taking some time off. No arguments, Jett," she added, when it was clear I was going to. "As an *experienced operative*, you know that pushing yourself's the easiest way to get sloppy. Come back refreshed, and I'll toss you into an op again."

So, really... it was Rocky's fault I was on a Dassault Falcon dressed in clothes that cost more than my monthly salary at ESP.

"You're fidgeting," Locke said, without looking up from his laptop in the seat across the table from me.

I swallowed and lied. "I've just never been on a private plane before. Isn't it more likely to crash?"

He nodded, still not lifting his head from his work. "Statistically speaking, yes. But not this one."

"Explain," I said, and then took the opportunity to study him while he spouted a bunch of stuff I already knew about how student pilots, single-pilot flights, riskier weather decisions, and lower maintenance standards negatively impacted the statistics for private plane safety records.

He was so fucking sexy. His button-down shirtsleeves were folded up his arms, revealing straight-up forearm porn. I was close enough now to see that his forearm tattoo was a combination of his company's anchor and compass logo. His tie had been yanked off and tossed onto the leather seat beside him the minute we'd boarded, and watching his thick fingers pluck at the tiny button of his shirt collar had made me want to take over the chore.

Now, a tuft of chest hair was visible in the open collar, above the white cotton undershirt he wore. Every time he shifted in his seat, those little hairs were either hidden or revealed.

"We have three pilots, and one of the flight attendants is also licensed to fly, although her experience is limited to her father's crop duster."

"Arial applicator," the flight attendant said with a soft chuckle as she set a coffee down in front of him and a bottle of water in front of me. "Your lunch will be ready shortly. Is there anything else I can get you in the meantime?"

I smiled at the attractive woman and shook my head. Locke finally looked up and met her eye, giving her a warm look that made me want to claw her eyes out. "Thank you, Kayla. We're all set."

She made her way forward and disappeared behind the galley wall. I shot Locke a look.

"What?" he asked.

I tilted my chin in the flight attendant's direction, then toward him, before lifting my eyebrows in question. *You and her?*

His forehead crinkled in confusion before smoothing. "Don't be ridiculous."

"What? Why is that ridiculous?" I lowered my voice. "She's beautiful."

He nodded and responded in the same lowered voice. "Yes. She is. She's also married to one of my pilots. And even if she wasn't, I don't fuck around with my employees."

I lifted my eyebrow again and grinned. "Aren't I one of your employees?"

He narrowed his eyes at me and gave me a slow up-down, which made his eyes darken. Then he turned back to the laptop, muttering, "Regrettably."

I snorted a laugh and glanced out the window at the ocean visible below us. The sun sparkled off the water in a blurry haze, making it look warmer than it was. We'd left the city on a beautiful, clear day, but it had still been cold as fuck. Thankfully, the forecast for Maiori was sun-warm and clear. Exactly what I needed.

"Surely you can find a way to occupy yourself," Locke said.

"Was I complaining?"

"You're fidgeting."

I studied him, unreasonably entertained by the fact that he was so aware of me. "Maybe I'm pent-up."

His eyes lifted from his screen again to pin me in place. "Maybe you need to go take care of that in private."

I grinned. "Maybe I could help you while helping myself."

The stern look on his face didn't change, but the skin above his collar turned pink. *Bingo.*

His voice was slow and deliberate. "Maybe you need to stop distracting me and let me work."

I shrugged and stood up, making a production of stretching so that my shirt rode up right at his eye level. He tried not to look.

He failed.

"Okay, then," I said cheerfully before heading back to the rear lavatory.

Before I got there, I heard the door to the rear section of the plane close behind me.

I turned to find Locke standing inside the closed door with his arms crossed in front of his chest. This section of the plane had two long sofas on each side that could clearly fold down into a giant bed to make it a bedroom. A stack of luxurious bedding sat neatly folded on one end of the sofa to my right, the sun warming a fat stripe across it.

"Did you need to use the bathroom, too?" I asked innocently.

He didn't say anything, simply crooked his finger at me and then pointed to the ground at his feet. The muscles in my stomach tightened with heat, and blood pooled low in my groin.

"Oh. You…" I swallowed. "You need a little help after all?"

"Stop talking."

"Stop fidgeting. Stop talking. So, so bossy," I said mock-sadly, even as I moved up the aisle to stand in front of him.

His lips were fucking sinful, and I wanted to taste them with my tongue, nip them between my teeth, and suck on them until he made guttural noises.

But that wasn't what I'd been hired for.

I slowly sank to my knees.

"Good boy."

Oh dear god.

I glanced up at him, trying to judge if the phrase had been intended to taunt or humiliate me. Locke's eyes were still heated, and the pink had crawled up his neck to his ears. His cock began tenting the front of his trousers, so I reached out and rubbed my palm across it before testing the shape of it with my fingers.

"I want to make you feel good," I said softly.

Locke's fingers moved into my hair. "Then take me out and let me fuck your throat."

My own dick was impossibly, painfully hard, and my breathing came out in sharp, shallow breaths. I fumbled for his belt and yanked it open, shoving his shirt up and out of the way.

"Easy," he murmured. "There's no rush."

His fingers moved gently in my hair as if learning the feel of it, but as soon as I fished his cock out and put the tip against my lips, his fingers tightened, tilting my head back.

"Let me see you open for me."

I looked up at him through my lashes and opened my mouth slowly, sticking my tongue out so he could see it wrap around the head of his cock.

"Fuck, that's good. You want this, don't you? You want to feel my cock in your mouth. Feel me using your mouth to get off."

I let my eyes fall closed as I made a sound of agreement and let myself enjoy the clean taste of him, the musky scent of him, and the slight pressure of his hold on my hair.

This was so fucking problematic. I knew it was. Straight assholes like Locke Maris were a dime a dozen, and I'd hooked up with plenty of them. Usually, I didn't give a fuck how they identified or how much internalized homophobia they were dealing with because I was only in it for a quick release. I wasn't their fucking therapist, and I'd accepted long ago that the world was full of shitty people whose dick could still give me a killer fucking ride.

But for some reason, this was different. Being used by Locke was both thrilling and degrading. I didn't want him to think of me as just a willing mouth. But at the same time, him treating me like nothing but a vessel for his need turned me on more than I expected.

And I was way more interested in an orgasm right now than trying to get to the bottom of this esoteric morality.

His cock was fucking perfect. Thick and long. Satisfying without being intimidating. I'd savored every moment of sucking him off more than three years ago in his kitchen. Had replayed the moment way too many times while getting myself off. And I was shaking with the need to do it again.

"That's it. You're doing so good."

His murmured words penetrated my lust-filled haze. I looked up at him and saw a flash of approval, of tenderness. But then it was gone, replaced by the intense, commanding stare he usually wore when looking at me.

"Get on with it," he said gruffly. "I have work to do."

His voice hitched on the last word because I'd already dialed it up a notch, deliberately letting myself gag as the head of his cock passed into my throat. Tears sprang from my eyes as I sucked in a breath and dropped deeply over him again, sucking and slurping, getting dirty and debauched. The sound of my gagging filled the small space and was soon joined by his grunts of pleasure and murmured encouragement.

"God, you're so fucking good at this," he said in a rough voice. His hand was still firm in my hair, and his other hand came around behind my head to hold me against his groin as his cock settled into my throat for several long beats.

When he let me go, I gasped in a deep breath and then took him in again, cupping his tight sac in one hand and reaching for my own cock with the other.

It didn't take much. As soon as I tasted the first spurt of his release and knew that I'd made him lose control, my own release took over. I quickly pulled off him to keep from accidentally biting him, which meant the last few threads of his release ended up on my chin as I threw my head back and gasped.

"Jesus fuck," he said in a graveled voice.

I opened my eyes and saw him staring down at me. Tears streamed from my eyes, and snot and jizz probably covered my mouth and chin. It was hard to tell from the watery view I had of him whether he was satisfied or disgusted.

But then he lowered himself to the nearby couch and reached for a box of tissues in a wall caddy, carefully pulling a few out and reaching for me.

I stared at him as he moved me to kneel between his spread knees and began wiping my face.

"You're a mess," he murmured, handing me more tissues for the cum on my hand and clothes.

One of his hands held the side of my face while he carefully wiped around my eyes, nose, and mouth.

Instead of cleaning up my dick with the tissues he'd handed me, I continued to stare at him in shock. Who the fuck was this guy?

When he was done, he cleared his throat and stood up, stepping away from me and straightening his clothes. "Maybe now you'll stop fidgeting."

And then he was gone.

The door to the compartment closed again, leaving me alone with cold cum drying on my cock and hand.

"Holy fuck," I breathed.

I stared at the door for another beat before hearing the muffled sounds of the flight attendant asking him a question about his coffee. I quickly moved to the rear lavatory and cleaned myself up, taking advantage of the healthy supply of luxury toiletries in a little cubby next to a stack of fluffy hand towels.

When I returned to the front of the plane, the flight attendant was setting the table with a white cloth and gleaming silverware. She made casual conversation with an attentive Locke, who was asking her about a recent visit home to visit her parents in Montana.

"Montana's beautiful. I've always wanted to spend some time there," Locke mused.

"My family has a place in Montana," I volunteered, stupidly wanting some of Locke's attention. "In a tiny town called Legacy."

I didn't realize my mistake until I saw the surprise on his face. "They do? What kind of place?"

Yes, Jett, what kind of place would go-go boy Jethro's family have? *Fuck.*

Why hadn't I thought to refresh my memory about the finer points of Jethro's cover story, when I'd literally lived a dozen lives since I'd last been Jethro? *Double fuck.*

The answer, I realized, was that I'd spent my time googling Locke instead. *Fuck, fuck, fuck.*

"Oh, uh... I just meant I have a couple of cousins who live there," I backtracked, waving a hand vaguely.

I tried not to think about what an understatement that was. My grandparents had bought a piece of land in Legacy years ago, large enough for them to give each of their children and grand-children a parcel. At any given time, there were at least a dozen Marians in town and tens of thousands of acres of land under Marian ownership.

I was incredibly glad Rocky wasn't here to see her "experi-enced operative" now.

"I know where Legacy is," Kayla said excitedly. "One of my

friends from high school lives there. What's your cousin's last name?"

I forced the name Marian back into its hidey-hole and shot her a friendly smile. "Johnson," I said. "They're actually my dad's cousins. Linda and Peter Johnson. Linda works at the grocery store in town, or at least she did the last time I heard anything about them. But it's been years."

I felt Locke's eyes on me as I carefully turned the conversation back around to Kayla, asking her where she'd enjoyed traveling with her job.

After the meal, I pretended to take a nap in order to keep from saying anything else stupid. Thankfully, my exhaustion took care of the rest and turned the fake nap into a real one.

11

LOCKE

I watched Jett sleep in the wide, leather chair across from me.

The man was a mystery.

Prior to bringing him to the Paxis tournament, I'd had my corporate security team run another background check on him to see if there was anything more to learn since I'd last run a check three years ago.

There was nothing new, with the sole exception of his address. Jett's current address was in Queens, which made no sense based on where Demarius had dropped him off the other night. But this wasn't a huge surprise. The man was a sex worker. Not, I imagined, a demographic known for consistently sleeping at their legal addresses.

Because of his background and the services I required of him, I'd insisted on a clear STI panel in addition to the updated background check.

It should have been enough to satisfy my curiosity about him.

Was enough, damn it.

I blew out a breath and let my shoulders fall.

I didn't need his life story to enjoy the services I'd hired him for. I didn't need to make small talk with him, or worry about entertaining him, or wonder what circumstances had led him to stay somewhere other than at his Queens apartment. He was here for one reason only.

I wanted to own him. If only for a little while.

The memory of him on his knees for me in the back room of the plane made me shift uncomfortably in my seat. Jett's mouth was as amazing as I'd remembered. Better, if such a thing were possible.

And he was being compensated for it generously, I reminded myself. I owed him nothing more.

But I did owe the Paxis Council my thorough knowledge of the global shipping landscape, the movement of contraband around the world, and recent technological innovations my company had been working on. So I went back to prepping for the tournament.

I tried not to notice every time Jett shifted or made a small sound. But when he wrapped his arms around himself, I nodded to Kayla, silently asking for a blanket and indicating she should drape it over him. He jerked awake when he felt the blanket land on his chest, but when he realized Kayla was only seeing to his comfort, he relaxed and shot her a grateful grin.

She returned his smile and disappeared back to the galley.

I pretended not to notice Jett's eyes move to me. But I felt the heat of them all the same.

After a few long moments, he shifted in his seat and turned to gaze out the window. Within a few moments, he was softly snoring once more.

And then it was my turn to watch him. Again.

Kayla might not have noticed Jett's knee-jerk reaction to being suddenly awakened, but I had. He'd looked ready for an attack.

Like someone who'd slept on the streets or been in other precarious situations.

Again, not surprising. But it was another piece of the puzzle that made Jett such a strange combination of contradictions.

He sometimes came off as wealthier than he was—an act, I assumed, to fit in better with wealthy clients. On the flight from Atlanta, he'd been wearing nicer clothes than he had in the past—more like a business traveler than someone planning to couch-surf with a friend while looking for a barista job or another dancing gig. He definitely didn't sound like someone from small-town South Carolina either, which might be for the same reason.

But I suddenly wanted to know... where else had he lived over the years? What jobs had he been taking to get by?

He'd mentioned a family card game his "dads" enjoyed, cousins on his father's side living in Montana, and a scar he'd gotten from a sister, though the background check had shown him only having a mother and no siblings.

Did he invent stories about an imagined family as a kind of coping mechanism? Or did he know and have some kind of relationship with his father? Were those chapters of his life closed? Was his family unable to help him financially?

My curiosity was piqued, which was annoying as fuck. I didn't have time to be so intrigued by someone I was only using for sex. He wasn't a security risk, and that was the only thing I needed to concern myself with.

I focused on the work in front of me for the rest of the flight and tried like hell not to let Jett's soft snores distract me.

We were met at the Salerno airport by a driver who quickly gathered our luggage and led us to my grandfather's old Rolls for the drive to the villa. I slipped into the back seat, expecting Jett to follow. When he didn't, I realized he was talking to the driver in broken Italian as he helped the man load the bags. The sound of his friendly attempts at conversation was unexpected.

"You speak Italian?" I asked when he finally took the seat beside me.

"Not really," he said with a laugh. "I did a few lessons on my phone over the weekend."

"Have you been to Italy before?"

Jett's cheeks flushed. "Is this where you reveal how small-town I am?"

"I didn't mean to embarrass you. But you've been to Amsterdam, so I wondered if maybe..."

"If maybe..." His eyes flicked up to the driver. "Another *job* had given me more travel experience?"

I shrugged and pressed the button to raise the privacy screen.

"I've been to some places. What about you?" he asked. "You've probably been all over the world with your job."

He avoided answering the question despite the privacy screen. I wondered if it was due to his desire to avoid mentioning other men he'd been with or if it was due to his embarrassment at his lack of travel. I decided to let him evade the question.

For now.

"Yes. I started traveling with my grandfather at a very early age. And my mother enjoyed tropical vacations." I glanced out the window at the bright sun reflecting off old tile-roof buildings. "I lived in London for a time. For graduate school."

"Did you enjoy it?"

I glanced at him. "You don't sound surprised."

Jett grinned. "Italian wasn't the only thing I looked up online this weekend."

I rolled my eyes. "Be careful what you read on the internet."

"Mm. So you didn't date the governor's daughter? I see."

Kalliope Andros and I had dated for six months around the

time I'd seen Jett in Amsterdam. When I'd returned, it had become clear to me that Kalliope and I would only ever be sexual partners and social friends. She was as politically driven as her father, and I didn't want any part of that. When she'd tried to manipulate my relationship with her father in order to impact complex port negotiations to his favor, I'd cut her loose.

I couldn't abide liars or double-dealers.

"That didn't last," I said. "And was never serious to begin with."

His eyes flicked back to the privacy screen, and he cleared his throat. "How can I best support you during this chess extravaganza, *Mr. Maris*?"

Right. Business.

"We'll spend a couple of days preparing the house and staff for the tournament. That means studying up on whatever information their people have sent ahead for accommodations, diet, et cetera, to ensure their comfort. I need you to take point on this with my housekeeper. Unfortunately, I have a lot of work I need to do before the guests arrive."

He nodded. "I can do that. My dads throw killer house parties, so I have lots of experience. What else?"

Again with the inconsistencies. But even if I couldn't control my raging curiosity, I'd be damned if I let it show.

"When the guests arrive, I'll obviously need you to help me make them feel welcome and comfortably accommodated. You'll be a liaison between our guests and the household staff."

He frowned. "Why don't you ask your mother to act as hostess? She's a society maven, right? Wouldn't she like this kind of thing?"

I shook my head. "My father wasn't a fan of Paxis, and he convinced her it was boring. She's never been to a tournament. Which suited my grandfather fine because he didn't trust her discretion."

The car pulled up to a dark metal gate, and a guard stepped out of the gatehouse to speak to the driver.

"Discretion." Jett pursed his lips. "What is there to tell about a chess tournament? How wild and crazy do these things—?"

I held up a hand to shut him up as my window rolled down so the guard could see who was inside.

"Ciao, Gianni," I said with a nod.

The familiar man smiled and waved us through. "Mr. Maris. Welcome home."

The words hit me in the gut. Villa Altomare was mine now. While I'd come to stay in January, to hide out for a week right after my grandfather's death, it hit me again that this was my house, not his. That he was gone, and he'd left me responsible for carrying on the Maris legacy.

"Are you okay?" Jett asked softly when the window was safely rolled up.

I ignored his concern. In fact, it was the last thing I needed. I had no time or inclination for being coddled.

"This tournament is made up of powerful people," I said, jaw tight. "Other men and women in positions like mine. Heirs to family businesses that have been around for a very long time. I mentioned Paxis is an old-world variant of chess? Well, this group has existed nearly as long as the game has. For generations. I play with people who have a lot of money and wield significant influence."

Jett turned toward me. "Like who?"

"Emil Sorensen, for one. His family remains the primary stakeholder in Soren Pharmaceuticals."

I could tell by the look on his face, Jett recognized the company name. "Who else?"

"Sheikh Saleem al-Qadiri is the son-in-law of the ruling Emir of Qadara."

Jett looked surprised before covering it up with his usual teasing manner. "I've never rubbed elbows with a real-life sheikh."

"And you're not going to," I snapped. "Your job around the players is to be seen and not heard. I want you to be wallpaper. When I'm playing the game, if you're in the room, you will stand silently behind me, awaiting my needs."

Jett's eyes darkened, and the grin he gave didn't meet them. "Sit still, look pretty. Understood."

"Most of the time, I won't need you in the game room. You're free to sit by the pool with the other non-players. Some will be spouses, some might be executive assistants, some will be..." I hesitated.

Jett grinned and curled his fingers into air quotes. "'*Assistants*' like me?"

"Mistresses, yes." I eyed him coolly. "I believe we addressed this when I made my offer, but as far as the others are concerned, you are very much my assistant and not my... '*assistant*.' Understood?"

Jet's eyes darkened even further, and his smile turned dangerous. "Oh, yes, sir. You're straight as an arrow, sir. I won't get any gay cooties on you while I'm sucking you off... *sir*."

His comment made my temper flare, but I ruthlessly quashed it. I had no time for anger either, and I didn't need to explain myself to him.

"While you're socializing, keep an ear open for gossip," I continued.

"You want me to spy on your friends."

I narrowed my eyes. "Not spy, exactly. You work for me. I'm asking for your help—"

"No. You're demanding it. In a particularly assholish way." Jett blew out a sharp breath as if calming his temper. "Fine. What am I hoping to see or hear?"

"That remains to be seen. And maybe you won't see or hear anything useful. Simply take note of anything that seems unusual. Anything that could help in a business negotiation, for example. The Maris family didn't get where we are today by underestimating powerful people. Just be aware. Use your head."

He bounced his eyebrows at my word choice, so I rolled my eyes.

"Remind me again why you didn't just bring a woman?" Jett asked. "Surely that would've been easier."

He was damn right it would've. I didn't want to think too hard about how easily I'd convinced myself that bringing Jett was the logical choice.

"I'm not in the habit of repeating myself," I told him as though it didn't matter one way or the other. "Please remember that this is a highly paid job, and one of the top requirements is discretion."

"And one of the bottom requirements is... my bottom?" His cocky grin appeared, which helped ground me for some reason. If he was feeling easy about the two weeks ahead, maybe I could also.

"Let's see if I've got everything," Jett said as the car pulled up to the house. "I make everyone feel welcome, facilitate their needs, act gregarious and charming enough for them to gossip at me except when standing silently as your beck-and-call girl, and carbo-load by the pool for long nights serving at the pleasure of your d—"

I was relieved that Jett broke off when the housekeeper opened the car door to welcome us.

"Good evening, Locke. Good to see you."

I stood and leaned in to give her quick cheek kisses. "Ciao, Concetta. I'm happy to be here. This is my assistant, Jett Davis."

She smiled warmly as Jett climbed out of the car behind me. "Welcome to Villa Altomare, Mr. Davis."

An attendant was already pulling our luggage from the vehicle as Concetta led us into the house, chattering happily about the visit. "We have your suite already prepared for you, and I've placed Mr. Davis in the suite's extra room as requested so you will have privacy for work between sessions. We will have dinner ready for you and Mr. Davis in the dining room in an hour if that suits you both."

Jett slowed down to take in the villa. "Call me Jett, please. This is beautiful."

It was open and airy, luxuriously fitted with modern but comfortable furnishings. The far wall was a wide expanse of French doors open to the cool evening air and peaceful view of the Mediterranean Sea.

Fresh flowers filled vases here and there, and the scent of orange blossoms came in on the breeze.

"Dinner in an hour sounds good," I assured her. "And thank you again. I know it is a lot of work on short notice."

"Not at all. We enjoy hosting this group and have been looking forward to it. This way, Jett. As I'm sure Locke has mentioned, feel free to avail yourselves of any of the house amenities, including the pool, fitness rooms, common areas, et cetera. If there is anything at all my staff and I can do..."

As she continued with her welcome spiel, I felt Jett's appreciation of the home. "It's breathtaking," he said. "Thank you for your warm welcome."

I nodded my thanks to her as she finished showing Jett the locked safe for his passport and the concierge tablet mounted on the wall of the suite.

My grandfather's suite comprised three rooms. A primary bedroom and sitting room with killer views of the Med, and a smaller second bedroom tucked next to the primary bedroom with only a small, arched window facing a garden. It had originally been used as a nursery, and then in my grandfather's older years, his personal attendant had slept there to be close in case my grandfather needed help.

It was strange to be sleeping here when I'd only ever stayed in my usual guest room.

There were a few details that had clearly been arranged to make the space feel like mine. A painting from the bedroom I'd always stayed in. A fresh coat of paint in a different shade. New fabric on some of the upholstered furniture. A larger table by the balcony doors so I could spread out and work.

It was the same, but different. I shot a smile of thanks to Concetta for her thoughtfulness. She returned it with satisfaction before leaving us to alert the kitchen about dinner.

Jett disappeared into the small bedroom but didn't close the door. He opened a suitcase, dug out a toiletry kit, and moved through the bedroom to his en suite bathroom. Instead of continuing to track his movements, I forced myself into my own bedroom to shower and change into more comfortable clothes for the rest of the evening.

Just as I turned on the shower faucet, my bathroom door clicked open.

Jett's hair was damp around the edges like he'd splashed water on his face. His shirt was missing, and his pants were open, revealing the same light blue briefs I'd noticed him wearing on the plane.

His eyebrows lifted, and he flashed a flirty grin. "Thought you might need help freshening up."

The thought hadn't occurred to me, not because I didn't want his mouth on me again, but because I'd assumed we'd eat dinner first and then retreat to the bedroom for some play.

But now that he was standing so close, my dick was eager to

take advantage of the opportunity. "Take off your clothes and get in the shower."

12

JETT

"Has anyone ever told you that you're awfully bossy?" I said as I pulled my clothes off a piece at a time and left them folded neatly on the edge of the nearby tub.

"*You* have." Locke's eyes tracked me across the open expanse of tile. Thankfully, wooden shutters had been closed over the windows, so we had complete privacy. "But I am the boss."

He was, I supposed. For now.

Part of me wished I were exactly what Locke thought I was. A rent boy whose primary concern for the next ten days was pulling orgasms out of him.

But I wasn't that guy. My father, Maverick, still found moments to repeat the mantra he'd started when I was very young. "Curious Cat is never content."

My mind had been whirling since we arrived.

Villa Altomare was different from what I'd expected. It was definitely a shockingly large villa. But it was also homey and warm, the way my uncle Jude's homes were. Despite Jude's obscene wealth from his music career, he didn't try to impress people with it. He was who he was, down-to-earth and family-focused.

It hadn't occurred to me that Locke Maris, heir to a multibillion-dollar fortune and the very definition of "old money," would own a place like this, let alone host global power players here. But then again, the housekeeper had implied they'd hosted before, most likely during his grandfather's time.

For as much as Locke often seemed rigid and closed off, seeing everyone welcome him here so familiarly and catching glimpses of his emotional reaction to arriving at his late grandfather's place had made me want to know more. Made me wish we had the kind of relationship where I could ask him those questions.

Fortunately for both of us, I also wanted his dick in my mouth again, which would be a good way to distract us both.

I grabbed an extra bath towel from a stack, and as I stepped into the large shower, I refolded it into a thick, long rectangle before dropping it in front of his feet and lowering to my knees.

Locke's body was obscene. Hard muscles with only the barest padding over his abs. Ink along his arm and one of his legs. The angles of his face and his narrowed eyes always looked fiercely intimidating in a way that got my dick up every single fucking time he looked my way.

"You look good on your knees for me," he murmured, folding his arms over his chest. "Wash me."

I would have taken offense if I hadn't been trained to look for even the most subtle tells in people's body language.

Locke Maris's jaw flexed.

I remembered it flexing several times before, and each time, he'd been anxious. The first had been in Amsterdam, when he'd been concerned about my health. The second in New York, when he'd made me the indecent proposal. Then again in the car just a little while ago, when he'd been concerned about his little gay secret getting out.

Locke wasn't nearly as chill as he was pretending to be.

Still, I thought about refusing him. Telling him to wash his own damned body. But my father, Beau, had always taught me not to spit into the wind no matter how mad I was, and denying myself the opportunity to caress every part of Locke Maris's body with my greedy little fingers seemed like a similarly bad idea.

I reached for the bottle of bodywash sitting on a small teak bench and poured a giant heap of it into a fluffy washcloth. Then I met Locke's eyes and began at his feet.

My fingers turned a utilitarian job into cultish skin worship. If he wanted me to wash him, I'd make him regret it.

By the time I reached the top of one of his inner thighs, Locke's dick was bobbing heavily in my face, and his quads were twitching under my fingers. His chest heaved on every loud inhale, and thick steam clouded the space around us.

"That's enough," he clipped, his voice gruffer than usual. "Suck my cock."

I blinked water droplets off my eyelashes and peered up at him again. "But I was just getting started."

He unfolded his arms and clasped the back of my head, pulling it close to his erection. "At this rate, we'll be here all night."

I hid a smile as I nosed the crease between his dick and thigh, still drawing it out to punish him for being an asshole.

When the hand on the back of my head moved to carefully brush the wet hair out of my eyes, I felt my own breath hitch.

Tricky bastard.

Using tenderness to get what he wanted was a dirty move. Fuck that.

I took him in my mouth, suddenly wanting to make him come as fast and hard as possible. He grunted loudly. The sound echoed in the tiled space, and his fingers tightened on my face. "Fuck," he snapped. "Fuck!"

His breath came in heavy pants as I worked his cock and balls with my hands and mouth like I was being paid for it. Which I was.

"Jesus, slow down. I'm going to... *fuck*!"

The warm, salty tang of his release hit my throat and tongue, and I swallowed quickly to keep up with it. My own dick wasn't nearly hard enough yet to be close to coming, but I was too annoyed to give a shit.

I stood up slowly, feeling the stiffness in my legs from being in the same position too long. Despite the folded towel, now soaked with water, the tile had still been a bitch on my knees.

Locke's neck and chest were streaked with red. Was it from the hot shower spray or how worked up he'd gotten?

His narrow eyes bored into me. "You think you're clever."

"You think you're straight," I replied pointedly, deliberately wiping the corner of my mouth with my pinky as if wiping away leftover traces of his release, even though I'd swallowed it all greedily.

I turned to exit the shower, but he grabbed my arm and yanked me back until the back of my bare body was plastered against the front of his. His softening cock pressed into one ass cheek, and one of his free hands came around to splay across my lower belly.

"Is this your way of asking for my mouth on you, Jethro?" he asked in a low voice in my ear. "Because you could just ask."

My eyes slid closed. My name wasn't Jethro. And while part of me hated that he didn't know that, I fucking loved hearing him call me by it in that teasing tone of voice.

"I dare you to suck my dick," I said, unable to hide a smile. There was exactly zero chance this man was going to reciprocate with another man's cock in his mouth. I'd been with plenty of "straight" men who would, but Locke Maris wasn't one of them.

"Mm. That's not asking."

His hand moved lower, fingers tangling into the hair at the base of my cock.

I sucked in a breath. "Please." My voice sounded ragged in the thick, wet air around us.

Locke's large hand wrapped around my hardening shaft, causing me to let out an embarrassing sound. I arched back into him, my hair getting caught on the late-day stubble of his chin and cheek.

"You going to come for me, Jethro?" He pulled experimentally, sending a shudder of pleasure through my groin.

My chest heaved. Water trickled into my mouth, making it clear I was open-mouthed in shock in pleasure. "Oh god."

"You like my hand on you," he said in an amused voice, bringing his other arm around me and spreading his hand over the center of my chest as if keeping me from doubling over. When he shifted, I realized he was keeping me from leaning forward and *blocking his view*.

"Fuck," I whimpered.

This was unexpected and so incredibly erotic. Locke Maris was stroking me off in the shower. Giving me pleasure instead of simply taking it.

Watching what he was doing to me.

"Good boy," he said in my ear before swiping a thumb over the precum escaping my slit. "You want to come, don't you?"

I needed to stop being a complete slut for him. It was embarrassing. I'd never in my life responded positively to "good boy" shit, so why the fuck did it get me every time *he* said it? Was it the way he made it sound almost like a taunt or a dare? I wasn't sure, but I wanted to claw a little power back.

"It's hardly your mouth," I said on a gasp as his hand twisted just right.

The rumble of his laugh vibrated through my back and balls. "Do you want me to stop? This not good enough for you? Not gay enough?"

The teasing in his voice made me smile. It was good to know I'd helped bring him out of the funk he'd been in when we'd arrived.

"There's plenty of time for you to prove your gayness to m— Oh *fuckkk.*"

"Come for me, Jethro." The command was whispered silkily. The man was a fucking maestro. He knew exactly how to play me.

I might have been embarrassed if I hadn't been in such ecstasy. I teetered on the delicious edge for a few long seconds before his fingers brushed my nipple. Then I nearly choked to death on shower water as I threw my head back and opened my mouth in a cry.

Thankfully, Locke clapped a hand over my mouth before it filled with water, stifling my shout at the same time.

"Shh, that's it. Just like that," he murmured.

Oh my fucking god.

Since when was a freaking hand job this powerful? This asshole had the ability to own me in a way no one ever had before.

If this was what an orgasm was like with only his hands on me, what the fuck would it be like if he ever let me come on his cock?

I shuddered again and felt his arms release me. He moved under the shower spray and finished cleaning himself off before stepping out of the shower and reaching for a towel.

My eyes followed him like rabid wolves stalking their prey. The wide planes of his back. The curve of his spine. The hard muscles of his calves leading down to slim but strong ankles and long feet.

I thought back to the men I'd dated in college before I'd sworn off relationships. They'd been the meek, nerdy sort. Sweethearts —at least I'd thought so until they'd proven otherwise.

Locke was nothing at all like them.

He was the complete opposite. The kind of guy best encountered in quick, furtive doses. Hot but meaningless. A dime a dozen in the city.

But somehow, this time, it was different.

And I fucking hated that. Because of all the men I'd hooked up with over the years, this one was the absolute least likely to give a shit about me in any way past what I could do for his dick.

I washed and dried myself, escaping back to my own room to clear my head while Locke went back to behaving like I wasn't anything important—a skill he excelled at.

And one I was determined to foil at every turn.

Just as soon as my legs stopped shaking.

13

LOCKE

I FELT NOTICEABLY BETTER after the shower. Not only had I experienced another fucking fantastic orgasm, but I'd also taken Jett by surprise, which was more fun than I'd expected.

After checking in with the office, I knocked on Jett's door to inform him it was time for dinner. He stepped out of the room, revealing a set of clothes I'd never seen him in. It was definitely not anything Minnie's shopper would have selected.

He wore a pair of jeans that were made to worship his body and a tight white cotton tank covered by a partially open denim snap-front shirt that looked like it had been through a thousand washes. The sleeves were rolled up, and he'd added a couple of necklaces, as well as a few silver rings on his fingers.

My heart rate increased. "I see you didn't take advantage of your new wardrobe."

He lifted his eyebrows in challenge. "You don't like the way I look?"

"That's not what I said." How I felt about his looks was irrelevant.

He nodded and tried holding back a smile. "Okay, then. Let's go."

As he passed me, I muttered an expletive that he caught. The sound of his laughter in the open hallway made me smile against my will. Being here with the provoking playboy was a nice distraction. Had I shown up alone again, memories of my grandfather might have overwhelmed me, which wouldn't have helped me get into the necessary mindset for the Paxis tournament.

I was counting on Jett to keep things shallow. Physical. *Distracting.*

When we arrived in the main gathering room at the center of the house, Concetta was there to lead us to the dining room.

"The chef kept it simple tonight with a salad, grilled fish, and a little sorbet for something sweet at the end."

"Perfect," I said, thanking her again and gesturing for Jett to take the seat next to mine.

As he pulled the cloth napkin into his lap, he made a point of eying the large table. "We could have eaten in the kitchen since it's just the two of us."

"The kitchen doesn't have the view," I said. "Besides, I'm pretty sure Roberto would have put a curse on us if we dared trespass on his territory. My grandfather was the only one who could sneak in there and share a coffee with the temperamental chef."

"Not misbehaving little boys like you?" Jett asked, a knowing sparkle in his eyes.

"He once smacked me with a wooden spoon. I won't be taking any chances."

The sound of his laugh relaxed me enough to smile back as an attendant came in with our salads. Once she was gone, Jett breathed out a "Holy shit, this looks amazing" under his breath.

"Welcome to Italy, where everything is fresh and local. You'll discover why I keep on an abusive chef."

He took a bite and groaned, the sound giving me pleasure in multiple ways. I liked watching him eat. Even though it had been over three years, I hadn't forgotten how skinny he'd been in Amsterdam. How he'd attacked the food I'd ordered like a man starved.

Feeding him was satisfying. Making him happy was addictive.

"What are your favorite foods?" I asked, trying to make it sound like nothing more than polite conversation. As his host, providing for him was my responsibility. That was all.

"Mm, well, this goes on the list now. Fresh tomatoes, balsamic. Basil. To die for. But I also like the usual suspects. Pizza, pad Thai, a good filet. Sushi, if it's fresh. What about you?"

The reminder that he had wealthy men buying him sushi and steak was unwanted. I batted it away in my mind.

"Agreed on the filet. There's a shrimp fra diavalo at a restaurant in LA I can't get enough of. And I'm secretly addicted to a chocolate tea biscuit you can only get online or in Europe. Minnie always has a stash in the office for very bad days."

Jett laughed. "I can't imagine you sulking in your office with a sneaky packet of chocolate cookies. What does that even look like?"

I pointed to my face without changing my expression. "Like this."

His laughter made me imagine pulling him into my lap. Something I would never do with a man in a million years.

"You're terrifying," he said through his smile. "People must quake in their boots on your bad days."

We finished our salads and started on the fish, which was served alongside a fresh lemon and caper pasta dish. Jett acted like he'd never had food before, the way he *ooh*'d and *ahh*'d over it. Concetta was in seventh heaven, and I could tell she couldn't wait to report back to Roberto that he had a new fan in the house.

"Tell me about your family," I said, curious whether he would explain the discrepancy between the single-mom story in his background investigation and the dads he'd mentioned. It was possible he had a single mother *and* a biological father who was married to another man, but he'd never mentioned a mother.

He swallowed and nodded, looking suddenly serious. "I, ah... I have two dads. I told you that. And a brother and sister. Gabe and Becca."

I nodded but didn't speak and risk derailing him. Maybe they were half siblings or stepsiblings.

"I grew up at the beach. Went crabbing. My dads met there as kids and then met again later." He glanced out at the sea. "We all like to go out on the water. Sailing, skiing, paddling. Doesn't matter. I love being on a boat."

He seemed to realize something because his eyes widened. "Sorry. I didn't mean to..."

"Sorry for what?"

"Your dad. Didn't he die in a boating accident? I thought I read online—"

I nodded and inhaled before explaining. "That's the official story. And it's true in a way. But he and his mistress had high levels of alcohol and party drugs in their system. The authorities think the two of them passed out before the waves pushed them into the rocks."

"Jesus. I'm... I'm sorry."

I shook my head. "Don't be. My father made his choices. He dishonored our legacy with his death. It crushed my grandfather. Imagine a Maris being such a fucking idiot on a *boat*. Besides, we were never close. He wasn't that type of father."

The kitchen attendant came in to remove our plates. Awkward silence filled the room after she left. Jett pushed his chair back and moved over to mine, pulling it away from the edge of the table until I was angled toward the view of the water.

Then he climbed into my lap, straddling me and wrapping his arms around my neck to hug me tightly.

I froze. "What the fuck are you doing?"

"We've talked about this before," he said with a familiar smile in his voice. "This is a hug. I'm hugging you."

"Nobody asked you for a hug."

"Aren't you lucky I didn't make you ask."

His breath was warm against my neck. I sank into the feeling and let myself hug him back for the briefest of moments.

He was solid and warm, provoking as fuck, but also somehow comforting.

I trusted him. Which was a distinctly bad idea.

"Oh!" Concetta came to a stop inside the door to the kitchen. Jett's entire body stiffened.

When Jett tried to leap out of my embrace, I tightened my arms around him and murmured, "It's okay."

He pulled back and stared at me in shock while I turned to Concetta. "He's feeling sorry for me because he accidentally brought up my father's death."

The transformation on her face was almost comical. If she'd been off the clock or elsewhere, she would have surely spit on the ground in disgust. Instead, she shook her head and murmured, "Che stronzo!"

Thankfully, it was clear she was referring to my father, not Jett.

Jett snorted in surprise and climbed off my lap before taking his chair again. "Tell us how you really feel, Concetta."

She grunted and pursed her lips before bringing us two bowls of lemon sorbet with a little delicate cookie on the side of each. "Dessert. Fresh made today. Enjoy."

She winked at me before turning toward the kitchen. As soon

as she was gone, Jett glared at me. "I'm not the first man you've brought here."

I was taken aback by his question. Rather, his accusation. As if my housekeeper's cheeky wink had implied I was a player or liar.

And it bothered him.

While I relished his obvious annoyance, I wasn't cruel enough to let an untruth stand. "That is correct. I once brought my college roommate." I hesitated before adding, "But I never touched his dick."

I could tell he was still unsure.

"Jett. I've never done anything sexual with a man before you. I'm simply not stressed about what Concetta thinks for a number of reasons. First, her brother is gay. I know this because she took me shopping in town one time, and we ran into him with his, quote, boy toy. Second, the staff here are discreet and loyal. They take great pride in protecting the Maris name. She would never tell anyone my private business, and she's rewarded handsomely for it. Finally..."

I leaned forward and reached for his hand, pulling him out of his seat until he reluctantly climbed into my lap again.

Then I continued. "I am not embarrassed by my attraction to you, Jett. Only surprised by it."

I moved my hands inside the denim shirt that perfectly matched his eyes. My hands cupped his rounded shoulders and then moved down over his chest.

Jett still seemed unsure. His eyes watched me with a thread of suspicion and disbelief.

"You've been very dismissive," he said carefully.

"How so?"

Instead of answering me, he stared at my lips before leaning forward and kissing me. He approached me slowly enough that I could have dumped him on his ass, but then I wouldn't have been able to surprise him again by accepting the gesture.

I cupped his cheek and kissed him back slowly. More slowly than he apparently wanted. He let out a grunt of annoyance that only made me smile and pull back a little.

"Patience, Jethro," I whispered.

"It's Jett," he grumbled before kissing me again.

I pulled back, just enough to smirk but not enough to risk ending the kiss. "Is it?"

He had to know I had his legal name now, and it was Jethro Benjamin Davis. I'd seen it on his passport myself.

His fingers tightened on the collar of my shirt, pulling me closer so he could deepen the kiss. My heart skipped along in my chest like I'd shotgunned a can of Red Bull instead of enjoying a nice glass of Pinot Grigio.

I could understand how this man made big money as an escort. He was sex incarnate. All I wanted to do was put my hands and mouth on him.

My fingers moved under his shirt and up the warm expanse of his back. Jett arched into me, grinding his ass on my dick. I barely kept myself from moving my hands down the back of his jeans.

The noises he made were definitely not appropriate for the dining room.

"Let's go," I said, pulling away and nudging him off me.

He made a cute sound of petulant disappointment before grinning at me. "Last one there is a rotten egg... *Jason*."

Then he took off running.

By the time I sauntered into the suite, he was completely naked in the center of my pristine bed.

Just the sight of him like that stole my breath.

"My first name's not Jason. And who said I wanted you naked in my bed?" I asked.

Jett's grin made his eyes dance. "Who said I cared what you wanted?"

I entered the room and closed the door behind me before leaning against it and lifting my chin. "Go on, then. Don't let me stop your fun."

He pulled on his cock with his fingers before tugging his sac with his other hand. His eyes remained on me. "I think you should see if you like sucking cock."

I didn't allow him the reward of my smirk. "I think you're pushing your luck."

He closed his eyes and let out a sound as his fingers teased the sensitive spot under the tip of his cock.

My phone buzzed in my pocket. I pulled it out, primarily to toy with him, but then noticed the message from the office was urgent.

"I'm sorry. I need to deal with this."

I turned around and made my way out of the room, ignoring the look of surprised disappointment on his face. A cyclone had strengthened a few hours ago, impacting two Maris vessels traveling between Brisbane and Nouméa. The ships were being forced into evasive maneuvers, with one of them carrying particularly high-value cargo for one of our largest clients.

After a few minutes, Jett came out of the bedroom fully dressed and offered to help. I let him read the information over my shoulder while I spoke with our chief of operations on the phone.

Surprisingly, Jett pulled out his own laptop and began scouring the internet for any updates on the weather, emergency preparedness in Nouméa, and any on-the-ground reports on social media.

I spent hours on calls and video conferences, monitoring the situation and arranging all the support we could for the crews and vessels, in addition to communicating with the impacted clients to assuage their fears. During all of those interminable hours, Jett brought me coffee and juice from the kitchen, the night staff followed later with the sorbetto we'd missed at dinner, and Jett continued to make himself helpful by printing off and pointing to legal-and-PR-approved language I could use when speaking to everyone.

By the time I finished my last media interview, thanking the Australian Maritime Safety Authority for their quick response and continued diligence, and my captains and crew for their stellar ship-handling and relentless care of our clients' cargo, the sky was turning pink, and I was exhausted.

I stood and stretched, grateful Jett had gone to bed a couple of hours earlier when I'd asked him to. I'd assumed he'd retreated to his own room, so I was surprised to find him sleeping in my bed, curled up in the dead center. I couldn't hold back a huff of soft laughter.

No more riding the rail.

I undressed to my underwear and slid in behind him, moving closer until I could fold him in my arms. He shifted and made a humming noise before settling back down with his hand over mine on his chest.

It was strange not to have the full swell of a woman's breast to hold on to as I spooned him or the soft floral scent of hair products in my nose. But the way I fit around him was somehow still strangely comforting.

He was strong and hard in places. Like I could wrestle the fuck out of him or force him into positions without taking care to be delicate with him, and that would be a *good* thing. Like I could shove him down to suck my morning wood before even greeting him in the morning, and he wouldn't be offended. Might even be turned on by it.

With Jett, I didn't have any worry that he'd wake in the morning and complain that I'd abandoned him tonight before we'd had a chance to fuck. Or that my job was super boring. Or that I put my work first every time.

Were these things the benefit of a professional sex partner or a man?

Or both?

I tried to steady my breathing to let go of the residual stress from the work emergency. Thankfully, everyone in the Maris Holdings family was safe. Our vessels and cargo were safe.

And for a couple of days, I could enjoy the freedom of being with Jett Davis without having to worry about what anyone else thought or what it might mean.

If only the cyclone had been the only storm on the horizon.

14

JETT

I woke in Locke's arms, plastered half-starfish-like across his chest and one long leg. There was no telling what time he'd finally come to bed, but I knew better than to risk waking him. Hopefully, his office wouldn't start bothering him for several more hours because of the time difference.

After sneaking out of his bed to my own bathroom, I showered and dressed. Concetta was nowhere to be found, so I followed the cooking sounds and smell of bacon until I found the kitchen.

There was music playing on an honest-to-god radio with an antenna sticking up, propped on the counter next to a stack of papers and two pencil stubs pockmarked with teeth imprints. A middle-aged man in a chef's coat and baggy black-and-white checked pants hummed along to the music.

"Mi scusi, potrei avere una tazza di caffè?" I asked in deliberately mispronounced beginner Italian. I fully expected the resident ornery chef to curse me out of his domain.

The man turned around and grinned. "Parli italiano?"

"Molto male, lo prometto."

He wiped his hands on a nearby towel and held one out to shake. "Mr. Davis. Please welcome. I am Roberto Sanna."

"Please call me Jett, and thank you for the incredible dinner last night. I've never had sorbetto like that. It was amazing. You'd better guard the leftovers. I plan to sneak in here in search of them one night."

He laughed. "You would be welcome anytime. Come, let's get your caffè. How do you like it?"

"Un cappuccino, per favore."

He gestured to a nearby attendant, a young man this time, who immediately got to work on the large silver espresso machine on the other side of the commercial kitchen.

Roberto turned back to attend to his food, asking me at the same time how I'd like my eggs.

When my coffee and food were ready, I planted myself on the other side of the large central island, where there were plenty of stools and where the other man had been peeling potatoes before stopping to make my coffee.

"Please don't make me sit at the adult table out there by myself," I said, flashing Roberto a humble smile.

He waved my concern off. "You sit here and tell us the news from America."

We spent the next forty minutes gossiping like TMZ fans. I'd spent a lot of time in the past several years chatting up people from all walks of life on various jobs. It was something that came easily to me, maybe because I had social parents and an enormous, gregarious extended family.

But I also appreciated the opportunity to have a break from it, so after scheduling a time later in the morning to talk to Roberto and Concetta about the upcoming Paxis tournament and its hosting needs, I decided to indulge myself with some time in the sun. I returned to the room and peeked in on Locke, confirming he was still dead asleep. Then I changed into swim trunks and made my way out the terrace doors to the pool. The sun was warm, and the sky was a deep, clear blue.

I covered myself in sunscreen and threw myself onto a chaise, barely restraining a pleasured groan at the expansive view and the feel of the warm sun on my skin.

This was the life. No wonder so many celebrities vacationed here.

While my body rested, my brain kept running at full speed. Was last night's emergency response a common occurrence in Locke's business? How had he known what to do? The man had been in charge of the company for less than six months, but he'd acted like someone with twenty-five years more experience.

Before I inevitably moved from appreciating his competency to remembering his hand on my dick, my phone buzzed with a text from my brother.

GABE

Where are you and why is it Italy?

You have to stop tracking me. Seriously, it's not okay.

I wasn't sure how he did it, but I worried he'd find a way one day to track me even when I left my personal cell phone at home on official missions.

GABE

Answer the question. Mav flew up to surprise you and you weren't there.

My stomach dropped.

> Fuck, seriously? Why didn't he tell me he was coming?

GABE

> You know the dads. They never want to ruin a vibe or be a nuisance.

> Since when? Beau is always in my shit, ruining all kinds of vibes.

GABE

> Okay, fine. Mav had a work thing in the city. But still. He was bummed you weren't there. Did you get a last minute consulting assignment? Amalfi Coast seems a strange place for it. Do they even have companies in that tiny town you're in?

> It's not work. It's pleasure.

The water splash-slash-cum emoji appeared. Even though I knew he was implying that I was somewhere nice getting lots of dick, I played dumb.

> Yes, in fact I'm in front of a swimming pool right now.

I sent him a photo of the water, tightly cropped so there was no identifying information in the shot.

GABE

> Who's the guy?

I hesitated. Thankfully, before I responded, another message from him popped up.

GABE

Guys, plural. I forget you don't do repeats.
Who are you with, though, and do they
need another Marian? Because I could be
free if needed.

Not sure Hunter would appreciate that.

My brother's bestie was territorial as fuck, even though Gabe
was oblivious.

GABE

Hunter doesn't care who I fuck.

Sure.

GABE

Why are you so fucking squirrelly? Why
can't you just tell me where you are and
what you're doing?

I'm in Italy with a friend. Why are you
awake so early in the morning?

GABE

Couldn't sleep. Which friend?

I closed my eyes and let out a groan under my breath. It was
impossible to do what I did for a living and be in the Marian
family.

You're worse than Beau. You're worse
than *Aunt Tilly*.

GABE

Take that back.

I closed my eyes and let the heat of the sun sink into my skin
again, but the phone buzzed a minute later.

GABE

I hate that you don't talk to me anymore.

I stared at the words, absently rubbing the ache in my chest. He wasn't wrong. And I felt the same way.

My fingers hovered over the screen before I typed a response.

I came to Italy with a straight guy. Someone I hooked up with before. Someone I should steer clear of. But I can't seem to stay away from. There. You happy?

GABE

Bro.

Don't say it.

GABE

BRO.

I clicked the screen off and tossed it on the chaise next to me to keep from typing more. There was nothing my brother could say that I hadn't already thought myself.

It was ridiculous to catch feelings for a straight guy. And even if Locke was coming into his own in terms of appreciating his walk on the wild side, he wasn't exactly the kind of guy who was going to start shopping for dildos and jocks and introducing his boyfriend at the annual Longshoreman's Ball.

It's just sex.

And I loved sex. Loved it. Couldn't get enough of it.

I also loved lying in the sun by a crystal-clear pool and a wide expanse of the Mediterranean Sea.

So this was enough.

In fact, it was plenty.

The perfect renewal and recovery before throwing myself back into the career I wanted way more than any relationship. Helping others and making the world a better place.

I ignored the subsequent buzzing of my phone and allowed myself to doze with nothing but the floral-scented air and the faint sound of a gardener doing work in the distance.

Being a highly paid escort had its upsides.

It was enough, I told myself again.

It was plenty.

15

LOCKE

WHEN I FINALLY WOKE UP, the sun was high over the house, and I felt much better. Jett was long gone, thank fuck. I wasn't interested in morning-after awkwardness, and right now, I needed caffeine more than an orgasm.

"Good morning, Concetta," I said, strolling into the dining room and heading for the table out on the balcony. "I would kill for a coffee and breakfast, please."

She flashed me a smile. "I heard about your late night. We will have something right out for you."

I held back from asking where Jett was, but a few minutes later, he was the one who appeared with my coffee.

"For shame, Locke," he said with a grin. "Don't you know American coffee preferences kill an Italian's soul? Your chef is back there sobbing into your omelette."

I shrugged and reached for it. "He hates me anyway, so my coffee order can't make it worse." I took a sip and groaned. "Thank you."

He propped his ass against the balcony railing. This time, he wore white linen pants and a navy tank top, fitted enough to show off the outline of every single muscle in his chest and abdomen. "I checked in with Minnie at the office to see if there was anything urgent, and there isn't. She did say you have a call at five this afternoon—Italy time—but that she will try to handle anything else that comes your way."

I blinked at him in surprise, replaying the words in my head since I hadn't been focused on what he was saying. "Uh, thank you. That... wasn't necessary."

Jett tilted his head in mock confusion. "Isn't that what your assistant is supposed to do?"

I shot him a look and took another sip of coffee, keeping my eyes firmly away from his body. "I need to talk to Concetta about the room assignments for our guests."

"Already done," he said. "Only, she wanted to warn you that Emil Sorenson and his wife are very loud in bed and—"

"Jett, you are telling tales!" Concetta said with a laugh, arriving through the open doors and setting my omelette down on the table. "I said he and his wife are not quiet guests. They sometimes argue and stay up late with requests for additional drinks. We used to put them near your grandfather's suite so they wouldn't bother the other guests, but remember, your grandfather was hard of hearing."

Jett met my eyes. "Anyway, since the room they'll be in is closest to mine, not yours, I think it'll be fine. But Concetta wanted to make sure you were okay with it."

I nodded, wondering if anyone would end up sleeping in Jett's bedroom at all. At this rate, the man seemed to have staked his territory in the center of my personal space.

Surprisingly, I hadn't minded sharing a bed with him, even though I usually preferred sleeping alone.

"I live in the city. Noise isn't a problem. Besides, Jett's right. It probably won't be heard in my bedroom. If he wants to be the one to suffer their marital spats, so be it."

She nodded and turned away but stopped before disappearing back through the doors. She returned and reached into the pocket of her skirt to hand something to Jett. "I almost forgot. Put this on the burns. It will help."

He took the small piece of aloe plant from her hands and beamed at her. "This is from Roberto, isn't it?"

She nodded, waved her hand over her shoulder, and disappeared into the house.

I watched in shock as Jett casually swiped the cut end of the aloe leaf over the tips of his finger. As the caffeine finally hit my brain, I realized what must have happened.

I shoved my chair back and stepped close to take his hand. "You burned yourself? How the fuck did he let you close enough to the stove for that? I told you not to go in there. He's a menace. You know what? He's fired. We'll have to find someone else for the tournament."

The tips of three of his fingers were redder than the others. I took the aloe from him and held his hand, palm up, smoothing the slick gel over the reddened fingers so he didn't have to try and use his nondominant hand to apply it.

He smiled at me. "Stand down. Do you think I'm stupid enough to get close to Roberto's stove? I accidentally touched a piece of metal that had been baking in the sun. It's fine. No big deal. It's my own fault for snooping."

I glanced up at him. "What do you mean, snooping?"

He turned slightly to point down by the pool, where there was a small flower garden.

"Ah. The little plaques by the roses," I said with a sigh. Each metal sign was engraved with the varietal and name and date of its acquisition. "I burned my leg on one when I was five. I would replace them, but my grandmother loved them."

"One of the rosebushes is from the Queen of England," he said, a tinge of awe in his voice. "Another is from Vraj Nanda. Do you know who that is?"

I nodded, returning my attention to his hurt fingers. "You'll meet him in a few days. He's one of the Paxis players."

When he didn't respond, I looked up at him. "What?"

"Vraj Nanda, the guy who wrote *Stillness is a River*? He's part of your nerd herd?"

Jett had refused to conform to my expectations at every turn during our short acquaintance, so maybe it shouldn't have been such a surprise that he was familiar with *Stillness is a River*.

But the way he spoke the title with a hushed reverence, like he'd not only heard of the book but read it and been impressed by it, hit me hard.

It made me wonder if Jett was a reader, and if so, what books he liked to read, and whether we'd read any of the same things and could discuss them. It made me wonder what other hobbies and interests Jett had, and how much there was to him that I didn't know—

Alarm bells clanged in my mind.

The reason I'd brought Jett—a sex worker, a former go-go dancer, a *man*—to Italy was so I wouldn't have to divide my attention between my sex partner and the Paxis tournament. The whole point was to bring someone who knew the score and was being well compensated, so there'd be no expectations on either side.

And now here I was, distracted and intrigued when I most needed to get my head in the game.

I released Jett's hand and tossed the remains of the aloe leaf on the table before returning to my meal. "I'm really hoping you don't refer to them that way when they arrive," I said stiffly.

He took the seat next to mine. "Who else is coming? Besides the ones you already mentioned on the way here."

I swallowed a bite of omelette before answering. "I thought you went over the room assignments with Concetta."

"I did. And she said things like, 'The Hartmanns are in the yellow suite,' and, 'Saleem and his wife prefer a view of the garden.'" Jett rolled his eyes. "I guess I didn't catch on to the fact that 'the Nandas' referred to a famous spiritual leader."

I shrugged. "I told you it was a gathering of powerful people."

He waited for me to say more, but I didn't. He'd see soon enough who else was coming.

And now that I thought about it, it was probably for the best that he didn't know too much in advance.

While I didn't think Jett would betray the NDA he'd signed with me, I'd be stupid not to remember that he was a player who'd probably learned to manipulate others for his own survival.

His entire career was about making men like me feel wanted. Feel seen and understood. That was how he got paid.

This was a job to him.

I was a job to him.

The reminder soured my mood, but it was necessary.

"I have a lot of calls today," I said, shoving another bite of food in my mouth. "You'll need to find a way to entertain yourself."

Jett frowned. "I can help with your calls, if you want. Just put me to work."

I shook my head once. "These are private calls. If you can't amuse yourself, ask Concetta what help she needs for the house party."

As I took a sip of coffee and gazed out at the water in the

distance, I felt his eyes on me. I knew he was trying to figure out the reason for my abrupt mood change.

No explanations necessary, I reminded myself.

"Sure," Jett finally said, a sliver of annoyance clear in his sticky-sweet tone. "I mean, of course, sir. Whatever you say, sir."

I continued to eat for another minute, the silence uncomfortable as fuck. My skin prickled with awareness. Of how he sat, how he moved. Every small sound of his breathing.

He leaned forward, and it took all my self-control not to tilt in his direction. Instead, I looked out at the water again. The endless stretch of impossible blue, several shades darker than Jett's eyes.

My skin felt like it was hooked up to an electric wire, the current so low I could barely tell it was there without stretching the limits of hyperawareness.

Jett stood abruptly and turned to push in his chair. I snuck a look at him, wondering what kind of underwear he could possibly be wearing with those pants. They were virtually transparent. The shape of his legs could be seen through the airy material.

His feet were surprisingly bare. The linen pooled around them and dragged on the floor a little. When he turned back to me, my eyes went to the loose drawstring at his waist.

He stepped closer and studied me for a moment. Maybe I'd been wrong about his eyes. They seemed the exact color of the Mediterranean at the moment.

Anger suited him.

"Come find me if you have need of me, *Mr. Maris*."

And then he turned and walked away, his lazy gait doing criminal things to his ass in those pants.

It was clear he wasn't happy.

But he was here on my terms. And he *was* an employee.

Anything else would be impossible.

~

Work kept me busy for the next several hours. A video conference with investors in Dubai. Email responses to the head of R&D, an official signature on a letter to the trade secretary of Portugal, and a call with the finance team to discuss expansion funding. Through it all, I was vaguely aware of gardeners working outside. The open doors to my balcony framed a view of the pool terrace and the sea beyond it, but to the left were also views of and a short staircase down to my grandmother's favorite garden.

It wasn't until everyone on the finance call except my sister hung up that I realized one of the men working outside my room was Jett.

He'd changed out of the linen pants and into a pair of running shorts and shoes. A dark tank exposed his shoulders to the sun, and his skin carried the sheen of sweat. The gardener he was chatting with seemed oblivious to the sheer temptation Jett Davis presented.

"Sure you can't come with me? Jasmine keeps asking me about you."

I tried to focus on what my sister was saying. "Come with you to the Caymans? No. I'm in Italy. I thought I told you that."

"You probably did. I've been buried in work."

I forced myself to look away from the scene in the garden in which Jett had been gathering clippings between making the gardener laugh.

"You're always buried in work," I told Celeste.

"Yes, well. There are worse things."

I hummed in agreement, thinking about the unspoken alternative. Our father hadn't worked enough. Had played too much. Our mother had never worked at all.

"Anyway, I really wish you'd come with me. You need a vacation even more than I do."

"I'm on vacation," I said. "The Paxis players don't show up until Friday."

Her laugh was clear over the line, familiar and comforting for all that she was making fun of me. "A couple of days in the villa to prep for your silly gaming week is hardly a vacation. Besides, I might believe you if you tell me you haven't checked in with the office today for more than a few minutes."

I ignored her implication, my eyes sliding to the balcony doors and back away from them. The old gilt mirror on the wall by the suite door caught my attention. My grandmother had checked her lipstick in that mirror every time she'd left the suite.

"It's weird being here," I admitted.

"But you were already there in January, right?"

"It's not the same. With everyone coming, I'm the host. They moved me into the primary suite."

"Is Willow there, too?" I could hear the hesitation in Celeste's voice.

"No, why?"

"I don't know. So you won't be alone? She's not my favorite person, but then again, I haven't spent much time with her."

"Which is fine because we're not dating," I said peevishly, my eyes moving back out through the balcony doors like little torpedoes whose navigation was completely fucked-up. Jett was leaning over, gathering a rogue branch from under a bush. Shorts pulled tight across his ass, and his hamstrings curved along the back of his thighs.

"Well, maybe if you were dating someone, they would be a comfort to you right now," she snapped back. "And maybe you wouldn't be such a fucking asshole to someone who loves you."

I blew out a breath and closed my eyes. "I'm sorry. I just..." I opened my eyes and let them find Jett again. "I haven't found anyone who'll let me be who I am."

"I'm not sure you've actually been looking," she pointed out.

That was probably fair. I didn't have the bandwidth for it.

"Who are you, Johnny?" she asked gently, using the nickname she'd used since she'd heard my fourth-grade teacher mistakenly call me by my first name. Jett had been righter than he knew when he'd teasingly called me John. "Tell me."

My sister and I had always been close. Maybe with the exception of the years when I'd been in college and she'd still been in high school, held in my mother's socialite thrall. But when I'd gone to London for graduate school and she'd done a semester at Oxford, we'd become close again, bonding over the impossibility of feeling sorry for ourselves while also having everything we'd ever asked for.

"'Cept decent parents," I remembered her muttering while sitting on the floor next to a half-eaten pizza in a takeout box.

"Except that," I'd agreed.

"Thank god for Grandpa," she'd added.

"Yep."

I dragged in a breath and thought about confiding in her. Telling her I was having a midlife crisis a decade too soon. Telling her I'd gone full Richard Gere and hired myself a Julia Roberts... er, a Julia*n* Roberts.

But it was a bell that couldn't be unrung. If I told her I'd found one man temporarily attractive and intriguing, she'd try to set me up with every gay man she'd ever met.

And that wasn't what this was.

"I'm a happy workaholic," I said, stretching my legs out in front of me and reminding myself I needed to do some kind of exercise if I wanted any chance of sleeping tonight. "My first priority is

Maris. And not many women are happy to take second place to the job. Or men. You know that."

She laughed again. "For a minute there, I thought you meant men as in *you* being with a man."

I squeezed my back teeth together. "Ha."

My eyes flicked back outside. To the man who was now carrying a patio umbrella out to a table, his biceps popping and shoulders catching the sun.

"You're not wrong," she continued wryly. "My new idea is to date someone at the office. We can be workaholics and still see each other."

Considering she worked for Maris, I was not impressed with her idea. "Absolutely not."

Her laughter rang out enough that I could picture her assistant smiling to herself through the door to her own office.

"Locke, I'm hardly going to harass an employee. It was a—"

"Everyone at Maris is my employee," I reminded her. "My responsibility. And we have rules for a reason. Promise me, Cellie."

She was suddenly quiet on the other end of the line. Enough that I pictured her silently fuming and began to feel like an ass.

"I'm sorry," I said.

"Wow. An apology from a Maris. I should buy a lottery ticket."

The old joke made me smile, but I was glad she couldn't see me. "I just—"

"I'm going to pretend you don't actually think I would date an employee," she interrupted. "It was a joke. You, of all people, should know that. This call is over. Feel free to try me again when you remember who *I* am, Locke."

The call ended.

I was crushed. She was right. I'd overreacted. I'd been so distracted by the goddamned go-go boy in my garden, I hadn't had my head on straight.

I shot her a text apologizing, but I knew she wouldn't accept it for at least a couple of days.

Accusing her of doing something our father had been notorious for was unforgivable.

And she wasn't even the Maris currently sleeping with an employee.

16

JETT

Dinner was awkward as fuck.

Locke seemed off in his head somewhere and uninterested in conversation. After trying and failing for the third time to engage him in conversation, I finally pulled out my phone and started reading through a memoir I'd been enjoying earlier.

Was it bad table manners? Absolutely.

Would Mav have made me do the dishes for a week for reading my phone at the dinner table? Yes. Even at age twenty-six.

Did I feel one shred of guilt? Nope.

The faint scrape of Locke's utensils was the only noise. I enjoyed the tender beef medallions with one hand while turning my page with the other. The Syrian refugee protagonist was now out of the boat and in the dark water.

"Vraj doesn't eat meat," Locke said.

I blinked up at him. "Correct. Neither does Selene Mercier. Roberto has it under control."

"Mm." He returned to his meal.

I watched him for another few moments until it was clear he was in his head again. Then I returned to reading.

When he was finished, he cleared his throat. "Did you have a nice day?"

I glanced up at him. "Me?"

His forehead crinkled as he gazed at me. "Yes. You."

"Oh. Er. Sure? Yes. In fact, I did. This is a lovely property, and you have a kind staff. It must be a joy to come here regularly."

Locke nodded and looked back down at his now-empty plate. Then he moved his fork around a little. If I hadn't been put in my place so emphatically earlier today, I might have helped him out of this awkward moment. Volunteered more about the day or asked him about his. But it was clear that wasn't what he expected of me. Or wanted.

I glanced back out at the sea, forgetting the doors were closed tonight because of a too-strong breeze and a chilly temperature.

My phone glowed from its spot under the table, resting on my thigh.

As soon as I gave up and snuck another glance at the page in the book, he spoke again, nearly causing me to jump.

"I thought about taking a swim after dinner."

What the fuck was he doing right now? This was excruciating. I tilted my head at him. "It might be cold."

"The pool is heated."

"Ah."

A young woman named Zuri came out from the kitchen, apologizing profusely for the delay. "I didn't realize you were finished with your meal. Pardon me."

I waved her off. "It's fine."

She shot me a grin. "Are you ready for cake and coffee?"

"Not yet," Locke said stiffly. "Maybe in about an hour. We'll let you know."

There was an awkward moment as her eyes flicked to me as if wondering whether the boss spoke for both of us. I gave her a reassuring smile and a shrug. It was fine. The boss was the boss.

Zuri's smile dropped as she ducked her head in a combination bow and nod. "Yes, sir. Whenever you prefer."

Once she'd removed our dishes to the kitchen and was completely out of earshot, I inhaled and exhaled carefully. "Pro tip, Locke. Being an asshole to your staff is an excellent way to lose them or, at the very least, lose their vaunted loyalty."

Then I stood up and dropped my napkin on the place mat in front of my chair. "Good night."

He let me get all the way to the end of the adjacent living room before he spoke. "Stop."

It wasn't angry or abrupt. It was soft like a plea. I didn't turn around.

"Please," he added after too long a pause. "Wait."

I forced myself to stand still. Not bolt to the bedroom in anger. Not turn and snap at him. Not drop to my hands and knees and beg him to fuck me. And not beg him to tell me why the hell he was so goddamn mercurial.

Locke's body stepped close enough for me to feel the heat of it through the thin cotton of my shirt. But he didn't touch me.

"Will you please join me for a swim? I need some exercise, and I'd really like your company."

The scent of his cologne surprised me. It wasn't just the scent of his bodywash. It was more. Like he'd made an actual effort.

For sex.

I reminded myself this wasn't a romance. It was an agreement for sex. Or, at the very most, seduction.

But I *had* agreed. And to be honest, I wanted it. I'd ached for him all day. I wasn't proud of it, but that was the truth. I wanted his hands on me more than I wanted to protect my ego or pride.

"I'd like that," I admitted.

He surprised me by moving up beside me and reaching for my hand, pulling me along to the suite, where we separated to change into swimsuits.

We moved together without speaking, out of the suite and down the nearby stairs to the terrace level, where we could exit through the fitness room doors to the pool deck. I'd spent plenty of time today touring the house with Concetta, so I'd already learned this shortcut. Watching him take it reminded me of all the times he'd been here before.

I imagined him as a kid, sneaking into hiding spots in a game with his sister. As a teen, lifting weights to impress a girl. As a young adult, most likely bored to be with the older set instead of somewhere more exciting.

It was almost impossible to see Locke as someone other than who he was. A too-serious businessman hell-bent on ruling everyone and everything around him. Someone too rigid to enjoy himself and let go, even for a little while.

Fuck. That.

"Best cannonball wins!" I declared, dropping my towel, yanking off my shirt, and taking a flying leap into the air off the edge of the pool deck. I soared into the cool night air, feeling the chill against my skin and hoping like hell he hadn't been lying about the pool being heated. When I reached the apex of the jump, I curled into a ball and flipped, wrapping my arms around my wide knees as quickly as I could before hitting the water with my shins and face.

Over-rotated.

When I came up for air to assess the damage my splash caused, I saw Locke standing at the edge of the pool with his mouth open in shock.

I let out a wet laugh, flicking my hair back and wiping my face. "Don't tell me you don't know what a cannonball is."

"Of course I know what a cannonball is. I was a twelve-year-old boy once, same as you."

"The ability doesn't expire, you know. You're in good shape." I eyed him up and down lasciviously. "Show me what you got... *Jimbo.*"

He rolled his eyes, then studied me for a moment, looking around at the wet splotches that reached an embarrassingly small ring around the edges of the pool. My siblings wouldn't have let me live it down if they'd been there to see such a paltry splash zone.

"I could beat that attempt with a clean swan dive," he muttered.

I raised an eyebrow.

He sighed and put his things down carefully on a nearby chaise before backing up a few feet from the edge of the pool. Then he took a few long steps and launched lazily into a perfect dive, graceful to the point of seeming like it was slow motion.

Fuck, he was beautiful.

When he came up, he flicked his hair and met my eyes. Water droplets in his eyelashes caught the light from the house in a way that made me suck in a breath.

"You, ah... hardly splashed at all," I said.

The edge of his lips curled up. "Because I'm not a barbarian."

I moved closer to him, suddenly eager to break his ridiculous poise regardless of how angry it made him. Before I could tackle him and shove his head under the water the way I used to do with my siblings, he reached out a hand for mine. When I gave it to him, he pulled me the rest of the way toward him until I couldn't help but put my legs around his waist as I landed gently against his front.

This part of the pool was the perfect depth. Even with my arms around his neck, the warm water came up almost to my shoulders.

"You're too serious," I accused. "Somewhere along the way, you forgot how to have fun."

His hand moved to cup the back of my head, and he kissed me—right there in the pool where anyone could see us from the house.

It was the first time this supposedly straight man had initiated a kiss. It was firm and overpowering. Nothing elegant and graceful like his dive had been. His large hand held me to him in a possessive way that made me dizzy with sudden need.

I arched into him, pressing myself into his lower belly, and he responded by slipping a hand down the back of my suit to grab an ass cheek.

My tongue wanted to tie itself in knots around his, taste every inch of him. Carry in its little moving boxes and unpack for good.

I pulled back with a gasp. "Why are you like this?"

His eyebrows furrowed. "You don't like the way I kiss?"

"No. Yes. Of course I like the way you kiss. Has anyone ever *not* liked the way you kiss? Jesus. But I mean..."

I hesitated, trying so hard to remember that this was not my place. He'd hired a sex doll, not a whiny bitch.

"Nothing," I said with a sudden smile. "Never mind."

He'd moved his hand from the back of my head to my chest, and now he moved it up to hold my chin. "Don't be an ass. Tell me what you were going to say without playing silly games."

I felt suitably chastised. Honestly, I couldn't blame him. I would have felt the same way if he'd backed away from something like that.

"You're so fucking changeable. It reminds me of the outdoor shower at my dad's house the year one of my dads went through a DIY phase. One minute, it was blissfully hot, and the next, it was an icy torture chamber. The unpredictability was worse than either temperature."

"What way would you like me to be?"

From this close up, I could see his dark eyes glinting, his eyebrows still sleek with water. The warmer light from the house hit the high planes of his cheekbones.

But I could also see a sliver of uncertainty in his eyes. A few rogue eyebrow hairs traveling in the wrong direction. A few tiny sunspots near his temple.

Imperfections. Cracks in the perfect image he tried so hard to maintain in front of the world.

"I want you to stop playing games," I said evenly. "Just when you start to be real with me, you pull away as if you're trying to make sure I don't read anything into it. I promise I won't. You fucking hired me for sex so you wouldn't have to deal with relationship expectations. I get it, okay? But can you not punish me for all the people who might have fucked you over? Can you at least let yourself have some fun? You're paying for it, after all."

His thumb absently swiped along my jawline, which was hella fucking distracting.

"Everyone always reads into it, Jett."

I batted his hand away from my face and dropped from around his waist to stand on my own two feet. Unfortunately, the water was deeper for me than it was for him, and our slight height difference became apparent again when the water covered more of me than him.

"Flatter yourself. You're not the only one who doesn't do relationships, you know," I said, feeling the now-familiar heat of annoyance.

"You're trying to tell me you aren't searching for a new sugar daddy?"

I couldn't hold back the bark of laughter. "I can say unequivocally, I'm not looking for a sugar daddy. Or a relationship. In fact…" I hesitated before pressing ahead. "I found a new job when I was in the city. It starts when we get back. I'm sure I'll be too busy for a relationship. You know how it is when you start a new… Well, you probably don't know since you've always been destined to work at Maris. But most people work their ass off to prove themselves in a new job, and that's what I plan to do."

Locke looked suspicious, as if he wasn't quite able to trust that I was being honest. "What kind of job? Where?"

"It's a consulting firm. I'm starting in a general admin position, but they try to promote from within. The kind of thing where I start off doing data entry or whatever, and hopefully, over time, I can work my way up to being an executive assistant. Or maybe work in marketing? I'm not sure."

Shut up.

"What's the name of the company?"

It was definitely time for me to remember some tradecraft because right now, I was sucking balls at it.

"And give you a chance to come snoop around my work? No way. Besides, I don't want to jinx it. I have a good feeling about it."

He crossed his arms over his chest. "I told you I could've found you something at Maris."

I lifted my eyebrows. "Yes, but then I'd be sleeping with the boss, and what would that do to both of our reputations?"

A strange look crossed his face. "No. That's… no. I wouldn't do that."

I reached out and touched his arm. "I know," I said softly. "I overheard you giving that guy at the Candy Bar hell about harassing one of your employees. You were fiercely protective, and I appreciated that. I knew you were one of the good guys from the beginning."

Locke's shoulders relaxed. "Good."

The serious nature of this conversation and how close it was coming to blowing the last scraps of my cover needed to end. I quickly dove under the water and yanked his legs out from under him, which wasn't as easy as I'd thought it would be.

He retaliated by yanking my shorts down and swimming quickly away from me. As soon as I came up sputtering after yanking my shorts back up, Locke dunked me.

The motherfucker dunked me.

We continued the water fight for at least twenty minutes, dunking, yanking, poking, and grabbing until we were both water-logged and breathless. I finally had to call a truce.

"Peace!" I cried through my laughter and rubbing my chest. "You yanked a chest hair, asshole."

He came up and slicked his hair back, wiping his nose and mouth before piercing me with those fucking eyes. His chest heaved with exertion. "You're pretty strong for a little guy."

I squawked in indignation before I realized he was joking. Then I launched myself at him again. Instead of pushing him into the water, I only managed to knock him one step back. Meanwhile, his arms went around me and held firm.

"No more," he murmured in a low breath. "Let me catch my breath before you try to drown me again."

I wrapped my legs around him again, happy to note the thick swelling of his cock under my ass. My muscles were warm and happy from the exertion, and I was smugly satisfied that I'd gotten Locke to have a little fun in the process.

The sound of our cries and laughter had echoed around the pool deck, joining the croaks of nearby frogs, the occasional gecko click, and the distant surf.

Suddenly, I wished we had more time together, more than just two days before his chess friends arrived. Long nights in which I could unwind his daily stress in creative ways like this. Something more than just sex, which was easy to come by, even though Locke insisted it was all he wanted.

I was beginning to wonder if what Locke Maris *needed* was something vastly different.

17

LOCKE

It was impossible to conduct an interview with a director of compliance candidate when all I could think about was the way Jett's fingers had tasted in my mouth as he'd sucked me off last night.

When we'd returned to the room after our swim, I'd stroked us both off in the shower. It hadn't taken much more than a heavy petting session under the hot spray before we both came over my fist and the shower floor.

Jett had settled himself in my bed before I'd finished brushing my teeth, which had prevented any awkward moment of my having to either man up and ask him to join me or let him return to his own room.

Which was why, when I'd woken hard and aching in the middle of the night, he'd been there to suck my cock. It had been dirty as fuck but had ended sweetly with him sneaking off to the kitchen and returning with the chocolate cake we'd never gotten to after the swim.

"... golf with Declan Hayward recently, and he said Truett Moore recommended..." The man droned on, dropping as many names as possible to impress me.

You want to impress me? Tell me how you'll do the fucking job, not who you're privileged enough to share a club membership with.

"I believe that's all we need for now," I said, trying not to sound as judgmental as I felt. "Minerva will keep you updated on next steps. Thank you."

After ending the video call, I started a new one with my assistant.

"I already know what you're going to say," Minnie said as soon as her face popped up on the screen. "But remember, you got mad at me for cherry-picking candidates last time."

I glared at her, ignoring her cute, familiar face and the new bangs I was still getting used to. "If this was my punishment, be assured, it worked."

She shrugged and grinned. "You should be more aware of all the ways in which I seek to carry your burdens, Maris. And be more grateful."

Minerva Willis and I had known each other for twenty years. Her father had been my grandfather's driver, and he'd had Minnie in the car or at the house with him enough for the two of us to become friends. When it had come time to hire an assistant, my grandfather had sat me down and discussed that almost nothing else mattered in the role more than trust and discretion.

It had been a no-brainer. There was no one outside my family I trusted more than Minnie. And since she'd already been working a few years by then as an admin at our office in Jersey City, she was also experienced. She was as much of a workaholic as I was, going even further in taking continuing education classes whenever she had time. When I'd taken over Maris Holdings in December, it had meant a life-changing promotion for her as well.

Thank god it hadn't resulted in her treating me any differently than she had when she'd been a sassy eight-year-old.

"I'm grateful, Min. Keep the riffraff away. Forget what I said about cherry-picking. Please only send me the best cherries from now on."

"My pick is Carina Bouchard from KLX. I'll set it up for later today if possible. How's it going there? Is everything ready for the tournament?"

I nodded, feeling a pinch of guilty regret that she couldn't ever know the truth behind the Paxis Council. "Yeah. All good."

She tilted her head. "And your new mistress is handling it all?"

I felt a cold flush roll over my skin like a rogue tide. "My what?"

"My replacement. Your new assistant. Gotta say, I'm a little jealous."

I tried blowing out a breath of relief without changing my expression. Minnie was still pissed I hadn't brought her. "Don't be. He's annoyed to be doing menial tasks. The man's a diva."

She knew I was teasing. "Where'd you find him anyway?"

"I told you, I met him in a bar a while back, then ran into him on that flight from Atlanta. He was looking for work. I needed someone friendly and gregarious for a short-term gig, so I figured it was a win-win."

"You really need to leave the hiring to me. Straight talk, Locke, he does not sound like a cherry."

I held in a laugh and hoped my face wasn't turning red. "No. No, he's not a cherry."

"I could have picked you a cherry for that job, too." She sniffed. I didn't mind it when she was territorial, but in this case, it was a subject that needed to be closed.

"This is a personal event, Min. You know that. It's not Maris stuff. Besides, you have enough on your plate as it is."

"Speaking of my not needing to sully myself with your personal nonsense… Willow's been trying to get ahold of you," she said, giving me a pointed look. "Want me to forward her to Mr. Davis? Let him handle your personal business?"

Before I could call her out on her petty jealousy, Jett came wandering into the suite, sweaty in running clothes and with the tinny sound of bass-beat music coming from his earbuds. He moved past me into his bedroom as if I wasn't even there.

Thankfully, the laptop camera was angled away from where he'd passed.

"No," I said, clearing my throat. "Just ignore her. Or give her a professional 'Mr. Maris is out of the office' type response. Believe me, she knows we're not in a relationship. She's just not happy about it."

Which was an understatement. The woman had blown up my phone before I'd finally blocked her number.

Minnie looked a little too gleeful. "Professional disdain. Got it. What else?"

"Will you please order Celeste lunch from Soletti's? If she already has plans, she'll eat it tonight."

She looked up from her tablet. "I thought Celeste was headed to the Caymans with her friends?"

"Shit. Right. Okay, can you find out where she's staying and send some flowers and a bottle of Dom to her room, please?"

She nodded. "I'd ask what you did to piss her off, but apparently, I'm not to involve myself in your personal—"

"Jesus, Min," I snapped. "Fine, okay? I hired the guy because…" A million words came to mind. *He challenges me. He's hot. He makes me insatiably curious. He gives incredible head. He's kind. He cares. He's a terrible liar. He's fucking beautiful.*

I want him.

Jett chose that moment to come back out of the room, this time dressed in stylish but simple twill shorts, a solid-color T-shirt, and leather flip-flops. Clothes Minnie had arranged.

He moved quietly past me and out the door to the suite, once again ignoring me or giving me space and privacy for my call.

"Because there's just something about him, Min," I finally said in a low voice. "And I need to figure out what it is."

I focused back on her after trailing him with my eyes. The look on her face was one of surprise but also affection and understanding. "Oh," she said.

I blew out a breath. "It's not a thing."

"Mmhm."

"Don't do that. I'm serious. You know how I feel about relationships. And Locke Maris is hardly going to come out as... what? Bisexual? Give me a break."

"What the fuck does that mean?"

I closed my eyes and remembered she, herself, was bi, even though the last three people she'd dated were men. She'd dated a woman in high school for three years. It was just that I hadn't liked Heather, so I tended to forget about her.

"You know what I mean," I said.

"I do, but you're still an ass. And I think your bad attitude is coming from fear. You can be bi without telling anyone about it, Locke. You can also be bi without doing anything about it."

Of course, she was right. And I could admit to myself there'd probably been other times I'd been physically attracted to men in my past, but I simply hadn't felt strongly enough to acknowledge it, let alone act on it. There'd always been plenty of women to hold my attention instead.

"Can we please stop talking about it? I'm bi. Okay? There. I said it. It's just a surprise, is all. And learning this about myself doesn't change my stance on relationships."

She blew out a breath, the air making her bangs flutter. "No. I get it. Maybe it would have been different six months ago, but now we definitely don't have time for anything serious."

It was a conversation she and I had shared many times. We loved what we did for Maris, even before my grandfather had died. And we both recognized we were in prime career-building years. We could find love later.

But hearing her say it now made me feel... annoyed. Cheated somehow.

Stifled.

"*You* do," I said. "You have time."

She laughed. "Right."

Her grin changed into a familiar expression of challenge. "If you don't have time, neither do I."

I knew what she was doing. We both did.

"Fine," I said, unwilling to have this discussion right now.

"But if things change, Maris... you let me know."

Instead of sitting in her smug righteousness, she jumped right back into work stuff, explaining the highlights of Carina Bouchard's resume and then moving on to the other urgent items she needed from me today.

When we were done, I was exhausted, even though it was only one in the afternoon. Thankfully, it was lunchtime, and that meant getting to sit down for a meal with Jett. Every minute spent in his company entertained me in some way. He was a joy to be around, even if he was provoking or angry.

Thankfully, today he was neither.

His face lit up when I stepped onto the balcony and joined him at the table. "Ah, the hardworking CEO spares time for sustenance. Come. I've slain some PB&J for you."

I took his outstretched hand and gave a mock bow over it. "If Roberto sends out such a sammy, I will literally suck your dick right here," I said in a low voice.

His eyes widened, and he called out toward the kitchen. "Zuri! Change my order, please!"

The young server came rushing out of the kitchen door with a small tray of lemonade. "Absolutely. What would you like, Mr. Davis?"

He frowned before glancing at me and looking back at her. "You don't need to be formal with me, even around the curmudgeon. It's Jett, please."

She looked nervously at me. How was it possible that everyone in my house saw Jett as the fucking messiah while they viewed me like a smoking volcano that might erupt at any moment?

"He's right," I said gently, trying to hide my annoyance. "It's best to treat guests the way they would like to be treated, and please don't be uneasy around me."

She gave a hesitant smile. "Yes, sir." Then she turned to Jett. "What would you like?"

"Any chance Roberto has peanut butter and jelly back there?"

She crinkled her face. "Zero chance. But he said he can make your favorite salad or grill you a piece of chicken if you don't like the farro and butternut squash dish he has prepared."

Jett smiled at her and shook his head. "The farro sounds amazing, Zuri. Thank you."

I murmured my thanks as she set the lemonade glasses in front of each of us and disappeared again. Then I turned to Jett. "How has your morning been?"

He looked pleased by my interest. "I spent the first part of the morning helping Concetta and Zuri with flower arrangements for the bedrooms. Concetta wasn't happy with the way they'd arrived from the florist. Then I consulted with my cousin Cas about which outfit to wear to what event this week because he has better taste than the person who picked out these clothes. After that, I checked my email, drooled over my Instagram feed, and got a workout in. You?"

We spoke about preparations for the upcoming week, my ridiculous interview with the name-dropper, the time Jett met Sabrina Carpenter and had no idea who she was. The most famous man Jett had ever hooked up with. The most famous woman I had. Throughout it all, I felt a strange combination of relief that the conversation was so shallow and disappointment that I couldn't keep listening to him talk. I wanted to gather more tidbits of his life like I was walking along an endless beach collecting the seashells Jett loved so much.

No matter how plain each one might seem, all of them were special. And together, they made a unique and interesting collection.

I wanted more. I wanted them all. My fingers itched with need of them.

But when our plates were empty, he hopped up. "Welp, I'm headed to town to visit the market with Roberto. He said I could carry his bags."

Before I could respond with anger, he laughed and fake-punched me in the stomach. "Joking, babe. Joking. Kind of."

It was a flirty move, one which I was supposed to return with a fake punch of my own, maybe. Instead, I reached for his wrist and pulled him to me until our chests collided. Then I inhaled his gasp before taking his lips in mine to remind him which man in this house he was supposed to be serving. Within seconds, I deepened the kiss simply to get more of him.

The little high-pitched whimper he let out was brief but satisfying. His surrender to my kiss was even more satisfying.

Until he pulled away.

"What time will you be done with work?" he asked with heated eyes.

I met and held them. "Whatever time you get back."

The smile on his face was electric. "Then I guess I'll hurry."

My head spun with the mixed-up bullshit I'd told Minnie. The mixed-up bullshit I'd told myself.

And the very clear evidence that I was a bold-faced liar.

18

JETT

For as much as I'd wanted to think Locke's good mood at lunch meant he was opening up a little, I knew better.

It was a trap.

Another of his mercurial mood swings.

The promise he'd made after lunch wasn't worth rushing our trip to town for—not that Roberto would have allowed it—because there was a high chance Locke would either be in a closed-off mood again when I returned or that he'd have work commitments he couldn't step away from.

And I turned out to be right.

When we returned from the bustling mercato in Maiori, bags overflowing with fresh fruit and vegetables, Locke was closed up in the suite on more fucking phone calls.

I helped in the kitchen for a little while, cleaning produce and putting it away, before I overheard a news headline on his radio.

"… deragliamento vicino a Brema…"

Train derailment near…

"Brema? Cos'è Brema?" I asked, not realizing I'd slipped into Italian without thinking.

Roberto frowned at me. "Penso sia in Germania."

Ahh, *Bremen*.

After making my excuses, I went outside to the far edge of the pool terrace and used my phone to look up the details. Thankfully, there were no fatalities, only minor injuries of two locals involved.

The photos showed several overturned train cars, their sides open and cargo spilled.

My fingers itched to contact Rocky and find out what the fuck was going on. This was exactly the kind of thing the team was worried about. It was killing me not to be able to at least ask if anything had gone missing during the derailment.

But I was on vacation, and the last thing I needed to do right now was anything that would cause someone at work to ask me where I was or what I was doing.

I gave up on the internet research after reading everything I could get my hands on and finally went inside. Locke was still on calls, so I changed into running clothes and hit the gym, alternating lifting with running and cycling until my legs were jelly.

I'd stayed in there well past time to dress for dinner, but since no one had come to alert me, I assumed the meal had been delayed. When I returned to the suite, Locke was on another call. Or maybe the same one—there was no way for me to know, really.

I walked past as silently as possible, but this time, the man himself called out.

"I'm sorry."

It took me a minute before I realized he was talking to me. When I turned back to look at him, he was half standing from his seat at the large table.

The look on his face was genuinely apologetic. "Something

came up, and I have to deal with it. I told Concetta to hold dinner until you were back and then serve it in here if that's okay?"

I nodded, and he blew out a breath.

"Okay," he said, exhaling. "Okay."

He moved over to the tablet mounted on the wall, the one that had controls for the lights, the temperature, and the household messaging system. After pressing in a message to Concetta, he returned to the call and unmuted himself.

I moved into my room, closing the door before grinning.

Locke had made a sincere apology, and he'd held dinner for me. Was it pathetic that I was touched by those things? *Yes.* Was I allowing it to do that toxic thing where you ignored all a guy's red flags? *Also yes.*

Because I wanted him enough to be with him despite the red flags. In fact, I wanted to have sex with him, even if he was covered in the damned things.

Give me all the red flags.

I spent a healthy amount of time in the shower and bathroom, prepping on the off chance he'd finally round all the bases with me. Then I changed into one of the outfits his shopper had selected.

I chose to skip the undies, fasten fewer shirt buttons than recommended, and dab on a little lip gloss—the kind a straight guy would never notice unless and until he kissed me and tasted it there.

Then I sauntered out to the suite's sitting room in time to see one of the night staff setting out our food while Locke wrapped up the call to take a dinner break.

It was already late. Past eight our time, which meant his team in New York was due for a late lunch. Once he'd closed the laptop, he stood and stretched. His clothes were rumpled, and the only reason the table wasn't littered with coffee cups and leftover snacks was because he had diligent household staff cleaning up after him.

"C'mere," he murmured, holding out his arms.

I walked into them happily but then acted awkward and confused. "What's this? What is this thing you're doing with your arms?"

"Smart-ass." His arms tightened around me in a hug.

"I didn't think you knew how to work one of these things. They're awfully complicated."

The smell of him made me want to climb him. Instead, I tucked my nose against the warm skin of his neck, catching a glimpse of the attendant as he flushed pink and hid a smile.

Even though Locke Maris was old-school about claiming his sexuality, his family seemed to have been good at hiring accepting people. The thought reassured me.

"I've been taking hug lessons," Locke said. "They're very expensive, but I think I'm getting the hang of it."

I pulled back and flashed him my biggest smile. "Worth every penny, though, right?"

He cupped my face and smiled, the kind of smile that suddenly made him look younger, more relaxed.

Happy.

"Worth every penny."

And then he kissed me.

When our food came, I strategically didn't eat. I had big plans for later that night, and I didn't want anything to upset them.

"Are you feeling okay?" Locke asked when he noticed my still-full plate.

"Yep," I said. "Very okay. And I'm looking forward to making you feel very okay as well."

He crinkled his forehead, clearly a hundred percent clueless about why I would forgo a meal before having sex. That was okay

—he didn't need to understand the ins and outs of prep to reap the rewards. And I could always sneak into the pantry later and steal shit from the fridge if I was hungry. There was a reason you were always nice to the person in charge of the kitchen.

When he finally finished his meal, I stood and moved toward his bedroom, crooking my finger at him.

"I have more calls," he said. "I'm sorry."

"Give me half an hour," I begged. "Your employees aren't even back from lunch yet."

I could tell he was tempted, and sure enough, he stood and followed me into the bedroom.

Once we were behind another layer of privacy, I started pulling off my clothes, keeping my eyes on him. "Fuck me."

Heat blazed through his eyes, but instead of a hearty "Hell yeah," he shook his head. "Not now. Not when I can't take my time with it."

I shucked off my pants and stepped toward him, completely naked while he was still fully dressed. "After your call?"

His hesitation was clear enough. His eyes roamed over me from head to foot as if assessing the risk versus the reward. "This is why you didn't eat."

I reached for the button on his pants. "This is why I didn't eat," I said softly. "I want you inside me."

His cock filled the front of his pants, tenting the fabric until I lowered the zipper and released him. One eyebrow went up. "I can't imagine your ass is more talented than your mouth."

"Mm." I lowered to my knees on the rug. "Then I propose an experiment. We do both, and then you can declare a winner in the morning."

Locke threaded his fingers through my hair. "My guests arrive in the morning."

I shrugged, running my chin along the hard heat of his erection. "A simple whisper will suffice. We can speak in code. 'Heads or tails,' if you will."

The sound of Locke's bark of laughter was electric, lighting up parts of me that had been asleep a long time.

"I'd make a dirty joke about putting my head in your tail, but I'm afraid I'd botch it," he said, looking down at me fondly.

I leaned in and rubbed my cheek against his shaft, inhaling the now-familiar scent of him. "Later, then," I murmured before opening my mouth and drawing the head of his cock inside of it.

The blow job was quick, mostly because he was already hard for me, but also because I was good at it. And I knew he needed to get back to work. As soon as he came with a ragged grunt, I flopped back on the rug to finish myself off.

Part of me expected him to pull up his pants and return to his computer, but another part secretly wanted him to stay. To watch.

The second part won.

Locke's eyes moved over my body as he fastened his pants, stopping and staring at the hand I had wrapped around my cock. I'd used my own saliva—still mixed with his release—to ease the slide. And then I went for it, stroking and arching under his intense stare.

"Look at you," he said in a low voice. "Writhing on the floor with my cum in your throat and on your cock. Does that feel good? Are you getting off with my cum, Jethro? The taste of it. The feel of it. The scent..."

I let out an embarrassing sound, but I didn't care. His words were doing it for me in a major way, and there was no one else here to hear them.

"Put a finger in your ass for me."

I moved a hand down behind my balls, pressing my taint before feeling for my hole. My knees were bent up and spread, and Locke moved to get a better view.

"That's it. Inside, Jett. Slide it in. Do it now."

I wasn't going to last. I was going to nut in half a second if he kept talking like that, kept tilting his head to the side and staring at me with narrowed eyes.

My finger breached my hole, and I felt the automatic squeeze response. Locke huffed out a breath and swallowed.

"Fuck yourself with it."

I pressed the wet finger further in, trying not to focus too much on the sensation since I was already on a hair trigger.

"Give me another finger," he said. His arms crossed over his chest, and his jaw flexed. "Stretch that tight hole for me, Jethro. I have plans for it later."

As soon as my second finger tugged my hole—before I could even slide it inside—Locke grunted deep in his throat. And that was it.

"Oh fuck!" I arched back, balls tight and nerves firing. With one last feeble attempt at fucking myself on my fingers, I groaned through my release, the hot splash of cum landing on my stomach and chest.

Somehow, I kept an eye on Locke, whose face remained mostly composed with the sole exception of his heated stare and the red flush of his cheeks.

"Good boy," he murmured before turning and exiting the room.

I lay there on the floor, chest heaving and sloppy with jizz, while the aftershocks continued to rack my body.

After cleaning myself up, I slid into his bed to wait for him.

But he never came.

19

LOCKE

The world was conspiring to keep me away from Jett Davis's ass.

First, I'd spent two hours on a call with Minnie, discussing some complex legal matters with my grandfather's estate. This had involved multiple embarrassing incidents of me staring off into space, thinking of the raw need and vulnerability on Jett's face when he'd finger-fucked himself.

Minnie urged me to follow up our call with the candidate interview she'd mentioned earlier in the day, and I agreed. Although the idea of sinking into Jett's body to lose myself for a little while was seductive as fuck, I was still head of Maris Holdings, and I knew what my priorities were. I just hoped Jett would understand the delay.

I couldn't believe I'd had to leave him like that, sexy as fuck on the floor, stretched out and desperate for release.

Having sex with Jett was completely different from having sex with a woman. Even when I'd had highly physical sex with women, it had felt performative. Like the woman was only acting "dirty" for my benefit and not because she, herself, was turned on by it.

With Jett, it was clearly equitable. He was physical as fuck, and dirty talk only seemed to ramp him up. If anything, he seemed to be holding back his responses to me. I had the feeling that if we were truly alone in the house, I could get him to shout and cry when he came.

I blew out a breath and refocused on work. The interview.

Carina was accomplished and smart—the perfect candidate for the position, just as Minnie had said. She was also very attractive. Exactly the kind of woman I would have been interested in pursuing, if she wasn't about to be my employee. This realization wasn't as disappointing as it should've been.

After shooting Minnie a "You were right" text, I finally closed down my computer and stood to stretch. I needed sleep and Jett, not necessarily in that order.

I'd taken two steps away from my desk when a message from Vukasin Draković, one of the Paxis players on the council, popped up on my phone.

The Bremen derailment involved Draković cargo which has since gone missing. Regrettably, it may negatively impact my visit.

I stared at the screen. Missing cargo from the Serbian company meant missing weapons. Which most likely meant the derailment was not an accident but a targeted offensive.

The manner of his message made it clear he thought it was related to the Russian activity, the reason for our tournament.

I shot him back a quick confirmation of receipt and benign reassurance that we'd handle any arrangements required.

And then I blew out a sigh and sat down to do much-needed research on the issue.

After a few moments, I heard a soft noise and looked up. Jett padded sleepily from the bedroom out to the main part of the house, obviously trying not to disturb me.

I followed him.

"Can't sleep?" I asked before he reached the living room.

He jumped and turned around. Then he smiled. "Hey. I was going to sneak some of Roberto's sorbetto." He shrugged. "I got hungry."

I realized with a pang that I'd missed the window. He'd waited for me—skipping dinner so we could have sex—and I'd blown it.

"I'm sorry."

He shrugged again. "I understand. Shit happens. and your job is very important. Get back to work. I'm fine."

He looked disappointed but not angry, completely the opposite of women I'd been in similar situations with in the past. As he turned to continue on to the kitchen, I followed him.

"Friends don't let friends midnight snack alone, Jethro," I said when Jett shot me a questioning look.

He grinned. "Shit, babe. If you're there, I'll have to restrain myself and only eat a mildly embarrassing amount of sorbetto. Maybe you should go back to work. Surely there's a cyclone somewhere with your name on it."

I shook my head. "And let you finish the sorbetto without sharing any of it? Not a chance."

We snuck into the darkened kitchen like little kids, in a way Celeste and I never would have actually done as kids.

"I don't even know where the fridge is," I admitted in a hushed voice.

He laughed. "It's your house, Locke. And the fridge is in here."

When I stepped into the small room off the back of the kitchen, childhood memories came flooding in. "Oh," I said, reaching out for the wide glass bottle on a nearby shelf. "My grandmother used to keep lemonade in this."

I twisted off the metal cap and imagined I could still smell the tang of it inside. "She made it extra sweet when Celeste and I were here." I let out a laugh. "Or she had the kitchen staff do it, I guess. There was a chef one time who added cut-up cherries to it. We thought we'd won the lottery that summer."

Jett looked at me over the arm he held the fridge door open with. "You enjoyed it here."

I nodded. "It was like a break from reality. And my grandparents were so... normal compared to my own parents. They didn't fight. Didn't express their frustration with my presence—" I stopped myself, realizing too late that I'd ventured into too-personal territory. "Yes. I loved it here. Still do."

Jett pulled the container of sorbetto from the freezer while I searched the shelves for the little cookies. We took our booty out to the kitchen and began looking for utensils. Jett knew exactly where they'd be.

"How do you know where the ice cream scoop is, for fuck's sake?" I asked.

He smiled up at me sheepishly while he rinsed it under hot water. "I've done reconnaissance. This sorbetto mission wasn't a spur-of-the-moment thing, Jerome."

After scooping some into the bowls I found, he returned the container to the freezer and waved me over to the small table in the corner. "Bring those cookies. I want more than one."

"You must be starving," I said. "I can make you something more substantial."

"Do you cook?" he asked in surprise.

"I mean... no. But I could wake someone."

He snorted. "You're lying."

I nodded and grinned. "Not sure what it says about me that you believed me. I may not be a great cook, but I can scramble some eggs and make a grilled cheese."

Jett plucked up a cookie and scooped it into the sorbetto before putting the entire bite into his mouth and groaning. "Fuck. I'm going to marry that man."

"You'll have to go through his wife first," I said with a laugh that quickly faded out. "You'd like her, actually. She's a nurse. She helped care for my grandmother before she died. Lung cancer. She came here for her final months a few years ago."

Jett eyed me over the spoon as he dragged it out of his mouth. If only he knew what that did to me.

"It sounds like you were closer to your grandparents than your parents, yeah?"

I nodded. "They were incredible people. Never stopped trying to make life better for everyone around them." I thought back to some of the amazing moves my grandfather had made in Paxis tournaments over the years. His generosity and goodness had helped the entire fucking world, not that anyone would ever know it.

I swallowed and dug into the sorbetto again. "My grandfather taught me Paxis, too," I said, lifting the conversation out of deeper places. "So I've been thinking of him a lot this week."

Jett's eyes were still on me. "Will you teach it to me?"

"Paxis?" I asked in surprise.

"Yeah. I'm kind of good at games, actually. And I already know how to play chess."

"You know how to play chess," I said, ignoring my excitement.

He tilted his head at me the way he did when he was going to tease me. "Don't take my word for it, Maris. Let's see what you got."

Which is how we found ourselves on the floor of our suite a couple of hours later, dressed in pajama pants and arguing over the placement of his rook.

"You said I could move it onto the yellow board," he accused. "This is my home rook, and yellow is the fire board, right?"

"Yes, but the blue player played his requesting pawn. And you're responding with—"

"With my home rook," he said. "Because I'm offering blue my home."

"Babe," I said, not realizing what I was saying. "You want to use your resource rook instead."

To be fair, he'd picked up the game incredibly quickly. I'd been surprised by the way his brain worked. It was understandable he'd made a simple mistake.

"Right, but if I offer him my home rook instead of my resource rook, when my home is located on vast mineral wealth, can't I then offer my resource rook to another player and make use of both in the same way?"

I stared at him before blinking at the board and realizing what he'd set up. "Fuck."

His chest puffed up. "The student becomes the teacher. You may blow me now."

I held his chin and turned his face away from me before blowing a hot stream of air behind his ear and down his neck until his skin broke out in goose bumps and his shoulders contracted. "Jesus fuck, Jeffrey," he breathed. "Why is that hotter than a real blow job?"

"You're not getting out of this game by distracting my dick," I warned, pulling away. "Make your second move."

He stretched his neck, tilting his head from side to side and groaning again. "You're purposefully distracting me. That's a dirty tactic."

"Yes, well, I may have forgotten to mention that according to family lore, my great-great-great-great-grandfather was a privateer. It's in my blood."

Jett reached for his influencing bishop and played it to the blue board, next to red's rook. Solid move.

"Why does it not surprise me that you're from a family of pirates?" he muttered, reaching for his glass of wine.

"Privateers," I corrected. "We pillaged for the crown and had the law on our side. It's different."

"Barely!" he spluttered with a laugh.

I took a minute to focus and move two countermoves. Then Jett moved for the red player, and I moved for the blue. We continued playing until he made another unexpected countermove.

"Audentes fortuna iuvat," I muttered. *Fortune favors the bold.*

He snickered. "Fata viam invenient." *The fates will find a way.*

I stared at him. "You speak Latin."

He blinked and flushed pink in the cheeks. "What? No. Jesus. I saw it in a movie once about the Trojan War. In history class? I can't remember."

"You sounded more sure than that," I said.

"I'm good at languages," Jett admitted. Which explained the blush. "I learned High Valyrian from *Game of Thrones* on Duolingo."

"No," I said, laughing.

He bounced his eyebrows, but his words were formal and solemn. "Skoros iksos hen lenton."

"And that means?"

"It's like, totes true," he said, using a cheeky, playful accent.

We took a few more turns before Jett suddenly boxed me in. "Ha! Now you're going to have to sacrifice your home rook if you want to save your king. Suck it, Paxis Daddy."

I sacrificed my home rook but then quickly took it back on the next move. "My company's called Maris Holdings, Jethro. Not Maris Take and Give Back. Once something's mine, I keep it. It's pretty much my family motto."

He didn't look very bothered by the loss. His eyes were bright from the wine and lips cherry red. "Pirates gonna pirate, I guess." He tapped his chin. "In *real* chess, you can't just do that, you know. In *real* chess, these moves have dire consequences."

If only he knew how dire real Paxis moves were in the game I usually played.

"You want to challenge me to a game of real chess, Jethro?" I teased. "Because I'll kick your ass in that, too."

The heat of competition flared in his eyes. He knocked all the pieces and boards away except the black set closest to us. He quickly set it up for a game of straightforward chess.

And then he wiped the board with me again. "Rematch," I said in disbelief.

His eyes were alight with victorious satisfaction. "Sure, babe. Whatever you need."

I may not have taken Jett's ass tonight, but at two in the morning, with both of us struggling to keep our eyes open, I finally took his king.

And it was somehow almost as satisfying.

20

JETT

EVERYTHING CHANGED when people started arriving.

By the time I woke up the next morning, Locke was already finishing his breakfast and talking to the security detail about how the new arrivals and their luggage would need to be scanned.

I felt a niggle of unease. Sure, most of Locke's guests would make high-value targets, so it made sense to keep a secure perimeter, but why monitor what his guests brought in?

That wasn't the only change. Staff I hadn't seen before bustled around, cleaning and seeing to details like additional floral arrangements, a pitcher of ice water and glasses by the entry door, a basket of prepackaged snacks on a drinks cart out on the pool terrace.

It was off-putting, the easy rhythm of our first couple of days gone as if it had never existed in the first place. I quickly shook off my selfish disappointment and reminded myself why I was here.

To be Locke's host and ensure this event ran smoothly.

"How can I help?" I asked Locke with a smile when the housekeeper disappeared.

"I need you to remember this is a serious event with very important people," he said, no traces of the warmth or humor from the previous night in his expression. Clearly, the pendulum had swung again. "Your manners need to be impeccable, and you need to listen more than you speak."

Anger sparked under my tongue, but I bit it back. "Yes, sir."

He blew out a breath. "I'm sorry. I... this has nothing to do with you. I just... I need you to understand this is a big deal. It's the first Paxis tournament I've hosted, the first without my grandfather, and I need it to go well."

While it helped to understand his shitty attitude was due to his nerves, it was still shitty.

"I promise I know how to behave around adults, Locke," I said firmly, wanting so fucking badly to add that I'd met dignitaries all over the world and was even tangentially related to the current king of Liorland. But of course, I couldn't do that.

He nodded. "Good. And you're my assistant. Nothing more. Right?"

I clenched my teeth. "I believe you've made that point, yes. Several times, in fact. Shall I remember it later tonight? When my mouth is on your dick and you're crying because it's so fucking good?" My voice was too low for any of the staff to overhear, but it still made his ears turn red.

Locke closed his eyes and inhaled. "Jett. You know what I mean."

"Of course. No acting gay around the very straight, very important people. Gotcha." I gave him a sharp salute. "I shall change out of my rainbow-colored jock forthwith and remove the dildos from the men's amenity baskets. What else?"

He rubbed his face with both hands and sighed. "Everything I say makes this worse. Tell me what to do to make it stop."

I studied him and noticed the small signs of stress. The divot on his forehead, the lift of his shoulders, the tightness in his jaw that looked like it might snap under the slightest breeze. "You could say, 'Jett, despite your beauty, charm, and obvious sex appeal, it's important to me that none of my rich nerd friends discover my dirty little secret. Would you mind, terribly, hiding your little gay light under a bushel while we play board games this week?'"

His jaw flexed impossibly tighter. "May I speak privately with you in my suite, please?"

"Fine." I stood and moved quickly to the bedroom, ready for the fight Locke seemed to be spoiling for. I would give him a piece of my mind. Hell, I'd give him *all* the pieces of my mind. And then—

He yanked me into a linen closet before we even reached the suite, pressing his hand against my mouth as he pushed me back against the door and murmured for me to just be still.

For a split second, I wondered if we were in danger. If he'd heard someone breaking into the house or something. But then I remembered the guards at every entrance, part of the professional security team required for the elite guests who would be staying here.

"It's John, isn't it?" I said, still white-hot with anger and disappointment. The word was meant to remind *myself*. "Your name is John. Which is handy since that's what you are to me. My *john*."

Locke's stormy eyes met mine in the dim space. A small, high window allowed a few threads of sunshine to filter in through the branches and leaves of a tall shrub.

"Just stay still," he repeated. "And don't speak."

He reached behind me for something, pulling out a thick wool blanket before dropping it on the floor. If he thought for one minute I was going to...

"What are you doing?" I hissed.

"You're incapable of silence?" he muttered as he sank to his knees. "Should've known. Maybe I need to learn how to say it in High Valyrian."

I stared in shock as Locke's fingers quickly fumbled with the front of my pants.

"Help me with this. We don't have much time," he said.

My hands moved automatically to fulfill his request. Was he for real? "You don't need to—"

"Yeah. I do."

He yanked my pants and underwear down to my knees and then licked the tip of my cock experimentally. I stared at the scene. *What the actual fuck.*

"You're already hard for me," he said, as though surprised.

I'm always fucking hard for you, I wanted to say.

"You're on your knees for me," I said instead. "Of course I'm hard."

"You have a nice dick."

I blinked. "So I've heard."

His eyes darkened. "You let anyone else touch your cock before I'm done with you, Jethro, and I will fucking end them. Do you understand?"

My dick got even harder while I nodded stupidly.

No one had ever been possessive over me. *Ever.* I couldn't help thinking about Locke's words during the game yesterday. *"It's called Maris* Holdings, *Jett."*

But those were just words. Ones that didn't apply to me.

His mouth on my cock? That was action.

Locke was sucking my dick. This supposedly straight man was on his knees for me, and I was crystal clear on the reason for it.

He wanted to prove something.

That he wasn't afraid or ashamed. And maybe, *maybe* that he didn't think of me as his whore.

"Fuck," I groaned when he finally stopped playing around and sucked me down enough to gag. I moved my hand to the side of his face and grinned. "Easy, Johnny."

His eyes flicked up to mine. I expected to see annoyance at the stupid nickname, but instead, his gaze was soft. *Wanting.*

Seeing him like that, his commanding mouth stretched wide around my cock, eyelashes wet with tears from gagging, was enough to bring my orgasm screaming closer to the point.

He pulled off and wiped his wet mouth with the back of his hand. "Tell me how you like it. Tell me how to make you feel good."

I guided his mouth back to my cock. "Any way you put your mouth on me is going to make me come," I admitted softly. "It won't take much, I promise."

He returned to the effort of pleasing me—sucking, licking, teasing—until I shoved him away and clamped my own hand over my mouth to keep from betraying our location and activities to the household staff. My orgasm hit hard and fast while Locke quickly grabbed a towel from a nearby shelf to catch my release.

His eyes were hot on my cock the entire time until it gave its last pitiful spurt, and then he glanced at my face with an expression of awe. "I did that."

I wanted to laugh. "Take it easy, big guy. It's not rocket science."

He pushed to his feet, his own erection obvious behind the fabric of his pants. "Are you saying I wasn't any good?" The knowing glint in his eyes challenged me to admit the truth.

"You did fine, young padawan, but there's always room for improvement. With tutoring, for example. And intensive practice."

He huffed out a laugh and pulled down another towel to wipe his face with. "I'll consider it."

I finished cleaning myself up and straightened my clothes. "Thank you," I began. "You didn't need to—"

He broke off my words with a hard kiss, his hand moving to hold the back of my head the way he always seemed to do. I melted against him, riding his mercurial fucking pendulum like a willful glutton.

When he pulled away, he surprised me. "I'm sorry for taking my stress out on you. While it is very important to me that my guests not discover our sexual relationship, there was no need to be a dick about it. I appreciate your discretion, and I trust you. If I didn't, I wouldn't have invited you here during such an important event."

I tried not to read too much into it. Trust wasn't the same as affection or respect. But it was nice all the same. Especially considering I was a damned liar.

I nodded. "I understand."

He nodded and took a breath. "Good."

I expected him to want me to reciprocate, but he exited the closet after first carefully scoping out the nearby area to make sure he wouldn't be seen.

Meanwhile, I gathered up the blanket and towels we used and shoved them into the hamper in the corner of the space.

The interlude boosted my spirits. When the guests started arriving, I was happy to play the cheerful event host, welcoming everyone to Villa Altomare and inviting them to let me or the staff know how best to make their stay comfortable.

The house staff was obviously experienced in handling such high-level guests, and if I hadn't been nephew to a major country music singer and comfortable around celebrities, I might have had a hard time remaining calm.

I wasn't there to greet everyone. Concetta's careful management of the day often required me to help in other areas of the house, and after lunch, she asked me to accompany Zuri to town to gather a few items one of the guests needed.

"She will pick the cheapest, and you will better understand to get the most indulgent," Concetta said quietly while Zuri walked around the other side of the car to get in next to the driver. I assured the busy housekeeper we'd be fine and spent a good part of the rest of the day away from the villa, procuring what she needed.

To be honest, it was a welcome break from Locke's immediate return to being dismissive. While he wasn't rude to me necessarily, he acted like I was simply a member of the house staff. Nothing important. No one of note.

Since I'd never thought of this adventure as an actual job, having to act like I didn't have a personal relationship with Locke was a bitch.

When Zuri and I returned from town, I avoided Locke like the plague to keep from having to face the roiling stew of mixed emotions the situation was provoking. Last night had been fun, and pretending it had never happened was something I wasn't doing a good job of.

Dinner had been a casual cocktails-and-canapés affair on the terrace for the people who'd already arrived, and I'd made a point to stand on the periphery and handle any issues that arose without interacting socially with people so above my perceived station.

It wasn't until we returned to the suite after dinner that I could no longer avoid him.

"I smell like Sorensen's cigarillo smoke. Come shower with me," he said as he hurried past me through the suite, pulling off his shirt and unbuckling his belt. The view of his bare back over his pants was a dirty trick.

"Why?"

"Because I've been in pain since you left me with blue balls in the closet earlier. Let's go."

I followed him into his bedroom and bathroom but didn't pull off my clothes. Instead, I folded my arms in front of my chest and tried to be serious. It was difficult when he continued to reveal more tempting body parts.

"I've hardly seen you all day." *And not even a single word of praise for how well-behaved I was.*

He didn't bother to look up, only reached for the bodywash and used it to stroke his already hard cock. "Why are you acting like my girlfriend right now? Get in here and touch me."

I closed my eyes and cursed myself. We'd moved from the happy host portion of my duties to secret lovers. Exactly what I'd signed on for.

And god help me, I *always* wanted to get naked with Locke Maris, regardless of how much the other aspects of our arrangement sucked.

If he wanted me to get him off, I would.

As quickly and aggressively as possible.

I had to admit it was my favorite trick. I'd already used it on him once before, but maybe it bore repeating.

You want to come? I'll make you come in three seconds.

I pulled off my clothes and dropped them in a pile by the door before moving into the shower and lowering to my knees. No towel this time. I wasn't going to be here long enough to need it.

Thankfully, he'd already rinsed off his bodywash. All that was left on his cock was the faint taste of soap and the overwhelming scent of sandalwood and vetiver. I couldn't even detect a morsel of his own scent, which was probably for the best.

Clinical. Quick. Professional.

I sucked his cock like a goddamned pro, massaging his nuts and taint and even ghosting a fingertip over his hole. Sure enough, the man came in record time, sucking in a gasp so quickly he nearly choked on shower water.

I wiped my mouth and stood up.

"Okay?" I asked with a forced smile. Unfortunately, my neat trick had resulted in my own blue balls.

I'd gone and spit into the fucking wind, just like Beau had warned me about.

Locke looked like he wanted to say something, but he shook his head and reached for the bodywash again. "I have a video conference in thirty minutes."

I nodded and murmured something about getting out of his hair, but as I moved out of the shower and gathered my things, I could see him watching me in the mirror.

"Jett."

I met his eye in the mirror but didn't say anything.

"Thank you."

My stomach plummeted. Whatever I'd been expecting, whatever I'd been hoping for, that wasn't it.

Thank you? *Fuck that.*

I gave him a quick nod, then walked to my room and closed the door. My boner was gone, and my resentment returned to a healthy boil.

How could the man blow so hot and cold?

I could deal with bossy asshole Locke. I might not like it, but I was more than capable. I'd spent most of these last few years playing roles that were a lot more dangerous and uncomfortable than being Locke's assistant. And at least this job came with the bonus of getting face time with the man's dick on the regular.

But he wasn't *just* a bossy asshole. And I never knew, from one moment to the next, which Locke I was going to get.

The caretaker who'd insisted on rescuing me in Amsterdam?

The charming, witty, open man who'd told me stories and taught me Paxis last night?

The generous lover who'd pulled me into a closet and sucked my cock this morning?

Or the cold, ruthless businessman who treated the people in his life like chess pieces and didn't seem to care when their feelings were sacrificed for the good of the game?

Every time I rebuilt my defenses, Locke would knock them down again.

After waiting until I could hear Locke on the call, I threw on running clothes and shoes, grabbed my earbuds, and went downstairs to the fitness center, which had the same amazing view of the pool deck and water beyond.

After hopping on a treadmill facing the open doors to the view, I pumped up my music and began running off my frustration.

About twenty minutes into my run, an attractive man about my age entered the room dressed in similar workout clothes. I hadn't seen him before and couldn't place him from the names on the list. His eyes widened when he saw me, and then he flashed a friendly grin.

"Mind if I join you?"

I pulled out an earbud and tilted my head at the room full of high-end equipment. "Help yourself."

Maybe I should have introduced myself as the event host and given him the rah-rah to make him feel welcome, but I wasn't feeling it.

Instead of choosing any of the equipment spread around the room, he chose the treadmill right next to mine and began a warm-up walk.

"Santiago Alvarado," he said with a genuine smile. "Call me Santi."

It took all of my training and self-control to keep from reacting to the shocking introduction.

"Jethro Davis," I said, nodding rather than risk shaking hands with the son of one of the world's most notorious drug lords.

While the name Esteban Alvarado had been on the guest list, never in a million years would I have expected it to be *this* Esteban Alvarado. Notorious drug lord Esteban Alvarado. The one who, along with his son Santiago, was constantly under suspicion for multiple criminal activities around the world related to the movement of drugs and money.

Suspicion by my employer, specifically.

What the actual fuck are the Alvarados doing at a chess tournament?

"Haven't seen you at one of these things before," he said with a friendly grin.

"I work for Mr. Maris."

"Ah," he said, lifting his chin. His bronze skin was perfectly smooth, with inky-black eyelashes that must have made his mother proud. His eyebrows were clearly shaped by someone, and his haircut had to have cost several hundred dollars.

"What about you? Do you play, or are you here with one of the players?" I asked with what I hoped was naive politeness.

He grinned. "I'm here with my old man. He plays. Wants me to learn alongside him, but we'll see. The game's boring as fuck if you want to know the truth."

I shrugged. "At least the weather is nice," I said, trying to remain boring and plain as I stopped my run and prepared to leave the stressful situation. Maybe this was why Locke didn't want me talking to anyone. He was friends with fucking murderers.

Santi stopped his own treadmill and stepped off.

"You want to go for a swim with me, chico lindo?" he asked in a sultry voice, white teeth flashing in a player's grin.

Not gonna lie, after not being able to experience my own

release in the shower, there was a part of me that wanted to let this man pull it out of me.

The trained agent in me was tempted to flirt with him, too. To lure him in to take advantage of whatever he might want to share with an intimate partner.

But there was no way I could do that while I was here with Locke. Not only was I not on the clock—well, not on ESP's clock anyway—but I also wasn't a jackass.

It was in Locke's best interest for me to be solidly straight as far as everyone here was concerned. More than that, I was loyal to a fault, whether Locke deserved it or not.

"I'm afraid I have an early morning tomorrow," I said. "Good night, Mr. Alvarado."

"Santi. Please," he said, reaching out to place a hand on my shoulder. "And the pleasure is mine, Jethro."

As I made my way back to my room, I wondered if Santi and Eduardo Alvarado's presence here was enough reason for me to come clean to my boss at ESP.

When I entered the suite, Locke was still on a call, discussing anti-piracy naval escorts through the Gulf of Aden. He sounded smart and commanding, determined and casually in control. The tone of his voice was enough to make my dick hard, which was embarrassing as fuck.

Since he didn't even acknowledge my presence, I slunk to my own room and jacked off in the shower to the memory of Locke Maris barking at someone to "get Defense on the line again."

Then I fell asleep.

Alone.

THE FOLLOWING morning came way too soon, considering how fucking uncomfortable I'd been sleeping in my own room for the first time since arriving. After dressing in an outfit from my new "assistant" wardrobe, I dutifully followed Locke to breakfast.

As soon as we entered the room, he was surrounded by people greeting him, including a few newcomers who must have arrived late.

"Ah, Locke. Well met. Very sorry about your grandfather's passing," Ted Harlan said, clapping him on the back. "But I'm sure you'll do well at the helm of Maris in his place."

Locke nodded and murmured a few words of acknowledgment, while the third person in line to the British throne gestured for him to take the seat next to his.

So, it really was *that* Ted Harlan.

I glanced around the main table and recognized several notables, including Santi's father, Esteban, Selene Mercier, who was currently the head of her family's tech company, and Vraj freaking Nanda, taking a sip of ice water as if he hadn't single-handedly changed people's lives with his words on healing and enlightenment.

It was the motliest of crews.

What the fuck kind of Paxis game was this? While I'd seen the names on paper, it was very different seeing the people in person.

Most of them were here with spouses, exactly as Locke had claimed, except for Alvarado, who'd unexpectedly brought his son.

Santi flashed me a grin as he gestured for me to join him at a smaller table off to the side. "Good morning, Jethro. How did you sleep?"

I felt Locke's gaze sear the side of my face.

"Good morning, Mr. Alvarado," I said in a politely restrained voice. "I slept well, thanks."

"Come join me at the kids' table," he teased.

Before I could take a step in his direction, Locke cleared his throat. "You must be Esteban's boy," he said, eying Santi. "Santiago, right?"

Santi's head tilted, but he grinned back and reached out his hand to shake Locke's. "Santi. Yes. And you must be Locke. Your reputation precedes you, of course."

"As does yours." Locke clasped my elbow. "I'm afraid I need Mr. Davis here with me. We have a few items of business to discuss before the first game session begins."

His smile was polite but cool. Santi's, on the other hand, was amused. "Sure thing, jefe."

Then he turned away and began flirting with one of the attractive young women in the room.

"Stay away from him," Locke commanded in a very low whisper. He pulled back the chair next to his and nudged me to take it.

Part of me wanted to argue, to make a comment about how I might as well be industrious and take side jobs since Locke hadn't wanted me the night before. But the tension was back in Locke's jaw, along with that stupid little line I couldn't stop wanting to smooth off his forehead.

I glanced around to make sure no one was paying attention to us as I quickly whispered back. "We met in the gym last night. Polite minimum only, swear."

He nodded and turned to accept another greeting.

Saleem al-Qadiri was dressed in immaculate white—a thobe so finely woven it moved like water. A slim Patek Philippe watch disappeared beneath his cuff, and it reminded me of the kind of watch my great-aunt wore. Ten times more modest in appearance than the actual cost of the thing.

Apparently, he'd given up his own family name in order to

marry into the ruling family of Qadara. He must have loved his wife very much.

Al-Qadiri, unlike Santi Alvarado, smiled with genuine warmth and happiness at Locke.

"My friend, may your grandfather be granted paradise, and may peace find your heart in time. If you need anything—my family's door and our table are always open to you."

I could tell by Locke's manner that he had great respect for the man—who only seemed about ten years older—and as soon as they finished speaking, al-Qadiri's wife approached and greeted Locke just as warmly. "How is Celeste? She sent my father the loveliest glass bird to sit in his window."

Locke's body language changed at the mention of his sister. He relaxed and smiled. "She's good, Liyana. Thank you for asking. How's your father? Please remember me to him when you call home."

She returned his smile, her expression fondly affectionate. "I will. He misses the game, but traveling isn't easy for him with his hips."

When the food was served, I had a chance to watch the interplay between the people at my table. It was easy for me to tell who Locke was comfortable around and who he was guarded with.

Since I was being watched now by Santi in addition to Locke, I tried to spend most of my energy politely listening to others like a good assistant... while mentally tallying the who's who of *what the everlasting fuck*, like the agent I was trained to be.

One thing I quickly realized was that there was no way I could keep this gathering a secret from ESP. It was too important. Too impossible to believe that this collection of power players had come together to play an extended version of chess.

But at the same time, I needed to figure out the best way to notify Rocky without also admitting that I'd basically accepted a temporary assignment as a highly paid sex worker.

Worrying about that was ridiculous, of course. I was embarrassed by my own decision, but I was also known for being curious and adventurous, even when those things got me into trouble.

Curious Cat is never content and all that.

"Ready for the first session?" Locke asked the room when we finished the meal.

Everyone nodded and began leaving the table.

He turned to me and lowered his voice. "Remember, there are no electronics allowed in the game room. If I need anything, I'll send someone to get you, and if something comes up at the office, Minnie will call you to come find me."

We walked back toward our suite so he could gather the special case that held his personal game board and pieces.

"What can I do to help you in the meantime?" I asked, trying to reduce his stress and remind myself of our original agreement.

Once we were behind the closed door, he turned me to face him. "Remember what I told you. I need you to be my eyes and ears—"

"Take a breath. I got it."

Locke moved to the buffet-type cabinet on the far side of the sitting room, where his game case was. "Okay. Thank you."

He opened his case, revealing an old wooden game board and a neat collection of intricately carved pieces. I moved closer to look at them since I hadn't had a chance to look at the set yet. "Holy fuck," I breathed. "Those are incredible."

Each piece was unique and obviously handcrafted. The wood was smooth and worn after generations of handling, but the designs and faded paint were still enough to see how special they were.

I'd never seen anything like it.

He smiled and peered down at them with obvious pride. "Aren't they? This set dates back to the late 1600s. My ancestor commissioned it from a French craftsman. Al-Qadiri's set is even older, and Harlan's is solid gold and jewel-encrusted. It travels with armed guards because it's technically part of the Crown Jewels."

"Will I get to see them?" I asked, suddenly wondering how different the game experience was using boards like this instead of the simple practice sets we'd used two nights before.

He closed the case and nodded. "Of course. You'll be in and out of the game room as needed. Just remember to leave your phone outside. The guard will remind you."

After he left, I sat down and tried to get my thoughts in order.

Maybe I was overreacting. Maybe this *was* purely a gathering of oddball Paxis enthusiasts.

If every other player was as obsessed with the game as Locke was, to the point where they all carried game sets that were museum-level specimens like his, then it made sense that the only kind of people he could enjoy a game with would be other old, wealthy enthusiasts. Especially since they were the only ones who could afford the kind of security traveling with these game sets required and who had two weeks of disposable time to spend on something so... quirky.

I changed into my swim trunks and pulled my assistant clothes on over them before heading to the pool to do reconnaissance.

If there was one thing I knew about a group of rich, bored spouses, it was that they were often an amazing source of intel.

Maybe one of them would help me figure out what the fuck Locke Maris was doing in a house full of some of the world's most influential people.

21

LOCKE

I HAD to force myself to concentrate on the game when my brain was intent on wondering what the fuck Santi Alvarado was playing at by flirting with Jett.

Santi was a playboy. He had a history of fucking anyone and everyone—which was, of course, none of my business. Unless he attempted to fuck with what was mine.

And right now, Jett Davis was mine.

"Locke, your move," Ted said, nudging me with his elbow.

My grandfather's words came unbidden. *If you're reacting, you're already losing.*

I cleared my throat and reached for my requesting pawn before touching my negative pawn.

The game moved quickly after that, the moves coming from muscle memory. Unlike the straightforward version of the game I'd taught Jett, each piece and hand movement, each feint and counter, meant something extra when the Paxis Council played.

I wondered idly what Jett thought of the assortment of players gathered here. Had he recognized Esteban Alvarado's name? Did he think it strange that Nanda, the spiritual healer, was keeping company with a supposed cartel leader? Or that I was keeping company with either of them?

When the council had first formed centuries ago, it hadn't been with the intention of becoming peacekeepers. A spirit of competition and a desire to prove themselves against other elite Paxis players from around the world had driven them together.

But meeting one another had opened their eyes to the problems outside their spheres of influence. They'd realized that where governments failed, they could use their private resources to affect change on a global scale. And where overt diplomacy was impossible, they could strategize through silent negotiation on a Paxis board.

No one who sat on the Paxis Council was a saint—not even Nanda, though he was probably the closest. We were all wealthy, influential people in our own right. Most of us had a tendency to be ruthless in our day-to-day lives and businesses. Some did things that weren't altogether legal. And from time to time, council members clashed in the real world.

But when we came together for a tournament, it was an opportunity for us to put all of that aside. To balance the scales and do some good.

The primary rule was that while we were convened, we would use our power to help others, with no thought of personal gain. To do otherwise was to betray the council... which never ended well.

As I watched the board now, information flowed out through a system of taps and game moves, making it clear that Russia was planning something big. From what we could tell from our combined intel, they were smuggling sanctioned chips, autonomous underwater drones, loitering munitions, and nerve agent antidote.

All of this painted a dangerous picture.

Our best guess was that they were planning an attack on undersea communications cables or LNG terminals critical to European natural gas supplies. And by the time we broke for lunch, we had agreed on a course of action in which each of us played to our strengths.

Emil intended to run down the source of the nerve agent through his pharmaceutical contacts. Al-Qadiri would trace the movement of Draković's missing weapons. Selene would seek updated tracking information on the lost chips. Esteban would get intel from pirate groups in the North Sea. And Draković would reach out to his Russian contacts.

Meanwhile, I was tasked with locating the smuggled cargo.

A few shipping containers on an unknown ship in a vast ocean.

Needles in haystacks were easier to find. And that was *if* the contraband was being moved on a vessel.

As we exited the game room, my head was pounding, and I could feel my own body vibrating with stress. There was no room for errors here.

Jett was waiting in the hallway as I exited the room, along with a few other assistants. Just seeing him there made my shoulders drop a fraction... which felt dangerous. I had no time for distractions.

I nodded at him and tilted my head toward our suite without saying anything. Thankfully, he took the hint and followed me silently.

"Get me something to eat," I said, yanking off the button-down shirt that felt like it was strangling me. I moved into my bedroom and dropped the shirt on the floor of the closet before grabbing a clean T-shirt and pulling it on. I looked at the bed longingly, wishing I could have just ten minutes to lie down, but there was too much to be done.

Responsibility chooses the worthy, not the willing.

When I turned back to the main room, I found Jett still staring at me. He quickly blinked and nodded.

"Yes, sir," he muttered before turning to go.

"Wait," I called.

He turned back to me, eyebrows raised in question.

The last thing I needed was an attitude problem in my space, but I could hardly blame him for his pique after the way I'd been acting. Being stressed didn't excuse rudeness.

"Get yourself something, too. And please find me some headache medicine. Then I want you to stay with me while I get some work done. I might need your help."

Instead of cracking a joke or bouncing his eyebrows, he frowned in concern and nodded. "Okay. I'll be back as soon as I can."

I sat down at the small table by the open doors overlooking the pool terrace below and the sea beyond. The air was sun-warm and smelled faintly of flowers. It was a strange contrast with the dangerous waters of the North Sea that might be hiding a war's worth of tech en route to a criminal nation.

The council had agreed the smugglers were likely going to transport their cargo to Russia via sea using one of two likely routes—Skagerrak Strait in the North Sea or the Kiel Canal.

Though Maris Holdings had been working on technology that could scan ships for certain electronic signatures—including the signatures embedded into Selene's missing chips and Drakovic's stolen weapons—those scanners only worked within a very short range. We'd need some intelligence to point us in the right direction, so I already had my people running CCTV footage from nearby ports to figure out which ship or ships could potentially be carrying the cargo.

In the meantime, we'd try to get as many vessels as possible to come through the canal, making them easier to scan. All we had to do was set up somewhere along the banks in an isolated area.

The first email I shot off was to my contact at a NATO inspection agency, reassuring him that the rumors of Maris ships moving contraband via North Sea routes were unequivocally false.

I want to assure you that we at Maris are diligent about pre-inspecting our cargo. There is no need for an increase in inspection activity involving Maris ships in the North Sea. This will only serve to negatively impact global commerce, as you know.

International inspection agencies had no love for shipping companies and saw all of us as enemies. If I asked for fewer inspections, they'd give me more. And more inspections for Maris meant more for everyone.

The second email was to my counterpart at Bakker Logistiek in Amsterdam, baiting him into rerouting his own ships. The man had loose lips. If I told him, I might as well have told the entire Baltic shipping industry.

Are you experiencing the uptick in inspections on North Sea routes? How's a man supposed to do business like this? I'm diverting most of my ships through the Kiel Canal for now.

I continued implementing my part of the action plan until Jett returned with a staff member pushing a cart with our meal on it.

Jett instructed the placement of everything and quickly brought me a bottle of water, along with a dose of ibuprofen from his own room. "Or I have coffee. The caffeine might help."

Once the attendant was gone, Jett nodded toward the pills in my hand. "I didn't know if you trusted the people here to provide you medicine. There are quite a few... interesting characters among the guests."

I threw the pills back and swallowed them with a gulp of water. "Who said I trusted you more?"

His eyes blazed up at me for half a second before he realized I was joking. Then he rolled his eyes. "You'd be way less fun to fuck while sedated than you are fully aware. What would my goal be? To steal your fancy chess set that probably has your family crest all over it? Hardly."

"I do not have a family crest," I said. "Only a business logo. And I assure you that isn't carved anywhere on the board."

Jett's eyes flicked to the ink on my arm. The company logo I'd caught him tracing with a finger in the middle of the night the other night when he'd thought I was asleep.

The thought reminded me of just how cold my own bed had been last night without him in it. When my work calls had finally ended, I'd considered waking him up and talking it out. Even confessing that I'd almost told him after the vengeful blow job in the shower—when the disappointment in his eyes had nearly brought me to my knees—that I'd wanted him in my bed.

Instead, I'd left him alone. And now I regretted it.

My stress had only grown with the first game session. Playing the game had made it real. Had reminded me there were actual lives at stake.

More of my grandfather's sayings rolled through my head on repeat.

If you falter, someone else dies for it.

Jett brought over a plate with a very large salad on it.

"What's this?" I demanded.

The edge of Jett's lip curved up. "So the bit about grad school was a lie, right? This is a... sal... ad. Say it with me. Sal... ad. Salad!"

I glared at him. This would never get me through the next game session. "Bring me a real lunch."

He shook his head. "Your actual assistant sent along dietary restrictions for you based on recent bloodwork. Since the evening meals are so rich, you're expected to eat healthy at lunch."

Jett looked tickled by my weakness.

"The bloodwork was wrong," I muttered. "It was taken after a late night and several travel days. This is Roberto's revenge on me for bogus infractions."

Jett's easy laughter helped loosen my shoulders again. He returned to the table and brought another large salad that matched mine. "I chose to join you in solidarity. Mostly because this looked ten times better than the sandwich option they had. Stop bitching and start eating. It'll help your headache."

"Mpfh."

I begrudgingly forked into the pile of weeds, making sure to spear a slice of grilled chicken as well.

"How'd your game go?" he asked after a couple of minutes. "Did you win?"

I shook my head. "A winner's not declared in a single morning. We play a long game."

Jett's fork poked through his salad until it found a strawberry. "When do you pick it back up?"

I watched the strawberry's route toward his mouth and the way his lips opened to pull it off the tines of the silver fork.

"Hm?" I asked.

"The game. When do you have to be back for it? I can set an alarm."

I glanced up at his eyes before refocusing on my own food. "They'll send for me. In the meantime, I need to work."

"Right. You mentioned I might be able to help?"

I thought about it for a long moment. I'd meant that Jett could help me stay focused and de-stressed. But the man had proven to be remarkably intelligent the other night while learning Paxis. He really *could* help with this.

I shoved the salad bowl away and reached for the small plate of cheese and crackers he'd also brought. "I need you to find me an isolated spot along the Kiel Canal."

Jett's fork paused halfway to his mouth with a sprig of greens hanging off it. "The Kiel Canal?"

I nodded. "It's in Germany."

"What do you need this spot for?"

"In case one of my ships needs to pull over for an emergency." I waved my hand dismissively. "Just find me a spot."

He was quiet for a moment. I looked up to see his eyebrows furrowed.

"Problem?" I asked. "Use Google Maps. Look for areas that aren't close to population centers. That's all I need."

He cleared our dishes away, retrieved his own laptop, and retook his seat across from me.

Within the hour, my contact at Bakker called.

"Locke, what the fuck is happening up there? Just today, I've had two ships boarded in Skagerrak Strait!"

We commiserated for a few minutes before trying to determine at what point it would make more sense to use smaller ships in order to use the Kiel Canal instead of the North Sea.

"I will reroute through Kiel," I insisted. "At least for the time being. Hopefully, the inspectors will lose interest soon."

When we ended the call, I felt Jett's eyes on me.

"What'd you find?" I asked. "Anything good?"

"Not yet. What's this for?" he asked, closing the laptop. "It sounds like something's going on. Does this have to do with inspections? Like cargo inspections?"

I took a final sip of the coffee he'd brought, realizing my headache was receding. "There's an increase in NATO agency inspections on maritime traffic in the North Sea. Inspections cost precious time. I'd rather avoid the risk and use an alternate route."

"The Kiel Canal," he supplied.

I nodded.

Jett studied me. "But... why are you concerning yourself with the routes your ships are taking? That seems... way below your pay grade. More of a job for operations."

The man would make a shit soldier. He'd mouth off to his commanding officer before doing a damned thing he was supposed to.

I reminded myself I wasn't his commanding officer. I wasn't his anything, really.

"You suddenly know global shipping management? Did you learn that on Duolingo, too?" I huffed and nodded at the laptop. "You said you wanted to help. So help."

Jett made no attempt to open the laptop. "I know a little bit about a lot of things. I'm smarter than I look. And I do want to help. But I can help better if you tell me what's actually going on."

It was on the tip of my tongue to say that Jett had already impressed me with his intelligence more than once. But instead, I sat back in my chair and crossed my legs, watching his teasing, bow-shaped lips and trying to read them for the truth.

"Impress me, then, with your knowledge of global movement of goods and the tech that keeps half a million metric tons of cargo moving across the world's waterways every day."

Jett's teeth scraped his lip while he hesitated. I considered how to release him from the small moment of awkwardness and potential embarrassment.

But then he opened his mouth and spoke.

"I went to high school with Hunter Berringer."

The last name got my attention. "Am I supposed to know who that is?"

"He's Cy Berringer's son. Cy runs Lowcountry Hazard Transport. They handle—"

I barked out a laugh. "I know what they handle, Jett. But being friends with a kid in high school doesn't give you—"

"He's my brother's best friend. I spent half my time at his house growing up. His mom was good friends with one of my dads."

I stared at him. "One of your dads."

His eyes opened infinitesimally wider. "Um, yeah. I have two dads. I thought I told you that?"

What was I supposed to say? *Your extensive background check revealed a single mother and no siblings, so what the actual fuck?*

"So explain what kind of exposure you had to hazmat shipments. As a high schooler." I folded my arms over my chest.

He sucked in a loud, annoyed breath. "Hypothetically, I was around when he had phone calls about finding creative ways to evade inspections, ducking into unexpected ports to wait out unpleasant traffic, timing certain runs to deliberately hit bad weather. I know that sometimes certain ships pull the fuck over to avoid getting caught doing shady shit. I know that the shipping business sometimes... skates the rules." His eyes met mine. "A little like privateers."

I huffed. "I'm not Cy Berringer. Maris doesn't do 'shady shit' anymore."

He rolled his eyes. "Oh, come on. You're no angel. You hired a fucking prostitute, for god's sake."

His last sentence was a gut punch that literally stole my breath.

When I'd asked Jett to accompany me, he'd joked about being my whore. The comment had rankled, but I hadn't rebutted it. In fact, I'd told myself it was better for both of us if we looked at our arrangement that way.

Then I'd reminded myself over and over, these past few days, that Jett was someone hired to do a job. Someone who didn't genuinely like me. Someone I couldn't trust. Someone I didn't have to give a shit about.

But hearing that word come off his tongue now felt wrong on every level.

"Watch your mouth," I growled. "I've never once called you that, and you shouldn't call yourself that either."

Jett's eyes widened, and I couldn't help but notice the way they caught the warm light from the open terrace doors. They were ten times more compelling than the actual water beyond the terrace.

His expression softened. "My point is, whatever you're doing in the Kiel Canal, you're not going to shock me. I can help you better if you tell me what's going on."

I hesitated.

Jett stood up and moved behind me, clasping the muscles of my shoulders with his strong hands and digging his thumbs in to massage tight muscles. "I signed an NDA, Locke. If you trust me not to tell anyone about the dick sucking, trust me not to tell them about the shady shit."

"I don't do shady shit," I grumbled. "I mean it."

The sound of his laughter helped ease the tightness in my shoulders. "Fine. I promise not to tell anyone about the strictly legal way in which you're planning in advance for one of your ships to pull over for an emergency."

I grunted noncommittally. Then I closed my eyes and allowed myself to enjoy the massage for a few minutes. After a while, Jett began humming something almost under his breath.

"What's that song?" I asked, tilting my head back to rest on his stomach as his hands moved to massage my chest. It felt ten times better than the massages I got regularly back home. "I know it."

He laughed softly. "Because it's played fucking everywhere. You can't escape it. Like an earworm from hell."

"What is it?"

"'Not Mine' by Lyra Vale."

"Mm, right. I saw her play the Super Bowl show last year with my grandfather."

"Tell me more about your grandfather. Aside from Paxis and football, what did you do together?"

I tugged his hand until he came around to face me. "We worked," I said regretfully. "Which is what you and I need to get back to. Sit."

Jett seemed a bit disappointed, but he didn't prod me again as he returned to his seat at the table. And maybe it was because he didn't press me that I felt comfortable giving him a little bit of the truth.

"I need to find something in a ship," I explained.

His brows furrowed. "Like what?"

I clenched my teeth as the tension Jett had massaged away immediately returned to my neck and shoulders.

There was no way I was giving Jett the details of the weapons and nerve agent antidote. I couldn't begin to imagine the risk if he had information like that—not just risk to others if it got out but risk to him for having it. And I didn't want to scare him either.

"I'm not sure. But I have technology that can scan the containers if I can get close enough."

Jett's eyes met mine, and I wondered yet again how it was possible the man hadn't been discovered by a modeling agency somewhere along the way. He was fucking beautiful.

Distractingly so.

"Smuggling," he repeated. "You're forcing ships into the Kiel Canal so you can search them for whatever's being smuggled. And you need a place to send your team with the scanning technology."

"Hypothetically." I met his eyes. "Find me a place."

Jett opened his laptop, muttering. "The Kiel Canal sees ninety ships a day. Can your tech scan them all?"

"I might not need to. I have people reviewing surveillance video to find out which ones could have been loaded with contraband."

He nodded and got to work.

And for some reason, it didn't occur to me to wonder why he knew the daily commercial volume of one of the world's most vital waterways.

22

JETT

I WAS A SHIT INTELLIGENCE AGENT. How was I still employed? I didn't hide my emotions well, and so far, I'd been so inconsistent with my cover story as to resemble the holiest of swiss cheese.

The notes app in my phone was full of the inconsistencies I'd spilled, either accidentally before I thought it mattered or on purpose to find a balance between what I'd already spilled and the need to keep some semblance of cover.

"Fuck," I breathed as I finally escaped to my bathroom for a break from the strange new tension rolling off Locke.

It was clear that whatever was happening during all those work calls was impacting his ability to enjoy the Paxis game. He'd come out of the game room coiled tighter than a snake.

He hadn't mentioned what contraband he was looking for, but for it to cause the amount of stress he seemed to suddenly be carrying, it had to be big.

Humans? Weapons? Hazardous chemicals?

Was it related to the work my fellow ESP agents were doing in Brunsbüttel?

If there were humans or weapons on a ship, ESP needed to know about it, but there was no way I could contact Rocky from inside this house. First of all, a text wouldn't be enough. She'd immediately pick up the phone to ask me a million questions.

And I was way too paranoid to have this conversation under the same roof with Esteban Alvarado, not to mention the sheer amount of guilt I already felt at betraying Locke. It would somehow be worse if I did it steps away from his own bedroom.

Maybe I could get out after dinner and take a run on the streets around the villa with my phone.

But—and add this to the list of reasons I was not going to be making ESP's Agent of the Year—none of those things were first and foremost on my mind the way they should've been.

The new thread of danger and intrigue was kind of... doing it for me.

Locke had been pretty fucking irresistible when I'd thought he was a boring, workaholic chess player. Now it seemed the boring chess player had secrets. And secrets were like candy to me.

The kind of candy that made me stupid. That made me spend too much time in the bathroom prepping for sex that Locke surely wouldn't agree to give me.

I left the bathroom and returned to the sitting room.

When I returned to the room, Locke glanced up from his work.

"Tell me about Santiago Alvarado."

I blinked. "I told you. I met him in the gym last night. He came in when I was almost done with my run."

"He spoke to you."

"I mean, yeah? It was just the two of us in a room, so it would have been strange not to at least say hello."

"What else did he say?"

I wondered what information he was looking for, exactly. "To be honest, I think he was flirting."

Locke let out a grunt of amusement, his shoulders finally lowering a little. "Yes, princess. He was definitely flirting. The man would fuck a statue if it stroked his ego."

His words were insulting, whether he'd meant them that way or not. It was enough to get my back up and want to repay the insult.

"At least someone around here wanted to fuck me last night," I said, raising my eyebrows in challenge.

Locke's nostrils flared. This time, there was no clenching of the jaw. No hesitation.

"Get on the bed. Clothes off. Ass up." His eyes narrowed. "If this is your way of asking for sex, I am not impressed."

I watched him carefully for a beat.

But you sure are interested.

I bit back the grin and moved quickly to his bedroom, yanking my clothes off so fast he wouldn't have time to change his mind.

"Lube in the bedside table," he said in a deep voice behind me. "Prep yourself."

If only he knew. This boy came desperately pre-prepped. My knees weren't interested in spending any more time at his feet for the time being, and my prostate was crying out for attention. Besides, I wanted to push his limits, see what he was and wasn't willing to do with me.

Apparently, possibly being involved in global criminal conspiracies wasn't a deal breaker for my neglected gland.

I wasn't proud, okay? I was desperate.

I'd seen the way he'd reacted to my body, but the heated look on his face when he'd watched me finger myself two nights ago was a thousand times more confirmation of just how badly he wanted this.

I moved onto the bed on my hands and knees before dropping to my elbows and waggling my ass.

"Stop fucking around," he said, although I could hear the laugh in his voice. "I'm supposed to be working."

After grabbing the lube and making a show out of fingering myself with it, I returned to the knees and elbow ass-waggle. "Let's go. Apparently, Grandpa doesn't have all day."

Locke moved up behind me and slapped one of my ass cheeks. "Smart-ass," he mumbled. "Maybe I need a little help to get hard for someone who gives me such grief."

I felt the heavy length of his erection brush against the back of my thigh. "I've heard that happens to men of a certain age." As soon as he pressed the tip of his cock into my hole, I sucked in a breath. "Oh *fuck*."

I wanted this, *him*, so much more than I cared to admit. He was hot and commanding. And he had a fucking incredible cock.

Even if letting him fuck me while I had so many unanswered questions about him required an unprofessional amount of cognitive dissonance.

Locke's warm palm landed on my lower back. "Breathe."

"I know how to take a dick," I croaked, trying to relax, even though it had been almost a year since I'd bottomed for anyone.

He leaned over me, the coarse hair from his abdomen scratching my skin and his hot breath warming the center of my back. "You don't know how to take *my* dick," he said in a low voice.

The whimper that escaped me was embarrassing. My face flooded with heat, and so did my dick. It hung heavily between my legs, but I was too busy bracing for Locke's thrusts to reach for it.

He continued to push forward, stretching me to the limits until my body began to sweat and my breathing shallowed.

"Breathe," he said again.

"You try taking this thing and breathing through it," I hissed.

He pulled out carefully, but before I could snap at him to get back in there, I felt the cool slick of lubed fingers instead. "I should be insulted that you didn't stretch yourself enough," he chuckled, his hot breath still landing on my back until my arms prickled in goose bumps. "You must think I'm small."

"Or I think I'm desperate," I admitted. "Hurry."

"Nah. I think I'll take my time."

"They're going to come get you for the game, fuck!" He hit my prostate with a long finger, sending my thoughts to the wind and all my nerves into live wires. "*Fuck.*"

"I don't care about the game right now. I care about fucking you into this mattress."

"Yeah," I panted, brain long gone on an extended vacation. "Okay. Good."

He took his sweet fucking time with it, stretching me until I could have taken a fucking barn if I had to.

By the time he finally gave me his dick again, I wanted to cry. Instead, I only whimpered a little bit more.

"That's it," he murmured. "Just like that. Good."

One of Locke's hands was on my shoulder, the other on my hip. I felt the length of his hairy legs against the back of mine and wondered for just a split second how he felt about fucking a man for the first time. But as soon as his cock moved against my gland, I stopped caring about anything other than getting off.

"Do not touch your cock," he warned in a commanding voice.

"Asshole," I choked out. "Why not? I want to come."

He sped up his thrusts until the sound of his hips slamming into my ass filled the space around us. "You will. But not yet," he gritted out.

And then he moved the hand from my shoulder into the back of my hair. Just when I thought he was going to push my face further into the sheets, his thumb moved to my cheek and gently brushed a line from my jaw up to my temple.

What the...?

The orgasm slammed into me without warning. After being on the knife's edge, I'd thought I needed to stroke myself off to find relief. I cried out in surprise.

He grunted his approval, sounding more satisfied than he deserved, before slamming into me a final time with a guttural noise and a bit-off curse.

Oh my fucking god. My chest heaved with strangled breaths while I collapsed carefully onto the bed. Locke pulled out of me, pressing a hand above my tailbone and then caressing my ass cheek before pulling away and climbing off the bed.

"Told you so."

I turned to watch as he disappeared into the bathroom, the clench and bounce of his ass a reward for my efforts.

I didn't have the oxygen to bark back a smart response, so I simply stared while my breath sawed in and out of me. The sound of the shower hit my ears.

"You coming?" he called before adding, "What am I saying? You already did."

I huffed out a laugh and pushed myself off the bed and out of the puddle of cooling jizz on the sheets. *Mental note to find someone to change those.*

When I entered the bathroom, he was already scrubbing himself. "Do you need me to wash you again?" I asked, unsure of my role now that the sex was over.

"Get in here."

I stepped into the shower and nudged him out of the way to rinse myself off. Surprisingly, he moved over and leaned against the cool tile wall. Then his eyes did a slow up-down I felt all the way to my damned toes.

"I enjoyed fucking you."

Jesus, this man had the magical ability to reinflate empty nuts.

"Glad you're getting your money's worth. Jeremiah. Jedidiah? Jucifer?"

"Nope. None of those."

He stepped forward and reached for my face with an open hand. I watched him carefully, unsure of what he had in mind.

The kiss shocked all the thoughts out of my head. When he'd first initiated a kiss with me—the night in the pool—I'd been shocked. But then he'd been wildly unpredictable.

Now, Locke Maris's mouth was on mine, and both his hands held my face like I was something special. His lips were wet with shower water, his skin already scented with the sandalwood body-wash. Within seconds, his tongue moved past my lips, and my knees nearly gave out.

I clutched his hips to keep from slipping or falling back against the tiled wall but then realized the way he was holding my face meant I would have fallen toward him if anything.

Because he'd pulled me closer. Our chests brushed together, and then he shifted, stepping between my legs until my cock pressed against his hip. Instead of hissing and backing away like he might have done our first few times together, he pressed back against it, getting even closer and deepening the kiss.

He wasn't in a hurry to end it. Even seemed to be enjoying it despite already nutting hard.

My head swam with the unexpected heat of the encounter. Locke's sheer talent at kissing and his clear interest in continuing.

Which was when a strong knock could be heard from outside the bedroom.

Locke stepped back with a curse. "Give me a minute!" he shouted through the noise of the shower. Then his eyes landed on mine.

"Get cleaned up. I want you to come to the game room in an

hour and bring me some fucking food. I'm already hungry." He turned to step out of the shower, muttering, "Fucking salad."

I washed myself quickly while watching him dry off, throw on deodorant, and comb his hair. Then he was gone.

What the fuck was that?

My entire body still shook with the aftereffects of that orgasm and the make-out session that followed. Since when did the man want to run laps around first base after already hitting a homer?

I pressed my fingers to my lips, feeling the leftover tingle of his stubble. My lips were probably cherry red right now. And I suspected I might have even had a minor hickey under my ear.

When I finally trusted myself to turn off the water and get out of the shower, the suite was silent. The only evidence of our sexual encounter was the absolutely destroyed bed and the bottle of lube lying open on the floor where it had fallen.

I quickly cleaned up and stripped the sheets after pouring and then spilling some of the coffee we had leftover from lunch onto the pristine white sheets. *Oops.* Instant non-jizz reason to throw the entire bundle into the wash.

The tablet mounted on the sitting room wall made the house-keeping request simple, and within minutes, a staff member had arrived to take care of it. When forty-five minutes had passed, I made my way to the kitchen and requested a snack and a fresh pot of coffee for Locke.

Roberto looked me up and down as he shook a frying pan on the stove. "Succhiotto?"

It wasn't a word I was familiar with, but I got the feeling it meant hickey. My hand flew to the spot I'd noticed in the mirror. Roberto's laugh filled the kitchen, enough to make several people turn and stare. He barked them back to work but then lifted an eyebrow at me.

"Stai attento con lui." *Be careful with him.*

"Troppo tardi," I muttered with a shrug.

Because it *was* too late. And being careful with Locke Maris at this point was like holding a ticket to paradise and not boarding the airplane.

When the tray was ready, I carried it back to the wing of the large villa that housed the game room and nodded to the guard.

"Electronics in the bin, please, Mr. Davis," he said, nodding at the rack on the wall with individual slots. Sure enough, Locke's phone was in one of the slots. I juggled the tray until the man took it from me so I could pull my phone out of my pocket and slide it into another slot. Then I retrieved the tray, and he opened the door.

I'd seen the game room before the guests had arrived. Since then, the plain round table had been replaced by one that was elaborately carved and painted, the decorations mesmerizing. Around the table were matching chairs, all carved similarly in detail that belonged in a damned museum. The intricately carved furniture looked even older than Locke's chessboard. For a split second, I imagined Lancelot and Gawain sitting around something much like it.

Where the hell had this thing come from?

As soon as I picked out Locke's position around the table, he waved me over. "Thank you. I'll take some coffee first."

I glanced at him before sneaking a look at the game to see all of the exquisite boards and pieces. Sure enough, they were amazing. Five boards sat in a circle, each filled with pieces from at least ten different sets. I wondered how they chose whose boards to play with each round.

The tray joined a few others along the room's long built-in cabinet while I prepared his coffee.

While I had done domestic chores as part of my cover on ops

before, this was the first time I'd done something so menial for another person outside my family or an op.

Just as the resentment began to whisper again, Locke pulled me down to whisper something in my ear. "I need you to check the email on my phone and tell me if there's a message from Arjen Willems. If so, come tell me what it says."

He met my eyes and lowered his voice further. "Phone password is the name of the card game you play with your family and the number of times you've refused me."

I stared at him until his nostrils flared, and he said, "Go."

Within seconds, I was outside the room, reaching for his phone and typing in *EgyptianRatscrew0* as fast as I could.

Had I told the man no before? Yes. Several times.

I'd refused him when he'd suggested I didn't need to give him the lap dance. I'd rejected his offer of a ride after we'd met again at the steak house. I'd declined his plan to fly me home from Amsterdam. And most recently, I'd balked at coming to Italy.

But we both knew that wasn't what he'd meant.

His Maris logo lock screen disappeared and revealed rows of tidy apps, most of them familiar.

Even though I'd cloned his phone three years ago and found nothing, I still wanted desperately to spend time alone with it, snooping like a motherfucker.

When, exactly, had he changed his phone password? And had he only done it for this reason, so I could be his message gopher?

Did it matter?

I quickly found the email app and skimmed the page, sucking in as much information as I could as quickly as possible.

There was an email from Arjen Willems with only one ship name and city name in it.

MV Helvig Star. Nyborg.

I locked Locke's phone and put it back in the slot before returning to the game room and waiting to be gestured to the table. Then I leaned down and whispered the names in Locke's ear.

The fading scent of his bodywash was almost enough to distract me from the look of concern on his face. "Thank you. Step back and wait a minute."

I stepped back and stood against the wall the way I noticed other people doing the same. One was a beautiful woman I recognized as al-Qadiri's wife, and another was a middle-aged woman in a suit who seemed to be keeping a close, maternal eye on Selene Mercier.

Locke leaned forward and reached for one of his pieces, nervously tapping it on the board while he considered where to play it.

To me, the answer was obvious. A blue bishop—Selene's piece, I guessed—was within striking distance. So when he set the piece on the board nearest Vraj Nanda, I was surprised. Why was he leaving himself open to Selene?

But the soft-spoken Indian man pursed his lips and nodded thoughtfully, like Locke had executed a masterful move, and I decided maybe Locke had gone easy on me the other night. Clearly, I didn't understand the game as well as I'd thought.

It made sense. It was just lame.

After a moment, Nanda tapped his chin and leaned forward to reach for one of his own pieces on a nearby board. After tapping his piece on the arm of his chair while he considered his options, he made one simple move and sat back, clasping his hands together over his stomach.

Ted Harlan shook his head and reached for his own piece, a beautiful knight. His move was more like Locke's, although he moved the knight first before reaching for a second piece and moving it as well.

What kind of strategy is at play here?

I couldn't get close enough to see everything, but it seemed like Ted's benign move was more than it seemed because the muscles tightened in Locke's shoulders again. From the look on the players' faces, you'd have thought they were fighting an actual battle, not a fictional one.

After several more players took their turns, complete with lots of nervous tension and tapping, the game seemed to come to a natural pause. Selene turned to her assistant and gestured her forward with a smile and a request for an update on a business matter. Esteban gestured for an attendant to fetch his son. Al-Qadiri penciled notes in a tiny notebook. Nanda closed his eyes as if taking a mini-nap or possibly meditating.

Locke crooked his finger at me. When I moved near his shoulder, he turned to whisper again. "We are going to be here a while. Please go outside and enjoy the rest of the day. I'll need your help again after dinner."

"Are you sure? I don't mind staying."

He shook his head. "Just bring me that food first," he said with an unexpected grin.

I stepped back to the tray and pulled up the little divided serving dish of olives, dried fruit, and nuts before setting it on the table in front of him next to his coffee and a fresh crystal tumbler of ice water.

"Perfect. Thank you."

"Can I get you anything else?"

He met my eyes, his grin now gone. "Please do as I said."

I nodded and turned away, stung, but as I exited the room and reached for my phone, I realized what he'd "said" was for me to go outside and enjoy the day. He was asking me to take a break.

And what better way to take a break than to go for a run outside and make the one phone call that could absolutely ruin my fucking career?

23

JETT

After changing into running gear and grabbing my earbuds and phone, I moved to the front door of the villa. Several security personnel were there, two from the team Locke's people had hired, one who was part of the British royal guard, one who worked for al-Qadiri, and one of Alvarado's men.

Alvarado's man frowned at me. "May we help you, Mr. Davis?"

"Just going out for a run," I explained with a friendly smile.

Al-Qadiri's man tilted his head toward the stairs to the terrace level. "You would be safer remaining on the property and taking advantage of Mr. Maris's fitness center."

"Am I in danger?" I asked, acting as sweetly naive as possible while wondering *what the fuck.*

The guard working for us shifted on his feet. "It is our job to ensure your safety."

Alvarado's man nodded. "You should stay here."

I tried to look friendly and clueless. "No, thanks. I'd rather enjoy this beautiful weather. It's a nice break from New York's cold."

I moved to the front door before Alvarado's man spoke again. As I left, I heard him murmur something to one of the other men, but I didn't stick around to hear what it was.

While I was too experienced and well trained to shake with nerves, I certainly felt them.

Now that my lust was temporarily slaked, my training was kicking back in, and the weight of all my questions about Locke was impossible to ignore. What were the chances that Locke's business in the Kiel Canal was unrelated to the very mission my fellow agents were on right now?

Pretty slim.

And why had those men warned me against leaving? They had no need to protect me. I was household staff and nothing more.

I started with a walk, then a slow jog, following a map of the area on my phone while listening to music in one earbud. After a mile and a half, I found a secluded area and stepped off the road into a large cluster of trees before making my call.

"Aren't you supposed to be on vacation?" Rocky answered with a smile in her voice. "Why am I not surprised to hear from you?"

I tempered my voice to keep it low on the off chance anyone was anywhere in range. It seemed impossible, but I'd been trained to never assume. "Hey, yeah, about that... Turns out work might have found me."

Her teasing tone shifted immediately. "So help me god, if you went looking for trouble..."

"I didn't. I swear." Well, not exactly. Not that kind of trouble anyway.

"Tell me."

I paused, sick to my stomach at the idea of lying to her. Rocky was solid. Had been supportive of me from my earliest days at ESP. But I couldn't bring myself to admit to her I'd taken a job as a high-paid escort.

It also occurred to me, way too late, that there might have been some kind of clause in my employment contract that forbade such a thing.

"There's a group here... some kind of chess tournament going on at a local villa," I began carefully, trying to avoid actual lies. "And it includes some heavy hitters. I'm talking Esteban Alvarado, Ted Harlan, Saleem al-Qadiri, Vukasin Draković—"

"Woah, woah. What are you saying? Where exactly are you?"

My heart thundered as I swallowed. "Italy. Near Maiori, on the Amalfi Coast."

"And there seems to be a gathering of... let's see. A notorious cartel leader, a British royal, an oil prince, a Serbian weapons dealer..."

"It sounds unbelievable," I said, blowing out a breath. "But it's true. I saw them."

"And you think they're actually there to play chess."

I opened my mouth to say of course, that I had seen the actual game and some of the play. But then I bit back the words.

"I... I'm not sure what they're doing," I admitted. *Truth.*

"Any chance you can find out?"

"I can try. Are any of these guys on our radar for specific reasons right now? I mean, besides Alvarado."

She asked me to wait a minute and then put me on hold. The sun had gone behind a cloud, and the slight breeze was enough to make my sweaty skin uncomfortable.

She came back on the phone, all business. "It was Draković's weapons lost in the CRL derailment. Selene Mercier owns a microchip company. The same chips Russia is desperate to get their hands on. Sorensen's pharmaceutical company makes various antidotes." She didn't elaborate, but I knew she meant antidotes to chemical and biological agents. "There's no chance this is a gathering of chess aficionados, Jett."

When she said it like that, I felt like a complete idiot.

"I, ah... overheard someone mention the Kiel Canal," I said, cringing in expectation of getting Locke into trouble or torching my own career.

She sounded incredulous. "In what context?"

"No context. I don't know. I just heard it while I was eating lunch. It got my attention. I don't know how it relates to any of this." *Also true.*

"Jesus."

"The conversation was mostly stuff about the game and general niceties. There was nothing at all about their businesses or anything clandestine."

"Well, there wouldn't be, would there? It's not like a gathering of bad actors is going to chat about their criminal enterprise at a restaurant."

I closed my eyes and inhaled. *It wasn't a restaurant. It's a private villa with armed guards, and I'm sleeping with one of the supposed bad actors.* "Right."

"Keep your eyes and ears open, Jett. In the meantime, I'm going to put together some surveillance tech and overnight it to you at your hotel."

"I'm staying with a friend," I said. "I don't want him involved. Let me find another place for you to send it."

I looked both ways and began walking on the road again in the direction of the town. As soon as I was warmed up again, I picked up the pace with a jog.

"Be careful," she said, sounding more serious than the situation seemed to call for. No one at the villa was going to suspect me of being an intelligence agent. A whore, maybe, but not a spy.

"I'll text you an address."

After ending the call, I quickly made my way into town, inquired about a place to receive a package, and discovered the local post office allowed *Fermo Posta*. I sent the information to her, signed the email *Jethro Davis*, and then cleared the relevant data from my phone before heading back at as fast a pace as I could manage.

By the time I returned, I was drenched and noodle-legged. I made my way through the front door, handing my phone and earbuds over to the guard before walking through the hidden metal detector bars that had been set up.

He nodded and returned my items to me, causing me to wonder how the hell I would be able to get the surveillance equipment through the door.

It was a problem for another time.

Just like the fact I'd held a single name back from Rocky on my list of who's who here at the Italian "hotel."

The thought of Locke getting pulled into an ESP investigation filled me with dread. I told myself I was protecting him. But the truth was messier. The moment I said J. Locke Maris's name out loud, he would be forever—officially—off-limits to me.

And that was a line I couldn't bring myself to cross.

24

LOCKE

I FOUND it hard to concentrate on the game that afternoon.

The memory of Jett's tight ass squeezing my dick was hard to ignore. It had never been like this for me before. With anyone. And I was beginning to wonder if the difference went beyond the physical. That the reason sex with Jett was so much better was because it was *him*.

And the only way to figure it out was to spend more time with him.

Throughout the afternoon session, I'd felt myself becoming more and more resentful of my role in the Paxis Council. I knew why it was important—how could I not when my grandfather had reminded me over and over? But today, I was annoyed as fuck.

Why couldn't European and American militaries run this shit down without turning it into a spiderweb of diplomatic posturing, double-dealing trade agreements, and useless sanctions?

Yes, it was efficient for the council to nip shit like this in the bud before it turned into something bigger. But it felt like the barrage of global clusterfucks we had to handle was as never-ending as the tide. And just as relentless and destructive.

"Good game today," al-Qadiri said, eying me from the seat next to mine as we all reset our pieces to their neutral positions in preparation for the morning's session.

"Maybe."

"You play like your grandfather."

I felt the compliment. My grandfather had been deeply respected by his fellow council members. "Thank you. I always hope to honor him and the rest of the council with my moves."

"You do. I am impressed." He continued studying me, but then his eyes flicked to Esteban and back to me. "Patience and action are difficult to balance. Do not expect to get it right all of the time."

"Mistakes are costly," I said carefully. When spoken about, the interaction we had during a Paxis session always had to be referred to in game language. "I fear losing."

He nodded slowly. "As do I. As do all of us. But there cannot always be wins. And remember, we can only do our best." He hesitated before meeting my eyes. "It is only a game, Locke. Your life is important also."

This was also a familiar chorus. "Now you sound like my grandfather," I accused with a smile.

Al-Qadiri returned the smile. "He was a smart man." He tapped a finger on the table over a symbol of family. "And he loved your grandmother very much. And his grandchildren and dogs and boats."

I huffed out a soft laugh, remembering summer days with my grandfather on his sailboat, his old black Lab asleep at his feet.

"That's not really my scene," I admitted. "I enjoy city life, and I enjoy my work."

He smiled and tilted his head toward Vraj Nanda, who sat on the other side of me. "Maybe you need to talk to our friend here about balance. He will do a better job than I will convincing you of its powers."

"What do you do for balance?" I asked.

"I have my family. My hobbies. We need things that help us remember we are men and not gods." His face widened into a smile. "A love of horses is something my wife and I have in common. Her passion is for showing, and mine is for racing." He chuckled. "I never go to the racetrack without my family. It is possible to enjoy such things together."

"Like when I take my sister shopping in London?" I suggested. "Because I do that more often than I care to admit."

He laughed and clapped my shoulder. "Celeste will keep you on your toes. But she is too much about work as well. The two of you need to remember to play."

I thought again about Jett. About using his body for my pleasure only a few hours ago. "I do play, Sidi," I said, trying not to smirk. "Trust me, I play."

He laughed. "I do not mean the ladies, Locke. I have seen your picture everywhere with pretty girls."

"If you ask me when I'm going to settle down, I'll think your wife has been in your ear too long," I warned before drinking the last sip of water from my glass.

Al-Qadiri pushed back his chair from the table and stretched. "Ahh, no. I am no matchmaker, and marriage and children are not for everyone. But I know that time away from work and stress *is* for everyone. And that is all I will say to you about that for fear of sounding too much like an old man."

Esteban must have been listening to our conversation because he came over to pile on. "Saleem is right. And it is time for me to play. It is hard to be cooped up in here while the ladies are laid out so lovely in the late afternoon sun. Let's go."

While I hadn't seen who'd traveled here with Esteban other

than his son, I knew the older man usually brought along a mistress or two. Never his wife, and never the same woman twice.

As we filed out of the room and collected our electronics, I caught sight through the open doors of the women laid out in chaises by the pool. Most of them were beautiful, slim and sexy in various types of revealing swimsuits.

But surprisingly, it was a man who caught my eye.

Jett was sprawled on a double-wide chaise alongside a sexy young woman in a tiny bikini. He was shirtless and wore only a pair of small swim shorts in a familiar blue checked pattern. Even from here, I could see ab muscles and the curves of shoulder and thigh muscles.

He laughed at something the woman said, and she leaned over to whisper something else, making both of them laugh again.

Jett Davis was fucking Kryptonite. Worse than that, he was like loitering munitions. Hanging around seemingly benign, but ready to cause mass destruction at any time.

My dick filled just watching him. Despite fucking him earlier, I wanted him again. To plant myself inside him over and fucking over until I couldn't get it up anymore.

"Mr. Maris, would you like me to call Mr. Davis back inside?" an attendant inquired softly after seeing me watching Jett with a scowl on my face.

"Yes, please. Tell him to meet me in my suite. Thank you."

The woman nodded and disappeared through a side door, moving swiftly down the stairs to the lower terrace level. I watched her approach him if only to see how disappointed he would be when his fun was interrupted, but disappointment wasn't what I saw.

His face brightened, and he jumped up, tossing unknown words over his shoulder to his chaise mate before grabbing his shirt and yanking it on. Within moments, he was hurrying toward the house on the lower level.

I turned to our suite and moved just as swiftly, not wanting to be caught watching.

Unfortunately, when I got to the suite, my phone started pinging with messages from the office, reminding me of a critical video conference I had with one of our largest customers.

"Just give me three minutes to change," Jett said, rushing into the room. "And I can help with whatever you... what?"

From this close up, I could see the sweat on his skin, the way the edges of his hair curled more than usual from it, and the noticeable outline of one of his nipples under the soft cotton tee.

I know what that nipple tastes like.

The thought made me salivate, and for a split second, I had the outrageous thought that this man had been deliberately planted to distract me from serious business.

I swallowed and ground my teeth together. "I, ah, have a meeting."

His brows furrowed in confusion. "Okay...?"

"I thought maybe you could..." I wanted him to rub my shoulders again, but it would be too distracting. Plus, he would be visible on-screen. I remembered the most recent Paxis session. "Email Minnie and ask her to get me an updated summary of all inspection activity from ships in the Baltic region, with special focus on North Sea and Kiel Canal itineraries."

He nodded. "Anything else?"

"C'mere."

He stepped closer until I grabbed the front of his shirt, pulling him the rest of the way into my personal space until his lips were close enough to taste. Jett's arms immediately went around me as I took possession of his mouth, my hunger for him flaring hot.

We kissed for several long moments until I finally had to force myself to pull away. "I missed you," I admitted gruffly. "Now go."

I turned to the computer, not allowing myself to see his reaction to my ridiculous confession. It was too embarrassing. Instead, I busied myself getting my tech crew in Brunsbüttel on the line to tell them where to set up along the canal.

"I want to test the technology on all passing ships," I explained. "Make sure the data collection is thorough, and report back to me with anything that pings."

Before I could put the phone down, I got a call from Arjen, my contact in security and surveillance tech, with an update on CCTV at the ports.

"I'd bet you money the ship you're looking for is the *MV Helvig Star* out of Hamburg. Looks like there are four additional cargo containers aboard that weren't listed on the manifest. It's headed to Helsinki. Was loaded yesterday."

"What makes you think this is it?"

"I pulled the footage from the pier. There's money changing hands and dock workers looking hella paranoid. If it's not what you're looking for, it's something else big."

"Where can I get close to it?"

A few clicks of the keyboard sounded. "Rounding Skagen now. ETA Nyborg tomorrow."

I thanked him and let out a breath. *Fuck.* We'd gambled that the cargo would be in the canal. Now we'd need to reassess. Fortunately, I had some ideas. "Jett?"

He came out of his room with his laptop. "Yeah?"

"I need you to request a dinner session of the game. Ask Concetta to notify the players and change dinner plans accordingly."

He looked at me with surprise and concern on his face.

I tried to give him a reassuring smile. "I have a few new moves

I want to try, that's all. Find out who's willing to sit down with me for a game."

I knew, of course, everyone would show up. It was expected, and the players understood the urgency.

"Locke..." Jett hesitated. "You seem to be juggling a lot between work stuff and Paxis."

Sure, baby. I'm just trying to stop a potential terrorist attack before noon tomorrow. Everything's fine.

"My work is stressful," I explained. "I was hoping to take my mind off it with more game play."

He studied me for another beat before nodding and leaving the room, murmuring that I would find Minnie's inspection summary in my email.

I quickly scanned the email to discover all inspections were normal and clear.

But the *MV Helvig Star* wasn't one of the ships that had been inspected.

I closed my eyes and imagined using the game to communicate the updated information to the council. We'd need to get someone near Nyborg to sneak on board that ship and find the stolen cargo. Esteban usually had the best crews for work like this. And while they carried out the clandestine maneuver on the eastern coast of Funen, we needed to create a distraction for all the media outlets and law enforcement agencies in the region somewhere else.

Which meant turning my scanning operation in the Kiel Canal into a blockade instead.

Any way you sliced it, this was a pain in the ass. I ran my hands over my head and wondered why my first Paxis tournament hadn't been one of the good ones. One of the easy ones. One in which we all came together to prevent the next pandemic, help rescue people from an oncoming storm, or silently bolster promising research.

When Jett returned to the room, I stood up and stretched.

"Hey, remember you tried teaching me about hugs?" I said, shooting him a pathetic smile. "Think you can show me how they work again?"

The relieved look on his face was all I needed. And when he came into my arms and tucked his nose in my neck, I remembered why the Paxis Council did what it did.

To protect people. To make sure their loved ones came home at night.

To preserve moments like this.

25

JETT

Something was definitely wrong. The tension in Locke's body was palpable. His muscles were coiled as if waiting for an attack. But it wasn't until my nose brushed the pulse in his neck that I realized how rapidly his heart was beating.

"Talk to me," I said softly. "Please."

Locke didn't move or speak, only held me tighter and inhaled me.

I moved my hands up and down his back before trying to massage the tightness at the top of his shoulders. "Mm, that feels amazing," he said.

"Why do you play Paxis with a drug lord?" I asked, pulling away and meeting his eye.

He didn't shy away from eye contact, but he didn't answer me either. So I continued.

"Because there's no fucking way all these important people are here for a friendly game of chess. I don't care how fancy the boards are."

His jaw flexed, the one reliable indicator that he was anxious.

Locke's hands came up to hold my face, his thumbs moving over my cheekbones. "I don't know what you're implying. When have you heard me do anything other than Maris work or game play?" he asked. "You've seen my email and slept in my bed."

He was right, of course. And when he said it like that, it sounded ridiculous. But so had this unlikely collection of supposed chess players, when Rocky had reminded me of it.

The instincts I'd developed as an agent were leading me in one direction. My instincts about Locke, the complete opposite.

Which was I supposed to follow?

"If I challenged anyone here to a game of Paxis…" I began, thinking of how dumbed down their play had seemed.

"They'd all kick your ass in an embarrassingly short number of moves," he finished, sounding very sure of himself.

"In case you forgot, I'm pretty good at games, John Locke Maris," I teased.

Locke smiled and ran his thumb over my lower lip, following the movement with his eyes. "You figured out what *J* stood for?"

I'd always known, of course. He was in the goddamned ESP database now. But it had been fun pretending to guess.

"It explains a lot. *John Locke*, like the philosopher. *'What worries you, masters you,'*" I quoted, running a finger along the ever-present divot between Locke's eyebrows. "Which of your parents had a love of philosophy?"

He shook his head, blushing slightly. "Neither. My mother met a famous hockey player at a fundraiser when she was pregnant with me. He was charming and successful, and his name was Locke Bennett. The John is from the original Maris who founded the shipping line. My mother was convinced I needed to be named after him to safeguard my legacy as the family heir. As if being the only son of an only son wasn't enough."

"If you wanted to play more Paxis right now, I could have

played with you," I offered, remembering how stung I'd felt when he wanted to play more Paxis instead of spending time in bed with me.

His fingers continued moving gently over my face as if memorizing it. And his eyes were filled with unexpected affection. "I appreciate that. It's not quite the same." He took in a breath and held it before letting it out. "After? Will you play with me later tonight?"

Locke's lips tightened into a thin line, and he dropped his hands to my hips. "Before you answer that, I should probably warn you that my session with the others might go long. And I don't want a repeat of other nights, where I say I'm going to be there and then don't show."

It was probably pretty sad that this basic courtesy made my heart leap and my stomach swoosh. But it was the first time I'd felt that, even while stressed, I still ranked among Locke's priorities.

I leaned forward and kissed his chin, then jaw. "I'll wait for you in your bed. If you feel like more Paxis when you get here, great. If not, we'll play another time, okay?"

His face warmed with satisfaction in a way that made me second-guess my suspicions. It wasn't until he'd left me to take a quick shower and shave that I remembered he'd never answered my question about Alvarado.

Curiosity hummed under my skin. I'd been distracted. Locke's pendulum was a dizzying ride, but it was time to focus.

Locke was right that I hadn't seen anything suspicious. I'd been in that room and watched some of the game play. No one spoke, or they spoke minimally. In and out of that room were serving staff, spouses, administrative helpers. The boards, while intricately adorned, were regular chessboards, and the pieces the same. They weren't electronic, at least as far as I could tell. Locke had brought his set back to the suite tonight before taking it again, and he'd set it right back in the same place it had been, nowhere near a charging cable of any kind.

I hadn't seen him pass paper messages, speak in code to anyone, or even spend much time with other players outside of the game session. At breakfast, he'd talked to me. At lunch, we'd been alone in the suite. Dinner was going to be eaten while they played.

Instead of retreating into my own room to change for dinner, I shoved one of my rings deep in my pocket and quickly moved to the empty game room. The guard outside the room lifted his chin at me. I made a production of taking my phone out to slide into a slot. I held up an empty hand with five bare fingers. "I think I dropped one of my rings this afternoon. Locke said I could come look before the game starts."

He nodded and let me in. I only had a few minutes to snoop, but what I saw was even more interesting than I'd noticed earlier.

The table itself was filled with symbols. The design was decorative from a distance, but when you looked up close, it was covered in things like celestial symbols, animals, human figures, structures, plants and flowers, arrows, and intricately scrolled roman numerals. Elaborate, symbolic design. The kind found on historic art pieces, ancient carvings, and other museum-quality items.

It took me a minute to wrap my head around what I was seeing, what I was thinking.

It's a fucking code.

My eyes drank it in as quickly as possible, and just as the guard poked his head in to ask if I'd found what I'd been looking for, I noticed the chair arms also had things carved into them, each one different.

What the fuck.

I remembered how each player had the same nervous tics,

tapping their pieces while they considered their moves. They tapped them on the board, on the arm of a chair, on the edge of the table.

Jesus Christ. It *was* all a front for something.

I held up my ring and smiled at the guard. "Thank you. My sister would kick my ass if I lost this. It was a gift," I said. Which was true.

When I finally arrived at the dining room to play happy host to the non-player guests, the only people there were Liyana al-Qadiri, Santi, and the young woman I'd talked to by the pool after my run. Rylee Melling was one of the three women who'd accompanied Julien Hartmann, the CEO of Stratos Aerospace. Her face lit up when I walked in.

"Jett! Come join us. I heard you went for a run this afternoon."

"The weather was beautiful," I said. "And so are you. That's a lovely dress. Sheikha al-Qadiri, Mr. Alvarado, good evening. I hope you're enjoying your stay."

Santi's eyebrow arched. "No comment about my beauty?"

"If you had dressed in silk chiffon, things might have gone very differently, Santi," I said with a smile, trying not to roll my eyes at his constant charm offensive when I hadn't given him any indication I was interested.

The women chuckled, and we were joined by a few more people. I helped Sheika al-Qadiri to a seat and then took the one next to her. She and her husband seemed closer to Locke than some of the others, so I wondered if I'd be able to learn anything from her about him or his past.

Or the true purpose of the fucking game.

"Mr. Maris mentioned you and your husband have horses," I began politely.

What followed was a passionate description of the two loves of her life. Kida and Makani were purebred Egyptian Arabians with million-dollar bloodlines and countless awards and medals.

"Do you ride often?" I asked.

She blinked at me, horrified but too well-mannered to show it overtly. "Not my show horses. Riding changes their musculature. But there are other horses in my program I ride."

When I'd finally learned way more than necessary about Qadiri horse culture, she asked me what I did for fun.

"Collect seashells," I admitted, knowing this was already part of Jethro Davis's lore now, the same as it was part of Jett Marian's real history. "I grew up near a beach and learned early on that hunting for shells was a good excuse to disappear into my head for a while to think big thoughts."

"Thoughts about what?" she asked with an attentive smile.

I shrugged. "Depends on the year. Some years, it was about who would win in an epic Marvel and DC superhero battle. Some years, it was why my crush didn't like me back. Other years, it was about what to study in school and whether I was going down the right path."

"And now?" she asked with knowing eyes. "What would you think about on your seashell hunt today?"

Why the hell am I jeopardizing my career for a straight guy who's obviously a big fat liar?

"Whether I'm living up to Locke's expectations," I said, offering a self-deprecating smile. I needed this conversation to bear fruit if I had any chance of figuring out what was going on in this house.

She patted my hand. "I'm sure he's very happy with your service, dear. You've done a good job making everyone feel welcome. Locke appreciates hard work."

"Have you known him a long time?"

She smiled thanks to the server who brought out our first course before turning to me. "Since he was a little boy. My own father played in these Paxis tournaments. I used to travel with him. When he got too old to enjoy travel, he passed his game to my husband, and I accompanied Saleem instead."

"Why didn't your father pass the game to you?" I asked. I leaned closer and added in a whisper, "Is it because it's boring?"

She laughed. "Not at all." Her smile became more guarded. "My father believes Paxis is better handled by men."

"Handled?"

She let out a puff of air. "Forgive me. My English. I meant played."

Right. The woman's English was perfect. She'd meant what she'd said.

"And what do *you* think?" I asked.

She smiled. "I think I want to send you a picture of a seashell I have at home to ask what kind it is."

Her deflection was understandable but frustrating. I gave her my cell number, and when I turned back to my own plate, I caught Santi looking at me from across the table.

"We should take a swim later," he suggested. Instead of his usual flirtation, this seemed more serious.

"Maybe," I hedged. Could he tell me anything? Would he know what his father was involved in?

"We could talk about *John*," he suggested.

I choked on a bite of salad while Santi watched me with dark eyes.

Had he overheard me calling Locke that? Had I somehow left the doors or windows open? Had we been naked at the time? *Fucking*? My face heated as I scrambled to remember.

I'd given Locke shit about his decree that we should hide our physical relationship, but that was mostly because I wanted the man so badly I was literally risking my career to be here, and it hurt that he didn't seem to want me enough to even claim me as a lover in front of his friends.

Even so, I'd understood his reasoning, and I agreed with Locke's desire to protect his own privacy. Ours wasn't a relationship. It was a business transaction.

I needed to find out what Santi knew about it.

"Okay," I managed. "Sure."

Thankfully, one of the other guests began asking Santi about a resort in Colombia, and he turned his focus on them. Meanwhile, my brain finally landed on the only time I'd called Locke John since Santi's arrival.

Today, when we'd been talking about chess. We'd been fully dressed. But I'd been in his arms. His hands had been on my face. I'd mentioned sleeping in his bed.

Fuck.

What would Locke do if he found out someone knew about our sexual relationship? And if that someone was from a known crime family who probably used information like this to control people, what would that mean for Locke?

Or was Locke part of it? Was all of this a front for a global crime syndicate of some kind?

I couldn't quite believe it. But I wasn't sure whether that was because the facts didn't line up... or because I didn't want them to.

Somehow, I made it through the dinner with more anecdotes from Liyana al-Qadiri's elite horse world, which sounded like an obscene way to spend her money. But then again, al-Qadiri was part of a billion-dollar oil empire. Liyana's father could buy her every horse in the world several times over, and it would still be pocket change to him.

When we finally finished, I took the opportunity to check in with Locke by slipping into the game room and standing quietly behind him until he had enough of a break in the play to summon me forward.

"Do you need anything?" I asked softly, keeping my hands behind my back to keep from touching him.

The scent of him filled my nose, and being this close perked up my dick. I hated that my response to him was so damned predictable. Especially in light of my discoveries.

"Ask Minnie to get me a list of all ships traveling through the Kiel Canal in the next twenty-four hours, not just ours, along with their positions," he murmured. "And please bring me a Sprite or ginger ale or something if you don't mind."

After bringing him the drink, I made my way to the suite to email his assistant with the request before changing into a swimsuit.

When I got out to the pool, Santi was already in the water. And we were completely alone.

26

JETT

"AHH, THERE HE IS," Santi said with his usual flirty grin. "Get in. It's cold as balls out here."

I pulled off my T-shirt and walked slowly down the steps into the illuminated water of the pool, glancing around in search of others. "Is Rylee joining us?"

He shook his head. "I told her to meet us in an hour. I wanted to talk to you alone."

The water was warm, and I sank down the rest of the way so it covered my shoulders. "Okay?"

His eyes moved up and down my body as if running a hand over my skin. My stomach tightened with unease.

"Why are you with him?"

"With who?" I asked, widening my eyes with what I hoped was manga-level innocence.

"Whatever he's paying you, I'll double it," he said with a smile. He moved closer to me and reached out a finger to touch the side of my face.

My stomach flipped with nerves. "You have it all wrong. I'm

Mr. Maris's personal assistant. I fetch his meals and make phone calls for him. My job is to help—"

"That's not what I heard when I was stealing a smoke in the garden outside your windows. You two seemed really fucking friendly. His hand on your face. Your mouth on his. Mm. Hot."

Fuck. "It's not what you think," I said out of utter desperation. And I finally understood how other people could say something so stupid when caught red-handed. What else was there?

He leaned in and made a production of sniffing my neck. "I can smell him on you, chico lindo," he said with a soft chuckle. "Stop trying to protect the man. He has nothing to fear from me."

I gritted my teeth, angry that anyone would dare poach on Locke's territory while a guest in his home. But I couldn't say that.

"You're wrong," I said again, this time through clenched teeth. "Locke is straight."

Says his mouth, anyway.

Santi ignored my words. "Then I'm a better bet, pretty Jett," he continued. "I actually like cock, so I won't have to pretend you're a woman to get it up for you."

I couldn't hold back a laugh. "So now you think he's sleeping with me despite not being attracted to me? Which is it, Santi? He's fucking me, or he can't get it up for me?"

His eyes darkened. "I don't care. Let me fuck you. What will it take?"

It was time to work.

I made a flirty little face at him. "Why aren't you playing the game tonight? I thought you'd be in there with all the other guys."

He waved a hand through the air, flicking droplets in an arc. "Boring bullshit."

"Is it? It seems like there's more going on than just a game. With all those important people? Surely there's side deals for work and stuff."

He rolled his eyes. "Not even. If only there was, maybe I wouldn't be so fucking bored. We come here and fall asleep from the boredom."

"Your father's bored, too?"

He shrugged and stirred a finger in the water, watching it swirl in a vortex. "He plays the game, he comes to the room to work or fuck. Plays the game, works, fucks. That's it. Like I said, boring." He winked at me. "Except the fucking, of course."

The man seemed to be telling the truth. I got the feeling he would have bragged if there'd been anything to say about the game or power moves outside the game. "What kind of work does he do between sessions? With Locke, it's all phone calls with the office and compliance stuff."

He snorted, his eyes dark on mine. "We're shadow movers, Jett. You want someone to do something without getting caught? That's us. That's what we do."

I nodded as if that was enough detail for me. "Sounds like something that's none of my business, sorry. I didn't mean to pry."

He took my face in his hand and leaned in until our noses almost touched. "Let me have you, pretty Jett."

I hated that he'd learned my real first name from Locke and the staff. It made me feel less safe somehow. There was a reason for cover identities, and I was a fucking idiot.

"I can't," I said carefully, pulling away and moving toward the stairs. "I'm sorry. I'm here to work. That's all."

He watched me as I stepped out of the pool and dried off with a towel. "Come find me when you change your mind. Whoever I'm with can find somewhere else to be, okay?"

Lovely.

"Thanks for the swim," I said with a benign smile. Then I turned and tried not to run into the house.

When I got to the suite, I took a hot shower, pulled on clean sleep shorts and one of Locke's T-shirts, and climbed into his bed to wait for him. This time, there was no chance I'd fall asleep before talking to him.

It was time to get some answers.

And I was pretty sure I knew how to get him to talk.

27

LOCKE

THE SESSION WAS INTENSE. Now that we knew where the smuggling ship was, we decided Esteban's people would board the *Helvig Star* when it docked in Nyborg tomorrow, while I used a couple of my ships, along with several from other companies, to block the Kiel Canal as a distraction.

While the authorities were busy flocking to Germany to clear the clusterfuck I was about to cause in the canal, Esteban's people would remove the smuggled weapons from the *Helvig Star* before anyone in the world was aware of how close they'd come to disaster.

My hands shook with nerves. The biggest challenge of being a member of the Paxis Council, according to my grandfather, was doing your part without attracting suspicion. Which meant I had to get several ships to turn crossways in the canal in such a way as to cause an international logistics situation without making even my own employees suspicious.

Thankfully, my grandfather had trained me for this.

When I got out of the session and grabbed my phone, I

checked it for the list Minnie had provided of the current ship positions. Then I compared this to the coordinates of the location Jett had found when we were working together the other day.

I moved through the house to my grandfather's old study. The room had already been cleared of his personal items, but not much else had changed. I cleared the decorative items from the top of one of the built-in cabinets, pried up the panel they'd been resting on, and entered the code to the safe below.

Inside lay several burner phones, stacks of cash in multiple currencies, alternate identification documents for the remaining members of my family, two handguns, and various other items that might be needed under extreme circumstances. I grabbed one of the phones and moved to the small powder room off the study that was even more soundproof than the study itself.

I dialed one of my contacts whose specialty was getting into software systems he wasn't supposed to be in.

Vox answered. "What do you need?"

I gave him the names of two Maris ships, two Douvernay ships, and a Nowak ship, all in the same section of the canal closest to the spot Jett had found.

"I need you to create a logjam. Turn the ships, confuse them, I don't care. I just need them to block the canal from six in the morning local time until about three in the afternoon. Then they can continue on their merry way. No casualties or property damage. Is that possible?"

"Yep," he said. "Not a problem."

The call ended without discussion of remuneration. He already had free access to Maris satellites, which was all the payment he could ever want or need in his line of work.

I blew out a breath and moved back to the study, returning the phone to the case and locking up. Then I moved over to the window and looked out at the Mediterranean.

The weight of Maris Holdings was heavy enough, but the weight of trying to stave off a war between Russia and the rest of the world was suffocating.

I closed my eyes and remembered Alvarado's request for a game extension after this week's issues had been resolved. He proposed helping in the aftermath of the cyclone in the Coral Sea since we were already gathered and able to arrange aid easily.

It had been an important reminder that we didn't just prevent evil. We also tried to do good.

The Paxis Council was a good thing. Worth any stress associated with it.

Still, I wondered... how did the other members of the Paxis Council handle the stress?

We need things that help us remember we are men and not gods, al-Qadiri had said.

Well, I knew of at least one person in the world who was under no illusion about my being a god. I blew out a breath and smiled —the first I'd felt in hours, if not longer—thinking about Jett's promise that he'd be waiting for me tonight.

It might be a weakness, but it was really fucking nice to think about someone looking out for *me* while I was trying to look out for the world.

I opened my eyes and stared out at the water again... just in time to spot Santi Alvarado leaning toward Jett with a hand on his face.

"What the fuck?" I muttered to the empty room.

After looking closer through watery shadows and blue-tinted light, I could make out that Jett's eyes were wide and his body language was all over the place. Not guarded. Not reserved. Not *staying the fuck away from Santi* like I'd instructed.

Anger flared. My back teeth felt like they were going to break apart. I stormed out of the office and nearly knocked Selene Mercier over.

"Pardon," I said. "I was just on my way—"

Her face was tight, and she looked upset. "Can we talk?"

I hesitated, torn between delaying to save Jett from Santi's clutches and calming the fuck down.

The choice was far harder than it should have been. Harder than it would have been even a few days ago. But ultimately, I forced myself to choose the latter.

"Of course, Selene. Come in."

She moved past me into the study, and I closed the door behind us.

"What's going on?"

She stood behind a chair, her long, dark hair glinting in the light from a nearby lamp. As the only other American on the council, she'd been social friends with my grandfather from time to time. This meant I knew her a little better than the others and naturally trusted her more. Whether I should or not remained to be seen.

She inhaled through her nose, then spoke. "I'm sure we shouldn't be speaking of this outside the game room, but I honestly don't know the proper procedure for this, Locke. And I'm not sure who on the council I can trust."

I frowned. There was a reason why the council didn't conduct our business through conversations. Selene knew this as well as I did. But the idea of her breaking protocol could only mean—

"One of the players has made an illegal move outside of the game," she said in a hushed voice.

"What kind of move?"

Her eyes met mine. "Using information in a game to expand personal wealth."

I stared at her for a moment, uncomprehending. Not *wanting* to comprehend.

Betraying the rules of the game was unfathomable. Because of the nature of what we did and the secrecy around our legacy, we couldn't simply boot someone out of the group. If someone left the Paxis Council, they left in a box.

This rule was so well-known, it hadn't needed to be enforced since before my grandfather's tenure on the council.

It was also the reason the entire council had to approve any new members, regardless of bloodline or legacy. Santi Alvarado wouldn't be allowed to learn the truth of the game unless he proved worthy.

Which seemed impossible now that I was going to drown him in my own pool.

"Which of us?" I demanded.

She shook her head and shrugged. "I haven't gotten that far."

I let out a frustrated breath. "How do you know this, then?"

Selene moved to take a seat in one of the two armchairs in front of the large desk, so I joined her in the other. "Remember the last tournament? Your grandfather and I made a collaborative move."

I thought back to the decision to invest in microchips to advance counterfeit-resistant medical supply tracking. As a group, we'd decided Mercier's own company couldn't be involved without raising suspicion, so she'd advised which of her competitors should get the contract.

"I remember," I said.

"A significant number of shares in my competitor's company were acquired mere hours after that move was played, for a sum large enough to have gotten the attention of Wall Street."

My gut cramped. "Who made the purchase?"

Her lips tightened. "A shell company. Malik Makida Ltd. Registered in the Caymans. My people brought this to me a few weeks ago, and they've been trying to trace the owners, but you know how impossible that can be, even with our resources."

"It might be a coincidence," I pointed out. "People buy stocks for all sorts of reasons all the time."

She nodded but said, "I don't know that I believe in coincidences like this."

I wasn't sure I did either.

"So what do you propose?" I asked. "We can hardly throw out a blanket accusation with so little information. It would incite mistrust and would only prompt the betrayer to cover their tracks even further."

"Of course." She leaned back and crossed one leg over the other. "I think we must set a trap. In the game. Dangle a lure—another lucrative opportunity—and see if anyone bites. That, at least, will confirm that my suspicions are correct and one of us is complicit."

"And if no one bites?"

Selene lifted one shoulder in an elegant shrug. "Then perhaps I'll start to believe in coincidences."

I pinched the bridge of my nose and stood up again to pace. "Okay... so we wait for the game expansion? Later this week?"

She shook her head. "We need time to act if and when someone takes the bait."

I groaned and considered the situation before landing on the answer.

We'd planned to quietly find the contraband on the *MV Helvig Star* and return it to Draković. But if, instead, we moved through official channels and allowed the Helvig line to take credit for stopping the plot... and then planted several rumors about Helvig's strong dedication to stopping terrorism in its tracks... it would boost the company's reputation in the industry, leading to global growth and profitability.

An unmissable opportunity for an investor.

"I have an idea," I said.

"What is it?"

"You'll see first thing in the morning when I make my move."

Her face widened into a grin. "Your grandfather would be proud of you, Locke. Not surprised, just proud."

I managed a ghost of a smile. "Thank you."

But while I might trust Selene more than the others, I knew better than to take everything she said at face value. That was why I wasn't sharing my plan.

As we parted ways, I dragged myself back to my suite. Every step felt like ten, and my eyes stung like I'd pulled an all-nighter.

I'd grown up knowing I'd eventually wear twin capes of power and secrecy, but in moments like this, the weight of them was almost too much to carry.

And there wasn't a single soul I could share that weight with either. No one in my life—not the sister I adored, not the people I worked with, not the women (or man) who'd shared my bed—could ever know the truth of Paxis. And I couldn't trust anyone on the council enough to get close to them.

The realization made me on edge and out of sorts.

And that was *before* I got to my bedroom and remembered I had a drug lord's son to murder.

"You're here," Jett said, glancing up from where he already reclined in my bed.

"I'm here."

His face was serious as he met my eyes. "We need to talk."

I crossed my arms and glared at him. "Agreed. Start talking."

Jett pushed himself upright and leaned against the headboard.

What exactly was he going to say? That the punk had made him a better offer?

If Jett thought for one moment I was going to let him out of his commitment to me before the end of this week, he was wrong. If he thought I'd allow him to move from my bed into Santi-fucking-Alvarado's, he was mistaken.

"Easy, tiger," he said with a frown as he patted the bed next to him. "Why do you look so angry?"

I tried ignoring his concerned expression. "Whatever you're going to say, the answer's no."

He made a funny expression, a little tilt of the head and purse of the lips, and then he looked amused. "Well, I was going to ask if you'd mind letting me fuck you. Since you said no, that means you won't mind. Great! Let me show you how to prep."

I ran a hand through my hair. "Don't be cute," I muttered.

Jett's sunshine smile was warmer than the Mediterranean sun. "I mean, I could *try*, but it's kind of my permanent state." He patted the bed again. "*Orrr* you could just tell me what got you upset."

"Damn it." I yanked the covers back and climbed in. I gave in to the urge to hold him, pulling him fully into my arms, where I was starting to believe he might belong.

It wasn't the same as being able to trust him, but the connection felt damn good anyway.

"Fuck," I mumbled. He felt fucking incredible, all lean muscle and coiled tension.

He snuggled against me with a contented sound before grumbling about how many clothes I was wearing. "Get them off."

I stepped out of the bed and stripped down to my boxer briefs before sliding in and pulling him down to lie face-to-face with me on our sides. Then I reached for his hand.

"Tell me what Santi wanted."

"How'd you know Santi talked to me?" he demanded.

I rolled my eyes. "Next time you have an assignation with someone, maybe don't do it where I can see you out the window."

Jett rolled his own eyes twice as hard. "Next time you think you've caught me having an assignation with someone, maybe remember that I'm not an idiot *or* an asshole... and that no one actually uses the word *assignation*."

Despite myself, I huffed out a laugh. "Touché. What did he want?"

Jett hesitated, his eyes flicking between mine. I could tell he was caught between telling me the truth or a lie. But when he blew out a breath and opened his mouth, I wasn't sure which he'd chosen.

"Santi said to be careful of you. That he thought something suspicious was going on here. With the Paxis players."

My antennae pricked, and I leaned up on an elbow. "Suspicious how?"

Jett hesitated. "He... he thinks the game is a front. He implied you're using your ships to help his father move drugs or... or people."

I stared at him. So much for Santi being worthy of the game. This was enough reason to ban him from ever becoming a player. Not to mention, it was a dirty lie.

"I'm not," I assured Jett, cupping his face so he could see the truth in my eyes. "I don't have a professional relationship with Esteban. And they don't use Maris ships. At least, not to my knowledge."

"You gonna tell me why you play chess with a drug lord, then?" The words were softly spoken, but his eyes pleaded.

It wasn't his first time asking, but it was the first time I was tempted to tell him the truth. Instead, I leaned down to kiss him.

He let me kiss him once, twice, three times, before he pulled away. "That's a good trick—the best—but I'm not falling for it."

I combed my fingers through his messy waves. "I can't answer that, Jethro."

"Are you into anything illegal?"

I didn't want to lie to him, so I hesitated, trying to find the right words.

"Correction," he said with the barest smile. "Are you into anything nefarious?"

"No," I said quickly. "Never."

He studied me as if my face were a lie detector. I tried to show him with my expression what I couldn't put into words.

"What am I missing?" he breathed, almost to himself. His eyes were still on me. "If you don't tell me, I can't help you."

Jett pushed me onto my back and moved until he lay on top of me, his knees to either side of my waist and his cotton-covered cock brushing mine. My hands went to his ass to pull him closer.

"I'm not sure you can help, baby," I murmured before turning to kiss the inside of his elbow.

Why did I feel better simply because he was here with me? Having him within arm's reach was an immediate balm to the tension that had been riding me all day.

His eyes were wide, lips plump in their usual bow shape.

"You called me baby."

I snorted. "No, I didn't."

"You did. You called me baby."

Heat flooded my face. "I... no. I wouldn't have."

Jett's eyes narrowed. "You don't need to be a dick about it."

He started to climb off me, but I grabbed him to keep him there. "Wait. Please. Just wait."

He sighed and slumped, as if giving up. I hated to see his

disappointment. In part because I believed him. I probably had said it. Let it slip, rather. I just shouldn't have.

I shifted to sit up, still holding him in my lap. "Don't go anywhere," I said softly. "Please."

He stayed in my lap but straightened and crossed his arms over the shirt he'd pulled on. I noticed absently it was my favorite, the one Celeste had given me this past Christmas as a joke. It had the company logo on the chest, but instead of Maris Holdings, it said Maris, Hold Me. It was a joke from when we were kids and she'd misunderstood the company's name.

I nudged his arms away from his chest and traced the logo over his chest.

Then I told him the story behind the shirt.

While I told him about my sister, about the months we'd let her get it wrong and other memories of her as a child, Jett listened with those denim fucking eyes trained on me like I was important. Like what I had to say was worth listening to. Like Santiago Alvarado was nothing.

"She calls me Johnny," I said, adding a non sequitur. "Like you have."

He chuckled. "Does she?"

I nodded and traced the logo again, enjoying the way it hardened his nipple. "Sometimes."

Jett leaned forward slowly and dropped open-mouthed kisses along my jaw, my throat, my cheek and forehead. By the time he made it down to my shoulders, I was breathing heavily and hard as a rock.

"Can I fuck you?" I asked, hope like a fragile balloon in my chest.

He bit his lip and smiled. "You make it sound like I'd be doing you a favor."

"You'd be doing me a very, very big favor," I said, feeling the joy of bantering with him.

He opened his mouth, and I knew he was going to make a joke about being on the clock, about being well compensated for having sex with me, but I didn't want to hear it. I put my fingers over his lips.

"I want you to want it," I said, feeling pathetic. "Not because—"

Jett yanked my hand away and leaned down to kiss me, holding my face in place. He kissed me hard before pulling back. "I have never done anything sexual with you I didn't want to do, Locke. I promise. If you'd offered me zero dollars to come here with you, I still would have agreed." He huffed. "Maybe even faster."

I held the back of his head and kissed him again, relishing the feel of Jett and his words. I trusted him. For once, I didn't worry he was telling me what I wanted to hear. Maybe I was a fool. Maybe I was just like all his other sugar daddies who'd fallen for pretty lies.

But I didn't think so.

I was finally able to admit that there was something different about our connection. If he were only with me for the money, he wouldn't have been as upset by the ups and downs this week as he had been. I'd seen his frustration when I'd dismissed him. He had to be used to being dismissed by other powerful men, but it was different with me. At least, I liked to think it was.

I sat up and rolled him onto his back, pressing him into the mattress with my hips. "I want you. Badly."

His eyes warmed, and his cheeks darkened. "Then what the fuck are you waiting for?"

I kissed him again, happy to lose myself in him, his body, his fucking undimmable light.

We kissed and touched each other like teenagers, grinding our cocks together and feeling each other up without going any further. As if we had an unspoken agreement to make it last as long as possible.

By the time I was ready for more, Jett's neck was streaked with red, his heaving chest and audible breaths the best rewards for my efforts.

"You're killing me," he murmured. "Please."

I reached down to shuttle a hand over his cock. Our clothes were long gone, and all of his bare skin was irresistible. I thought back to the first time he'd blown me in my kitchen, when I'd thought of him as an easy mouth.

Liar. You never thought of him that way.

Jett's face tightened with desire so strong I had to close my eyes. "You're so fucking beautiful."

His lips brushed my ear. "Then why aren't you lookin' at me, Johnny?"

If I opened my eyes, saw the affectionate, open look on his face, it would change everything. I knew it as well as I knew my own name. My family legacy.

The Paxis code.

"Can't," I said, giving him a lazy smile instead.

The low sound of his laugh moved through me as his mouth continued teasing me. "Liar," he breathed against my skin.

Every part of me was engaged and wanting. It wasn't just my skin itching for his. My cock thickening for him. But also my chest pulled tight with need. My gut twisted up in him.

"Jethro," I murmured.

"I like it when you call me that," he said.

"It's your name," I said, knowing maybe it wasn't. From that very first night at the Candy Bar, he'd introduced himself as Jett, as if Jethro was a fake name he'd put on his employee paperwork and then forgotten about.

Could that be it? Could that be the reason so many details about him didn't add up?

"Mm."

I opened my eyes to look at him. "Tell me."

His smile was strangely off. If I hadn't been so aware of him, I might not have noticed.

"Baby," I said, feeling the truth of it. The plea and the cracked-open chest of it.

He tucked his face into my neck. "Yes. That. Definitely that."

I moved through the motions of loving him like I was two people. One handled the physical side. Lube, stretching, sucking his cock until his eyes rolled back in his head and he was begging me to get inside him.

The other made sure he was turned on, out of his mind with pleasure. Protected. Adored. Safe and satisfied.

His body squeezed hotly around my cock as I thrust into him from above. His knees bent up toward his shoulders, his toes already curling.

"So fucking sexy," I couldn't help but say. "So hot. Such a good boy for me."

Jett's cheeks were flushed and eyes glassy. "Want to make you feel good."

He was transparent as glass, and in that moment, I realized I didn't need to know his real name to know who he was.

And who he was to me.

"Come for me, baby," I whispered into his sweaty temple when I couldn't hold back any longer and my body pounded into his.

"Oh god," he whimpered. "Fuck. I can't... oh fuck!"

His release was intense, overwhelming both of us and sending my brain and body flying.

By the time we recovered, I was cum-drunk and not in my right mind.

And maybe I wanted to be real with him for a minute. Connect with him in a way that might help him understand why I was the way I was.

Which was my only excuse for what I said a little while later.

"Santi's right. The game isn't just a game," I said into the darkness, after we'd cleaned up and returned to the bed. Jett's head rested on my shoulder, and I was drawing lazy shapes with my fingers up and down his arm.

I couldn't tell him everything. But I could give him this.

"We use it to communicate things that can't be said aloud or written down. Each move carries meaning beyond the board."

He blew out a long breath. "Okay," he said softly. "That's what I thought."

I moved my hand into his hair. "Please forget I told you that. Santi should never have brought it up, but since he did... I just... don't want to keep secrets from you."

The silence stretched.

"Santi didn't say anything."

I shifted until I could see his face in the dim light from the edges of the shutters. "What do you mean? You said he told you—"

"I lied."

28

JETT

IF LOCKE WAS GOING to make a confession, then I was, too. Because this wasn't just sex for me, and I was beginning to realize it wasn't for him either.

The angles of his face in the shadows carried the usual tension, something that had returned after I'd softened them earlier with pleasure.

I hated seeing him unhappy and stressed.

"I knew something more was going on," I admitted. "But I didn't know how to get you to admit it."

His jaw moved, but he said nothing.

If he was upset with me, he didn't have a leg to stand on. His silence was a pain in the fucking ass.

I shoved him away and sat up, turning to flick on the bedside table lamp so I could see him better. "You're going to be mad at me?" I asked incredulously. "That's rich."

"You manipulated me."

I crossed my arms over my chest. "Join the fucking club, Locke.

You've been manipulating me, too. Or were you really having me look up a location in the Kiel Canal just to test some tech?"

The accusation hit its mark. His nostrils flared, but I also saw a brief look of contrition before he wiped it away.

"Because it was none of your business why I wanted you to look that up. It had nothing to do with you—"

Is he serious?

"You made me feel like an idiot! I kept asking you, *begging you* to tell me, and you kept insisting that *I* didn't know what I was talking about. And this whole time, you've insisted you were playing goddamned chess, and in reality, you were—"

Locke's strong hand over my mouth kept me from finishing the sentence. "No."

When he finally let go, I lowered my voice even more. "I want to know so I can help."

"You can't."

"I definitely can't if I don't even fucking know!"

"I'm not allowed to tell you anything about this," he hissed. "Telling you puts you in danger."

"I can handle danger," I said, unable to spill my own secrets but unwilling to let him worry about me.

He scoffed. "Right." He stopped and sucked in a breath. "Jett, there's a difference between living on the streets and going up against people this powerful."

I let out a soft, incredulous huff. If only he knew what kind of situations I'd been in before. What kind of danger I'd faced and continued to face every day in my job.

The words piled up in my throat, but I didn't let them out. The reality of asking him to spill his secrets while being unable to spill my own made my stomach churn.

I had more reason than ever not to trust him. But I wanted to trust him more than ever, too.

What the fuck am I doing? When did this get so fucking complicated?

Locke's eyes stayed on mine. When he spoke, his voice was soft, but his message was firm. "I need you to stay out of this. Stop asking questions. Please."

He'd moved closer, and I hadn't even realized he'd been holding my hand until he squeezed it. The warm strength of him was reassuring, and I was a sucker for the fantasy of letting him protect me.

Locke's other hand came up to cup my face. "Baby. Please."

There was no way I was staying out of it, but I suddenly wanted to be Locke's "baby" more than just about anything. So I crawled into his lap and kissed him. "I know a lot of people, Locke. I can help if you'll let me."

"You're helping enough by being here with me," he said softly.

I knew he meant it, and it felt good. But not being seen as someone with vital information or skills to help in whatever it was they were doing stung.

I kissed him back, hungry for connection despite my frustration.

The kissing turned into Locke's fumbled reach to pull my cock against his and stroke us off together. It was fast and desperate, his grunts hot against my skin and my face eager to stay pressed as close as possible into the crook of his neck.

"That's it," he urged in a broken voice. "Oh fuck, Jett. Baby. Fuck."

I spilled over his hand and belly, wondering how it was possible to feel this close to someone who didn't know me at all. Someone who kept secrets just like I did.

Later, when he was already breathing regularly against my shoulder, his body slack from sleep, I couldn't stop myself from considering the impossibility of the situation.

I wanted Locke. And not just in bed.

I wanted more time with the sweet man who'd taught me Paxis. The one who took care of his people.

I wanted to kiss his jaw when it got tight and smooth the worry from his forehead. I wanted to see his eyes lighten and the tension bleed from his shoulders when we shared a joke or a meal or a touch.

But in what fucking world could the two of us have something other than this?

No world.

He thought I'd been lying to him about Santi when in reality, I'd been lying to him about *everything*. Who I was. What I did for a living. The reason I was curious about Paxis.

How could he possibly forgive me if I told him the truth? And that was assuming I'd ever be authorized to tell him the truth without losing my job. Which I wouldn't. Jesus, even the people who shared my DNA didn't know.

I finally fell into a fitful dream, and when I awoke, Locke surprised me.

"Have you ever heard of Malik Makida?" he murmured sleepily.

I was sprawled on my front with Locke half on top of my back. His stubble prickled on one of my shoulders, and his morning wood nudged my hip.

"No. Who's that? Am I supposed to know them?"

He sighed and rolled onto his side. "Not at all. I wondered— hoped, I suppose— that you might've overheard someone here mentioning the name. But it was a long shot."

I turned to face him. "I went to school with a Malik, so I would have noticed someone mentioning that name. But Makida..." I frowned.

"Never mind. Forget I asked." Locke pushed back until he sat against the headboard and rubbed his face. "I should shower."

My brain shuttled through information, trying to puzzle out why Makida sounded familiar. "Wait, you're sure it's not just *Kida*, right?"

"Positive." He frowned. "Why?"

"This is gonna sound silly," I said, sitting up as well. "But Liyana al-Qadiri has two horses. Their names are Kida and Makani, which is kind of like Makida?"

Locke's eyes widened in surprise before narrowing in thought. "No. This wouldn't involve al-Qadiri."

Since I didn't know what *this* was, I couldn't argue the point. "Okay. Malik means king, lord, or master in Arabic. Does that make a difference? The way Liyana dotes on those horses, I could see her referring to them that way."

His forehead crinkled. I could tell I'd presented him with an idea he didn't like.

"What's this about?" I asked carefully.

He hesitated. "It's about a possible... game infraction. One of the players here may have been taking advantage of information from the game to grow their personal wealth through stock trades. That would be a breach of our code, and we take that sort of thing very, very seriously. Malik Makida is the name of the shell company that did the trades."

"Doesn't seem like the oil sheikh needs more wealth," I said. "Right?"

"Right. Al-Qadiri's father-in-law controls an oil fortune, and Liyana is his only child, so it will all flow to Saleem one day," he agreed, still deep in thought. "Could it be Esteban? Can you think of a way to tie the name to him? Or Ted Harlan?"

"Macana in Spanish means stick," I offered. "Malìa means... enchantment, I think? In Italian. That's the closest I can think of, but no one here is from Italy... What about Polish for Draković? Malik is an actual Polish surname... malina is raspberry... makani is to dip, like a chicken nugget..."

I continued muttering through various languages based on who the players were.

Maybe it was because it was so early or because I felt too safe around Locke, but I'd completely forgotten that the man didn't know just how multilingual I was. Even if I spent my days doing nothing but studying language apps, that kind of fluency would be far-fetched.

When I glanced up at him, he was staring at me. I'd thought he was intense before? That was nothing. His eyes burned into mine.

"Who the fuck are you?" he growled.

I tried giving him the manga eyes, but he wasn't having it.

"Jethro... or whatever the fuck your name is... you need to tell me what you're doing here right fucking now."

Instead of waiting for me to answer him, he struck, wrapping his hand against my throat and pushing me onto my back and climbing over me to glare down at me. "Who. The fuck. Are you?" he demanded again through gritted teeth.

My chest heaved, and my heart hammered, but I didn't fear his aggression, only his disappointment.

"I promise you I am only here because you invited me. No one sent me, if that's what you mean."

"Answer the fucking question. Who are you?"

I grasped his wrist but didn't try to pull his hand off my neck. He wasn't strangling me, just holding me in place. If I weren't so worried about mishandling the situation, I would have been rock hard for him.

"You saw my passport."

"I have a few of those myself, Jett. A name on a passport means nothing."

I thought about a new lie. One closer to the truth. About telling him I was Jett Marian, consultant. The same Jett that everyone in my life knew outside of work. The same story my family knew. My friends.

But I couldn't bear to lie to him again.

And I wasn't about to give him my real name in a house full of powerful people neither of us trusted.

"Please believe that I'm on your side. No matter what," I said, trying to make him see the truth of it on my face, in my expression. "That's the truth. I need you to believe it."

"Why should I?"

"B-because I…" *Because I'm falling in love with you.* I swallowed. "Anything I say right now, you're not going to believe."

His thumb moved the tiniest bit, smoothing down over my pulse. I tried not to let my eyes flutter closed to focus on the feeling and imagine it being a caress.

Bzzt-bzzt-bzzt.

Our phones both went off at once from the bedside table. The only thing it could be was a breaking news alert.

He moved to grab his, tossing mine at me in the process.

Blockage in Kiel Canal prevents mass casualty in factory explosion.

I stared at the headline before clicking through.

"Are you seeing this?" I asked, reading about an explosion at a plant not far from where I'd found Locke's spot on the canal. Because of some kind of "accidental ship blockade," there was no canal traffic nearby when the explosion sent fireballs of flaming debris raining down over the water.

"Fuck. This… this is…"

"Did you cause this explosion?" I asked incredulously. "Is that why you wanted me to find a place on the canal? To minimize casualties?"

He looked up from his phone. "What? No! I didn't have anything to do with the explosion."

"You can't tell me you didn't know about it, Locke! You had me fucking scout for the spot. This exact fucking spot!"

He reached for my hand, but I yanked it out of reach. "I swear to you, Jett. I knew about the blockade, but I didn't even know there was a plant there." His eyes glittered with anger. "I did not cause this."

"Then who did?"

"I don't fucking know! How would I?"

"Was it someone here?" I asked.

Locke shook his head, his dark hair still sleep-rumpled. "No. No one here needed to do this. The purpose of the blockade itself was to create a diversion from something happening somewhere else. The canal blockade was enough. It should have been enough. But..."

"But what?"

He glanced back down at his news app. His phone was lighting up with notifications. Then he looked back up at me. "This is better."

29

LOCKE

THE WHOLE TIME I was showering and dressing, I couldn't manage to wrap my head around what was happening with Jett.

For the first time last night, I'd reached out to someone and tried to make an actual connection when the world felt too heavy. And he'd repaid me with lies and manipulation.

Hell, he'd been lying to me from the very beginning about who he was—he *had* to have been. There were too many inconsistencies in his story. Too many facts that didn't add up. And now that I saw them, I couldn't unsee them.

I fucking hated liars and double-dealers. Half the reason I didn't get close to people was so I wouldn't have to lie about what I did. So I should want nothing more than to toss Jett out of the villa on his ear.

And still—*still*—when Jett begged me to believe that he was on my side, part of me genuinely wanted to.

And when he'd thought I might have had something to do with the explosion at the plant near the Kiel Canal, I'd been panicked with the need to convince him I hadn't.

So much for keeping things simple with a man who wouldn't require explanations or excuses from me. So much for not being distracted.

I refused to waste another minute thinking about any of that. Not when there was an operation being carried out. Not when there was a potential double-dealer on the Paxis Council. I knew what my priorities needed to be.

"I need your help today," I said abruptly, stalking out of the bathroom fully dressed.

Jett was still sitting on my bed, still looking shell-shocked and uncertain. I ached to hold him, to murmur reassurances... but they would have been lies.

Head in the game, Locke.

Jett looked at me with suspicion but nodded once.

"Keep checking my phone and email while I'm in the game room. If any news comes in on a ship called the *MV Helvig Star* or anything involving Nyborg, I need to know about it."

I could tell he wanted to ask why, but he didn't. He simply nodded and moved off to his room to shower and dress.

After notifying the group of an earlier start to the morning's game session, I quickly dressed and found Concetta to request coffee and pastries in the game room.

When I got in there, the only person who'd arrived before me was al-Qadiri. His warm smile welcomed me as I took my seat. "Locke! I am glad you called an early start."

I blew out a breath, shrugging off my concerns about the situation with Jett, and felt the familiar ease of Saleem's company.

Saleem al-Qadiri was one of the players here I could trust. Like Selene, al-Qadiri's family had always made a point to extend their friendship to my grandfather beyond the game and the council.

"It's strange not having Mehmet here," I said, making small talk while we waited for the others.

He made a dismissive flicking gesture with his hand. "My

father-in-law is better off at home. His physical health is not good." His smile faded. "I worry he is declining cognitively as well."

It was a strange comment. While Liyana's father had required hip replacements that had hindered his travel, his cognition had never been in question. "Has he been ill?"

"No, no. Simply old and stubborn. When he's not ruling his empire, he likes puttering around his home and his gardens where he can pretend the world hasn't changed in twenty years."

"Ah."

Saleem smiled. "Liyana is a kind and patient daughter who reminds me that sometimes it's difficult for us men as we age. We become set in our ways and only see the world from one perspective. Especially when we don't have a partner to open our eyes."

I nodded politely, my thoughts turning to Jett. *Again.*

He was right that Jett had opened my eyes. Had made me realize that I really wished I had someone I could trust. But now everything felt up in the air and out of control.

"What about the young man you're with," Saleem asked as if reading my thoughts. He watched me closely, gauging my reaction.

I frowned and hoped he couldn't see how the innocent comment made my pulse race. "Are you referring to my assistant? I'm not *with* him in the way you're implying." I imbued the words with as much power and persuasion as I ever had before.

He held up both hands. "Easy. It is okay if you are. Do not make assumptions about Qadara, habibi. We accept people's differences more than you may expect."

While that was reassuring, I was no longer concerned with Saleem or any of the council members learning that I was sleeping with a man.

I was more concerned that letting anyone know Jett was

important to me might risk his safety, especially if it was true that someone had betrayed the council.

Before I could formulate a reply, Liyana al-Qadiri appeared and placed a hand gently on her husband's shoulder.

"You forgot your glasses," she said softly, glancing at the board before smiling benignly at me. "Good morning, Locke. How did you sleep?"

Saleem was right. She *was* patient and kind. Soothing, even. "Fine, thank you. I hope you're enjoying your time here."

She nodded and patted me on the shoulder before handing him his reading glasses and stepping back toward the wall when the remainder of the council appeared. "I will wait until they bring in the food so I can help."

It was time to begin. I caught Esteban flicking a concerned glance at Selene, but otherwise, everyone seemed to be acting normal.

Vukasin Draković made the opening move, using his inquiring pawn.

Who caused the explosion?

We all looked at each other before Esteban leaned forward and reached for his offering pawn and then his "influential connection" bishop, indicating he already had feelers out.

Falko Brandt was calmer than I expected. For someone whose rail company probably served the petrochemical plant that had exploded, the man seemed perfectly at ease.

He took the board next.

Accident. Coincidence.

Ted Harlan was the next up. The quick movements of his requesting and positive pawns demanded confirmation of Brandt's information.

Emil Sorensen reached for his own bishop and set it beside

Falko's. Then he met Ted's eye and moved his knight to the same square.

Confirmed, by influential connections and a government source.

Vraj Nanda reached for his queen and tapped it in two specific spots on the arm of his chair before setting it next to Falco's resource rook. *Relief. Gratitude.*

Selene let out a little huff of laughter. Small smiles of relief on other faces.

I reached forward to take another turn, surprising a few players. As I made the elaborate combination of moves to explain the additional plan to credit Helvig with foiling the Russian plot, thereby keeping attention off Paxis Council resources, I couldn't see any dissent.

Next, it was al-Qadiri's turn. He quickly played his positive pawn, supporting the suggestion. Everyone else took turns playing their positive pawns, with the exception of Esteban, who played his caution pawn and spelled out *NATO inspection agency* as an alternative idea.

Ted lifted his eyebrows and sat back, considering the idea. Esteban's disagreement made sense. We usually didn't make moves that would deliberately enrich other companies unless there was good reason.

But in my opinion, there was good reason in this case, with or without potential insider trading.

A few played moves to discuss it, and they were well considered by the others. If I hadn't been trying to trap a traitor, maybe I would have voted a different way.

The game play took longer than any of us wished. The need to make it look like an actual game of Paxis in the meantime was just as critical today as it had always been. As always, there were attendants, assistants, and family members in and out of the room, which made it a critical cover.

My plan was finally approved, and we agreed to a brief break so that Esteban could inform his people of the new plan. Someone on one of his crews would tip off the captain of the *MV Helvig Star* to search certain specific cargo containers, and we would let them play the heroes.

Before I left the table, Jett came into the room and caught my eye. I gestured him forward.

He placed a hand on my shoulder to lean down and whisper in my ear, and I... I made a critical error.

As soon as I felt his hand on my shoulder, I reached up to cover it with my own hand. I didn't even notice the automatic gesture until I felt him whip his hand out from under mine as quickly as possible.

Fuck.

My palm fell to my lap, where it lay open and guilty. *Empty*. No one but al-Qadiri, who was sitting directly next to me, seemed to notice. As it was, he turned to speak to Liyana and hand her a small piece of paper from his notebook.

Fuck.

Jett cleared his throat. "Sorry, sir. Uh, Minnie says Maris involvement in the blockade should be cleared in the next two hours." He paused. "They are aware it was a software security test gone wrong, and all apologies are going out."

I turned to meet his eyes. "Thank you."

He nodded and moved over to the counter to freshen my coffee.

When everyone settled back at the table a short time later, Jett stepped back out of the room, offering his arm to Liyana, who seemed a little unwell.

When we resumed play, Esteban leaned forward and made a move on the board indicating that he'd passed on the message and his crew was acting on it immediately.

Julien made a move informing us that the missing drones had turned up in the possession of an international intelligence agency who'd found them during an inspection and was in the process of returning them to his company.

By the time we'd breathed a sigh of relief about that, Santi Alvarado was already moving back into the room to whisper something in his father's ear. Esteban nodded once and waved him off. A moment later, he moved his pieces indicating Helvig's intended announcement at finding the smuggled goods as part of its commitment to integrity, professionalism, and global peace. Or something like that.

We blew out a collective breath. Done.

Mission success.

We'd won the tournament.

After finishing out the game, Vraj sat forward and reached for his glass of water. "Victory is sweet, but sharing it with you makes it sacred. Cheers, my friends." He tipped the glass and took a sip.

We each reached for our own drinks to tilt in his direction.

Ted nodded happily and tilted his mimosa glass. "To effort, to togetherness, and to the joy of playing."

More players exchanged statements of victory and relief.

Esteban reminded everyone that the tournament wasn't over, only the game. "Let us meet back after lunch for the next game?" he suggested eagerly. The next game was to arrange aid to victims of the cyclone.

We agreed and stood up, ready to take a break and eat some lunch since all we'd had so far were a few pastries.

I moved back to the suite first to check in with Jett. As soon as I closed the suite door behind me, I realized he was pacing back and forth, running fingers through his hair until it was even messier than usual.

"It's okay," I said. "The only person who noticed me holding your hand was al-Qadiri, and he won't—"

"I don't care about the hand thing," Jett interrupted. "That's your rule, and I followed it to protect you."

I moved closer to him and put my hands on his hips to stop his movement. "Then why are you so upset?"

He licked his lips. "Because al-Qadiri owns Malik Makida Ltd., Locke. I know it for sure, and—"

"Jett." I squeezed him more tightly. "I told you, the horse thing is a stretch. Besides, I *know* al-Qadiri. He has been friends with my grandfather for years, even before he became a Paxis player. He's known for his kindness and generosity. His integrity."

Jett was already shaking his head. "I'm sorry. I know it's hard to fathom about a... a friend. He handed his wife a note, and she looked upset. Like she was going to murder someone. And then—"

"You're being dramatic. She looked like she wasn't feeling well, I admit, but— Please sit down. You're stressing me out."

Jett closed his eyes and put his fingers over his eyelids as if gathering his patience. "Liyana left." He moved to sit next to me, then turned on the small sofa to face me. "Whatever note he gave her caused her to call for her driver and leave the villa."

I reached for his hand and pulled it up to drop a kiss on his palm. "Take a breath, Jethro. That doesn't mean anything. She's probably shopping. That's what she's known for at these tournaments."

He turned his hand in mine and threaded our fingers together, squeezing firmly as if to make a point. "Johnny. You know that I... that there are... *ugh*." He took a deep breath and blew it out. "I think you already have an idea that I'm... not just a go-go dancer, right? So please believe me when I tell you that Malik Makida, Ltd. is owned by al-Qadari. I know people. I... asked around."

I felt the hot, unsteady flush of betrayal and dropped his hand like it was the sharp end of a knife. "You told someone about... Paxis? About what was going on here?" My voice was deadly, even though I was trying my hardest not to kill anyone. *Yet.*

"No. I swear. I haven't spoken a word about that."

"You just said you asked around. About Malik Makida Ltd. Who did you ask, Jett?" I took a breath and let it out. "Who did you break your NDA with, huh?"

"That's not important." He stood and began moving toward the door. "I just need you to believe me. And then we need to find out where Liyana went. Because my gut is screaming, and I really think she—"

"Stop," I said.

He automatically halted and turned toward me the way he always did.

Something inside me wondered if maybe things weren't completely fucked between us yet, even though I wanted to tear my hair out wondering what the fuck was going on.

"What's your role in all of this? Who do you work for?"

Jett hesitated, and I could see the gears turning in his head. "I can't tell you, but please believe you weren't ever a target. I'm here because I wanted to be here. I wanted to be with you."

I thought back to when I'd first encountered him. At the Candy Bar, when I'd only shown up there to give a dock boss a piece of my mind.

We'd met almost four years ago. *I* was the one who'd invited Jett here. In fact, at every single stage of our acquaintance after the Candy Bar, I'd been the one to pursue him.

The night at the steak house. The hotel bar in Amsterdam. Handing him my card on the airplane.

The indecent offer to come with me to Italy.

He'd initiated exactly none of it.

"Who *is* the target?" I asked in a low voice.

"No one. I told you, I don't have a target. I'm here for you. I..." He huffed out a laugh. "I genuinely thought you were bringing me to a chess tournament."

He looked regretful, sad, even a little scared.

"Are you in trouble?" I asked. "Do you need help? I can help you. Just tell me what's going on."

Jet shook his head firmly.

I imagined him under the thumb of one of the men who'd owned him before me. Someone who'd used him to gather information about other power players. Was that what this was?

"The explosion in the canal was an accident," I blurted, breaking the rules of the game. "No one caused it."

He slumped. "I know. I'm sorry I blamed you."

"Wait, *how* do you know? Who's your source? I don't understand any of this."

Jett's arms flapped from his sides and back down again. "That makes two of us. You won't tell me everything, and I can't tell you anything."

His phone buzzed in his pocket. He pulled it out and swiped it open. Before he even had time to read it, I was moving, lunging in his direction.

There was one message on his text screen.

You are in danger. Get out of the house now.

He wrestled me for the phone, but it was too late, and my arms were longer. "Who's this text from, Jethro?" I growled, seeing it was from an unknown number.

"Come with me," he said in a panicked voice. "We'll both leave, and I'll explain what I can. Please."

I shook my head. "It's my house. And I haven't done anything wrong."

This was a lie. I'd broken the rules of the game, just like al-Qadiri might have.

And every player knew the punishment for breaking the rules. Death.

I handed Jett's phone back, suddenly tired of all of it. I hadn't even made it through my first Paxis tournament before epically fucking up my grandfather's legacy.

Whatever my fate was, I would face it the way I'd faced so many things already this year.

Responsibly. Honorably. Upholding the Maris legacy...

And alone.

30

JETT

I WAS desperate to get Locke out of here. That text message hadn't been from a number I recognized, but I assumed it was from Rocky.

It had to mean she was sending people to the villa, either because she'd accurately connected the dots between my elite vacation buddies and the Kiel Canal blockade and explosion... or because Trevi had tattletaled after I'd asked him for information on Malik Makida an hour ago.

Either way, I didn't want Locke going down with the rest of them.

"Please, Johnny," I begged as I rushed after him, reaching for his elbow. "Just go into town with me for the afternoon. Or take a drive with me."

I was an idiot. As soon as I'd told Rocky who was here, she'd likely started pulling satellite surveillance to pinpoint a location for the elite visitors.

Locke shrugged me off. "I'm not leaving my guests."

As we neared the front door of the villa, one of the hired

guards was letting Liyana back into the house, and both of us stopped short.

Just as Locke had expected, she'd been shopping. She had armloads of packages and bags.

"Ah, Jett," she said in surprise, handing a big paper-wrapped bunch off to an attendant. "I wasn't expecting to see you here. You were right about the market stall with the flowers. I brought those as a thank-you for the housekeeping staff."

I frowned, noticing that the flowers were wrapped differently than the way the flower seller had wrapped them for Zuri and me that first day. Not that it mattered.

"Oh. Well... good," I said.

Locke seemed surprised when Liyana started to hand some of her shopping off to him like he was one of her servants, but he accepted the bags and played it off with a wry smile. "Jett was worried. Said you might not have been feeling well earlier."

"Thank you for being concerned. I hope to someday repay your kindness." Liyana gave me a warm look and patted my hand. "I *was* feeling a bit off. But all I needed was... retail therapy, I think they call it?" She looked around at the multitude of bags and beamed.

I managed a smile in return, but inside, all kinds of alarms were blaring. There was *no way* Liyana had had enough time in town to buy all of this. My sister Becca was an Olympic medalist shopper, and even she couldn't have gotten a haul like this so quickly. Something was off.

I reached for Locke's arm and pulled him back. "Can I talk to you? I just remembered something about—"

While I scrambled for a cover story, al-Qadiri strode into the entry hall. "Ah, there you are, my beloved. Back so soon?"

Liyana transferred her smile to him and kissed his cheek in greeting. As her lips brushed his skin, she closed her eyes for the briefest moment, as if memorizing the feel of him. Then she pulled away. "Saleem! I want to show you a picture one of the girls sent me." She patted her head and glanced around as if looking for something. "Oh! Would you be a dear and check to see if I left my glasses in the car?" She laughed. "I'm becoming as forgetful as you, aren't I?"

"I'll go look." Locke stepped forward

I tightened my hand on his elbow to hold him in place. Something was wrong. I'd been in the spy world too many years not to feel it. My gut was screaming.

Liyana shot him a smile. "No, dear. Your hands are full. Saleem will get them. Jett, dear, could you possibly arrange for my purchases to be sent to—"

As Liyana chattered about logistics and wandered further into the house, I watched from the corner of my eye while her husband moved out the open double doors toward the sleek black town car on the far side of the gravel drive. He waved to their driver, who stood close to the house, talking to one of the gardeners.

It struck me as odd that instead of standing to help his boss, he sat and watched—

And that's when I knew.

"Locke!" I hissed. I yanked him back with as much force as I could, just as al-Qadiri reached for the door handle of the vehicle.

The explosion was instantaneous—a single, concussive bloom of fire and metal that punched the air out of my lungs. The town car lifted off the ground, the blast folding it in on itself like paper. Heat slammed into us a half second later, a rolling wave that tore through the entryway and shattered the windows nearby. Shards of glass and blackened trim arced through the air, the driveway gravel peppering the house like hail.

Locke turned and covered me just as I tried to do the same to him. It resulted in a mini-wrestling match before he succeeded in shoving me under him, wrapping his arms around my head and tucking his face next to mine.

My arms banded around his back to keep him from popping back up and going to investigate.

The only sounds I could hear were muffled shouts and high-pitched ringing. Within seconds, Locke's face had pulled back enough to look at me, to scan every inch of me for injuries. I could see his mouth moving, his eyes wide and panicked.

Baby, are you okay?

I reached for his face and pulled him down to me to press a firm kiss to his mouth. It was the only way I could think to reassure him. And me.

Dust and smoke seemed to float all around us as my hearing started returning in patches.

"Chiama l'ambulanza!" someone shouted. One of the guards.

Another guard snapped at Liyana in Qadiri, rushing to keep her from running outside to her husband. From what I could see through the open front doors, Saleem definitely hadn't survived the blast.

Locke climbed off me and pulled me up, moving his hands over me and asking again if I was okay. His expression was so worried, it made my chest ache and my throat close up. I nodded. "'M'okay," I tried to say, even though it didn't sound right.

The fear in his eyes as he looked at me was stronger than any declaration. I wanted to cling to it, climb up its length and tangle myself in its vines until his affection and care were a part of me. But as my hearing returned, so did my brain.

"We need to leave," I said again, squawking like a panicked broken record. "The authorities are coming."

I could not be here when they arrived, and neither could Locke. I would lose my job. I would lose the ability to remain anonymous and unattached to an international incident. Locke...

well, he could lose a lot more. If the authorities arrived to find his crew of guests here—including Esteban Alvarado—there was no telling what conclusions they would come to or how long they would hold him.

He was better off leaving, getting back to the States and under the protection of his high-powered attorneys, and then figuring out how to respond to official inquiries.

If he stayed, local and Italian national police would want to investigate him thoroughly, and they might make it difficult for him to leave Italy for a while.

"No, Jett." Locke gripped my hand tightly as he pulled me toward Liyana.

Her shopping bags and flowers now lay strewn all over the filthy floor. Gravel and broken glass crunched underfoot. The woman herself was remarkably poised, standing calm amidst the destruction while the guards and drivers tried to contain the vehicle fire.

Locke reached for her. "Sheika," he murmured respectfully. "Are you injured?"

She turned to him with mournful eyes but a determined expression. "My injuries will heal." She pressed something into his hands. "I will see you at the next game."

And then she turned around and stepped out of the house, where her driver spotted her and quickly ushered her toward another car further down the driveway.

I followed Locke's eyes as he held up the small item she'd put in his hand. It was a piece of torn-out notepaper with *HELV.HE* written on it. The same note al-Qadiri had handed his wife during the game earlier for her to pass to his assistant.

"What does that word mean?" I asked.

"It's the stock symbol for Helvig. You were right. It was him," he said in a dull voice, looking from the paper to the destruction outside. "Makani and Kida. *Makida.*"

I tilted my head in the direction Liyana had gone and raised an eyebrow in a silent question.

He quickly shook his head and said in a low voice while staring out the door, "More likely her father. He would have been the one to arrange her escape, as well."

"We need to go, too," I urged, trying to pull him toward the door in the direction Liyana and her driver had gone. "Please, Locke. I'll explain later. I need you to trust me. We can't stay."

He spun me around and kissed me hard, like a punishment. When he pulled away, he shook his face. "I won't flee my own home. But you're right. You shouldn't be here when the authorities arrive. I can handle this myself. I need you to go."

I'd never been so torn in my life. Stay here and try to make it right, explain to the authorities what I knew about everything— what I knew about *Locke*?

Or get out of here and protect him by playing stupid with my employer? Acting like I'd never been close enough to the people involved to have more information than I'd already given Rocky?

If I stayed, I'd get caught up in the investigation. They'd learn I was here. That I'd been closer to it than Rocky had thought. Not only would I lose my job, but my connection to Locke and the Paxis tournament would bring a level of scrutiny that Locke himself might not be able to escape from.

I couldn't see any way of denying a relationship—no matter how innocent—with Locke Maris if I were here when the authorities arrived. It would be way easier to play dumb to ESP if I could say I'd never even been here. And if I could play dumb, I wouldn't be asked to reveal anything else about the Kiel Canal, al-Qadiri, Alvarado, or any of the other suspicious topics Rocky would inevitably ask me about.

The best way to help Locke was to... leave him.

Fuck.

"I'm sorry," I said, my heart wrenching with uncertainty and helplessness. "I..."

"Go, Jethro," he said softly. "Give me one less thing to worry about. Please."

I kissed him again and then bolted through the door. No passport, no money—those were still locked in the suite's safe, where Locke would protect them from the authorities.

The only thing I carried was my phone.

But I knew it was enough.

All I had to do was hop on a train and pay with my phone. Travel up the coast and make my way to Liorland. Beg mercy from my cousins. Contact Rocky and ask for help repatriating.

The hardest part would be coming up with a story to explain it all. As if I hadn't been in the thick of it.

As if I hadn't helped cause it all.

31

LOCKE

I watched Jett walk away, torn between wanting to pull him back inside to keep him with me and yelling at him to go faster. The sirens were already blaring, and I had no idea how he would ever get to town without being spotted on the road.

Who the fuck was Jett? What did he know? Who did he work for? Was he going to get in trouble?

It was killing me not knowing, but I cared about him enough to protect him from whatever consequences he was afraid of.

I only wished he'd understood that the Paxis Council hardly ever faced consequences. Our combined wealth, power, and connections were virtually impenetrable.

And as far as anyone knew, no one here had motivation to take out Saleem al-Qadiri, a friend of the family who'd come for a brief visit to pay his respects after the loss of my grandfather. Liyana and her driver were long gone, whisked away by whatever plan her father had made for them this morning.

I spent the next few minutes checking in with my security team and the remaining driver to make sure everyone was okay, and then I found Concetta. I made sure the staff had been briefed and that every member of the council who could evacuate had left immediately when the explosion happened. By now, they were already on boats speeding away to Tunisia, where their planes would inevitably come fetch them later tonight.

Having an emergency evacuation plan in place so the council wasn't caught together was a requirement at every tournament, though I couldn't recall the last time one had actually been implemented.

According to emergency protocol, I should be the only council person left on-site since I was the owner.

I heard shouting in Italian as first responders finally arrived on the scene. It felt like it had been hours since the explosion, but in reality, it had only been minutes.

First came the local police, but within half an hour, a team of national police arrived, and with them was an Interpol agent. When he learned I didn't speak enough Italian to answer questions properly, he switched to English.

"My attorney is on his way," I said, radiating innocence and confusion. "The man in the vehicle is… was… Saleem al-Qadiri," I explained. The name was enough to get his attention.

"Who else is here?"

I shook my head and pointed at my ears. "I'm having difficulty hearing you."

"We're looking for this man," he said loudly, turning his phone.

The picture on-screen was of a slightly younger Jett wearing a suit and tie and staring seriously at the camera. The sight made my heart ache and crack.

I wanted nothing more than to have that face here in front of me. To hold it in my palms. To see those lips tip up in an irreverent, teasing smile. To tell him... all the things I hadn't trusted myself or *him* enough to say when I'd had the chance.

I met the Interpol agent's eyes. "I don't know that man," I said, my voice ringing with absolute truth.

Because one thing was for sure.

Jethro Davis, the man I'd fallen for, was a ghost.

IT TOOK three days before they finally left me alone. The crime scene techs had come and gone. The attorneys and investigators had exhausted their attempts at getting information from me or access to the house.

Thankfully, Liyana's father—Mehmet al-Qadiri—had started a rumor that Saleem had upset a powerful opposition group when he'd begun pushing a new profit model for his father-in-law's oil holdings in an attempt to reap more of the earnings for himself. And it seemed Esteban Alvarado had helped him find the group to pin it on, because now the authorities were chasing their tails, investigating a bunch of leads that would never pan out.

The feint had worked in part because it was based in truth. Al-Qadiri hadn't been content to wait for his father-in-law to hand over control of their vast fortune. In the end, his greed had led to his downfall.

I could only imagine the guilt and pain Mehmet al-Qadiri was feeling. He'd brought Saleem into the Paxis Council. Taught and mentored him before letting him take the family's place at the table. He'd thought he'd known who his son-in-law was and believed he was trustworthy.

And he'd been wrong.

Maybe this would finally change al-Qadiri's opinion about Liyana's abilities. After all, she had to have understood enough of the game to recognize her husband's betrayal and act on it. And she'd shown her loyalty to the sanctity of the council over any affection for her husband.

I imagined sacrificing Jett for the council, but that was a nonstarter. I would never in a million years choose the council over Jett. Maybe this was selfish. The Paxis Council saved countless lives and prevented wars. What was one man's life in comparison? Still, I knew without a doubt I wouldn't have been able to do what Liyana did.

No matter how much it hurt to know that Jett had lied to me, I still missed him every damn day.

"Please eat, stellina." Concetta's voice was laced with concern as she stepped out on the balcony and eyed my untouched dinner. "I am beginning to worry."

I looked up at her and attempted to smile, but before I could reassure her that I was fine, a familiar voice came through the balcony doors, accompanied by my sister's rapid steps.

"Maybe he just needs some good dinner company."

Celeste was a sight for sore eyes. She was sun-tanned and healthy, dressed in a simple light blue T-shirt and soft, wide lounge pants with stylish sneakers. I stood immediately and moved to embrace her.

"Shit, Johnny. Since when are you a hugger?" she murmured into my chest.

The old nickname on her tongue made my eyes sting for reasons that had nothing to do with her.

"I've been practicing," I admitted. "And I could really use one."

She pulled back and fake-punched my chest. "Why didn't you call me? I didn't hear about the explosion until we docked in Grand Cayman."

I held out a seat for her to join me. "You hungry? Roberto made one of my favorites."

She glanced at my full plate and up at me. "So I see."

Concetta had already gone off to the kitchen, not giving Celeste an option of saying no.

We settled into our seats, and I gazed out at the sea, lost in thought again without realizing it.

"Concetta's worried about you," she said unnecessarily.

"I'm fine."

"What happened?"

I turned back to face her. "Saleem al-Qadiri's car blew up. Killed him instantly."

"Right, but why?"

I shrugged. "He has some powerful enemies. Apparently."

"How did they get access to the vehicle? Your security is meticulous."

That was a great question. One the authorities had asked numerous times. Fortunately, I literally didn't know the answer, so I could answer truthfully.

"I have no idea. My only guess is that it happened off-site. Liyana took the car into town right before it happened. There's no telling who had access while she was in the shops."

Celeste made a sympathetic noise. "I spoke to Liyana on the way here. She seems to be holding up okay. Her family is around her. Their kids are obviously devastated."

I pressed my lips together but didn't say anything. Since I'd never seen or met their kids—or heard Saleem mention them by name, come to think of it—I had no idea how they'd handle his sudden death. Maybe it would be like the way Celeste and I had handled our own father's. Mourning the loss of the parent you never really had.

She took my hand in hers. "Talk to me. This seems to have really hit you hard. I know you looked up to him. Respected him."

I stretched my shoulders, tilting my head from side to side.

"I'm okay." This was mostly true. I thought I'd known Saleem because of the pretty words he'd said. But his actions showed how wrong I'd been. "Tell me about your trip," I said, attempting to change the subject.

She went along with it, launching into the story of her trip to the Caribbean, a man she shared a clandestine kiss with there, and the tired refrain of how much one of her friends wanted Celeste to set the two of us up.

I was happy to see she hadn't held on to her anger at me over our last phone call.

Her food arrived, and she shoveled in bites between stories. I, on the other hand, couldn't stomach any of it. My gut was twisted with worry and loss.

All of it centered on the man I'd fallen for. The man whose real name I didn't even know.

"You going to tell me what's really going on?" she finally asked. "Because Minnie called me. She's even more worried about you than Concetta is."

I glanced out at the water. At the turquoise pool below, where Jett had challenged me to a cannonball contest and then wrestled with me like a kid. I hadn't laughed that hard since Celeste and I had celebrated her twenty-first birthday at a Magic Mike show in Vegas.

I closed my eyes and remembered the male bodies on display, none of them nearly as sexy as Jett's.

Why him? Why *fucking* him of all men?

"Talk to me, Johnny," she murmured.

"I'm in love with someone," I said, not shocking myself at all, even though the confession itself was a surprise. I'd already admitted it to myself a million times since he'd left.

"Who? And why do you sound so miserable about it? Is she married or something? Is that it?"

Concetta kept her eyes down as she gathered our plates, but I felt the empathy and understanding in her body language nonetheless. She knew. The entire household staff knew. And they missed him almost as much as I did.

"His name is Jett. Or... at least that's the name he gave me."

"The name he gave you—Locke, what the hell?"

I started telling her the story, beginning with the Candy Bar lap dance, the way he intrigued me, the attraction I felt—although I kept that part free of details—and how I came to bring him to Italy. I didn't mention the job proposition, only the invitation to help me out. To be with me physically at night and help host the event during the day.

"As your boyfriend?" she asked in surprise.

"No." I inhaled and exhaled, thrusting my fingers into my hair. "I wanted to keep it a secret. It was... I don't know. Like an experiment at first. I wasn't ready for it to change my life or anything." I huffed out a laugh. "How fucking ironic."

"What makes you think he's not who he says he is?"

This part was hard to explain without breaking confidences—both his and the Paxis Council's.

"Because I had HR run a background check on the name he gave me," I said shortly. "That's not the man I knew."

She nodded slowly. "Well, maybe you didn't know him as well as you thought you did."

"Maybe." I pushed back my chair and gazed out over the water.

In a way, Celeste was right. I didn't know Jett's real name or his address. I didn't know his birthday or who his mother was.

But I knew he loved seashells, and that his blue eyes glowed when he teased me. I knew how it felt when he chided me to eat healthy salad and forced me to take a break from the stress of my job. I knew how his mind worked when he assessed a Paxis board, and that he was equally kind to everyone, from my gardeners to the British king's cousin. I knew that when I'd been floundering under the weight of responsibility, he'd reminded me that I wasn't alone. I knew he could communicate in a million languages, including *mine.*

And I knew that he'd tried to take me with him when he left.

If I were judging the man by his actions...

"Mmm," Celeste said, watching my face.

I blinked and turned my gaze to her. "What's *mmm* mean?"

"It means... maybe you should track this guy down and talk to him."

I shot her a look. "You don't think I've thought of that? He's a ghost, Cellie."

She frowned. "Because of a measly human resources background check? You own one of the world's most advanced satellite and navigation software companies. You have pretty much unlimited money and resources. You'd think you'd have access to a hacker at the very least." She shook her head disapprovingly. "Like, what are you even doing with yourself, Johnny? Jeez."

I snorted. Then I thought of my contact—the one who'd arranged for the blockade. Now it was my turn to say it. "Mmm."

The edge of her lip curled up, and she nodded, clearly satisfied. "Uh-huh. There's the Locke Maris I know and love. Focused and determined, not gonna let a tiny little detail like not knowing a guy's name or location stop him. Let the hunt begin."

Concetta had retreated out of hearing distance, so I waved her over and requested a glass of whiskey.

As soon as she was gone, I turned to Celeste. "You're so fucking right. I *am* going to find Jett."

"Damn straight you are," she agreed. "You'll *make* him tell you the truth."

I looked out at the water and thought of Jett's eyes.

"And I might tell him a few truths of my own."

32

JETT

My phone battery had long died by the time I made my way to the palace and pled my case. Honestly, if the princeling hadn't been coming back from a fucking polo match or some shit and recognized me, I would have been screwed.

"Jett?" Chris asked incredulously.

"I need help," I said, suddenly feeling overwhelmed and exhausted. Even though we weren't exactly close, we were distantly related through our great-grandfathers and had spent several kick-ass family reunions and celebrations together over the years.

He took me in and treated me like a royal guest—which I guess went without saying—but once I was cleaned up and well rested, he and his fathers demanded answers.

"I need help getting home," I said. "I lost my backpack that had my wallet and passport in it."

King Lior nodded. "Of course. I'll send you home on one of our planes with a diplomatic pass."

Uncle Felix smiled, his face open and welcoming as usual. "You'll stay for a visit first, though, right?"

I shook my head. "I really need to get back. I was in the middle of a case at work, and there's some follow-up I need to do in the office."

He looked disappointed, which made his husband frown. "You will stay for dinner, at least," Lior said.

Chris elbowed me. "That's his commanding voice, in case you didn't realize it was supposed to be scary."

His fathers both shot him a look, but Chris only grinned. He was known in our family as a showboat, which didn't surprise anyone, considering the immense wealth and privilege he'd grown up with here in Liorland and Uncle Felix's huge, irreverent Wilde family in America.

"I'm suitably terrified. But also hungry, so I accept. Thank you."

The evening that followed was a nice break from reality, but as soon as I got back to my room, my now-charged phone was buzzing like an angry yellow jacket stuck between a window and the screen.

The first call I returned was to Rocky, who answered the phone with a "Jesus Christ, Jett! Where are you?"

"Liorland."

She huffed out a breath. "*Liorland*? What the fuck are you doing there?"

"Well..." I blew out a breath.

On the train here from Maiori, I'd had nothing but time. Time to think, and rethink, and overthink.

Time to look over that warning text I'd received from an unknown number the day of the bombing and remember that Rocky didn't know I was staying at Locke's house. Time to remember Liyana saying, *Thank you, Jett. I hope someday to repay your kindness.* Time to realize that good and bad, truth and lies, loyalty and honor, weren't the black-and-white concepts I'd thought they were when I'd first become an agent.

I'd had time to regret, too.

I'd foolishly gotten way too involved with a supposedly heterosexual billionaire. A man who literally controlled the world like pawns in a game. A man whose determination and responsibility were melded into his very soul. A man who'd stood alone, acted alone, for so long, that when I'd begged him to leave, he'd stubbornly insisted on staying behind—*alone.*

No loyal ESP agent would risk his career over Locke Maris by being less than a hundred percent honest with his boss...

Unless that agent had a damn good reason, like being head over heels in love with the man and determined to protect him at all costs.

"I'm visiting my cousins," I lied with no compunction whatsoever. "They invited me, and I figured, 'Hey, I'm on vacation, and Rocky specifically told me to stay out of trouble, so why not?' But don't worry, I'm heading back to Italy first thing tomorrow. I'll collect the package you sent to the post office and set up surveillance—"

"No!" she almost shouted. "Jesus, no. Under no circumstances should you go back to Maiori, Jett. I mean it."

I sat on the bed, stacked the pillows behind my head, and tried to think what the Agent Jett Marian that she knew might say. "What? Why not? Come on, Rocky! It's been almost a week. I'm so relaxed by now my muscles are starting to atrophy!"

"Have you not checked the news in the last forty-eight hours?" she demanded. "There's been a blockade in the *Kiel Canal.*"

"No way." I sank further into the pillows. "You mean... you think the convo I overheard was actually them... what? Plotting something? Shit."

"We don't know," she admitted. "It's not related to the explosion near the canal. That's confirmed by CJ and the others. The official cause is a software glitch. If there was an unofficial cause, we haven't figured it out yet. But listen, Jett, Trevi said you contacted him for information about a company..." Papers rustled in the background.

"Yeah, yeah, yeah. Malik Makida. I remembered someone mentioning that at lunch, too. Trevi said it's owned by Saleem al-Qadiri, so it makes sense that's why they mentioned it, right? Did that have something to do with the canal thing?"

"No. But..." Rocky hesitated. "Saleem al-Qadiri was killed by a car bomb at a villa just outside Maiori yesterday."

"What the fuck? I was just there! I left first thing yesterday morning. Damn it. I knew I shouldn't have left—"

"No, it's probably better that way. But that's why you can't go back. The investigator showed your picture around to the owner and staff at the villa—"

"Why?" I didn't have to feign shock now. I sat up on the bed and glared at my phone. "Why the fuck would he do that and blow whatever cover I would have had?"

"Because I couldn't get in touch with you! Because we were concerned that you might have tried to get close to the players. And that you might have been hurt in the process."

"Jesus Christ," I groaned.

I wanted to say that she should know me better than that... but based on recent events, she obviously knew me exactly the right amount.

"Anyway, if you go back to Maiori, you'll raise a whole lot of suspicion. And anyway, the investigation's not centered there anymore. Chatter says al-Qadiri upset the wrong people in the process of a power grab from his father-in-law. They've got a couple leads they're following up in Qadara."

I closed my eyes. I was sure that story was a plant, and I raised a mental toast to the Paxis Council.

"One thing that's bothering me, though," Rocky mused. "Two of the ships involved in the blockade were Maris ships. And al-Qadiri was assassinated at Locke Maris's house."

Interrogation 101: don't answer questions that weren't asked.

I waited her out until she finally said, "But then again, there were other ships involved. So there's no clear evidence pointing to Maris." She sighed.

"Do we have a mandate here?" I wondered. Because we could be curious cats all we wanted, but if there was no indication of danger or illegal activity that could lead to global instability, then what was our interest in al-Qadiri's death? "I can look into it?" I tried to sound eager. "Ask around—"

"No. God no. Go back to your vacation. Keep staying out of trouble. We'll see you in a week and not before."

I hung up the phone and squeezed my eyes shut.

I should have felt like I'd crossed a Rubicon, I was pretty sure. Yes, I was not Rocky's most rule-following agent. Yes, there were times I'd taken risks—like staying under way too long in Germany—that she didn't agree with. But I had never overtly disobeyed an order. I'd never questioned or tested my loyalty to ESP.

But if I were being brutally honest, my frustration with the job had been a constant drip, drip, drip that had, over the years, built into a tidal wave. So many times, I'd seen higher-ups—people who'd never had their boots on the ground in the agency—make decisions that enabled small-time criminals like Ronald Gillen to keep living their best criminal lives, with no thought to the people they hurt. So many times, I'd been pulled from cases *right* before they broke because diplomatic channels broke down and our authorization to operate was yanked.

I'd joined ESP because I wanted to do good in the world. I'd told myself that it was worth all the sacrificed time with my family and friends. That it didn't matter that I'd lived more of my adult life as a made-up persona than I had as Jett Marian.

But more and more often, I'd felt caged.

Worse, I was afraid I'd started to forget who Jett Marian even was or what he wanted...

Until Locke Maris had helped me remember.

The following morning, I flew home from Liorland in a private plane and spent twenty hours asleep in my own bed. Then I woke up and caught a ride to the airport.

If I didn't get the hell out of this city, I would drag my pathetic ass to Locke's doorstep and throw myself on his mercy.

If Locke was still being watched, which I had to imagine he was, this would have made it very clear to my employer that I was a lying asshole.

None of which I needed right now as much as the loving arms (and horrible Dad-joke humor) of my parents.

THE SUN WAS SETTING as I drove over the bridge to Rabbit Island. The familiar expanse of my hometown was like serotonin mixed with Valium. The stress began to melt away as if I were passing through a protection barrier that surrounded the island.

The streets were peppered here and there with kids riding their bikes or people walking a dog after supper, but when I got to the house I'd grown up in, the one that had been in my dad's family too long to remember, no one was outside.

I climbed the stairs to the front door and opened it, not surprised it wasn't locked since doors on Rabbit Island rarely were.

Inside, my family was shouting at each other. Familiar voices raised in incredulity competed for dominance.

"You scratched me!" Becca wailed with all the drama of a telenovela.

"To be fair, sweetheart," Mav said calmly, "Gabe's still bleeding from the last round where you smacked his face instead of his hand."

Gabe's friend Hunter muttered, "And yet you won't let me murder her."

"Alright," Beau said, heaving himself up from his chair at the game table in the corner of the family room. "Refill time. Who wants another glass of wine. Gabe, another beer?"

As I came into the room, the dog ratted me out. Pepper's nails scrabbled on the hardwoods as she woke up and bolted toward me. Beau looked to see what had woken her and found me standing there.

"Jett! We didn't know you were coming. Get in here."

I finished giving the dog a head scratch before moving toward him for a hug. But as soon as I saw they'd been playing Egyptian Ratscrew, I felt overwhelming emotion.

Loss. Loneliness. Familiarity and comfort. Fear. Grief. *Want.*

Utter and devastating heartbreak.

"Jett?" Mav said, standing up and frowning. "What's...? Oh dear."

They surrounded me just as I broke down, Beau on one side of me and Maverick on the other. I turned into Mav's chest and tucked myself into his arms, feeling Beau move in behind me to make a hug sandwich.

I'd come by my incredible hugging genius honestly. I wished I'd been able to tell Locke that.

"Honey, whatever it is, we're here. It'll be okay," Beau murmured.

I could see my brother out of the corner of my eye, his forehead creased with concern. Becca blinked and stood up, moving to reach through the group hug to scratch lightly into my hair, a gesture she'd always used to soothe me when I was upset.

"Glad you're home, Jetty-boo. We missed you."

I tried to keep my sobs silent as my breath heaved, and hot tears slid down my face and into Mav's shirt.

"Maybe I should go," Hunter said softly to Gabe.

"What? Fuck off, you're family, too," Gabe replied.

Beau moved away from the hug, gently shoving Mav and me toward the sofa. "You three go pick up the pizza we called in. Hunt, make sure they don't kill each other on the way."

Once they were gone, my dads sat on either side of me and waited for me to catch my breath. Beau had brought over a box of tissues, and Mav had whistled for Pepper to get over here and stop whining. Once she'd shoved her fat ass between us on the sofa and dropped her chin on my lap, she calmed down.

Mav's calm presence had its usual effect on me. "You want to talk about it?"

"How'd you decide to leave California for Beau?" I asked, voice hoarse and nasally from crying.

I'd already heard this story plenty of times. Mav was a veterinarian. He'd been preparing to take over the San Francisco practice from my grandmother when he'd reconnected with Beau in South Carolina and fallen in love. Leaving an established practice hadn't been easy.

My dads exchanged a knowing look.

"Easy," Mav said at the same time Beau said, "Bribery."

Mav put his palm on Beau's face and pushed him back. I didn't miss how gentle the touch was. They'd always been sweetly affectionate with each other. It made my teeth hurt.

Mav focused back on me. "I could decide to stay in California and be Beau-less, or I could move here. It really was that easy. It's kind of like asking someone to choose between living in a shoebox with their heart or living in Rabbit Island without their heart. Rabbit Island isn't worth living in if you're not *living*."

"A shoebox, babe? You suck at metaphors," Beau muttered before turning me to face him. "Who's the guy?"

I told them as much as I could without mentioning ESP, Paxis, global intrigue, or the whole sex-for-money thing. If I ever had a chance—even if it was a slim one—of building a future with Locke, that would remain our secret and ours alone.

"It's hard to explain," I continued. "But I can't have him and my career at the same time."

"Why not?" Beau asked, sounding angry enough to ride at dawn, guns blazing.

I stroked the silky-smooth fur of Pepper's head with my thumb. The little dip where her noggin met her ear fit my thumb perfectly like it always had.

"I just can't. Okay?"

Beau bent a knee up on the sofa so he could face me better. "If I had to choose between your dad and my business, it wouldn't even be a question."

Mav made a little sound of appreciation in his throat. Sometimes I hated these two and their perfect love.

"That's easy for you to say after thirty years together!" I snapped. "Hindsight is twenty-twenty, Beau. I barely know this guy. He's the head of a multibillion-dollar company. And he... he's fucking straight, okay? I didn't tell you that part, but of course he is. Or he claims he is, anyway." I heaved a breath. "And he doesn't do relationships."

Beau snorted, but Mav reached over and poked him.

Then Mav moved to sit right behind Beau so I could see both of them at once. His arm came around Beau's middle without thinking, pulling his partner close and leaning his chin on Beau's shoulder. It was a position I'd seen a million times before, but the casual ease of it, the way they had such... blanket permission to touch each other without asking or worrying about what anyone thought... it gutted me.

Would I ever have that?

"Sweetheart," Mav said patiently, "it doesn't sound like your guy is actually straight. Not if there's something between you. And just because he's some kind of important businessman doesn't mean he doesn't want or deserve love."

Beau pulled Mav's arm more tightly around him. "You know who else didn't 'do' relationships?" he asked, using air quotes.

"Uncle Teddy," Mav finished for him with a grin.

"Be real right now," I muttered. My uncle Teddy was stupid for his husband. Always had been since before I could remember.

"And Uncle Derek was 'straight,'" Mav added.

This, I already knew. I had the gayest collection of uncles on Earth, and they'd all had different paths to love. But it seemed like maybe the Marian family had already used up our allotment of happy ever afters before it would ever be my turn.

I smoothed Pepper's fur, watching the small movements of her whiskers. "How did Jamie and Jude convince them to... to give a relationship a try?"

Beau's grin widened. "They didn't. They were just lovable sons-a-bitches, and their men came to them. Maybe give that a try. It worked for me, too."

Mav moved his arm up to put Beau in a gentle headlock. "Do not listen to this father. Listen to me. The better father. The father with a level head." He winked. "You should go talk to him, sweetheart. Maybe after San Francisco."

"After... San Francisco?" I asked.

"Tilly's bachelor party," Beau snickered. "Remember?"

"No," I said, feeling dread curdle in my gut as I remembered the family commitment. "No way."

"Command performance, I'm afraid," Mav said before kissing Beau on the head and shoving him off so he could stand up. "Come on. Let's eat. I hear your siblings squabbling in the driveway."

"Dad, for real, I can't go. Aunt Tilly's whole point in throwing that ridiculous party is to set us all up with people!"

Beau stood and reached out a hand to pull me up. "Aw. Nice use of the word 'Dad,' but it's still not getting you out of this. Tilly played the 'next year I might be dead' card, so we're going."

I scoffed and followed him to the kitchen, past rows and rows of multicolored salt and pepper shakers of all sizes and shapes. "She's never gonna die. She drinks from the holy grail."

Gabe set three huge pizza boxes on the counter. "Tilly texted me and told me that if we don't show up, she might sign us up for a subscription to blue-cheese-of-the-month again."

We both shuddered at the memories.

"Fine," I said. "But I'm not talking to any men. And I'm sure as hell not kissing any of them."

Which was, it turned out, just another one of Jett Marian's lies.

33

LOCKE

It took me five days to track my prey down.

"Jett Talmadge Marian," Vox said. "Born and raised in Rabbit Island, South Carolina. Son of Maverick and Beau Marian. Graduated from local public high school and attended the University of Virginia, where he double-majored in global affairs and linguistics. Enjoys long walks on the beach and getting caught in the rain."

I ignored him the same way I ignored the sunlight glinting off the Manhattan skyline outside my office window and scrolled through the information coming onto my screen.

There was a picture of Jett from his student ID card at UVA, a candid shot of him standing on a dock by a marsh, grinning in the sun, a much younger image of him at a podium in what looked like a high school debate tournament.

And then there was an office ID badge photo of him that looked eerily similar to the way he'd looked after Amsterdam. Skinny and tired.

The company name on the badge was ESP.

"What is Ecumene Stability Project?" I asked, squinting at the address in the financial district.

"An Interpol-related agency," he said before slurping something through a straw. "Buncha do-gooder special agents."

I closed my eyes and exhaled for the first time in a week. He didn't work for the Alvarados. Or any other criminal group. He worked for the good guys.

Kind of.

The Paxis Council did what it did because governments were notoriously bad at it. Self-dealing and rarely prioritizing the welfare of the people they purported to protect.

Agencies like Interpol were rife with corruption and bias, and they were often hamstrung by regulations and "official channels."

Additionally, intelligence agents were often used up and discarded like pawns in a never-ending game. I hated to imagine Jett becoming jaded over time or, worse, finding himself in inescapable danger. I'd already seen the result of his job conditions once before.

"What would ESP have been doing in Amsterdam three years ago?" I asked, almost to myself.

"No way to know, dude. Undercover shit, most likely."

Undercover.

Fuck.

He'd cried in my arms. Fresh off whatever assignment where he'd pretended to be... what? Homeless? An addict? Or had it been worse? Had he been caught and held somewhere? Interrogated?

I remembered him waking up from a nightmare. The stark terror in his eyes and the thundering of his heart.

My fingers itched to hold him again, comfort him, support him financially so he could quit that fucking job, even if he wanted nothing to do with me ever again.

"Oh, this is unexpected," the guy said. "His uncle is Jude Marian. You know, from Jude and the Saints? My mom used to listen to them all the time when I was a kid."

"Uh-huh." I couldn't care less about Jett's famous relatives. "What's his address?"

"You want the kid's apartment in New York, parents' place in Rabbit Island, or—"

"All of it," I said, standing up and reaching for my suit jacket. "Give me every single fucking place I might be able to find him."

I threw my jacket on and called out to Minnie. "Get my driver and have my pilot prepare the plane."

"Wait," Vox called through the phone. "If you're looking for where Jett is right now, he's at his parents' place."

I took a breath and thanked him before ending the call. "Minnie, tell the pilots I need to go to South Carolina."

When I finally made it to the house on Rabbit Island, a younger man opened the door. "May I help you?"

"You must be Gabe," I said. "Is Jett here?"

He shook his head. "No. Gabe and everybody left for California this morning. I'm just looking after the dog. My name's Hunter."

I eyed him. "Cy Berringer's son? Jett told me you were friends with his brother."

Hunter nodded, suddenly looking less open and friendly. "And you are?"

"Sorry. Locke Maris. I've met your dad at a few industry events." I reached out my hand to shake, and he took it. My name seemed to relax him, but he still looked at me with suspicion.

"What do you need Jett for?"

"It's a private matter."

Suddenly, his eyebrows lifted as if he'd just put two and two together. "Oh, shit! You're the reason he was crying last night."

The image of Jett, *my Jett*, crying for any reason made my stomach turn. "Crying."

Hunter crossed his arms in front of his chest. "I take it if you're here, you care about him."

I opened my mouth and then closed it. How I felt about Jett Dav... *Marian* was none of his business. "I need to find him."

He studied me for a moment. "I was just getting ready to take Pepper out. Walk with me. In return, I'll tell you a story about Jett."

Maybe the man was as cunning as his father, because he'd effortlessly tied a leash around my throat. Within moments, I was trailing him on the beach, barefoot in the warm sand.

"Speak," I said when he wasn't immediately forthcoming.

He chuckled. "You're not like the guys he usually dates."

"I thought he didn't date," I said, falling willfully into his trap. But then again, I'd thought Jett was a sex worker. A go-go dancer. A player. For all I knew, he was a serial monogamist.

"He doesn't. I mean you're not like the guys he dated in high school and college. Other geeky types like him. Sweethearts."

I clenched my back teeth. Great. So I wasn't Jett's type? Didn't matter. I hadn't thought he was my type either, had I? When I got a hold of him, I'd convince him to date me anyway. Fuck type.

"Why doesn't he date?" I asked, assuming it was most likely because of his job.

I felt Hunter's eyes on me. The dog, a tubby black Lab who seemed entirely too trusting of strangers, loped happily after a group of birds at the edge of the surf, sending them flying and squawking away.

"Did you ever see the viral TikTok of the guy who got broken up with by AI? It was probably five or six years ago now. Maybe seven."

The idea that I'd ever had much time in my life for social media was laughable, but he didn't know that. I shook my head.

"Well, that was Jett. His boyfriend used ChatGPT to break up with him after almost a year of dating seriously. It crushed him. He swore off relationships after that, but then he ended up giving another guy a chance. Noah."

I could tell this was going somewhere I didn't want to go.

Didn't want to, but *needed* to.

"What happened with Noah?"

"They dated for a while. Jett really liked him. It took him a while to trust the guy, but when he finally brought him to meet the family one Christmas in Montana, Noah tried hooking up with Jett's cousin Wolfe."

"What the fuck?"

"Yeah, it was bad. I mean, Wolfe's hot, and he's got that shy, moody thing going on. He's also a celebrity's son. Best I can figure, Noah wanted to get close to the fame? The money? I don't know. But Wolfe's other dad is an ex-Marine. Honestly, Noah's lucky he didn't get murdered that weekend. Jett was shocked. Embarrassed. And, well, hurt. As you can imagine." He blew out a breath. "And poor Wolfe was horrified. The whole thing seemed to scare him off men completely, whereas Jett just swore off relationships."

I didn't say anything, my mind spinning as I tried rearranging what I knew of Jett now that he was no longer the man I'd thought I knew.

The knowledge of just how much I didn't know about him enraged me. I wanted to wring the man's neck.

As soon as I could get my hands on him.

"I need to find him, Hunter," I finally said.

We'd already turned to head back, the dog running ahead to the house.

Before he could respond, I stopped and stared down at something that caught my eye.

There, in the semi-packed sand, was a tiny, perfect shell. A miniature conch.

A triton.

34

JETT

I'D ALMOST BEGGED off my great-aunt's ridiculous matchmaking dinner party. In fact, after leaving Rabbit Island, I'd flown back to New York in a moment of weakness and found myself at Locke Maris's front door.

His housekeeper had answered and looked at me with reserve. "Mr. Maris is out of town."

"For how long?" I'd asked, feeling stupid that I didn't know. "He's not still in Italy, right?"

She'd shaken her head. "No. But I don't know how long he'll be gone. He didn't say." She eyed me. "And if he did, I wouldn't tell a stranger his business."

"I'm sorry. I'm... not a stranger. I promise. My name is Jett." I'd swallowed and then made a decision. It wouldn't make a difference to her, but it made a difference to me. "Jett Marian."

Her smile had softened. "Well, Jett Marian. I can tell him you stopped by the next time he checks in, alright?"

I'd smiled and thanked her before walking away.

And I'd spent the entire flight to San Francisco vowing to

take it as a sign. Locke Maris wasn't meant for me. There were too many reasons to count. The sheer number of lies between us. The fact that he didn't know the real me. Both of our histories with being workaholics and avoiding emotional entanglements.

And that didn't even take into account the fact that he might still identify as straight.

So I'd arrived at Aunt Tilly's "bachelor" party—to which she'd invited nothing but bachelors, for the most part—fully intending to put Locke Maris behind me—at least for the moment—and be the usual fun-time guy my family knew.

Fake it till you make it.

I was the king of faking it, and I certainly wasn't going to fail now. The hotel ballroom was filled with eligible bachelors of all kinds, and I wasn't going to be the one to bring the mood down.

"He's cute," I said, tipping my champagne glass discreetly at a tall man with smooth, medium-brown skin and a killer fade.

My cousin Caspian eyed the man up and down and turned beet red. "He's also a famous influencer who does videos about sexual health," he whispered. "I could never."

My brother glanced at the tall man and turned back to Cas. "Why not? He's hot."

Cas shook his head quickly. "No, yeah. But like... he probably knows things. Things I don't know." He lowered his voice even more. "Skill-level things."

"Think of all he could teach you," our cousin JJ said, bouncing his eyebrows. His wife rolled her eyes and walked away to get another drink.

I reached my glass over to clink with his. "Smart man."

Gabe clapped Cas's shoulder and suggested they move to the table where their place cards were. The two of them were at a different table from me.

"We're meeting up after for shots, right?" Gabe asked. "All the cousins?"

I looked at the place card two over from mine. "I haven't seen Wolfe yet. Is he here?"

Gabe looked around the large room. "I haven't seen him yet. He was supposed to be here, though. Did something happen to him?"

Cas appeared worried. "Aunt Tilly will be pissed if he doesn't show. He's her favorite."

It was true. She had a soft spot for the guy, but then again, she was a sucker for old souls and interesting characters. Men with bleeding hearts.

She was less impressed with those of us who kept it casual.

She was the quintessential matriarch who seemed to want everyone to fall in love and settle down.

Needless to say, I'd been avoiding her like the plague all evening.

As Cas and Gabe moved off toward their table, I turned to take my own seat. I snickered at my coupled-up cousins who'd been stashed together at an old-people's table in the corner of the room. They seemed perfectly happy, especially my cousin Alex and his boyfriend, Judd—the man I'd almost hooked up with in Amsterdam a few years ago.

What would have happened if I'd kissed the other man in Amsterdam? If Judd hadn't gone to the men's room and we'd headed up to his room before Locke arrived?

I shuddered to think of it. But that's what was going through my head when I continued the sweep of the party, looking for Wolfe... and saw Locke Maris come striding into the room looking like he was there to lay waste to an entire village and take revenge upon his enemies.

It was a hallucination. Or a dream. Or a stroke.

A psychotic break, maybe?

In the time it took me to realize he was actually here, I panicked.

There was no way I could talk to him *here*, of all places. Not with my entire family around. Cousins, siblings, friends. I had a history of crying like a baby when overwhelmed with emotion. I'd already done it at least once before over Locke, and chances were I'd do it again the minute he asked me to explain myself.

The minute he realized I wasn't anything like the man I'd pretended to be.

As I bolted from the room, all I could think about was getting to my hotel room. I said a silent prayer of thanks for Gabe's insistence that we get separate rooms in case he wanted to bring a guy back to his. With any luck, I could have my big sobbing breakdown in private.

I stabbed the elevator button several times. "Come on, come on," I muttered, staring up at the digital display.

"Don't fucking move," I heard Locke say in a low voice as he strode quickly toward me, his long legs eating up the ground between us.

The elevator doors slid open, and I darted inside, hammering the button for my floor over and over while saying a prayer to all the elevator gods.

Just as the doors began to slide closed, he shoved his hand between them and held them long enough to squeeze in.

My entire body shook with fear. Fear he would confront me. Be angry with me.

Reject me.

But I also shook with need. He was right here. So fucking close. One deep inhale of his familiar scent would fucking gut me.

Don't breathe. Just don't breathe.

This elevator didn't have enough oxygen. I could hardly pull in enough air to breathe anyway.

"You're here," I said stupidly.

His dark eyes narrowed and then began to take inventory. For seventeen floors, that man's gaze moved over my body like it was reestablishing lost territory.

"I am," he finally said.

The tears were coming. I could feel them. My nostrils stung, and my chin wobbled. *Dammit. Fuck.* Nobody wanted this. Absolutely no one.

Locke pulled the Stop button and jammed the elevator. Then he crossed his arms in front of his chest and waited.

As if the alarm wasn't blaring.

As if security wouldn't respond.

As if he had all the time in the world for me.

I started babbling. "I'm sorry! I'm sorry I left you. God, I am so fucking sorry for that. I wanted to protect you, but still, thinking of you handling everything alone... And I... I'm not who you think I am, Locke. I lied. I know you hate liars and manipulators. I know you'll never be able to trust me after that. And..." Then I got angry. Defensive. "And besides, you're not even comfortable with your sexuality! You don't want a relationship. The whole reason you picked me was because I was easy!"

His bark of laughter made me jump. "I picked you because I couldn't keep my fucking hands off you. Because I couldn't stop thinking about you. Because for four fucking years, I looked for you. Thought of you. Dreamed of you."

This couldn't be real. If I woke up in my bed right now, I was going to be fucking livid.

"W-what?" I asked stupidly.

He uncrossed his arms and stalked forward, backing me into the wall. Six feet of angry Locke Maris made my head spin. Took up all the oxygen. Burned me from my toes to the top of my head. And convinced me that this was really happening.

"Don't fucking leave me again," he growled, splaying a hand high on my chest and softly shaking me. "Whatever happens from now on, we handle it together. Do you understand?"

I lurched forward, crashing my mouth into his. My throat let out an embarrassing sound, but I didn't care. I couldn't hold back anymore, couldn't stop myself from touching him, from having him. From tasting his mouth and inhaling his scent.

His mouth was possessive, punishing me hard enough to leave bruises. It didn't matter. I yanked his shirt collar, pulling him as close as I could until my arms were wrapped around his entire head.

Locke's hands were everywhere, on my chest and abs, under my shirt, up my back to grip my shoulder blades.

His thickening cock ground into me, pressing against my own. It was too blunt, too separated by layers. Too *not close enough.*

"Please," I begged against his mouth. It came out too high. Too revealing. "Please," I said again, in case he hadn't heard it the first time.

"Give me an answer, Jethro." He sounded angry. "Give me an answer right fucking now. You and me. Yes or no."

My remaining fear tumbled past my lips without warning. "I... I don't want to be your dirty secret."

His face hardened, and he pulled away. Slammed the Stop button with his hand, then selected the Lobby level button.

"W-what's happening right now?" I demanded.

Locke didn't answer. He faced the doors as if ready to stride out and return to New York, giving me up as a bad bet. An ungrateful or distrusting partner.

I stepped up behind him and pressed my forehead to the back of his neck, taking a moment to breathe him in. "Please don't leave," I whispered. "Please give me a chance to understand."

"No."

A sickly beat of silence convinced me to step back while anger threatened to return. How fucking dare he reject me like this? But then he spoke again, right when the elevator chime dinged.

"I told you already, Jett. From now on, where I go, you go. You're coming with me."

He grabbed my hand and pulled me along, back toward the ballroom where my great-aunt's bachelor party was presumably in full swing.

"We can't go in there," I said in a panic when I realized where he was taking me. "They don't know about you." It wasn't completely true since my parents and siblings knew, but the dozens of other Marians and Wildes didn't. And if they found out about my connection to Locke Maris, they'd never stop asking me about it.

"Who's the dirty secret, then, Jethro?"

"My name isn't really Jethro," I admitted.

He spun to face me. "I know, Jett. But you're *my* Jethro." He ran a hand over my hair, cupped my jaw, and stared into my eyes. "I'm tired of living my life making all the most important moves in secret. So tell me right now if you want to be with me. For real."

"Of course I do," I snapped. "That's not the problem."

"Good." He turned and entered the ballroom, yanking me over to the small stage that would have a band for dancing after the dinner. He strode up to the microphone and tapped it. "This thing on?"

Everyone's face swung toward us, a hush overtaking the room.

"Guess that means yes," Locke said. "Hi. I'm sorry to interrupt, but I have a small announcement to make tonight."

My entire body was taut as a bowstring, torn between shocked pleasure that Locke was *here*, that he'd come for me, that I might be *his* Jethro... and anxiety because I'd tried to give my heart away twice before in my life, and both times it had been shoved right back at me with a "thanks but no thanks."

"No, wait!" I grabbed Locke's arm and tugged him away from the microphone. "If you do this," I whispered. "If you make this real... if I give you my heart, Locke Maris... you'll *own* it. For good. Understand?"

The divot between Locke's eyebrows smoothed, his jaw loosened, and his lips parted on a grin. Locke leaned in to press a small kiss below my ear and whispered, "I told you before, Jett. It's called Maris Holdings. Not Maris Take and Give Back."

He flashed me a wink before straightening up and speaking into the microphone again.

"I heard this is a bachelor party of sorts. Well, I'm claiming my bachelor." His hand tightened around mine and lifted it as he continued. "Jett Marian is mine. *Forever.* He's not available. He will never be available again. Is that clear?"

Wide eyes followed his every word. I heard someone whisper, "Is that Locke Maris?"

My sister's grin was ridiculous, and my brother Gabe shot me a thumbs-up and mouthed, *So hot.*

I turned to Locke, just in time to have his mouth crash into mine, kissing me like a man just home from months at sea. My legs wobbled, but Locke's arms banded around me to keep me from melting to the floor.

"Oh *fuck*," someone said. Someone else wolf whistled, and I was pretty sure my cousin JJ yelled, "Get it."

As soon as Locke pulled back, I glanced out at the sea of beautiful men and noticed the sheer number of heated gazes pointed straight at him. I shoved in front of the microphone. "Same goes for him. Obviously."

I didn't get to enjoy the smattering of laughter since Locke was tugging me back offstage and out of the room. As quick as we'd come, we were gone again.

"Where are you taking me?"

Heated eyes found mine. "Your hotel room."

When we were alone in the elevator again, I looked down at my shoes instead of at Locke. "Why aren't you mad?"

"Who says I'm not?"

"I really am sorry I couldn't be honest with you," I blurted, glancing back up at him. But instead of anger, I saw tender affection. The expression on Locke's face took my breath away.

"I know, baby," he said. "And so am I."

I moved closer to him and tucked my nose into his neck. "I missed you so much," I whispered.

Locke cupped the back of my head and placed kisses on top of it until the elevator dinged and the doors slid open again.

Thankfully, the key card worked on the first attempt, and I was able to push inside my room. As soon as I felt him behind me, I turned to find out what was supposed to happen next. Was this where we talked it out? Confessed all of our lies and started over again?

"Take off your clothes."

Apparently not.

"I think we should talk," I said, trying to be an adult and accept the consequences of my actions.

"Is that what you want right now?"

I stared at him. "No."

He stepped forward and cupped my face. "What do you want, Jethro?"

His expression was sweeter than I deserved. Kinder. Affectionate. Every move of his hands was gentle and tender. Almost too much.

I didn't deserve it.

And despite his announcement downstairs, it was too good to be true.

Part of me felt like this was all part of an elaborate ploy. A revenge plot expertly targeted to enact the most amount of damage.

I'd been here before. But neither of the men I'd trusted to love me in the past were even remotely able to hurt me like this man was.

If this was all a joke, it would end me.

Which was why it finally happened. The dam burst, and the first tear came.

I'd learned from my dads a long time ago that crying was nothing to be ashamed of. But just as long ago, I'd learned from my school friends that it was. The result was my brain being completely on board with a good cry and my heart being mortified by it.

"I'm sorry," I said quickly, moving as far away from him as possible and dropping down to sit on the far side of the bed. "Ignore me."

He didn't let me hide. Instead, he followed me around the bed and pressed me down onto it, lying on top of me and covering me in his warm strength. He pressed soft kisses to my cheeks, forehead, eyelids.

Lips.

"I will never ignore you, Jett Talmadge Marian," he said reverently.

I blinked up at him, remembering he'd known my name when making his big public declaration. "How do you know my name?"

"I know people," he said with a soft smile.

"And now you know me," I said, stupidly, trying to make a joke on the off chance it would stop my meltdown. "The real me, I mean."

The look on his face was making it hard to breathe. He still looked fondly affectionate. Adoring.

In love.

"I always knew the real you, Jethro," he said.

He moved a hand to my forehead and smoothed back my hair, the movement comforting and sweet. The smile was still there. And the kind eyes.

It was too much to take in.

"I came here to tell you that I need you," he said. "But I think I had it wrong. Well, partially wrong, anyway."

He leaned down and kissed away the line of tears across my temple. "I think you need me," he whispered. "Just as much as I need you."

My breath hitched, and more tears spilled. "Please don't mess with me," I begged. "I want you so much. I want to keep you and have you be mine."

He pulled back to meet my eyes, both hands now cupping my face. "I'm already yours, baby. I think I was that night at the Candy Bar. When you told me to 'sit my sexy fucking ass down' and proceeded to sass me, Magic Mike–style."

A helium laugh bubbled up. "You tried so hard to act unaffected."

"I was affected, Jethro. Very, very affected."

His smile was more relaxed than I'd ever seen it. And there was a light in his eyes that hadn't been there before. "Your Jethro?"

"Mmhm. If I have anything to say about it—which I do because you will do what I say—you'll be my Jethro forever."

"So fucking bossy." More tears. "Forever?"

He pursed his lips and shrugged. "Unless you send me away.

And even then... I gotta be honest. I don't take well to being denied by you."

I barked out a wet laugh. "When have I ever denied you?"

His thumb brushed more tears away. "Because you're my good boy," he teased softly.

My stomach tightened with need. "I want to be," I admitted.

The moment sat heavily between us. Monumental. Toes off the edge of a diving board and all the weight shifting forward.

"I love you," I said, words featherlight and hopeful.

His smile widened. "I know."

"How could you know anything? I've been keeping so many secrets from you."

Locke leaned down and kissed me slowly before pulling back up to peer down at me. "Not as many as you think. Not the stuff that counts."

"How could you possibly know that?"

He pressed a kiss to my temple, taking in the last of my tears. "Wait here."

He got up and found his pants on the floor. And then he pulled out a tiny box. For a split second, I recoiled in uncomfortable shock. This was way too soon for tiny boxes. We had days and weeks of conversations that needed to happen first—

"Relax, baby," he said with a chuckle, shaking the box gently. Then he moved next to me on the bed. We both sat up and leaned against the headboard. "Open it."

I pulled the lid off and peered inside. There on a tiny little handful of sand was a perfect triton, the brown and white spines forming a familiar spiral design.

My heart leapt in excitement. "I love tritons! Where did you find this?"

He reached in and pulled the tiny shell out of the sand. "Rabbit Island. I went walking with Hunter and Pepper."

I blinked at him in astonishment. "You what? How? Why?"

"I was looking for you. Wasn't sure if maybe I would throttle you or fuck you. I was in the process of figuring it out. And then I found this."

I lifted an eyebrow at him, remembering his command when we'd first entered the room. *Take off your clothes.* "And you decided to fuck me."

"I decided to do both." He placed the shell in my palm and curved my fingers around it.

Locke's gaze warmed. "I decided to keep you."

35

LOCKE

WHEN I FINALLY CALMED JETT DOWN WITH reassurances and promises that I meant every word I said, he began to relax. But it wasn't until I was deep inside his body, murmuring how much I loved him over and over again, that he seemed to finally let go and trust me.

"Not leaving," I said into the side of his face as I thrust into him excruciatingly slowly. "Meant what I said. You're fucking mine."

"Thought you were straight," he slurred, eyes having a hard time staying open as my cock hit a good spot.

"This feel straight to you?"

Jett's skin was damp with sweat as he struggled not to come. "You feel so fucking good."

"I feel incredible," I agreed.

"Not what I m—oh fuck! Locke! Please, don't stop. Right there."

I picked up the pace, feeling the familiar heaviness in my balls. The idea of coming deep inside him made my stomach clench and the nerve endings sing.

Jett's fingers dug into the skin of my back. He still carried fear and desperation, which only made me love him more. I could already tell that getting Jett Marian to let go of his fear and trust me would be the most incredible gift I would ever receive. And that was worth anything. Even putting up with his unexpected career choice.

I'd meant what I'd told him. Whatever happened from now on, we'd figure it out. Together.

His body squeezed around me, hot and tight, as I moved in and out of him faster, trying to keep the same angle.

Watching his reaction, the slurred words, the glassy eyes, turned me all the fucking way on until I needed him to come before I blew.

I reached for his cock and wrapped my hand around it between us. He was rock hard and leaking. "Let go, baby. Give it to me."

His eyes met mine, soft denim blue that would always remind me of how he looked in the Amalfi sun, with the changeable sea stretched out behind him.

One more tug of his dick, and he was mine, head back and cry escaping. The heat of his release on my hand and the tight pull of his body on my cock were enough to finish me off. I thrust inside him one final time as my orgasm hit, sending me into ecstasy only Jett could make me feel.

"Can't believe you showed up," Jett said when the sensations finally settled down.

I pulled out of his body and leaned up to kiss him. "Can't believe you thought for a single moment that I wouldn't."

His eyes followed me to the bathroom, where I gathered a hot cloth to clean him up with. When I returned to the bed, he was still watching me.

"What do you think you know about me?"

I busied myself wiping him down, nudging his hand away when he reached for the cloth. "Well, I know that you were trying to protect me there at the end. By getting me out of the house before the authorities showed up."

Jett nodded.

I tossed the cloth back toward the bathroom and climbed into bed next to him, pulling the covers over both of us and wrapping him in my arms.

"I know you don't like grapefruit," I said, intent on playing this game as long as he needed me to. "And that you would murder the single mother you don't actually have for a lemon sorbetto."

He couldn't hold in a snicker. "True. I'd date you just for access to Roberto if I had to."

I huffed out a laugh. "'Date.' It sounds like such a weak word for what I want with you."

The light was back in his eyes. "What word would you use?"

"Love," I said. "You would *love* me for sorbetto. And I would accept."

He smiled. "Okay. What else do you know about me?"

I reached out to caress his face with the backs of my fingers. "I know I love you. Very much."

His eyes were luminous. Not shiny but almost. "Locke," he breathed.

I smiled and kissed him softly on the lips. "I know you work for ESP. That you're an intelligence agent."

His smile dimmed, but he kept his eyes on mine. "I guess you don't know me as well as you thought." He put a hand on my chest, over my heart. "Because I no longer work there."

I covered his hand in mine, disappointment sharp and anger ready to rear its ugly head in his defense. How fucking dare they? "I'm sorry, baby. Maybe... maybe I could talk to someone for you.

Try and get your job back. Or find something similar with another agency."

His lips curved up again. "That might be kind of awkward since I'm the one who quit."

A breath of relief whooshed out of me. "Thank fuck. But why?"

Jett moved to lie on top of me, propping his chin on his hands over my chest. "I don't want to keep secrets from you. Ever. Never again."

I leaned up and kissed him gently. "Same," I promised.

"Does this mean you're going to tell me about Paxis?"

"Yes." Even though it would put him in danger. He was too savvy to allow me to keep secrets from him, and I was too selfish to risk losing him. "But in a way that makes sure you're protected."

Jett reached out and caressed my cheeks. "I'll always be protected. My boyfriend is pretty good at taking care of me. And I've got skills of my own, too."

Annoyance grumbled out of me. "Not boyfriend. That's too... I don't know. Too small for how I feel about you. Find something else."

"My *love* is a pretty good protector," he suggested, eyes dancing.

"Yes. That." I pulled him close again for another kiss, but when Jett tried to deepen it into something else, a prelude for sex, I stopped him. "Tell me what you want to tell me. You're still not here with me. Not all the way."

Worry continued to crease his forehead and shadow his eyes. I could tell he wouldn't be completely free of it until we'd shared more of our truths.

"I never targeted you. You were never part of an op. ESP doesn't know that Paxis exists, as far as I know. Definitely not as anything other than a variant of chess."

It was a relief to hear it, even though I suspected as much. If an intelligence agency had suspicions about the council, they wouldn't have cleared me so quickly in al-Qadiri's death. Or they at least would have asked very different questions of me in Italy.

"Go on."

"They didn't know I was going to Italy. They only knew I was on vacation." He stopped and took in a breath. "Until I called them."

This part, I definitely didn't know. "You called them? When?"

"After you asked me to look at the Kiel Canal. We had a team responding to a situation regarding smuggled drones. It was too much of a coincidence, and I was worried we didn't have the full picture." He hesitated. "I told them there was a strangely high-powered group of people gathered and that I'd overheard mention of Kiel. But..."

"But?"

"I didn't tell them about you. I didn't even mention your name."

The admission that he'd risked his job for me was significant. "Why not?"

Jett's cheeks flushed. "I didn't want you to get in trouble."

He told me more about the op, about how he'd wanted to go— expected to go—because of his experience on other German missions and his fluency. Then he told me about being undercover there before we met in Amsterdam and why he'd been so broken when I'd found him.

I pulled him into my arms until he could barely breathe. He finally pulled away enough to lie side by side with me and continue sharing. "I wanted you so badly that night in Amsterdam. But you rejected me."

"You needed coddling, not fucking," I reminded him. "And I held you in my arms all night. I held you during your nightmares. I kissed you that night."

"I kissed you," he corrected.

"I went home with blue balls," I grumbled, remembering the long flight. My anger. My fear for Jett's safety.

He hesitated. "What's the real purpose of your nerd herd, Locke?"

I reached out to smooth his worry away, my thumb pressing gently into the crease between his eyebrows. "World peace. De-escalation of tensions. Providing aid. Gentle disruption of terrorist plans. Prevention of mass suffering."

My grandfather's words moved easily out of my mouth as I passed along part of the secret to him—something I'd thought I would never do. "It started with whispered words during regular Paxis tournaments. A dozen very powerful men began to recognize the power they held outside of any government. It was power due to immense wealth but also connections. Why depend on fickle or corrupt government leadership to act when the council could act much sooner and without the obstacles of international diplomacy and red tape?"

Jett tangled his legs in mine. "Ah, a cadre of superheroes."

"More like a cadre of people with enough resources to make a difference. And the one thing these men had in common was a desire to do good with those resources instead of hoarding them."

"How can you trust everyone in the group?"

"You can't. Al-Qadiri proved that."

I went on to explain about the insider trading, why that kind of activity was against the rules, and how the only way to protect the Paxis Council from a vengeful ex-member was to eliminate them.

"So the Paxis Council planted the bomb?"

I shook my head. "His father-in-law did. We think Liyana called her father after Saleem asked her to buy the Helvig stock. Mehmet was the one who brought Saleem onto the council. He knew it was his responsibility. Saleem's actions shamed him."

"Liyana betrayed her husband for the sanctity of the council?" he asked in disbelief. "How could she?"

His outrage warmed something in my chest. "You wouldn't do the same?" I teased.

"Fuck no. Would you?"

"Of course not. But I'm not sure she loved her husband more than the game. She'd grown up around the council and felt betrayed when her father passed her over for her husband."

Jett's eyelids were drooping. "What if the council finds out I know the truth about everything?"

I rubbed his back slowly, in hopes of soothing him to sleep. The poor man looked wrecked. Like he'd been as upset by the past week as I had.

"First of all, they won't," I promised. "Because we'll come up with a plan. Our own code. Secondly, your agency will have your back, Jett. Even if you no longer work for them."

He snuggled closer to me. "Maybe I could be an asset for the council," he murmured sleepily.

"Mm, maybe. Get some sleep, baby."

"Don't leave. Want to suck you later."

I couldn't hold back the laugh, and I felt his grin against my chest.

"Duly noted," I said. "I'll wake you for the sucking."

Several long beats of silence passed. Enough that I thought he'd fallen asleep. Until Jett's soft breath moved across my skin differently. "Want to introduce you to my family."

I moved my hands up and down his back, then moved my fingertips lightly through his hair. "You won't be embarrassed by the caveman who claimed you in front of every gay man in San Francisco?"

"No one's ever claimed me like that before," he admitted softly. "'S nice."

"You'll move in with me when we get back to the city, right?"

"Meh," he said.

"Meh?" I asked, staring down at the side of his face. "*Meh?* What the fuck does that mean? Yes or no, and the answer better be yes, Jethro."

His lips curled up, but he didn't open his eyes.

"Some decisions are best made hungry, Johnny."

I laughed, remembering what I'd told him when I'd made the original indecent proposal. "You don't even know what you're talking about. That makes no sense."

His lips stayed curled up as he finally fell into a deep sleep, tucked safely in my arms.

EPILOGUE
JETT

THIS WAS A VERY BAD IDEA.

Teaching my cousins and siblings any game was a recipe for disaster, but doing it after we'd spent the better part of the day at one of Alex's wine tastings was taking it to a whole other level.

I'd tried to warn Locke, but he was too naive for this crowd. The man was a baby lamb in a room full of rabid and tipsy wolves hell-bent on initiating him the Marian way.

"It's not a horsey," Lennon explained to Ella. "It's a rook."

"Knight," Locke murmured, reaching for his scotch and taking another gulp.

The huge patio table on the deck behind my grandparents' lodge in Montana was big enough to hold everyone. The summer sun was setting behind the mountain, shooting warm rays across the yard and deck. Chill music played softly from hidden speakers, and various dishes of appetizers dotted the table between practice chess sets.

"It's literally a horse," Ella said, holding the knight from the red set. "And it's pretty. I'm naming it Frank."

Locke finished helping my cousin Rosie with the yellow pieces, which she kept knocking over since she couldn't stop staring at my hot fucking boyfriend.

"Eyes on your board," I told her.

Locke's hand moved under the table to my upper thigh and then quickly toward my inner thigh until his fingers were nearly brushing my balls. "Mm," I hummed in a too-highly-pitched tone. "Mmhm."

"Okay," he said to everyone, as if he wasn't causing a nuts situation under the table. "Who remembers the eight types of pawns?"

Tommy started rattling them off. "Positive, negative, requesting, offering—"

His fiancé, Foster, stage-whispered, "Kiss-ass."

Their dog lifted her head from the floor by Foster's feet, sniffed when she realized he wasn't talking to her, and put her head back down with a huff.

Avery took a sip of wine while her wife raced around after their toddler in the grass. "I'll trade someone all my pawns for their queen," she said seriously, shooting me a wink.

"That's not..." Locke took a deep breath. "That's not an allowed movement within the game regulations."

Gabe shot me a look before blinking innocently at Avery. "I'll trade you my queen if you'll let me have your first few moves."

"No," Locke said. "Let's, ah... let's play a round without variations first. Okay? Good."

Benji nodded and focused on the board in front of him. "Agreed. And there's no point in trading for the queen when she can only trade with the bishop anyway."

I almost snorted.

Locke's forehead crinkled. "No. The queen doesn't trade at all. And neither does the bishop."

Lennon leaned forward. "Unless it's the blue one, right?"

Locke looked at me with wide eyes. The sheer frustration and overwhelm was kinda cute, I had to admit. "I'm not sure we should..."

"It's fine. They'll pick it up when we get going. Let's start with a sample game. A trial run."

JJ nudged his wife. "You start. You're the one with the pink race car piece. That one always starts first."

All of us waited a beat while the ridiculous line finally clued Locke in to what was going on.

Suddenly, his face cleared. "You assholes! *Fuck*, you're all horrible human beings. I can't believe you had me going."

Everyone broke into laughter. Beau grinned over at him. "My baby girl was captain of the chess team in high school," he said. "When all our friends were packing stadium chairs and coolers for football games, we were loading up the SUV with nerds."

Locke glanced at Becca. "That true?"

She grinned. "I play a mean horsey."

He turned to me with a look of betrayal and accusation. "Your sister is a chess nerd, and you didn't think to mention it?"

"Why do you sound so surprised when I've already kicked your ass many times in the game?"

Mav rocked back in his seat with his beer bottle propped over his stomach. "He comes by it honestly. It's a Marian thing."

"Our cousin Wolfe is the only one I can't beat consistently," Becca bragged, but then I noticed the glint in her eye. "Jett's easy to beat unless he's playing with someone he's attracted to. Then he takes it seriously."

My face flushed hot as Locke's expression made it obvious he was remembering the times I'd beaten him at chess. "That so, Jethro?"

"Pfft."

As everyone continued to talk around me, I took a moment to

wonder where the hell Wolfe was. He'd been a no-show at the bachelor party, and he was still in the wind. Uncle Jude had explained that Wolfe had taken off on a solo camping trip, but I knew he and Derek were starting to worry.

"You okay, baby?" Locke murmured close to my ear. "Did you need to go lie down?"

I snorted. "You'd like that, wouldn't you?"

"Yes. Yes, I would. And it beats the hell out of trying to teach anything to these fuckers. It's a good thing I learned how unwelcoming your family is before I committed to you even more than I already have."

I turned his chair out and climbed into his lap, wrapping my arms around his neck and ignoring all the groans and catcalls from the drunk Marians surrounding us. "Oh yeah? You thinking of jumping ship, Johnny?"

He pulled my face down to kiss me. I loved that he was never awkward or hesitant about showing me affection, no matter who was around.

"I can't. I'm locked in now."

I could tell he was teasing me. "Oh yeah? You on the hook?"

Locke had already explained everything to me about the Paxis Council, and we'd spoken for hours over several days about our shared interest in doing similar work on our own. Helping people with his money and mine. Our combined skills and connections.

A Paxis pair, of sorts.

He would continue to serve on the Paxis Council, but we would also look into doing the good parts, the helping parts, on our own. We already knew we could use many of our same contacts—him with the council and me with ESP—to help make the biggest impact.

Locke kissed me again on the mouth, the cheek, the ear.

"Can't leave you now. I'd have to pay out your contract. It's cheaper just to keep you."

I wrapped my arms around him and squeezed. "So sensible with money," I said. "I love that about you."

"You giving me another hug lesson, Jethro?" His arms came around me just as tightly, and his voice was the deep kind of rumble that made foreplay look like child's play.

His big hands moved up and down my back.

"I *do* think I need to go lie down," I admitted softly.

"Mmm. And I think you deserve a little punishment while we're up there. For letting your family play dirty tricks on me."

I stayed in his arms for another beat. "I love you so much."

"I'm gonna need you to prove that," he said in a warm voice. "Get upstairs, baby. Let's go."

His hand smacked my ass as I stood up and tried to make my way into the house without everyone seeing my physical interest in Locke Maris.

He was right behind me, and when we got upstairs and into the privacy of our own room, I spent hours and hours proving my love to him.

Showing Locke that my heart belonged to him.

That I was his.

That he owned me completely.

And that I owned him right back.

Want more of Jett and Locke? Sign up for my newsletter now to read a sexy Owning Jett *bonus scene → https://readerlinks.com/l/5162718*

Up next in the Made Marian Legacy series is Tracking Wolfe. *Is sweet*

Wolfe is going to follow in his cousins' footsteps and find his HEA? Find out here → https://readerlinks.com/l/5161190

Wondering about Jett's family? Maverick and Beau get a second chance at love in Moving Maverick, available here → https://readerlinks. com/l/1437602, while Felix and Lio fall in love in Felix and the Prince, which you can grab here → http://readerlinks.com/l/1437598

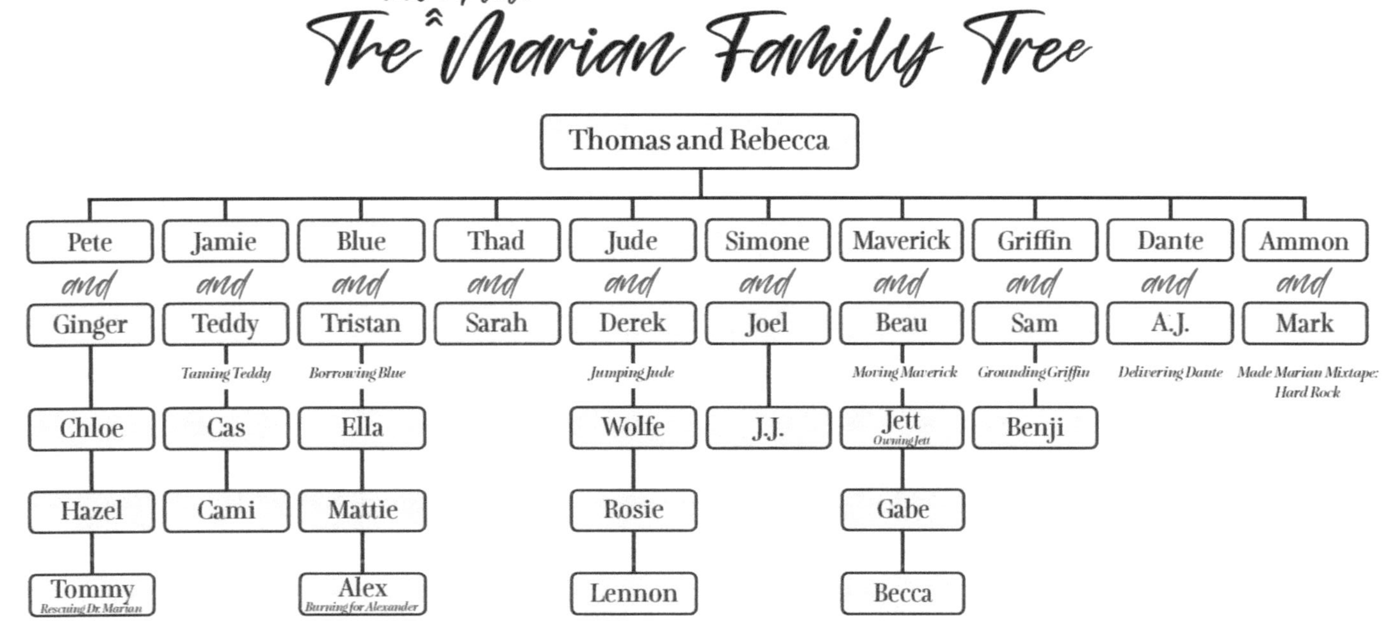

incomplete
The Marian Family Tree
Thomas and Rebecca
Pete and Ginger
Chloe
Hazel
Tommy
Rescuing Dr. Marian
Jamie and Teddy
Taming Teddy
Cas
Cami
Blue and Tristan
Borrowing Blue
Ella
Mattie
Alex
Burning for Alexander
Thad and Sarah
Jude and Derek
Jumping Jude
Wolfe
Rosie
Lennon
Simone and Joel
J.J.
Maverick and Beau
Moving Maverick
Jett
Owning Jett
Gabe
Becca
Griffin and Sam
Grounding Griffin
Benji
Dante and A.J.
Delivering Dante
Ammon and Mark
Made Marian Mixtape: Hard Rock
For a detailed reading order, visit lucylennox.com/reading-order

A LETTER FROM LUCY

Dear Reader,

Thank you for reading *Owning Jett*. I had so much fun with this one! It reminded me of *King Me*. If you like the "spy" type romantic suspense elements, you might also like the art thief cat-and-mouse set-up in *King Me*.

Up next is Wolfe and Trace's story! I know everyone has been excited to finally get sweet Wolfe's story, so check out *Tracking Wolfe* in my shop or on Amazon. There is also a mini-fic on my Patreon called "Sunstruck" that shows us the original spark of this relationship. For more information, feel free to visit my Patreon here: https://readerlinks.com/l/5161222

Be sure to sign up for my newsletter to get bonus content, sales announcements, and more, including discounts on the next releases!

You can also follow me on your favorite retailer site to be notified of new releases, and look for me on Facebook for sneak peeks of upcoming stories. You can also join me right now on Patreon for exclusive content and behind-the-scenes glimpses.

Please take a moment to write a review of *Owning Jett*. Reviews can make all the difference in helping a book show up in searches.

Feel free to stop by www.LucyLennox.com and drop me a line or visit me on social media. To see inspiration photographs for all my novels, visit my Pinterest boards. The Pinterest board for *Owning Jett* can be found here.

Finally, I have a fantastic reader group on Facebook. Join us for exclusive content, early cover reveals, hot pics, and a whole lotta fun. Lucy's Lair can be found here.

Happy reading!
Lucy

ABOUT LUCY LENNOX

Lucy Lennox is the USA Today bestselling author of over fifty gay romance titles including the GoodReads Hall of Fame winner Wilde Love. Born and raised in the southeast USA, she is finally putting good use to that English Lit degree she earned before the turn of the century.

Lucy enjoys naps, pizza, and procrastinating. She stays up way too late each night reading romance because it's simply the best.

For more information and to stay updated about future releases, sales and audio news and to grab some free and bonus reads, please sign up for Lucy's author newsletter on her website at Lucy-Lennox.com or to stay in the know, join her exciting reader group, Lucy's Lair on Facebook.

facebook.com/lucylennoxmm

instagram.com/lucylennoxmm

amazon.com/Lucy-Lennox/e/B01N0IOYPT

bookbub.com/authors/lucy-lennox

patreon.com/lucylennox

pinterest.com/lucy_lennox

ALSO BY LUCY LENNOX

Get my <u>New Release Alerts</u>

Join me on Patreon

Follow me Everywhere Else

Read my books:

<u>Made Marian Series</u>

<u>Forever Wilde Series</u>

<u>Aster Valley Series</u>

<u>The Billionaire Brotherhood Series</u>

<u>Made Marian Legacy Series</u>

<u>Standalones</u>

<u>Novellas</u>

<u>After Oscar Series</u> (with Molly Maddox)

<u>Twist of Fate Series</u> (with Sloane Kennedy)

<u>Licking Thicket Series</u> (with May Archer)

<u>Champion Security Series</u> (with May Archer)

<u>Honeybridge Series</u> (with May Archer)

Visit my website at <u>www.LucyLennox.com</u> for a comprehensive list of titles, audio samples, freebies, suggested reading order, and more!